They *would* be getting together.

this kiss taught him anything, he thought in the last
tional part of his brain, it was to stop deluding himself
at he could keep his hands off her for very much longer.
t just to prove he wasn't completely helpless, to let her
ow she wasn't the one in charge, he broke the kiss.

He didn't push her away, wrapping his hands around her
d staying all but mouth to mouth with her. And although
could feel her muscles tense, she didn't test his strength.
her own.

"The next time we do that," he said, "we won't be out-
le, where half the village gets a free show. We'll be some-
ere we can finish this."

"You keep making threats—"

"Not a threat, a promise." This time, when he felt her
uscles bunch, when those brilliant blue eyes narrowed
his, he turned her loose. Not because he was afraid his
ength wouldn't be enough.

Because he might not let her go.

Temptation Bay

ANNA SULLIVAN

FOREVER

NEW YORK   BOSTON

Forever
Hachette Book Group
237 Park Avenue
New York, NY 10017

www.HachetteBookGroup.com

Printed in the United States of America

Originally published as an ebook

First mass-market edition: December 2013

10 9 8 7 6 5 4 3 2 1

OPM

Forever is an imprint of Grand Central Publishing.
The Forever name and logo are trademarks of Hachette Book Group, Inc.

The publisher is not responsible for websites (or their content) that are not owned by the publisher.

The Hachette Speakers Bureau provides a wide range of authors for speaking events. To find out more, go to www.hachettespeakersbureau.com or call (866) 376-6591.

To Erin and Jake, setting off on the road to your very own Happily Ever After

Temptation Bay

Prologue

October 16, 1931. Windfall Island, Maine.

Christ, Giff, pay attention. You nearly swamped us."

"You're the one who overloaded the boat," Hank Gifford ground out, bending his back to the oars with renewed concentration.

"You won't be complaining when we rake in the dough this stuff'll bring on the mainland."

"If we live long enough to run it over to them hoity-toity, soft-handed city slickers," Giff muttered.

His contempt for the wine-with-dinner crowd ran deep, but his love of life ran even deeper. The fishing boat they'd "borrowed" was little more than a thirty-foot canoe, and the waves were wicked tonight, slapping the bow and splashing over the gunnels. It took all their strength to keep the little boat from foundering, but even with death at the hands of the frigid Atlantic mere inches away, Giff found it hard to concentrate.

His eyes kept straying back to the trio of ships, loaded with liquor brought down from Canada or up from the Caribbean, riding at anchor twelve miles out from shore at what bootleggers had dubbed the Rum Line. The distance did little to discourage the smaller boats that steamed, sailed, or rowed out from shore in order to place bids on the contraband, and to ferry bootleggers and their flapper girl-friends, musicians and gamblers to join the nightly floating party—a party all the livelier for taking place within nose-thumbing distance of the U.S. Coast Guard.

The 18th Amendment, intended to deliver America from the evils of alcohol, had instead created a whole new category of crime, where even the average citizen flouted the law and huge fortunes were made practically over-night. And not just by your run-of-the-mill lawbreakers, Giff thought with a sniff. The hoi-polloi were in on the fun as well, making great gobs of money with no risk, seeing as they hired men for the cloak-and-dagger, and kept their own backsides safely in their parlors. Those like Giff and his friends took their own risk and lived or died by it.

Then again, what was life without a little risk? And those rich men, well, they'd gotten themselves into a shitload of trouble—and the rest of the world along with them—what with all their speculating and high finance. Likely the only thing keeping them from throwing themselves off the roof of a New York skyscraper was the booze, whether they ran it or drank it.

Giff laughed at that, and wished again they could row back to the ships instead of on toward the cold and lonely shore. His old grandma would have warned him he was going to perdition, and she'd be right, seeing as one of those rum-runners went by that exact name. Giff supposed the moniker was apt, but he'd have a hell of time, well, going to Hell.

Norris fired up the small outboard motor, now that they were far enough away from the big ship named *Perdition* to be obscured by the moonless night and the ugly mood of the Atlantic. Even if they caught the noise of the motor, the eager beaver Coast Guarders would have a hell of a time pinpointing the sound in miles of dark ocean. As they swung in a wide arc that would keep them safely in the dark as they made their way back to shore, Giff's hopes were well and truly dashed.

"Don't see why we couldn't stay a tad longer," he grumbled.

"Weather's turning," Norris said, his breath steaming on air gone icy in the hours since they'd motored out from shore. "A tad longer and there'd be no getting back tonight."

"Then I'd be cozied up with that pretty little floozy we ferried from one ship to the other."

"Like she'd have you."

"I woulda talked her around to it, if you hadn't dragged me away."

"Oughta be grateful," Norris muttered. "Loreen woulda smelled that skirt's perfume on you and then where'd you be?"

"Bunking with you, I guess."

Norris snorted. "Your feet smell like that rotten French cheese they got at the grocer's by mistake last spring."

Giff ignored him, listening instead to the jangle of the music floating back to them, enjoying the way the lights shone in the moonless dark and reflected off the surface of the heaving ocean. He could still smell the booze and the perfume of the dancing girls, and the sour sweat of the losers at the clattering roulette wheels.

Their boat hit the rocky shingle of beach in the sheltered curve of Temptation Bay, and he put his mind back on reality, turning to stare expectantly at his partner.

"Thanks for nothing," Norris said, jumping out to tie the boat off to an old metal pole sticking out of the ground for just that purpose.

A figure appeared out of the darkness, his boots swirling through the thin mist crawling across the ground.

"Bitch of a night," Floyd Meeker said, setting a dimly lit lantern on the ground so he could blow on his hands to warm them. "See you made it. Took you long enough."

"Like waiting's a problem for you, Meeker," Giff said as he climbed out of the boat. "Your best talent is doing nothing."

"Giff had his way," Norris put in, "We'd've spent the night."

"Just wanted to keep warm. And mind you there's all kinds of warm on that big boat out yonder."

They all laughed.

Even Meeker, notoriously sour of disposition, cracked a smile, although he had a dire pronouncement to chase away the humor. "You'd've likely waited out the weather, but not the Coast Guard."

Giff snorted. "Lousy Coast Guard." Which was the reason they worked at night, and went miles out of their way to keep to the darkness, for Christ's sake, so there'd be little chance they'd be seen.

"Ahoy," their fourth partner called out, appearing, as Meeker had, out of the darkness, his young son like a shadow a step behind him.

Norris was already hefting a wooden crate, the bottles inside it tinkling musically, when Jamie Finley stepped up beside the boat.

"Might's well earn your keep," Giff said to Finley's son Emmett, handing the kid one of the smaller crates.

Surprised, grinning hugely with the joy of a boy being treated like a man, Emmett took the crate. And bobbled it.

"Hey."

Three men lunged for the crate. Norris managed to

rescue it before it hit the rock, then tucked it under one arm to cuff Giff on the side of the head with the other hand. "What the fuck's wrong with you, giving the good stuff to a scrawny kid barely old enough to piss standing up?"

Giff grabbed Norris by the collar, cocked his fist back. Finley hooked his arm, pulled him off. Giff stumbled back a step or two, but he dropped his arm. He'd be damned if he rubbed his head like a sissy, but he wasn't above digging the toe of his boot into the rocks and shying one Norris's way.

Finley took the crate from Norris and handed it back to his son. "May be scrawny, but you're strong, aren't you, Emmett?"

Speechless with the trust his father showed, Emmett took the crate and carried it—very carefully—toward the old horse-drawn wagon they used to ferry the stuff to their hide.

"Mind you put that up front, and be careful," Norris called after the kid, turning back to Finley. "Why'd you bring him, anyway?"

"His mam—"

"Has you whipped?" Norris said, Giff and Meeker laughing and tossing in their opinions of Laura Finley's hold over her man.

"Wanted Emmett out of the house," Finley said quietly. "Maddie," he finished. That single word was all it took to have the others choking back their humor.

They fell silent, but for the shuffling of crates and the crunch of rocks underfoot, all of them contemplating the measles epidemic cutting like a scythe through the island's children. Older kids, like Emmett, caught it and seemed to sail their way through. The smaller children and the babies . . . They were another story.

A few of the island's families were already in mourning, and so many of the other children were sick. Including Finley's baby daughter. They'd almost lost her twice already, but the doctor from the mainland said the longer she survived, the better her chances. And if it seemed like he was sticking his nose in, well, what were neighbors for? Windfall Island was a one-for-all kind of place. They gave each other hell on a regular basis, Giff allowed, but they counted it as a right—and a duty—to know their fellow islanders inside and out. How could you watch someone's back if you didn't understand what they were facing?

"Jay-sus," Meeker spat on the ground, "what are we, girls?"

"Only an asshole like you'd begrudge Finley and all the families a moment of respectful silence." Giff clapped Emmett on the shoulder. "C'mon, kid, sooner we get this lot unloaded, sooner we can get away from sourpuss over there, and cozy into our racks."

Emmett lifted his head, all four men ignoring the way his eyes shone in the meager light from the flotilla three miles out. And then those young eyes widened when, clear as a bell, they heard a thin, reedy wail.

"That sounded like a—"

"Baby," Emmett breathed, and as four grown men stepped back, he moved forward, following the cries to the bow of the boat. There, in a tiny space between some crates that had been braced apart so they wouldn't shift, he found what looked like a bundle of blankets. A bundle that moved and cried.

Emmett leaned into the boat and gathered up the bundle. He pulled back a corner of the blanket, saw the glint of gold surrounding some sort of jewel that proved a deep red when he carried her a few steps so he could hunker down next to Meeker's lantern. In its light he saw the letters embroidered onto the silk lining of the baby's blanket—an ornate S bracketed by a smaller but equally embellished E on its left and an A on its right. He hastily covered the jewelry, telling himself it would be best to wait for his mam. His mam always knew what to do.

"She's about the same age as Maddie," he said, thinking of his baby sister. He stood and turned to the watching men. "Fair soaked, too, and probably chilled clear to the bone."

"Rough waters," Meeker said. "She likely caught her death."

Finley gently rearranged the child so that she rested against his son's chest, then pulled Emmett's jacket around her. "We'll hurry," he said, squeezing the boy's shoulder.

"Aye," Norris chimed in. "We'll take her back once we've finished—"

The *Perdition* exploded with a roar that sounded like the end of the world. The ship they'd just left riding the high waves and the high times shot flames and debris a hundred feet into the air, then subsided into an inferno—fueled by a hold full of liquor—that no one could have survived.

Emmett stumbled back, lost his footing and sat down hard on the rocks. He never dropped the baby, just sat there staring, as if the crackle of the burning timbers, the hiss of debris hitting the water, even from twelve miles away, might tell him where the little girl had come from, and if there was anyone left to know she was lost. Or care.

Chapter One

"Portland Tower. This is N277HK requesting approach."

"N277HK hold your position. We have outgoing."

"Roger that, Portland Tower, holding," Maggie Solomon said from the cockpit of her AS355 Twinstar helicopter, hovering at a safe distance and altitude over the Maine coastline east of Portland International Jetport.

She didn't mind hovering. Things were so much more appealing from the air. Less...messy. A little distance was never a bad thing. A fitting rule of thumb, she thought, for life in general.

"You got a fare, Maggie, or just cargo?"

"It's a suit, so I guess it depends on your outlook."

The radio was quiet for a few seconds while the controller dealt with the outgoing traffic, which turned out to be a small commercial jet taking off. "Roger that, N277HK," the controller said once the plane was airborne and safely away. "By suit I take it you mean some sort of corporate stiff."

"Lawyer." Maggie patted her control panel lightly. "I'll have my baby fumigated later."

A slight laugh crackled through the radio static. "Come on in, one thousand."

"Roger that." Maggie brought the 'copter in for a landing, and saw her fare, standing at the edge of the tarmac like one of those Easter Island statues she'd seen in *National Geographic.* Inscrutable expression, oddly compelling, just a little scary.

Most people hunched automatically, instinctive fear of thirty-five feet of rotor blade edged with stainless steel spinning at approximately 400 rpm right about head level. Dexter Keegan just stood there, not moving, even though the wind was fierce enough to scour the paint from the buildings, not to mention mold his suit to his body—his long, lean, nicely muscled body. The kind of muscles that came from a gym, she told herself, and when she realized she was staring, she took a good long look at the suit again, because the suit, with its crisp white shirt and almost military cut, instantly put her back up.

Too bad, because she liked looking at him, in spite of the bland lawyer expression that said "trust me," and made her want to do exactly the opposite. His hair was dark and just a bit too long, his features a shade too handsome, and his attitude struck her as self-confident, with an edge of swagger. Swagger irritated the hell out of her.

His gaze found hers through the chopper's windows, dark eyes cool and shadowed. There were depths there, Maggie thought, and despite her better instincts, she found herself intrigued. Maybe if he relaxed enough to get out of that suit he'd be worth a fling. She didn't have them often, and not with anyone she could get seriously involved with. But this man didn't strike her as being any more interested in entanglements than she was. Entanglements were a while off in her life plan.

She powered down the helicopter and put on her business face as she climbed out. "Dexter Keegan?" she said, holding out her hand.

He took it. "Call me Dex, Miss..."

"Solomon," Maggie said, taking her hand back and telling herself he hadn't held it a bit too long. And that she hadn't been flattered by it.

"You have a first name?"

"Yes." She stepped around him to retrieve his luggage.

"I'll get that."

"Part of the service," she said, shouldering the hanging bag and snagging the roller. She noted the quick flash of irritation that crossed his face and remembered her first rule of operation: *make the customer happy*. Word of mouth traveled a long way in the blogosphere, and he looked like a guy who knew his way around a cutting phrase.

And maybe the keyboard was mightier than the sword in the twenty-first century, but she'd be damned if she let the potential for bad press compromise—

He reached for the suitcase. She nipped it away. "Really," she said through her teeth, "It's no trouble."

"Something to prove?" he said equably.

Maggie shrugged, a lift and drop of one shoulder. She always had something to prove. And if it rankled that Dexter Keegan had read her so easily, at least she looked away before he saw the little snap of peevishness in her eyes because she was attracted to him, and she didn't want to be.

But that wasn't his fault.

So she handed him the shoulder bag—compromising as much as she could manage—and waited until he stowed it, then lifted in the roller and secured the luggage net.

She opened the passenger door and stood back while he climbed in, and nearly took a right to the jaw when he reached for the door handle just as she leaned in to buckle his harness.

He lifted both hands, his expression missing only a pair of waggling brows.

"I need to make sure it's properly latched," she said, adding in a deadpan voice, "Wouldn't want you to fall out," cinching the straps tight before she stepped back. "I'd hate to have wasted the trip. Fuel is an ugly price these days," she said before she secured the door and headed around the front of the Twinstar.

He gave her a look through the glass, mostly amusement. At least the man could take a joke, she allowed, and by the time she'd boosted herself into the pilot's seat, she was almost optimistic about having to spend the next twenty minutes with him.

She completed her pre-flight checklist before slipping on her headphones, unhooking the ones hanging behind the passenger's seat and handing them to Keegan. "All set?" she asked him.

"You're driving."

She smiled, just a little, and put him out of her mind. Or rather labeled him, which amounted to the same thing. Instead of an attractive man he was simply a tourist. She knew how to handle tourists.

"Portland Tower, N277HK requesting clearance."

"N277HK, this is Portland Tower. You're cleared for liftoff. Keep it under a thousand, Maggie, I'll hold traffic until you're away."

"Roger that, Portland, and thanks."

"Maggie," her passenger said.

She ignored him, grasping the stick on her left that lifted the bird and the control lever in front of her that moved them forward. Her feet were already resting on the pedals that served as the rudder, determining the pitch of the tail rotor and turning the helicopter left or right. In a choreography that was as natural to her as breathing, she lifted the Twinstar off the tarmac and put it into a smooth turning climb that took them out over the Atlantic coastline, her spirit soaring along with the bird.

She loved this, loved that weightless moment when she hit altitude and leveled off, when her stomach dropped out and she went a little breathless and a lot awestruck. No matter how often she flew, plane or helicopter, it was never anything less than pure magic. Utter freedom. It was the only time in her life when she was truly at peace and absolutely her own woman because she'd built a thriving business around something she loved, something she never allowed to be just business. And even though she knew Mr. Dexter Keegan could see the childish delight on her face, she didn't care. She simply let herself *feel*.

When she reached the height and distance she wanted, she checked in with the tower, reported her stats, and was given the all clear, meaning she was out of range to present any impediment to airport traffic.

"If you look to your right there's a wonderful view of the city of Portland, Mr. Keegan," she said.

"Dex."

"If you have some time on your way back through, the Old Port district is a great way to spend a day," she continued evenly, more at ease than she ever was on the ground.

"I doubt I'll have time for shopping and sightseeing."

Maggie glanced over at him, and saw a veteran flier, calm and relaxed. To all appearances. What she felt from him was different. What she felt was alertness, energy, focus. His eyes never stopped scanning the skyline, and yet she felt like she was being watched.

She didn't comment; those were personal observations, and personal observations invited personal questions. Instead, she swung the Twinstar wide in the usual flight pattern, and lost herself in what she loved.

"The extreme point of land below us is Cape Elizabeth," she said, filtering the radio chatter and keeping an eye out for birds from the other charter services that worked the Portland area. "As we move northeast, you'll see dozens of islands, large and small. In all there are nearly 3,000 islands along the Maine coast. Only Louisiana and Florida have longer coastlines."

"Fascinating," he said, with a tinge of sarcasm Maggie told herself she'd imagined, as when she looked over she didn't see it on his face.

Then again, self-control was a vital tool in his line of work, and winning or losing might hinge on how good a show he put on. "I can lose the spiel, but I have to stick to the flight plan."

His eyes shot to hers, boredom sharpening into irritation that was quickly smoothed over. "Lot on my mind," he said, the practiced, chagrined smile making it an apology as well as an explanation.

Maggie had nothing to say to that, so she said nothing.

"For a tour guide you're not very talkative."

"I get the feeling you prefer it that way."

"I don't want the spiel," he corrected her. "I'm not against conversation in general though, and since I'm the customer, and it's your policy to make the customer happy..."

"It's not usually this difficult," she said, and she'd ferried some pretty wobbly fliers in her time as a pilot. Then again, an airsickness bag wouldn't solve this problem. Maybe a cold shower. Or a bullet. She glanced over at him. A silver bullet. And maybe some Holy Water. Dex Keegan had wolf written all over him, wolf with a veneer of civility, which was a devastating combination. What woman didn't want a gentleman in the dining room and a beast in the bedroom?

"What's going on between the headphones?" Dex wondered into the silence—silence being a relative term in a helicopter.

"Thwarting gravity."

"Nope, flying for you is like driving for most people. You do it without even thinking."

"How about landing, can I think about that?"

"Sure, but you weren't thinking about landing, either."

"I'm beginning to think about crashing."

Dex chuckled, and it was such a rich, infectious sound she couldn't help but smile. At him. That wasn't good. Especially when she caught the glint in his eye. That glint told her he thought he'd won. Which meant she'd lost.

Maggie hated losing. "Mr. Keegan, why are you baiting me?"

He sat back in his seat, and just when she thought she'd gotten the last word, he said, "I'm a lawyer. It's what I do."

She slanted him a sideways glance. "You cross examine every stranger you encounter?"

"You're more likely to get truthful answers when you keep people a little off balance, don't give them time to think."

"So I'm not just a liar, I'm neither smart enough nor imaginative enough to lie on the spur of the moment."

"Everyone has an agenda," he said mildly.

"Including you, Mr. Keegan?"

"Including me. But you knew that already."

"Very cynical."

"It saves time."

Maggie huffed out a breath, as much humor as derision. "Suppose you ask your questions, and I'll do my best not to mislead you. Or at least confine my lies to the little white kind."

He laughed, full out this time, a contagious peal of sound that tugged at some part of her she had no intention of acknowledging. She didn't so much as smile, tempting as it was.

"Tell me about the island."

It surprised her enough to have her glancing over at him. Their eyes met, held. The air between them began to . . . sizzle, she admitted, before she turned away. And warned herself not to look at him again—or at least not to get so caught up it took her a moment to remember where she was in the conversation. She recovered admirably, she decided. "I figured you knew all about the island, seeing as you have business there."

"It would be helpful to get the impressions of a native."

"Isn't it a shame I left my grass skirt and coconut bra back at the hut."

"I've been to Hawaii," he said, although the once over he gave her, complete with the kind of speculative edge that said he was imagining her in the bra, gave her a nice little ego bump. "I'm more interested in what Windfall Island has to offer."

"Windfall," Maggie echoed, and although she knew he had ulterior motives, suspicion couldn't drown out the surge of warmth she always felt. Windfall Island wasn't just a dot on the map; it was, simply, home.

Her father had meant it to be a prison when he'd banished her there. He'd never know the amazing gift he'd given her, could never understand what it meant to love unconditionally. Windfall was hers; it had been since the day she'd set foot there.

"You strike me as a man who does his homework," she said, "but if you want a firsthand account, I can give you the island's background, tell you how it got its name, that sort of thing."

"I'd rather talk about the present."

"Not big on history?"

He shifted a little in his seat, and she could feel his eyes on her. "Is there a reason you don't want to discuss the island?"

"Oh, I don't know, because I feel like I'm getting the third degree? I'm your pilot, not your witness."

It was his turn to use silence as a response. He settled back in his seat, eyes forward again, oozing nonchalance.

Maggie glanced over at him, not buying it.

"I'm really just trying to get a feel for the place," he finally offered.

Maggie smiled a little, fondly. Growing up, she'd never really felt she belonged anywhere. That just meant she got to choose her home, and she was lucky enough to have been welcomed with open arms to Windfall Island. The place might be peopled with the truly eccentric and the down-right loopy, but there was no place on Earth she'd rather live. "Windfall has to be experienced."

"That's my intention."

"And I'm happy to provide transportation."

"It's a small community, a small, close-knit community. And I won't be around long enough to—"

"To what? To waste your time getting to know people?"

"Maybe you missed the part about my time crunch."

"No, I got that loud and clear," she said, shooting him a wry grin. "Just like I didn't miss your reason for coming to Windfall, because you didn't give me one."

"Can't," he corrected, "On the instruction of my client."

Maggie snorted. "That sounds like a line."

"It is a line. From the Bar Association."

"Have they met you? Because you do fine without a script."

"Be careful, I think you just complimented me."

"That wasn't a compliment; it was a commentary on your ability to prevaricate."

"Yeah, I'm taking that as a compliment too."

"Well, prevarication is probably a required course in law school. I bet you got an A."

"You just can't help yourself, can you?" He sat back, crossed his feet at the ankles. "Keep the compliments coming; I can take it."

She grinned over at him, caught him grinning back, and when her pulse scrambled she turned forward again. Before he could see it too. And comment on it. Not that she couldn't fend him off—once she got her nerve endings to stop throbbing so her brain could kick back in. She just had to stop thinking about how much she liked the shape of his mouth, not to mention the rest of him—including his brain, which she was finding delightfully agile. Probably like his body.

She closed her eyes, took a deep breath, dug for strength.

"Admit it," he said in his richly amused voice. "You're enjoying this."

Maybe, Maggie thought, but she didn't like being called on it, especially with Dex Keegan's brand of smug confidence. In fact, it pissed her off enough to want to put him in his place. "You want to know about Windfall? These aren't the families who came over on the Mayflower looking for religious freedom. You won't find any Brewsters or Bradfords or Aldens in the phone book. Windfall was settled by outcasts, by escaped slaves and shipwrecked sailors, some of them just one short step up from pirates. They took native American women for wives, and they're proud of that heritage, proud enough to make *native* an insult."

"I didn't mean—"

"It was the way you tossed it off," she said, still riding that defensive surge. "They didn't build stately mansions on huge tracts of land, and every man of every color was free, or as free as possible on an island run with an iron fist. It was a hard place inhabited by hard people."

"The apples haven't fallen far from the tree."

"Johnny Appleseed never made it to Windfall."

He shifted, and she could feel him watching her again. "Are you always this hostile to men you're attracted to?"

"Has your ego always been this big?" she shot back.

He considered that for a beat, then said, "Pretty much."

Maggie shook her head, amused despite herself. Amused and wary. Best to keep her guard up around Mr. Dexter Keegan, at least until she found out what he wanted with Windfall Island and its people.

"So you've lived on the island all your life?" he said at length.

"No."

Maggie heard a soft huff of air over the headphones before he said, "The look on your face can't be good."

"What look?"

"This isn't a contest."

"Everything's a contest. Life is a contest."

"Who raised you? Attila the Hun?"

Close enough. Admiral Phillip Ashworth Solomon had treated his only child with as little care as Attila had the men he sacrificed for conquest and glory. If she'd been a son...But she hadn't, and she'd stopped wishing otherwise a long time ago. She'd made the life she wanted, and if it couldn't be enough for the Admiral, well, it was his loss.

"I thought you were curious about the island."

"I'm curious about everything," he said, sounding like he found it a blessing and a curse.

Maggie looked at the landscape laid out below her like a picture postcard. "Take a look out the window," she said.

"What direction?"

"Down." Hundreds of islands dotted the inlets and waterways of the coastline, some of them so small they were no more than a pile of moss-covered rocks, only a dozen or so large enough for year-round habitation. The sight always made her catch her breath, the blue, blue water with its mosaic of browns and greens like a huge fascinating jigsaw puzzle that changed mood and appearance from day to day. It never looked the same twice, but it was always familiar. Always hers.

"Islands everywhere," Dex observed, maddeningly underwhelmed. "I'm only interested in one."

"To understand Windfall you have to understand that," she said, pointing down, "and that," gesturing to the endless, blue-gray stretch of the Atlantic Ocean, eerily calm today.

Dex didn't say anything, just looked at her expectantly, waiting for her to fill the silence.

She obliged him, answering the initial question he'd asked her. "I wasn't born on the island. My mother and I moved there when I was a teenager."

"And your father?"

"Didn't. But you're interested in the island, and we'll be landing in about five minutes."

"So you'll be rid of me. Without finding out why I'm asking all these questions?"

"If Windfall Island was a country, gossip would be our national pastime. It won't be long before everyone knows your business."

"Does that go for you, too?"

Maggie bumped up a shoulder. "I manage to keep to myself. No crime in that."

"So you're not the least bit curious about why I'm here?"
"In that suit it's probably bad news for someone."

Bad news for someone. Maggie Solomon left it at that. So
did Dex. He couldn't tell her why he was there, but he could
have assured her it had nothing to do with her. There was
no way she could be descended from Eugenia Stanhope,
taken more than eighty years before at eight months of age.
Eugenia's kidnapping had come to be known as the crime
of the century, considering the Stanhope family was not
only insanely wealthy, but also boasted connections in all
the highest circles of business and politics, including the
White House.

Dex had good reason to believe Eugenia, if she'd lived,
had ended up on Windfall Island. And if she'd not only
lived, but married and given birth as well, her descendants
would either still be living on the island, or he could at least
pick up the trail there and follow where it led. Not having
been born on the island, Maggie wouldn't be on that list...

Except there were her eyes, brilliant, almost turquoise
blue. Not exactly the Stanhope eyes, but close enough that at
first he'd thought his search had ended before it really began.

Still, while her eye color was rare, it certainly wasn't
isolated to the Stanhope family. Maggie had no reason
to lie to him about her origins, and questioning her any
further would only raise her suspicions—and the whole
island's, considering her huge and obvious loyalty to her
adopted home.

If his reasons for coming to Windfall became public
knowledge, it could pose serious problems for the investigation. There was money involved, big money, and even
the most level-headed people went a little crazy over millions of dollars.

He had a reputation to build, and nothing could get in the way. Especially not a woman with all the warmth and welcome of a north Atlantic iceberg. And the strength. His eyes shifted sideways. He would have admired her for it if he wasn't so sure she was going to cause him trouble.

He reminded himself yet again that he should remain objective, but in his mind's eye he was seeing her stride from the helicopter as she had moments ago, that long, slim body encased in a dark blue flight suit no doubt intended to project skill and professionalism. He found it ridiculously sexy.

She wasn't classically beautiful, he thought. More like effortlessly arresting, with perfect, milky skin set off by a cap of sleek black hair, spiky choppy bangs on her forehead and just curling over her ears and the collar of her battered flight jacket. Dex saw character there, in the lift of her chin and in her eyes, those brilliant blue eyes that told him she liked nothing better than to laser through bullshit.

Then there was the way she moved, energy and confidence in every economical step. Her words were just as spare, and while she'd made her opinions of him and her home clear, she kept to herself. Not his usual type, and he figured there must be something perverse in him that he found the sulky set of her mouth appealing, something a little self-destructive that he looked forward to her next cutting comment. And he delighted in not knowing what that comment would be. He'd never enjoyed the predictable.

The woman definitely had dimensions, unexpected dimensions, to her. Take the way she flew, a symphony of movement and emotion so beautiful and raw that watching her made him feel like a voyeur. The fluid grace of her body and the striking, stirring, orgasmic—there was no better way to describe it—bliss on her face made him envy her for the amazing good fortune of making her living doing something she so obviously loved.

If he'd had to choose the one thing about her that intrigued him the most, though, it would be her kiss-my-ass, get-the-hell-out-of-my-way attitude. She was independent as all hell, Dex thought, and in his line of work—no, that wasn't true anymore. He'd left the military and his Special Ops unit behind a long time ago. Problem was, the I-could-die-tomorrow philosophy was hard to shake, especially when he'd chosen a profession that could be every bit as dangerous—and not just to the one in peril.

Hadn't he watched his own sister simply dissolve when she got the news that her cop husband had gone down in the line? Hadn't it broken his heart when she fell apart, killed him to stand by when his parents took her and her two small children in while he could do nothing? Even as he'd grieved, he'd promised himself he'd never do that to someone who loved him.

He glanced over at Maggie Solomon and relaxed. She didn't want anything to do with him, so as long as he resisted his baser urges he'd be fine. Hell, even if his urges got the better of him she'd send him packing, probably by putting him in the dirt—a mental picture he deep-sixed since the idea of a nice, sweaty bout of wrestling with her wasn't doing a whole lot for his self-control.

She glanced over and caught him staring. He looked away, feeling ridiculous that just a meeting of gazes had the heat rising to his face. He hadn't blushed since he was eight and Jenny McWhorter had leaned over and kissed him on the cheek in front of God and his entire third grade class. But he wasn't in third grade anymore. Any heat he allowed himself to feel on account of Maggie Solomon was going to be a hell of lot farther south than his face.

"You sure know your way around a silence," he said, and if keeping his voice even was a struggle, well, he'd managed it, hadn't he?

"You change your mind about the spiel?"

"No, I still don't want to be lectured like a fifth grader. Although," he gave her a long, speculative look, "you wouldn't happen to have any horn-rimmed glasses around, would you?"

"Yeah, I keep them next to my snood, sensible shoes, and the wooden pointer I spank my naughty pupils with."

"Now you're talking."

"You don't set the bar very high, do you?"

"I'm a simple man."

Maggie snorted softly, derisively. "Every woman's fantasy."

"Including yours?"

She didn't dignify that with a verbal response, but the way she set her jaw spoke volumes.

Dex grinned at her. "Did I hit a nerve?"

The helicopter dropped suddenly. Dex grabbed the door handle.

"I'm sorry," she said as she leveled the Twinstar off, "Did you say something about nerves?"

Dex considered and discarded a dozen different comebacks.

His silence was all the response she needed. "That's what I thought," she said, smiling one of the small, wry smiles he already knew represented a major display of emotion for her.

And she'd gone silent again. Dex swore under his breath, but he made sure his tone was light when he spoke for her benefit. "So you were wondering why I'm on my way to Windfall Island."

"Not really, but I gather you want to talk about yourself."

"Your lack of curiosity is unnatural."

She glanced over at him, still amused. "Okay, I'm positively dying. Why are you here?"

Dex smiled so it felt like she was laughing with him, not at him. "Business."

"Who's getting sued?"

And now his smile had some actual humor in it. He'd laid his back trail carefully, and he'd worn the suit for a reason. Nice to know it had paid off, especially with a woman who not only sliced her way through bullshit with the skill and finesse of a master chef breaking down a side of beef, but kept her opinions to herself. If he could fool Maggie Solomon, the rest of the island's population would be asking him for legal advice five minutes after they touched down.

"Why else would you be coming to Windfall with small bags and a big briefcase?"

"If I'd known you were here, I'd have left the briefcase behind."

"Flattery?"

"Not entirely."

She looked over at him, and Dex lost his breath. The heat in her eyes seemed to incinerate all the oxygen in the cockpit. He should have thought about the case, but he was caught, mesmerized. Hungry. And Maggie Solomon, he thought in amazement, was the only one who could satisfy him. She was testy, sarcastic, and way too smart to be fooled for long, and he wanted her beyond reason.

"Maggie—"

"N277HK, I have you on radar," crackled the voice from Windfall Island Airport.

Dex hissed out a breath in frustration. But he thought

better of what he'd been about to say. He needed to stay far, far away from Maggie.

She radioed back, requesting final approach. She didn't look at him again, just sent the helicopter into a banking turn that redirected his attention. He watched the ground rushing up at his face with something approaching gratitude. Of all the dangers he faced on Windfall Island, Maggie crashing the helicopter wasn't the worst that could happen...

Chapter Two

Windfall Island sat a couple miles from the far end of one of the long, thin peninsulas stretching out from the mainland. Houses dotted the shoreline, modest, year-round dwellings rather than the sprawling glass-fronted vacation homes that had begun to spring up on the smaller islands. At the seaward end of the island, clustered around a pretty little bay, sat a handful of buildings, hunkered together against the Atlantic winter about to sock in. At the land-ward end was the marina with its weathered docks and spearing masts, and the village, population nine hundred eight—not counting three babies on the way.

From his current altitude, Windfall looked welcoming with its quaint settlement, its checkerboard of neat fields already harvested for fall, and its quiet, forested shorelines. But Dex knew better. Even if his research hadn't already clued him in to the kind of welcome he could expect, geography would have provided a warning.

Roughly half the island had direct exposure to the Atlantic. Even on a day like this, with blue skies and mild winds, the surf foamed and sprayed along the jagged, rocky shore. Dex could only imagine what it must be like in a gale, winds whipping the ocean into a frenzy, surf thrashing the exposed coast; even the wide channels separating the island from the mainland would be impassable.

Geography, however, was only part of the story. Isolation might be a physical reality, but the history of the residents made it a way of life. Dex expected a warm welcome. Tourism made up their main source of income, after all, and he was arriving at the tail end of the season. But they weren't stupid or unobservant. What they were was rarified, and a lone man asking a lot of unusual questions wouldn't go unnoticed or unremarked for long. It would make his job that much harder, but he never let a little adversity stop him. His eyes wandered left again and he thought, *Nope, one impossible undertaking at a time*.

"Not much to it," he observed, making an obvious visual survey of Windfall Island.

"We have everything we need. Where are you staying?"

"I'm at the Horizon."

"Really?" She slanted him a look, surprised. "That's an efficiency. AJ only rents by the week. You planning to be around a while?"

"It's a possibility."

She didn't respond, too busy landing the helicopter, Dex figured, so he left her to it. Not surprisingly, she climbed out as soon as she'd powered down the bird, coming around to unlatch his door before it occurred to him to release his harness. And then he left it on because having her lean across him was irresistible…until her scent went to his head. Since he needed his wits about him he let her step back. But he drew the line at watching her schlep his luggage again.

Of course, she was still being unreasonable, so he simply took her by the waist and shifted her aside.

"What the hell?"

"Finally."

"As in finally you're going to die?"

"Not exactly."

"Put your hands on me again—"

Dex crowded her back against the Twinstar. He didn't put his hands on her. "And what?"

"And you'd better be prepared to swim off this island, because I won't take you and I can see to it that no one else does either."

"Already desperate to keep me around?"

She plowed a fist into his stomach.

Dex's breath whooshed out, in surprise more than anything else. She couldn't have put much behind it with barely six inches between them, but he stepped away from her, slow and easy. And he was grinning. "I just wanted to see the real you."

"This isn't the real me."

"Maybe not," he said, rubbing a hand over his ribs, "but it's a hell of a lot more interesting than the tour guide who flew me in from Portland." Interesting, hell; she was glorious, blue eyes blazing, chin stuck out, that long, lean body all but vibrating with temper. She didn't show the slightest hint of a pout or sulk, she didn't pull out the tears or try to inflict guilt. In fact, she looked like she might pop him again. He rounded the helicopter to retrieve his luggage.

"You didn't rent a car," she said, surprising him again by how easily she reined in her anger. A woman who'd had a lot of practice, he'd bet, and found himself wondering why.

He let that go, too. What made Maggie Solomon tick was none of his concern. "I was told everything is in walking distance."

"As long as everything you want is in the village."

"Do you live there?"

"I live here."

Dex looked around, belatedly realizing they'd landed on the seaward end of the island, about as far from town as they could get, thinking, *why am I not surprised*, but saying, "Maybe you could put me up. I'm not very picky. I'll sleep just about anywhere."

"Well, then, you definitely need to stay at the Horizon. You'll be the biggest thing to hit the place since the hurricane of ought six."

"Not a lot of single men in town?"

She gave him a look, down, then up, definitely laughing at him again, although at least this time he got the joke. "Single won't be the deciding factor. On either side."

"Should I take that as a compliment?"

"I'd take it as a warning. Most every man on Windfall has a gun, and there's a long history of territoriality."

That wiped the smile off his face. "You sure there's not a spare room around here? You're hostile, but I don't get the feeling you'd shoot me."

"Pull what you did a minute ago, and I wouldn't be so sure."

"Maybe you should loosen up a little, have some fun."

She sent him another look. *Not if you were the last man on earth.*

He'd never thought of himself as a guy who needed the pursuit, but he got a kick out of being rejected by Maggie Solomon. "I'm always up for a challenge," he said.

"Then you came to the right place." Maggie turned for the office, her long-legged stride eating up the ground. "I'll have my business manager, Jessi, drop you at the Horizon."

He abandoned his luggage to trail after her. "I appreciate it."

"She's about to head home anyway, so if you don't mind it'll save me the trip. If there's anything else you need, she can point you in the right direction."

"Can she get you to have dinner with me?"

"That's not a direction she'll be pointing you," Maggie said lightly. She glanced over her shoulder, her expression...If she'd been any other woman, he'd have sworn she was flirting with him.

He smiled back. "I rarely stop for directions."

"Then it's a good thing you won't be driving."

Okay, not flirting, Dex decided, but still smiling, at least. The thing was, he couldn't take no for an answer. If he knew his small towns, and he did, gossip would be the hobby of choice for just about everyone on the island. Except for Maggie Solomon, apparently. That meant any information he could drag out of her would be reliable. "Are you always this standoffish?"

"If I can help it."

"Good, I was afraid this place would be boring."

The Solomon Charters waiting room was a calm, clean space with old-fashioned tile waxed to within an inch of its life, serviceable, if dated, chrome-and-black Naugahyde furniture, and a long unmanned counter. The wide office beyond was like getting too close to the sun, all heat and bright light and crackling energy. Maggie was used to it. Dex looked a little shell-shocked.

Music played, the printer hummed, the radio squawked, and every inch of wall space was covered with charts, maps, bulletin boards, and random notes tacked up at odd angles with multi-colored push pins.

Jessi Randal, Maggie's best friend and Girl Friday, stood in front of a desk crowded with office equipment, her son's school projects, and haphazard stacks of paperwork. She had a phone jammed between her ear and shoulder, and she was bent over the desk taking notes with a fuzzy purple pen, her butt waggling to a song that was thumping bass and not much else.

Maggie tossed the clipboard she'd brought in from the Twinstar on top of a stack, sending papers and file folders slumping sideways to bank up against the old-fashioned rotary office phone.

Jessi looked up. Her gaze landed on Dex; her usual warm smile turned appreciative. And considering. She turned to Maggie and pointed at him, shaking her hand like she'd burned her fingers.

Maggie shook her head.

Jessi rolled her eyes.

Dex cleared his throat.

They both ignored him.

"Really, Mrs. Delacourt," Jessi said into the phone, "I understand the plane is small, but you know, that means it's lighter, so it's a lot easier to defy gravity…No, Maggie hardly ever crashes, and never when she's flying. Let her behind the wheel of a car and you better watch out, but in a cockpit she's golden…Yes, you could take a boat, then rent a car and drive ninety miles to the airport then catch a commercial flight to New York, but that'll cost you more than hiring Solomon Charters, and—oh, wait, you don't drive, do you?"

Jessi listened for a second or two, then, grinning, she wrote *Delacourt* on a scheduling board next to her desk. She finished with "Thank you," and hung up, barely pausing to draw breath as she turned to Maggie. "Is this a gift for me? And if it is, why is it dressed for a funeral?"

Dex glanced down at his perfectly respectable black suit, then at Maggie. "I doubt she'd call me a gift."

"Not even close to being on the list."

Jessi took another look at Dex, an embarrassingly long and thorough look. Dex didn't seem to mind, until she started talking.

"Good looking," Jessi said. "Focused, healthy ego but he's probably earned it, and if he wasn't interested in you, I'd be all over him."

"Are you a business manager or a profiler?" Dex said.

"Jessi likes to think she can read people."

"Jessi likes to think that because it's true," Jessi said.

Maggie shook her head. "If I had a clue how to find anything in this mess you call an office, you'd be history."

"Right, and then who'd pay the bills, answer the phone, and deal with Mrs. Delacourt?"

"I have skills," Maggie said.

"People skills?"

"Those, too. Sort of. I deal with the tourists."

"As long as you keep to the script," Jessi said, and then she caught the smirk on Dex's face. "Look, Mr. Keegan agrees with me."

"Dex," he said, "and the script isn't all that great, either."

"See? I told you he was into you."

"He's a gift for you, remember? Start unwrapping. Don't mind me."

Jessi burst out laughing, so did Maggie. They both looked at Dex, and laughed harder.

"This is very entertaining," he said, "but maybe you could use some actual words."

Maggie hooked a thumb in his direction. "Lawyer."

"They do like their words," Jessi said, "and their arguments. I can see why you'd butt heads with him."

"Maggie doesn't argue," Dex said.

"Wait until you get to know her better."

"I don't climb."

Jessi frowned. "How did we get from Maggie to mountains?"

"Not mountains, walls," Dex corrected, his gaze switching to Maggie. "High ones."

"Not just words; you like metaphors, too." Jessi sidled closer, grinned up at him. "I'll bet you were a nerd in school, black-rimmed glasses, and with that dark hair," she sighed, "I always had a thing for Clark Kent."

"Clark Kent I could do, but I don't have a red cape."

"Too bad. Superman could leap tall buildings. Maggie's walls would be no challenge to him."

Two pairs of eyes slid sidelong to her.

Maggie rolled hers. "If you two are finished, Mr. Keegan needs a ride into town, Jess. And since you're off the clock," she consulted her watch, "ten minutes ago, I volunteered you to drive him to the Horizon."

"You're at the Horizon?" Jessi said. "You must plan on being around a while."

"Depends," Dex said. "Maybe I could pick your brain while we head into town."

"Sure. Wanna play twenty questions?"

"I've got more than twenty questions. Maggie wouldn't answer her share."

Maggie took a deep breath but it didn't help much. It had been a long day. She stared at Dex, bonding with Jessi. A long, trying day. "Yes, Jessi has lived here all her life," she said, "yes, she'd love to know why you're here. You can duck her questions, and she can tell you about growing up on the island. It should be a fascinating conversation. Go have it in the car."

"You grew up here?" Dex said, focusing all his attention on Jessi.

"Don't you have to go?" Maggie asked Jessi before she could answer.

Jessi looked at her watch and freaked out. "Sh—, Da—, Fudge Popsicles," she shouted, a blur as she raced from one side of the office to the other, collecting her purse and coat. "I should have picked up Benji by now, and Dottie Hampton is always so snotty when I'm late. Maggie, you'll have to take Mr. Keegan into town yourself."

"Call me Dex," he said, getting out of her way as she streaked around her desk.

Maggie stepped between Jessi and the door. "Jess, you have to go right by the Horizon."

"Absolutely true," Jessi said, smiling suggestively, infuriatingly, at Maggie, before she shoved by. "Nice meeting you, Dex. Welcome to Temptation Bay," she called out as she slammed through the office door, then the outer one. A few seconds later, Maggie heard her ancient Explorer cough to life and roar off.

She glanced at Dex. His expression was a lot like Jessi's, except more smug.

"Temptation Bay?" he said.

"Is that amusing?"

He gave her a thorough once over. "Appropriate is the word I'd use."

The heat that was rising to her face spread, but before it could get real traction she funneled it into annoyance. "I could make you walk," she pointed out.

His grin only widened. "But you won't."

Chapter Three

Dex could see Maggie struggling between wanting him gone and having to be the one to make it happen.

"I could just stay here," he said.

"I could call George." Maggie leaned against the desk and crossed her arms. She made him ask the question.

She didn't know he already knew the answer. "Who's George?"

"George is the sheriff."

As threats went, it was a pretty good one. Dex had done his homework on the local heat before he'd come to Windfall Island. A lot of people would take George Boatwright for a loser who couldn't cut it in a larger urban arena. A lot of people would be wrong. George had been an army sniper, but it wasn't his perfect aim that concerned Dex. It was his instincts. George would take one look at him and run a background check. Dex had laid a false back trail for himself, but it wouldn't stand up to too much scrutiny. "If you're afraid to spend any more time with me..."

She gave him a look, then disappeared into a smaller office behind the main one, reappearing with a set of keys. She didn't say a word as she exited the office, and she didn't offer to carry his luggage. Hell, she barely gave him time to toss his bags into the trunk of a sleek black Mustang GT before she slammed it closed.

"I'm headed into town, Mort," she yelled at an overall-wearing, scrubby-looking, twenty-something guy who gave her a half wave as she got in the car.

Dex barely spared him a glance as he shuffled off in the direction of a building that had to be a hangar. "You were going to tell me about the island," he said, settling into the passenger seat.

"Persistent, aren't you?"

"When I want something badly enough."

Maggie held his gaze as she started the car and put it in gear, turning her attention forward again as she peeled out of the airport lot with a squeal of rubber. For someone so closed off, Dex mused, she didn't realize just how much she actually gave away.

She drove like a maniac on the narrow, winding road that molded itself to every twist and turn of the shoreline. Her car, as deceptively sleek and pretty as its owner, hugged the curves like automotive Velcro. Whatever else could be said about Maggie Solomon, the woman appreciated fine machinery, and she knew how to use it. She worked the gears, clutch, and brake pedal like a race car driver, her face bright with the same delight as when she'd been flying—until he spoke, and she closed off again. It was like the clouds covering the sun suddenly. The light, the warmth was still there, and you knew it had to shine again some time. But not for him. Dex regretted that, more than he cared to admit.

But he couldn't let it matter.

"How far is it to the village?" he said as she powered the car through a series of curves winding around the rocky outcroppings along the shoreline.

She glanced over at him, one brow arched, the corners of her mouth lifted into a slight smile. "Why don't you ask me what you really want to know?"

"Because you won't answer my questions. I wonder why that is."

She bumped up a shoulder, let it fall. "Like I told Jessi, you're trouble."

"Maybe I'm here on behalf of someone on the island."

"I'd know about it. Which means you work for an outsider."

Outsider. He didn't so much file that term away as he took note of the way she said it. She might not have lived on Windfall her whole life, but she was an islander now, through and through.

"And if I said I don't intend to cause harm to anyone?"

"Good intentions are little comfort after the fact."

"They're not much good now, seeing as you're determined to think the worst of me."

She throttled the car down, then punched it through another curve. "In order to understand Windfall," she said, no hesitation, no defensiveness, no apology for putting him off before, "you need a little context—history.

"There's not much in the way of industry here. Never has been. The soil is fertile, but the island isn't big enough for more than subsistence farming. Fishing can be profitable, but boats are expensive to own and maintain. Even if the early settlers of the island had had collateral, there weren't banks on every street corner waiting to give out loans. But there were a lot of ships going in and out of New World ports."

"And the Atlantic is anything but predictable."

She shrugged again, with the same take-life-as-it-comes attitude he imagined the first settlers had possessed.

"There was always a captain willing to push the season,"

she continued. "They'd sail well into the winter, when crossing the north Atlantic was treacherous. In the event a ship didn't make port, the same owners who'd paid those crews to risk their lives didn't want to lose their cargo.

"Most of the organized salvage crews operated farther south, along the heaviest-traveled shipping routes between South America and Europe, but there were many communities like this one along the Atlantic coastline, where crews put out at a moment's notice to offload cargo and rescue passengers from ships that ran aground, usually at great personal danger to themselves. History calls them salvagers; rumor calls them wreckers."

"What's the difference?" Dex asked.

"Salvagers were opportunists who took advantage of ships driven onto the rocks by the Atlantic. Wreckers weren't that patient. Allegedly. There was a lot of money to be made, enough that the leaders of some of the salvage crews were said to have ordered lights to be carried along the shore."

"To wreck them."

"Tall tales," she said dismissively. "Lanterns shone at shore level don't carry far across open water, and even if they did, they would have warned ships away from the shoals, not suckered them in."

"What about survivors?"

"In the early days, who knows? Congress passed the Federal Wrecking Act in 1825. The Act regulated compensation for salvagers, including conditions involving survivors. It also decreed a death sentence for anyone found guilty of shining false lights or extinguishing real ones."

"It must have been a hard life."

"Harder, I think, than you and I can imagine. And it was only compounded by the attitude from the mainland. Salvage crews were insular, secretive, and dangerous. No one, including wives and children, discussed their business with outsiders. It's a powerful legacy."

"There aren't many shipwrecks nowadays."

"There's no real need for a monarch in England, either."

Tradition dies hard, Dex interpreted. Mess with one Windfaller, mess with them all. Including Maggie. She'd told him the other residents were armed to the teeth and junkyard-dog ornery, and he'd still rather take them on than Maggie Solomon. She had an edge to her, a quality that told him she'd do whatever it took and not think twice.

"My point is," Dex said, "there hasn't been any salvaging income in more than a century. You said farming and fishing weren't viable undertakings. How have the islanders survived?"

"Any way they could. Working on the mainland, running booze during Prohibition, tourism nowadays. Necessity is the mother," she finished, "a mother who turns out some pretty tough children."

"You fit right in here, Maggie."

"You don't," she said, no heat, no threat, but a warning all the same. "Tread lightly."

"And carry a big stick?"

She laughed a little. "I wouldn't. People around here see a stick, they just naturally feel threatened."

"Or when they see a lawyer?"

"This is the Horizon," she said, angling the car into a parking space in front of a weathered, two-story, wood frame building. The sign over the door looked like it had been carved out of driftwood or the broken plank off an old shipwreck. A wavy line bisected the sign from left to right. On top of the line was a half circle with rays coming out of it, painted a faded yellow. The wood below the line was painted an equally faded blue.

"Any chance we can continue this later?"

Maggie turned to face him, and suddenly the car was way too small. It filled with the scent of her, fresh salt air with just a hint of motor oil, strangely irresistible. He felt the heat pumping off her, saw the pulse beating in the hollow of her throat. She wasn't as calm and disinterested as she appeared.

He'd known her barely an hour, but he already craved her like a drug, could all but taste the hot magic of her mouth, feel the silk of her skin, knew how her long, slim body would fit to his.

She'd make it a contest, Dex mused; she'd take as much as she'd give. And how much sweeter the surrender would be.

"Maggie—"

"No."

"You're not being honest with yourself."

"Maybe not," she said, meeting his eyes, letting him see the desire, and the uncertainty, in the brilliant blue depths. "The real question is, how honest are you being with me?"

"As honest as I can be."

She smiled slightly. "That's how honest I'm being with myself."

She leaned forward and for a second, just a second, he thought she was going to kiss him because her face turned toward his. He felt her breath whisper over his lips...and then she popped his door open and shifted back into her seat, but not before she brushed against him and the world shuddered to a halt. Or maybe the lurch he felt was his nerve endings all shrieking to attention at the same time. It felt amazingly, electrifyingly good. He might never open another door again as long as Maggie was around.

"This is good-bye, Counselor."

"Not if I have anything to say about it," Dex murmured. But he stepped out of the car, disgusted with himself, and not just for mishandling the situation with Maggie.

He should have done more research, but damn it he'd thought lawyer would be a good cover. Now he wondered if the truth might've given him something in common with these people; after all, right and wrong were concepts with blurry lines. Then again, lawyers were called sharks for a reason.

And sharks, from the sound of things, weren't all that different from Wreckers.

After Maggie dropped him off at the Horizon—or, more accurately, kicked him out—there hadn't been much of the day left. Dex chose to spend it in his hotel room, factoring in what he'd learned from Maggie and re-thinking his game plan. He hadn't expected the case to go smoothly, or for Windfall Island to be a simple place just because it was small, but he'd come, he admitted, with expectations, which, if Maggie was to be believed, the place defied.

He was nothing, he told himself, if not flexible. Patience, however, was another story, and sleep hard to come by with his body still wired and his brain spinning scenario after scenario, all of them ending the same way: with him solving Eugenia Stanhope's kidnapping, a case that had baffled the best investigators, in and out of organized law enforcement, for the better part of a century. Making a name for himself.

Any name but failure.

He took out his cell and speed dialed, smiling when his old man's voice came over the line. "Hey, kid," Carter Keegan said heartily. "Still tilting at windmills?"

"You know me," he replied. "Never could resist a lost cause."

"Plenty of lost causes right here in the big, bad city of Boston. Take the other day..."

Dex smiled, listening to Sergeant Keegan's voice, with its broad Southie accent, as he talked about the Boston Police Department and the insanity that took place on a daily basis. His old man, a cop through and through, thought he was crazy to give up a perfectly respectable career as a fourth generation Boston cop to go out on his own.

Considering Dex was almost down to his last thin dime, Dad wasn't too far wrong.

"Your mother's gone out to the store. She'll be sorry she missed you," Carter was saying. "I swear, she worries more now than she did when you wore a uniform and walked a beat in some of the city's worst neighborhoods."

"I was close to home then," he said, completely understanding how his mother felt. Phone calls could be made, e-mails sent, but there was no substitute for seeing the face of someone you loved. "How's Lou?" he asked, wishing he could see her for himself, but knowing his father wouldn't sugar coat it.

"Louise is doing better, I think. It's still day by day, but she's getting tired of your mother being, what do they call it these days, a hovercraft?"

"A helicopter mom," he said, his mind going just for a moment to Maggie. She and his sister were a lot alike: strong, independent. Fighters. It took a lot to bring Lou down. If she was tired of being coddled, then she was on the mend. "That's good to hear," he told his father.

"It's damn good to see. You should drag your sorry butt up here and find out firsthand."

"I'm on a case, Dad. I'll get home first chance."

"Hell, kid, just make sure you call your mother later on. Otherwise she'll find a reason to blame me for it."

Dex laughed, feeling restored. Traveling around the country chasing missing persons cases meant he couldn't be there for a sister whose life had imploded, a sister who'd always been there for him. Hearing she was doing better, hell, hearing his old man call him kid, went a long way toward soothing his conscience.

And made him even more determined to solve Eugenia Stanhope's mystery. After all, he thought as he exited the Horizon, he wasn't the only one living with the choices he'd made.

Dex slipped his phone in his pocket and walked out of the hotel. The sky, far off at the horizon, was a mass of purple and gray where Mother Nature warred with Neptune in some distant, empty stretch of the Atlantic. The angry color bled to a clear, deep blue above Windfall Island, but the breeze off the water had a bite, both in temperature and tang. And attitude, Dex thought, fancying he could feel just a light slap in it from the storm raging miles away.

Fall had come with a vengeance, not just in the snap on the air, but the beauty of leaves shining red and yellow against that intense blue sky—the color, he couldn't help but notice, so much like Maggie Solomon's eyes. And wasn't she just like the morning, he mused, placid on the surface, all her emotions pent up and seething just under the surface.

He'd seen the depth of her generosity when it came to her friends, but something about him rubbed her the wrong way. It probably hadn't helped when he'd put her up against the helicopter. But he'd do it again. Hell, given the chance, he'd do more, push her past that iron control she seemed to wield over herself as automatically as she drew breath.

It would probably be glorious, but it wouldn't gain him her trust, and he needed her trust.

Even though he'd already betrayed it.

And if that didn't set well with his conscience, well, it was too late to turn back now, with the deal struck and the down payment already spent. And he wasn't a man who dealt in regrets, he reminded himself, turning his attention back to the case as he set off through the village.

The single road Maggie had taken from the airport at Temptation Bay contorted itself around rocks and hopped over small streams in a seeming race to make it to the village, but there it meandered suddenly, like it had been laid out by a drunken sailor—which it probably had. Businesses sat cheek-by-jowl on the inland side of the street, with a scattering of houses nestled in the curve behind them. Shanty-style buildings tottered along the shoreline side, some so old it looked like the next strong breeze might set off a domino effect. Signs were posted on the end walls: *No leaning.*

Each building was unique, some of them painted in garish tones with gaudy striped awnings, others less in-your-face, their colors softened by the sun, salt air, and the harsh weather that spewed off the Atlantic Ocean. Like the Horizon, each business sported a pictograph sign, holdovers from a time when few of the residents could read. None of the narrow lanes had names; the residents likely found it unnecessary. The tourists would find it charming, Dex imagined, and the tourists were very necessary.

True to Maggie's word, Dex saw no industry of any kind in the village. A trio of fishing trawlers were moored at the rickety docks, along with two Solomon Charters boats—for the crossing from island to mainland and whale watching, Dex assumed—but tourism was clearly the island's main source of income. He could use that; merchants who depended on tourism were invariably chatty, open to satisfying the curiosity of strangers.

He set out with high hopes; Windfall Island dashed them in record time. He hadn't gone a block before he realized nearly every tourist-centric business was already closed for the season. That left the businesses that catered to residents' day-to-day needs.

He chatted up Mr. MacDonald, sole proprietor and, this time of year, stock boy, cashier and bagger of the single grocery store. And by "chatted," he meant he'd talked and Mr. MacDonald had stared like a basilisk at him. Dex spent a little money at the five and dime, where the only conversation consisted of how much change he got back. Then he visited the hardware store, the pharmacy, and the pizzeria, grabbing lunch in the aromatic heat and fending off questions while the owner and her son revealed absolutely nothing about themselves or the island.

He'd even poked his head inside the doors of the Clipper Snip, telling himself it was the overwhelming odor of chemicals that made his mind reel rather than the eight pairs of female eyes that had swiveled in his direction then lit with some variation of avarice. They were only after information, Dex assured himself. It didn't stop him from feeling like he was about to be gobbled up like the last hot dog at a Fourth of July party.

Still, he loved this part of a case, when the clues could lead him anywhere, straight ahead or back the way he'd come or halfway around the world. Where everyone was a suspect and the most innocent tidbit of information could turn out to be the linchpin. And this case...this case carried special weight, just by being so damned historically significant, not to mention its importance to a family like the Stanhopes.

He should have been having the time of his life. And what was on his mind? Maggie Solomon. She was hardheaded, sarcastic, argumentative, uncomplimentary, and a general pain in the ass. And he couldn't wait to see her again. He'd known her less than twenty-four hours, but the world seemed so much brighter than it had yesterday, so much more filled with possibilities. Which was saying something when he stood on the brink of the biggest opportunity of his life. He solved this case and clients would be beating down his door, clients with substantial cases that didn't involve who was doing whom in some tawdry out-of-the-way motel room.

And he couldn't keep his mind on the prize. Okay, not only his mind.

Christ.

He took a deep breath, put Maggie in a tiny little box he locked away in an obscure corner of his brain, and swung through the door of the Windfall Island Antique Store. And stopped dead.

Hoarders: The Antique Chronicles, he thought, taking in the haphazard stacks of merchandise crowding the place with absolutely no sense of order.

A Chippendale dresser sat against the wall, its top crowded with vases, one of which could have dated to the early Roman Empire, others to the post–World War II trinket trade in Japan. A cheap dinette table was flanked by a six-pack of chairs; at least one of them looked to be a Windsor, if Dex remembered even a tenth of the research he'd done for an elderly client whose nurse had systematically stripped her house of antiques, replacing them with halfway decent fakes.

Ottomans sat on chairs, which rested on tables propped up by statuary, all of it balanced precariously, sometimes to the rafters high overhead. Dex stepped in and found himself in a maze of winding aisles barely wide enough to navigate. Around every corner something new caught his eye, items ranging in age and value from priceless museum quality to cheap flea market. Ten minutes later and with no idea where he'd left the door, he came to what appeared to be the front counter, if the gold and silver-plated antique cash register sitting on a glass display case was any indication.

Beside the counter stood a tall, gaunt figure with a white, slightly shiny complexion, dressed in the clothing of a nineteenth-century magistrate. Wax, Dex decided, despite the eerily lifelike eyes.

And then it spoke. "Can I help you?"

Dex pasted an open and friendly expression on his face and stepped forward. "You must be the proprietor." Josiah Meeker, or so the discreet gold lettering on the front window had informed him.

"And you'd be Dexter Keegan, lawyer from Boston," Meeker said, staring distastefully at the hand Dex held out.

Dex might have been offended if he hadn't seen the way Meeker's own hands rubbed against his pants legs. OCD in some form, he would have bet. Dex glanced around. That would explain why it looked like the man had never parted with a single piece of merchandise in his entire life.

"You after anything in particular?" Meeker said, still looking like he'd been sucking on a lemon.

"No." Dex wandered over to a trio of cabinets made of lacquered wood fronted with age-spotted glass.

Smalls—little collectible items—crowded the warped wooden shelves. He pretended to study the worn and well-loved old toys, costume jewelry, miniature china figurines, and matchbox cars that took him back to his childhood. But his eyes shifted to a pair of doors in the corner. Both doors bore signs limiting access to staff members, but one of those doors was narrower, with an external lock and a small thermostat on the wall beside it. Temperature- and, he'd have wagered, humidity-controlled.

"What's your business on the island?" Meeker wanted to know. "Maybe it will help me steer you to something likely."

History. But Dex stopped himself from saying it. There was something about Meeker that made his gut talk. Dex always listened to his gut, especially when caution was the message it sent.

"I'm just getting to know my way around the village."

"You're that lawyer checked into the Horizon yesterday."

"Word travels fast."

"I haven't heard anything about who you represent."

"Why would you?"

Meeker's face shifted into a smirk. "You tell me."

Dex borrowed Maggie's signature shrug, let his gaze drift around the place before they landed on the door with its telltale little thermostat. "I'm a sucker for a good cigar."

Meeker glanced over his shoulder, and when he turned back, those black eyes of his narrowed on Dex's face. "Don't sell tobacco products of any sort."

"That's not a humidor, then?" Dex said with a tinge of disappointment, indicating the smaller door behind Meeker.

"Cigar smoking is a nasty habit," Meeker said sourly. "I keep books in there. Which, no doubt, AJ Appelman told you."

"AJ Appelman? At the Horizon? Why would he tell me you keep books in a humidor?" Dex asked.

"Why indeed? Just who do you represent, Mr. Keegan?"

Frowning a little, Dex turned to look at Meeker. "What does my client have to do with anything?"

"Because they're more than just books. They're journals,

some of them going back to Windfall's beginnings." Meeker's mouth lifted in a slight, self-satisfied sneer. "I've had museums, universities, and all manner of research people begging me to loan them, to image them, and whatnot. I've turned them all down, with their letters and e-mails and phone calls."

"None of them bothered to come in person." Which would have given Meeker the respect he thought his due, even if he tried to deny his ego had anything to do with it.

"An outsider is still an outsider, even when he deigns to show up in the flesh. What makes you think I'd let you waltz in here and have them just for the asking?"

"Who said I was asking?"

"Are you meaning to tell me you're not here at the behest of some museum or university, to convince me to part with the only written history of this island?"

"I can assure you my client has no idea those journals exist." Which he could say with such absolute conviction that for the first time Meeker seemed uncertain.

"Oh," he said, moving to fuss nervously with a display of little china boxes on a nearby shelf.

Mission accomplished, Dex thought, all but shaking with the effort to keep his expression placid. Those journals might yield nothing, but the possibility they'd help him solve this case…It made his head spin a little, the idea that he could be the one to discover the whereabouts of a child kidnapped nearly a century past. And not just for himself. Eugenia Stanhope had a family who were still alive, still searching for her. He could only imagine what it would be like for them to finally see an end to all those years of wondering.

Yeah, he wanted those journals—as much as he wanted his next breath. Instead he turned away, taking small consolation in knowing he must have convinced Meeker he wasn't interested in them, or the man would still be hovering in front of that door like his skinny frame and nasty disposition posed any real obstacle.

Getting out of there before he did something stupid seemed like his only option, so Dex pointed himself into the maze, the natural light filtering in the front windows his only directional beacon.

Meeker followed along behind him. "Is there something I can help you find, then?" he said, sounding pained that he'd lost a sale.

Dex turned back at the door. "Didn't see anything that appealed to me."

And that was the absolute truth, he thought as he pushed through the door and stepped out onto the raised boardwalk. He hadn't laid eyes on the journals, but he'd discovered their existence—although Dex doubted Meeker's assertion that they were a written history.

On an island like Windfall, a community that operated as a sort of corporation to salvage shipwrecks and mete out shares, likely some of those books were more ledgers than anything else. The rest would be personal accounts, most probably written by women since they were more apt to keep diaries or journals than men.

Still, he might find a nugget somewhere in them, a bit of information that could lead him to Eugenia Stanhope's ultimate fate.

Just as soon as he found a way to get his hands on them.

Chapter Four

Within a week, Windfall's few remaining vacationers would be gone. Maggie knew, as she'd be flying them out herself.

Though the seasonal loss of the tourists, with their pockets full of mad money, meant lean times, Maggie preferred it that way. No outsiders meant the residents weren't reenacting a historical salvagers' community. They were themselves, and that, she thought with an indulgent smile, suited her so much better.

She swung through the door of the island's only fuel station, her smile widening into a full-out, time-to-have-some-fun grin.

Jed Morgenstern, all five and a half feet of him, had what looked like a bed sheet wrapped around his waist with a tail of it draped over one shoulder. He wore a t-shirt under it, a rope belt around his waist, and a slight look of embarrassment on his craggy, weathered face.

"Maggie," he said by way of greeting.

She could all but see him bracing himself. She didn't disappoint, taking a half step back and looking him over with a critical eye. "Could use something," she pondered. "Maybe a crown of olive branches."

"Jeez—"

"Or some gold sandals, and if you really want to pull off that look you should lose the t-shirt."

"Knock it off."

"What do Romans wear under their togas, anyway?"

"Maggie," he said again, casting a cautious glance over his shoulder before he added, "You know Martha."

"Not as well as you." But she did know Martha. Everyone on the island knew Martha and her affinity for the tragic romances of history: Arthur and Guinevere, Romeo and Juliet, Burton and Taylor—they didn't all have to end with death. Combine that with her constant search for novelty, and Jed's comfort zone didn't stand a chance. Then again, he probably had the best sex life of any man on Windfall. Not to mention more variety. "So who are you supposed to be, anyway?"

"Anthony and Cleopatra."

"I think you mean Antony."

Jed gave her a look, not caring a rat's ass about the distinction.

"Did you just roll your eyes?" Martha called from the back room.

"How does she *do* that?"

"Hey, Martha," Maggie called back to her.

"Call me Cleo." Martha appeared and struck a dramatic pose in the doorway, looking like a forty-something version of Elizabeth Taylor, if Elizabeth Taylor had been a five-foot ten inch beanpole with magenta hair. Martha got the costume right, though—hair done in spit curl ringlets, heavy black cat's eye makeup, white toga, chunky Roman-esque costume jewelry. "I didn't hear you complaining last night," she said to her husband.

Jed's complexion went about three shades redder, and he ducked his head. "I'm thinking you didn't come in here to bust my chops, Maggie."

"No, that was just a bonus. My fuel coming in Friday?"

"Maybe."

Maggie shrugged. "Maybe I'll get it somewhere else."

"On this island?" Jed said, getting a little of his own back.

"It'll be here Friday," Cleo put in.

"It's not coming by chariot, is it?"

"Funny," Jed snapped before his wife elbowed him away from the small front counter so she could lean on it, her eyes avid as they latched onto Maggie's face. "Tell me about the outsider you flew in from Portland the other day."

"Lawyer," Maggie said, "staying at the Horizon."

"And?"

"He paid me to bring him to Windfall, I brought him."

Cleo/Martha gave an impatient little huff. "You didn't talk on the way? For crying out loud, Maggie, didn't you ask him one blessed thing?"

"Oh, I grilled him," Maggie said. Mostly because he'd insisted on it, but still, the questions had come from her own brain, right? "He wasn't giving anything up. The lawyer-client thing, I guess."

Martha planted her hands on her toga-draped hips. That close-mouthed lawyer crap might be all right for the Supreme Court, her expression said, but she wasn't buying it. Martha smelled gossip, and she wasn't giving up until she got some. She opened her mouth to let Maggie have it, but the bell over the door jangled, and Trudie Bingham, blond, bright-eyed, and barely twenty, breezed in and sang out, "Ma-il."

Maggie didn't waste any time thinking she was off the hook.

"Here's yours," Trudie said, handing Maggie a stack of random advertisements with one or two junk envelopes on top, addressed to *occupant*. "I heard you brought a man to the island."

"Lawyer." Maggie dumped her "mail" into the wastebasket behind the counter. "Staying at the Horizon."

Martha threw her hands up.

Trudie was more optimistic about her chances of learning something useful. "Is he cute? Is he tall? Is he single?" she wanted to know.

Cute? Cute definitely was not the right terminology for Dex Keegan. Dangerous, secretive, potent, but not cute. "No, yes, and I didn't ask him," she said to Trudie. "In that order."

Trudie stuck out her bottom lip. "Mean." Which didn't, unfortunately, put her off. "Is he at least famous?"

"Never heard of him before," Maggie said.

"Oh. Then why are there reporters down at the Horizon?"

"What?" Martha streaked around the counter, clamped a hand around Trudie's wrist. "There are reporters at the Horizon?"

"With cameras. Mom went down there to find out why." Trudie's pout turned into a sulk. "She made me stay behind to man the counter at the post office."

Martha let her go. "I'll bet it's Paige Walker."

Maggie froze, her heart thundering in her ears so loud she barely heard the conversation buzzing around her. Not that she gave even half a damn about Paige Walker, Windfall Island's most famous daughter, gone to Hollywood to be a big star.

Paige might have gotten herself all polished up, earned fame and fortune, but while the surface might be as gold as the little statues Paige had earned herself, it seemed the base alloy was still just cheap metal.

She'd been a friend once upon a time, a good friend, back when they were both schoolgirls. Before Paige had betrayed her.

"Last I heard she was in Cannes," Martha was saying, her broad New England accent making it sound like something on a market shelf filled with pork and beans, rather than a playground of the rich and famous. "That girl never stays in one place long, even when those tabloid bloodsuckers aren't hounding her to dish up a scandal. And she never comes home.

"'Course," Martha continued, "this ain't her home anymore, and a sex tape with a married director is more than a scandal."

"I read the wife is going to sue her for," Trudie screwed up her face in a Herculean effort to remember the exact wording, "alienation of affection."

"I doubt there was much affection on that director's side—or Paige's, for that matter. Right, Maggie?"

"Don't know, don't care."

"Well, I doubt the girl'd come back here to lick her wounds."

Maggie figured Martha was right about Paige; she'd brushed Windfall Island off like so much beach sand a decade ago, made it clear just how much better she thought she was than everyone here. No way Paige would show her face while her precious reputation was in tatters.

But there were cameras down at the Horizon, and Paige Walker wasn't the only famous name with a Windfall Island connection. In Maggie's estimation, she wasn't even the worst.

"You going down there, Maggie?"

"No." But as she turned away from Martha and walked out the door, she knew she didn't really have a choice.

Maggie pulled her Mustang to the curb a block away from the Horizon, then sat there until her legs were steady. The sky was the clear, aching blue of a bright fall day, the air wafted in crisply through the open window, and she could smell the tang of the sea. Everything was familiar and dear to her. And the heart she'd thought was shattered beyond repair was breaking again.

A fair-sized crowd of Windfallers had gathered in front of the inn. She couldn't see who they'd gathered around, but she knew. If Paige Walker, star of stage, screen and, just lately, the Internet, had set foot on the island, there'd have been enough paparazzi swarming around her to pick up the island and carry it away.

And if she'd had any brains at all, any inherent sense of self-preservation, Maggie told herself, she'd turn the car around and give the Horizon and its plague of reporters a wide berth, just get the hell out of Dodge. It would have been the smart thing to do, easier on her nerves, better for her pride, even if slinking out of town made her feel like a felon. Better a felon than a tool.

And better, she thought with a vicious oath, to be a tool than a coward. She slammed out of the car, strode the half-block with her mind carefully blanked, and if her stomach was swimming sickly, if her legs wanted to buckle, who had to know? Definitely not the man who appeared at the other end of the narrow aisle that opened when those in the crowd caught sight of her.

Phillip Ashworth Solomon, Admiral of the United States Navy and her father, was nearly blinding in his dress whites. He was handsome and fit, his hair threaded with just the right amount of silver to denote the wisdom and experience of age without diminishing his strength one iota. He wore command like a comfortable old shirt, held himself uncompromisingly straight; and Maggie knew there was no softness in him, no pity for anything he judged a weakness. Like emotion.

That didn't mean he couldn't feign a good sentiment if he thought it useful. He caught her into a hug that had the camera flashes, press and civilian, firing wildly.

And in her ear he hissed, "Behave yourself."

All she could think was how much it hurt. She couldn't even be angry, just sick and achy and feeling like a kid again, too young to understand why she seemed to disappoint him, just by being.

He turned her to face the reporters, and she froze, miserable and lost and indecisive, telling herself it was the lights flashing in her face that made her eyes want to tear up.

"For God's sake, Margaret, smile."

The words struck her like knives, but when he reached for her, it was too much. She tried to push him off, but he grabbed her wrist and pulled it behind her back, as though he'd slung an arm around her waist.

"Don't go rebellious on me now," he murmured with a wide smile on his face, keeping his voice just under the level of the crowd. "I won't let you ruin this, too."

Too? "This has nothing to do with me."

"Of course it does. Joint Chiefs of Staff, Maggie," he all but crowed, the smile on his face sincere this time, and just a little fanatical. "To the president."

"No. You mean the actual president?"

His eyes narrowed, but he kept his smile firmly in place. "You stand to benefit, too, rightly so as the daughter of a high-ranking man. All you have to do is fall in line. For once."

Maggie twisted her arm free. She wrenched her shoulder in the process, but the pain was worth it. She should have known he wouldn't be thwarted so easily. He took her by the upper arms, turned her so her back was to the crowd, her expression hidden from the cameras.

She could have shoved him off; the physicality would have gone a long way to salving her nerves. But not her conscience. She couldn't bring herself to humiliate him in public. To cut all ties. The notion that she was still holding out hope for some sort of normal father-daughter relationship put an extra snap of disgust—for herself as much as him—in her voice. "Campaign not going well?"

"I'm up against Worthington," he shot back, his smile going a little grim. "He has three sons, and they're all serving their country."

"Too bad you only have one worthless daughter."

"You wouldn't be worthless if you'd do your duty."

Maggie absorbed that blow and wondered why, after all these years, hearing him toss off his subterranean opinion of her so casually should still hurt. But it did.

"How you could fail to understand this after living all your life as a military brat escapes me, Margaret," he said. "Having a daughter with military wings on her flight suit would trump Worthington and his sons, all three of them."

"Maybe you should have thought of that when it might have meant something," she murmured. Again, she tore free of his grip, this time walking away without a backward glance.

"You'll have to forgive my daughter," she heard him say, voice raised as he played the proud, loving father and made excuses for what he'd see as her unforgivable behavior. "I'm afraid Margaret has a schedule to keep. She has her own airport here on the island. It's small, to be sure, but growing by leaps and bounds."

The crowd parted again to let her through. She kept her eyes, achingly dry and hot, aimed carefully forward, pretended she didn't hear the murmurs of sympathy, feel the hands that reached out to touch her arm. Sympathy, even the mere idea of it, made her chest tighten painfully, had tears burning in her throat.

Running into Josiah Meeker was just the ticket to put the steel back in her spine. The crowd opened up and there he was: tall, cadaverously thin, with all the warmth of the winter Atlantic and the slime quotient of what washed up on its shore. His gaze slid over her, head to toe and up again, and took her back to a tiny storeroom where she'd been trapped, helpless. Until she kneed Meeker's balls up into his ribcage and made her escape.

She'd kept it secret, in deference to his family and with the understanding that if she even thought he was up to his old tricks, all bets were off. Meeker lived in fear of the knowledge she carried. And hated her for it.

"If you've overcome your loathing of publicity, Joe, there are some guys from the local news over there. They're probably only second-string reporters, but I bet they like a good story. I've got a doozy—"

He looked around, saw the faces turned toward them, and the twist to his mouth slid away, along with all the color in his face.

Maggie stepped around him and continued on her way.

The crowd closed behind her, swallowing Meeker, and good riddance. She'd pretty much eaten her limit of crow, even with getting the last word on Josiah Meeker. So, of course, as she headed for the blessed peace of her car, who should fall into step with her but Dexter Keegan?

"Will this day never end?" she muttered, not quite under her breath.

"Inevitably," he said, "and on a high note if you'll have dinner with me."

"You want high notes, find yourself an opera singer."

"Hmmm, not up to the wit I've come to expect from you, Solomon. Something weighty on your mind? Or someone?"

You, she wanted to say, *you and your preoccupation with me*. It wasn't ego; it was suspicion. And fear. Admiral Solomon had sent his spies before, digging into her life, her relationships, looking for a weakness he could exploit in order to drag her onto the path he'd mapped out for her life.

It hadn't occurred to her at first, but Dex was being so damned persistent.

"I would have thought you'd moved on to grilling the rest of the population by now," she said, keeping her face turned carefully away from him.

"Maybe we just happen to be going in the same direction."

"Maybe you should find yourself another lab rat. You've learned everything you're going to learn from me."

"Including the fact that your father is a four-star Admiral, currently on the short list for appointment to the Joint Chiefs of Staff."

"Congratulations. Now go away." And then she swore under her breath, because Dex had gotten a look at her face.

"Maggie, I'm sorry."

She kept walking.

"I've got a couple of shoulders here."

"I have a pair of my own."

"And you don't lean on anybody." He glanced back the way they'd come. "Suddenly that makes sense."

"Are you a lawyer or a psychiatrist?" she asked, but she held up a hand before he could answer. "Whatever you are, you can save the five-dollar words and fancy diagnoses. I know exactly what my problem is." When she met his eyes this time, hers were absolutely emotionless. "At the moment, it's you."

He grinned over at her.

Her mood lightened, marginally, and only because she could dig at him. "Not the kind of reception you're used to from women?"

"I've had worse." Again with the grin. "But not often."

A few more steps took Maggie to the driver's door of her Mustang. She almost regretted it—until she reached for the door handle and Dex got there first.

She stared at his hand, one eyebrow raised.

"Not used to men with manners?"

"I'm used to men who know I can open my own door."

Dex opened it anyway and stood back, leaving her no choice but to climb in. "Nothing wrong with accepting a hand when it's offered."

Except in her experience, there was always a price involved. And she'd already learned enough about Dex Keegan to know that, for all his big talk about manners and help freely given, his visit to Windfall was going to cost somebody.

Chapter Five

The decor in the big dining room of the Horizon consisted of wood-paneled walls, wood floors and wood ceiling, all stained nearly black from centuries of fires in the two big fireplaces that had been used not only to heat the place, but to cook the fare, once upon a time. Tallow candles had contributed to the patina; so had the pipes, cigars and cigarettes that had finally been banned by state law, to the annoyance of many citizens who considered the island its own little fiefdom, no matter what the stuffed shirts in the state senate dictated and George Boatwright chose to enforce.

Even without secondhand smoke, the air was a little murky and a lot aromatic from a grill that had never really vented properly. A fire crackled in the big fireplace; Zeke Gifford, Sam Norris, and Han Finley—joined at the hip since high school—argued good-naturedly over a game of darts. Cutlery clinked on dishes, glasses banged on tables, jokes were laughed at, thighs were slapped, and music poured out of an ancient jukebox, just the tinny high notes and pumping base audible over the buzz of conversation and the shouts of greeting when Maggie strolled through the door.

Home, she thought, had nothing to do with white picket fences and DNA. Home was where you found it. She'd never really had one, but that didn't mean she couldn't recognize it when she felt it.

Same with family. The Horizon was lousy with family.

Every chair in the place was occupied with islanders chowing down, drinking up, and embellishing gossip. *Or trying to score it*, she thought, with a grin that faded when she spotted Dex Keegan at a table in the center of the room, surrounded by all sorts of new friends. Trudie Bingham, with her blond hair and her dimples, sat close, her hand on his knee.

Maggie had known he would be there, decided she wouldn't let it keep her away. Hell, if she was being strictly truthful with herself, she'd admit she'd been looking forward to the interaction.

In the two days since her father's...invasion, Maggie had hunkered in, buried herself in work, kept her own counsel. She enjoyed solitude, she loved her work, but even flying, for the first time in her life, failed to give her mood a lift. After a couple of days keeping her own company—morbid as it was—got to be a little much. So, she'd brought herself down to the Horizon for a bit of cheering up.

This place and these people always did the trick. Surprisingly, so did seeing Dex Keegan. A man, she mused, and an outsider. Another first.

Still, Dex Keegan had a quick wit, and she did love a verbal duel. Too bad he wasn't getting in the game.

In the screenplay she'd written in her head, she would have breezed in and been lavishly greeted by her friends and neighbors—it was her place, wasn't it? Dex Keegan would be sitting by himself. His eyes would be on her, only her, those dark eyes that made her itch for things she rarely indulged in. And that wide and wildly talented mouth—or so she imagined—would be tipped up at the corners just enough to tell her he knew she was ignoring him on purpose and that it was their little joke.

So much for her imagination, Maggie thought. She sauntered over, watched his brows lift and his smile widen.

"Have a seat," he said.

"I like to separate business and pleasure."

"Which one am I?"

She turned it over in her mind for a second or two. "Come to think of it, neither. Give Jessi a call when you're ready to leave Windfall."

"So you can slot me into the business category again?"

"Yep." And then she could put him out of her mind once and for all.

"That's a narrow little world you live in, Maggie."

She laughed a little, shook her head, "I misjudged you, Keegan," she said, and started to walk away because she knew dismissing him would rankle. Like seeing him cozied up with Trudie rankled her, she admitted.

"What's that supposed to mean?"

She stopped, turned back, and because she kept her eyes straight on Dex's when they wanted to shift to Trudie, she saw it strike home when she said, "I pegged you as a guy who likes a challenge."

She had to give him credit; he laughed. Even as she watched his temper fire, he held it together and laughed. And when she felt her lips curving she let them.

"Maggie," AJ Appelman said, laughing with the rest of the Horizon's patrons who'd been close enough to overhear the exchange, and since all other sound in the place had died out for that brief minute, that meant everyone. "Haven't seen you in a couple days."

"Been busy," she said. "No time to entertain the tourists."

AJ laughed again, a deep belly laugh—and he had the physique to make it ring from the rafters.

Tall and barrel-chested, with hands the size of hams, skin ruddy from the sun and wind, and a prize-fighter's face, AJ Appelman was just the opposite—jolly, cheerful— and those huge hands were so skilled and delicate when it came to cooking he could have been a great chef anywhere. Instead he owned and ran the Horizon. His love and respect for Windfall Island ran clear down to the bone, and Maggie's love and respect for him was just as deep and strong. If she'd been able to choose her father...

She shook off that thought, but the feeling hung around, so she couldn't ignore AJ, even when he walked over and stopped right next to Dex Keegan.

She deliberately skimmed her eyes over Dex, putting everything she had into the smile she aimed at AJ.

Dex laughed, and even though she was careful not to look at him again, she could hear the ease and good humor in it.

AJ looked a little stunned.

"Who says I don't have people skills," Maggie muttered to herself, adding, loudly enough to be heard over the thumping bass of the song someone had punched up on the Wurlitzer, "S & M?"

"Rihanna's an islander, too," AJ said. "Different island, but still, gotta love a girl who's not shy about getting her freak on."

Maggie just shook her head as she made her way to the bar, slid onto a stool. "I've got a new one for you. Aloysius Joseph."

Laughing, AJ took up his position behind the bar, which wasn't just shaped in a long, fluid curve like the side of a ship, it *was* the side of a ship, at least part of one that had wrecked long ago off the island's coastline. "Still on Aloysius?"

"I guess you look like an Aloysius to me."

"That's too bad, because I'm not."

"Aha." She pointed a finger at him, mimed taking out a notebook and crossing it off her imaginary list. She ran a finger down it, grinned at him. "How about Alphonse?" Which she knew was next because she'd been prepared.

AJ just boomed out his big, rich laugh and slapped a hand on the bar. His mother had named him, of course, but like everyone else, she'd never called him anything but AJ. Not that he'd been a junior, either; his father had been a son of a bitch who'd run out before AJ had even been born.

Maggie had that in common with him, not that her father had poofed on her, not physically, at least. She'd always known where he was, even when his career took him away for months at a time. But he'd been absent even when he was in the next room.

AJ turned back from the pass-through window, where he'd carried on a short, pithy interchange with his line cook. "You're eating," he said.

"Don't change the subject. I'm going to figure it out, even if I have to ask Ma."

"She's been keeping it to herself for five decades."

Maggie snorted. "I could get it out of her."

AJ laughed again, this time the boom softened by affection Maggie knew was, at least in part, for her. The rest was for his mother, who was tough as nails, with a soft, sweet center that was even more surprising and endearing because of the prickly exterior. Everyone on the island knew her, and everyone called her Ma—not necessarily to her face. She chose who got to see that soft, sweet center.

For everyone else, she was Mother Appelman, the woman who ran the island with an iron fist, if not an actual title. Windfall had a mayor and a city council, but nothing got passed, or even considered, without Ma's stamp of approval. She was the Queen, the Boss, the Don, without any compensation but for her own personal satisfaction. The island and its citizenry, even the ones she didn't like, were her first priority. Not everyone appreciated her interference, but no one could argue with her results, or with tradition. Windfall had always been exactly what it was, an island unto itself. Ma kept it that way.

"She won't tell you," AJ said, "if only to keep you visiting her."

"That's a first. Usually people are trying to get me to leave."

"Maggie."

That one word, just her name weighted with sympathy and delivered with a mild undercurrent of rebuke, had a lump forming in her throat. When AJ reached across the bar and gave her a light, understanding cuff on the shoulder, it was almost more than she could bear.

Knowing Dex Keegan might be watching, watching and interpreting, was enough to make her suck it up. "What's on the menu?" Maggie asked him, because the normal helped to steady her, and because, while AJ always served burgers and fries, the rest changed frequently, sometimes more than once a night depending on his whim.

"A little of this, a little of that," he said. "You'll eat it and you'll love it."

She gave him a smile, a real one. "I always do."

"He flirting with you again?" AJ's wife, Helen, wanted to know. She was a short, scrawny, wild-haired, chain-smoking virago, and she was more Maggie's mother than her own had ever been.

Not that Nancy Solomon had ever done anything objectionable. Nancy Solomon had cooked and cleaned, and she'd given her husband one child, a daughter. She'd spent the rest of her life atoning for that failure, not making waves, and catering to a husband who had little respect for her.

Helen Appelman wouldn't have tolerated that. She had an opinion about everything, sure, and sometimes she beat you over the head with them, but at least Maggie never felt like an afterthought or a disappointment. Or a burden.

"He's a pain in the ass most of the time," Helen said, "and when my ass isn't wondering why I married him, my feet want to know why I let him work me like a dog in this hole in the wall."

"You always say you're going to kick me to the curb," AJ shot back, "but you never do."

"So it's my own fault, is that it?"

Maggie grinned hugely.

"Okay." Helen drilled a finger into AJ's arm. "You're on notice, Mister."

"On notice for what?"

"As if you didn't know."

AJ turned to Maggie. "See what you started?"

"Don't worry, Alphonse. If she sends you packing, I'll take you in."

Helen brayed out a laugh, bumping AJ with her hip. "In his dreams."

AJ shooed her away, winked at Maggie. "Just give me the high sign and I'm yours, Maggie."

Maggie snorted out a laugh. "I'm immune to your flirting."

"Folks around here are beginning to think you're immune to men in general," Helen put in.

"Folks around here need to stop worrying about my love life."

"Up until today they had nothing better to do. Now they can get into Dex Keegan's business."

"Better him than me," Maggie muttered, frowning as AJ slid a plate in front of her.

"What?" he said. "Not in the mood for meatloaf?"

More like she wasn't in the mood to be reminded of Dex, especially when she could feel his eyes boring into her back—which was foolish, of course. The man had better things to do than stare at her.

"You know if you don't at least try that he'll sulk for a week," Helen said to her.

Maggie took a bite of the whipped potatoes and gravy, closing her eyes while the flavor burst on her tongue and warmth spread from her stomach outward.

AJ, how do you always know? Every couple of nights she wandered into the Horizon in order to quiet the hunger pangs, and each time AJ and Helen filled a whole other emptiness inside her.

She ached to say it to them, the good kind of ache that made her want to press a hand to her chest and wax sentimental. Thankfully she caught herself before she embarrassed everyone. "You'd better be nice to AJ, Helen, or I will steal him away."

"I made the potatoes," Helen said.

"Then I guess I'll have to steal you away."

Helen threw her head back and laughed. "Like I'd have you."

"How do you put up with her?" Maggie asked AJ.

"Habit," he said, "and poor hearing. And sometimes I can get her to shut up for a little while—at least then she's not capable of forming words."

Helen went red in the face. "Don't get your hopes up tonight," she snapped.

AJ leaned over, whispered something in her ear that made the red of embarrassment deepen. She swatted him on the arm, but by the time he straightened, she was smiling, too, and they shared a look so intimate Maggie couldn't bear to watch.

Not looking didn't mean not feeling, though, and what moved through her was surprising. The loneliness she was used to. But the yearning caught her off guard. She wanted that, she realized, adding *someday* with enough conviction to have her stomach settling.

"Eat up," Helen said in her usual tone, which could only be described as the equivalent of vocal steel wool. But when Maggie looked up she saw sympathy in Helen's eyes, felt it in the hand she laid briefly on Maggie's arm. "Don't want people thinking there's something wrong with the fare."

Maggie took another bite, let the simple task and the amazing food nudge her back into the normal again.

"So what's the story on that guy you brought in?"

"Lawyer," Maggie said, "Staying at the Horizon."

"Ha. That might work on the rest of the Bozos on this island."

"But you're different?"

"Just answer the question. In great detail. Quote him if you can."

Maggie lifted both hands to make air quotes.

"Cute." Helen reached for her plate, slid it a few inches away. "Talk, or the meatloaf gets it."

Maggie dragged her plate back. "Nothing to tell."

"Are you—Is she—" Helen turned to AJ.

"Yeah," he said, just as disgusted. "She's actually claiming she doesn't know anything about the guy she just needled in front of God and everyone."

"He's staying here. How come you haven't squeezed out his life story by now?"

"He makes himself pretty scarce," AJ said. "Up and out early, wandering the village. He asks a lot of questions, but he hasn't met with anyone in particular."

Maggie bumped up a shoulder. "He's working for an outsider."

"Came to the same conclusion. You're running the floor tonight, Helen; go find out why he's here."

Helen stabbed AJ with a look. "I could barely get near him long enough to snag his order." She gestured to his table and the constantly changing crowd around it.

Maggie glanced over her shoulder. Couldn't resist. Trudie was gone, but a couple of the other island hotpants had pulled up chairs, as close to Keegan's as humanly possible.

His gaze shifted, pinned her.

She felt it all the way to her toes before she looked away.

"Every woman in town has hit on him in the last three days," Helen said.

"And every man is pissed off about it," AJ put in. "Somebody should warn him."

"Already did," Maggie said.

"Now, that's going to take some explaining."

"All you have to do is look at him. That face, that body. Factor in the predilections of some of the local female population, the inevitable reaction of the men, and bingo. Cause and effect."

Helen put on a sad expression, shook her head. "Cause and effect."

"Poor slob," AJ said. "He really can't help it."

"Nope." Maggie took another bite of meatloaf, feeling almost cheerful.

"Nice of you to warn him, though."

"Wouldn't be fair otherwise."

"Or nearly as entertaining." AJ shifted, gave Helen a baleful look when she started to primp. "He's coming over."

"Probably going to pay his bill," Maggie said.

"Way he's looking at you, settling up ain't on his mind," Helen observed blandly, "Unless you did something to piss him off."

"Something?" Maggie said, "Hell, I did everything I could."

Chapter Six

If Dex hadn't already realized just how much of a challenge he was facing, five minutes in the Horizon's big, overcrowded dining room/bar would have given him a pretty good idea. The citizens of Windfall Island spent a lot of time picking his brain, and not so much answering the questions he sent back at them.

While he would have preferred an out-of-the-way seat that put his back to the wall, he'd gone along gracefully when he'd been guided instead to a table in the center of the room. Put on display. That made his job a little harder, since he could only see half the room without playing musical chairs, which might have seemed a little odd. A little odd, it turned out, was as close to normal as it got on Windfall Island.

There was the couple who were channeling Antony and Cleopatra, a guy who wanted to check Dex's DNA for alien nucleotides, an elderly woman who spoke without using the letter E, and Maisie Cutshaw, the owner of the island's gift shop, who turned out to be part comic relief and part cringe factor. Maisie believed in being her own best advertisement and that meant wearing as much of her merchandise as she could drape on her pear-shaped frame, including a baggy, faded sweatshirt sporting a picture of a half-sunk schooner and a caption that read, *Nothing Ventured, Nothing Salvaged.*

And it wasn't just about history with Maisie. Apparently she'd made that her personal motto. "I guess I should have kept my appointment at the Clipper Snip last week," she said, pushing at her frizzy blond hair.

"I can't imagine why you'd need to."

"Well, aren't you the smooth one."

Dex smiled affably. He could do affable, when it suited his purposes.

Maisie dropped into a chair, leaned her elbow on the table and rested her chin in her hand. "How about I buy you a drink, Mr. Keegan."

"Dex."

"Dex." She smiled dreamily. "Let's get that drink, and then we can talk. For starters."

Dex picked up his half-empty beer, tipped it in her direction. "All set," he said, "But not all talked out." It was a great theory, too, but by the time he'd nursed himself through the rest of his beer, Maisie had shown herself to have a one-track mind. And he was the train riding that track.

As things went, though, Maisie was tame. Maggie had been right about the female half of the population. *Gentler sex, hell,* he thought. He'd gotten some propositions that made him blush, and there'd been one or two women he'd be afraid to meet in a dark alley. And it wasn't their looks that scared him; it was their appetites.

The good news? His popularity had given him the opportunity to observe the natives and draw conclusions about who might be able to help him on his search. The bad news was, he didn't hold out much hope of getting a straight story from any of the people he'd met so far. And then Maggie had walked in and he didn't care anymore.

It took a while, but Dex extricated himself from the latest group of islanders hounding him for information, and made a beeline for the bar. He didn't bother to wander or make it look like he got there by happenstance. He headed directly for Maggie, taking the stool next to hers.

She pretended not to notice.

"I thought maybe you came in to see me," he said.

"That's what you get for thinking," she said between bites.

She ate with a single-mindedness that made him grin. "Food's good."

"So's solitude."

She angled away from him, taking her plate with her and turning her attention to the small television perched in a corner behind the bar. Using it as a distraction, Dex figured. He would've bet she wasn't much of a watcher. Maggie Solomon lived her life; she didn't spectate others'.

She dropped her head to concentrate on her meal, then whipped it up again to stare at a local news report, the picture flipping between a perky blond reporter and Admiral Phillip Ashworth Solomon. She cocked her head, but unless she had the ears of an elephant, she'd only be able to pick up a word here and there over the din in the Horizon's big barroom. He saw the frustration on her face, the way her hand fisted.

"Maggie."

AJ's voice didn't carry far, but it got her attention. She looked up at him, then glanced at Dex, embarrassment putting some of the color back in her cheeks that misery, the misery he saw in her eyes, had leached out.

"Got a blueberry pie in the back," AJ said. "Fresh baked this morning."

Maggie pushed her plate away. "I think I've had enough."

AJ cleared the bar in front of her, giving her hand a quick squeeze before he took her dishes to the pass-through and went off to handle business at the other end of the bar.

"So," Dex said. "Where have you been hiding the last couple of days?"

She snorted softly. "Just because you didn't see me doesn't mean I was hiding. I had work."

Strike one. "It's just a figure of speech, Maggie, like... out of sight, out of mind."

"Yeah, that's one of my favorites. If you take the first part literally, I can handle the second."

Strike Two. "I only have one more question. Where did your sense of humor go? I could have sworn you had one the day we met."

She opened her mouth, then closed it, sighing heavily. But in the slight smile that followed he could see the ball sailing out of the park. "It's been... an interesting couple of days."

"At least it's not my fault this time."

"Leave now, and you'll be going out on a high."

"Still trying to get rid of me? I wonder why?"

"There's that curiosity again. You a lawyer or a private eye?"

His heart started to hammer, but his voice stayed even, thank God. "There's a little bit of PI in all lawyers, at least the good ones."

"And you're good?" She turned to face him, frowning a little. "Just what are you doing on Windfall? You haven't met with anyone."

"I've only been here a few days."

Maggie sat back a little, studied him long enough for him to think, *Damn, why'd I ever want her to be curious?*

"It occurs to me that if I hired a heavy hitter from the mainland," Maggie said slowly, working it out in her mind as she went along, "I'd make sure to be handy when he showed up. Wouldn't want him racking up billable hours alone in a hotel room and harassing innocent women..."

She turned her head slowly, until she was staring into his eyes. "Is he why you're here? My father?"

"No. But you don't believe me."

"You have to admit the timing is pretty convenient."

"Coincidental is the word I'd use," Dex said, hating that he sounded defensive. "I didn't even know Admiral Solomon was your father until the other day. And you still don't believe me."

"Give me a reason to."

The only way to convince her was to tell her the truth. Which was the absolute last thing he could do. At least not his truth. "Trust me, somebody in Washington already did their due diligence where you're concerned. If they hadn't come up empty, your old man wouldn't get anywhere near the short list for the Joint Chiefs."

"If I'd known that I would have stashed a skeleton or two."

"You don't have secrets, Maggie. I knew that five seconds after I met you. You're too direct."

"He'd think me too boring and unimaginative."

"Then he's an idiot."

She gave him a long, measuring look, one that had him reigning himself in.

"My being here has nothing to do with your father," he assured her, "Or you."

"Maybe not directly, but this is my home. I know everyone here, and I like most of them. Whatever your purpose, it involves me."

And as long as he withheld the truth, there'd be no convincing her. But he could wear her down. "Have dinner with me."

That got a smile out of her, if only a slight one. "Too late."

"Tomorrow."

"No."

Dex heaved a sigh, heavy on the theatrics. "I'm tired of eating alone."

"Didn't appear to me you were eating alone."

"You know what I mean. A nice meal with just one person, maybe some polite conversation—or as polite as you get. And after dinner—"

"No. Absolutely no."

And now who's defensive, Dex thought, suppressing a grin. "You could at least let me hope."

"I can do better than that."

His heart picked up speed, God help him, and it wasn't all about the job.

Then she turned and faced the room, lifting her voice above the noise level. "Mr. Keegan is in the market for a dinner date."

There was a humming five seconds of absolute silence. Even the juke box was between songs. Then a lone female voice called out from the depths of the gloomy room. "I'll buy him dinner, as long as he takes care of dessert."

The rest of the crowd erupted, cat calls and downright graphic suggestions from the women, laughter from most of the men, with one or two half-hearted threats tossed in for good measure. At least Dex hoped they were half-hearted.

But it wasn't the men who worried him.

Jessi came through the door, sidling around a pair of women who'd jumped to their feet, escalating from name-calling to hair pulling.

"What's with the riot?" she asked when she made it to the bar and stopped by Maggie's stool.

"Dex is looking for a date."

"Which Maggie announced to the entire room."

Jessi smiled hugely. "I'm available," she said, "and I have a babysitter."

"If you try to take him up those stairs, Jess, you're going to have a fight on your hands."

"Oh?" Jessi winked at Dex. "You going to try to kick my ass, Maggie?"

That had Maggie grinning. But the expression before that, the split second of panic and anger, told Dex a hell of a lot.

Maggie was attracted to him, and she didn't like it. The attraction was mutual—attraction, hell. That was too mild a word, and if he could feel this depth of want in so short a time...

Dex glanced over at her, let out the breath he realized he was holding. The last thing he needed was to complicate an already complicated situation. He might have reassured her of that, if he didn't know for certain she'd take it the wrong way. What he told himself was that he'd do his damnedest to keep any interactions he had with her on a professional level.

But God help them both if that cold shoulder she gave him ever thawed out.

"Well," Maggie began, sliding off her stool, "I have an early charter—"

"Not so fast." Jessi grabbed her by the wrist, began towing her toward an empty booth in the back. "What were you two talking about? I won't breathe a word, I swear, but I have to know."

Maggie smiled a little, because it was Jessi, but a smile was all she was willing to give away. "None of your business."

Jessi's mouth opened and closed. "I—You—" Her bottom lip poked out. "Mean."

"Trudie Bingham accused me of that very thing, with that very same pout on her face."

Jessi sucked her lip back in, her green eyes narrowing.

"Wow," Maggie said, "something finally made you speechless."

"Are you kidding me? I'm not letting you get away with this." She took a firmer grip, but Maggie just planted her feet.

"All you have to do is ask, Jess."

"Oh. Okay. Want to get a drink?"

"Not really."

"Pretty please, pretty, pretty please? With sugar on top?"

"Who let you out on a school night? And how much caffeine have you had?"

"Ha. I let myself out so I could get in on the fun. New man on the island, and it's Friday night. No school tomorrow, but I figured all the crazies would be here."

"And?"

"I've let you stew for long enough. And don't tell me you're not stewing. I know how your father twists you up."

"And you raced over here to keep me from tossing myself off the nearest dock into the icy embrace of the Atlantic?"

"Actually I was afraid you'd toss Dex off the nearest dock into the icy embrace of the Atlantic."

"He's too heavy to lift. He'd probably fight, too."

"And you'd probably enjoy it, if you let yourself relax a little."

Maggie chose to ignore that. "I threw him to the she-wolves instead."

They both turned around to enjoy the show, which seemed to be winding down, compliments of local law enforcement. George Boatwright, Sheriff of Windfall Island, stood between two spitting, screeching women, and was eyeing a third who looked like she might jump into the fray.

"Aw," Jessi said, "who had to ruin it by bringing in the cops?"

"Helen probably didn't want the place destroyed."

"Well, she's no fun at all."

Dex agreed, Maggie decided. He was still where they'd left him, facing the room, elbows lounging on the bar and a wide smile on his face. She was tempted to trip George and see what happened when the winner of the catfight claimed her prize.

"Not the outcome you expected, huh?"

"I don't know what I expected."

"But it makes you mad," Jessi observed, grinning from ear to ear.

"Glad I can entertain you," Maggie said, wiping the frown off her face. "I just wanted him to leave me alone."

"Are you sure of that?"

"What is this, psychoanalyze Maggie Solomon night?" At Jessi's puzzled look, she said shortly, "Keegan."

"Oh, now we're getting somewhere."

Maggie spun on her heel, strode the rest of the way to the back corner booth. She slid into the side facing the room, lifting her butt automatically to avoid the duct-taped section of the old leather seat.

"You know you're not getting off that easily."

She sighed, gave in. Jessi would hound her to hell and back if she didn't get all the details. But at least Jessi would keep them to herself.

"Keegan was there the other day, when my father and I played out that charming domestic scene in front of the whole island and a handful of imported news people."

Jessi snorted softly. "Your old man was his usual oblivious, posturing self, you played nice, and Dex saw right through the pair of you. And now he knows too much about you, and you don't like it."

Maggie let her gaze wander his way. Dex claimed he had nothing to do with her father, and she was inclined to believe him. After her confrontation with Admiral Solomon, he would have called off any dogs he'd sent—out of pride if nothing else. That didn't mean he'd give up.

"Dexter Keegan won't be around here any longer than he has to, and Phillip..." Won't be around here at all, she'd started to say. But she knew better.

She wanted to resent Jessi for bringing up the past, but ever since that newscast it had been there, on the edge of her mind, nagging at her. Her father was up for an appointment that would be the culmination of any military man's career. He'd stop at nothing to get it, which meant she'd be hearing from him again. The only time he remembered he had a daughter was when he had a use for one.

"I can't stop him from contacting me," she said to Jessi, "But I'll be damned if I waste a minute of my time worrying about it." Not one minute of dread or regret or wishing things could be anything but stiff and unpleasant between them. Phillip Ashworth Solomon wouldn't bend, not even a little, for her. And he'd taught her well.

What she'd learned on her own, Maggie thought, was to not look back.

"He's not like the men you usually date. Dex Keegan, I mean."

"I know who you're talking about, and we're not dating. Even if he was going to be here longer than five minutes." She stopped, shook her head.

"What?"

"He's no more interested in complications than I am."

"So have meaningless sex with him."

Maggie looked away.

"You can't, can you? You're afraid it won't be meaningless."

"He's got some hidden agenda, Jess. Whatever it is, I won't be used to further it."

"Bawk."

Maggie snorted out a laugh. "Did you just cluck at me?"

"Baaaawk."

"Make all the barnyard noises you want. If I want meaningless sex, I'll get it elsewhere."

"Well, I vote for George. Except it wouldn't be meaningless. And you'd have to forgive him."

"I forgave George a long time ago," she said, but what she felt this time was guilt, a tidal wave of it swamping her, drowning even the pinch it caused her to remember how much he'd hurt her.

"He doesn't see it that way."

"I trust him with my life."

"But not your heart."

"I don't love him, Jess," she said, "not like that."

"That's too bad because he still loves you."

"He'll get over it."

"All indications to the contra—uh, hi, George."

He smiled at Jessi, gave Maggie a long, even look that told her he knew they'd been talking about him. Not that it bothered him. Very little bothered George, as a matter of fact. He was one of the steadiest people, male or female, Maggie had ever known.

"Ladies," he said.

"George," Maggie returned in the same deadpan tone. "I'd ask you to join us, but you appear to be rescuing one of my favorite people from the vicious mob."

Emmett Finley, ninety years old and arthritic enough to lean on George's arm, wheezed out a laugh. "That'd be the day I let a bunch of women scare me off."

"He was egging them on." George's tone was severe, but he was fighting back a smile.

"Just a bit of harmless fun," Emmett said. "Not that I haven't deserved to land in a cell on occasion, and when I were a lot younger'n you pretty ladies."

Jessi patted the seat next to her. George helped Emmett slide in, then said, "I'll go get us something to drink," and took himself off in the direction of the bar.

"Make mine whiskey," Emmett called after him, "and none of that cheapo stuff AJ passes off on the tourists." He turned back, winked at Maggie. "Always go for the good stuff. Say, did I ever tell you about the time my old da took me bootlegging, and I bobbled a whole case of prime booze? Damn near dropped it."

Maggie smiled encouragingly. She'd heard all of Emmett's stories, even though they came in bits and pieces now, one cobbled with another. The rumrunner called *Perdition* was one of his favorites, although she couldn't recall in all her years on Windfall Island ever hearing him finish the story before his mind wandered off on one tangent or another. But what, she thought as she settled in to listen to Emmett talk about his youth, did it cost her to listen, except time?

All the time in the world wasn't nearly enough repayment for the incredible gift the people of Windfall had given her. The gift of home.

Chapter Seven

Dex watched the Sheriff of Windfall Island make his way from the corner where Maggie sat to the bar. So did everyone else except, possibly, Maggie, listening intently to the old man George Boatwright had deposited in her booth. By the time George stopped by his stool, the noise level in the room had dropped enough for Dex to hear the faint buzz of the hockey game playing low on the TV over the bar.

"Does this happen a lot?" Dex asked George.

"You mean the silence?" George smiled. "It's not what you'd call a natural state on Windfall, but eavesdropping is the best way to find out what's really going on."

"Or you could just ask questions."

"You could, but the answers aren't always truthful."

The exact point he'd made to Maggie, Dex thought. His eyes strayed to her, the corners of his mouth turning up a little when he remembered how she'd thrown it back in his face.

"She the reason you're here?"

Dex brought his gaze back to his beer, took a long drink to cool his throat and give himself a few seconds to bite back on the instant denial that sprang to his lips. It would be true; he wasn't there because of Maggie, but firing back would give the opposite impression. "Is that an official question?" he said instead.

George took up a cop stance, feet spread, one hand on his cop tool belt, a stern, just-the-facts-ma'am cop expression on his face. "Should it be?"

"The only thing on my agenda was dinner."

"I don't think you came all the way to Maine for AJ's meatloaf. No offense," he said to AJ, who stood behind the bar polishing glasses and listening unabashedly.

"None taken. And that's mostly because I want to hear the answer to that question."

The question Dex had known was coming, even though neither AJ nor the sheriff had actually asked it.

"I hear you're a lawyer," George said.

"Then you know I can't talk about why I'm here."

"You must be pretty smart, seeing as you went to law school and passed the bar exam and everything, so I figure you know all about what you can and can't do."

"But you're going to warn me anyway."

George gave him a humorless smile. "Windfall is a close-knit community. Everybody knows everybody else. There might be personality clashes and petty arguments between folks around here, but they'll band together when circumstance calls for it."

"And they're armed, I hear."

"To the teeth. Mostly legal."

"Mostly?"

George smiled. The humor reached his eyes this time, and once he lost the flat cop tone, New England crept in to slow down and draw out his words. "Every now and then somebody comes up with a weapon that's not strictly on the books. Confiscated a blunderbuss from Pascal Higgins a few years back. 'Course, time I knew the thing existed it was too late for the fellow on the business end of it. Soiled himself good, suffered some real humiliation, which might've been a lot worse had the fool thing not misfired. Pas was lucky, too. No telling what might explode when a gun hasn't been fired in a few decades, but he only ended up with a powder burn on his neck." His eyes sharpened on Dex's face. "Every day's an adventure around here."

"I'll keep that in mind."

"A smart man would, and like I said, I figure you for a smart man. You'll send a round to Maggie's table," he said to AJ and, having done his duty by the island and provided refreshment for his friends, he headed off without a word of farewell or a backward glance.

George slid in beside Maggie, bumped her shoulder with his in a way that bespoke long friendship. When he stayed pressed up against her, when she looked up into his face and laughed at something he said, no walls, no holding back, just a lot of affection, Dex had to roll his shoulders to work off... something.

"Careful there, son," AJ Appelman said.

"Always," Dex returned, taking another swig from his longneck and feeling like he'd dodged a bullet since neither Maggie nor the sheriff had noticed him staring. George Boatwright seemed inclined to take his cover story at face value. Dex got the impression that would change if he paid too much attention to Maggie Solomon. So he'd keep his distance, mentally and physically.

Apparently his mouth didn't get the message from his brain. "Quite a surprise to find out Admiral Solomon is Maggie's father."

AJ gave him a bland look.

"I should have known she was a military brat. She acts

like she's walking a post," Dex explained into the silence. "All she's missing is the gun."

AJ took up a towel and a glass from the drainer next to the little bar sink, and set to polishing. "This is her home. No surprise she feels protective."

"It's more than that."

"Observant fellow, aren't you?" AJ put the polished glass on the clean rack and took another, meeting Dex's gaze. "I 'spect a lawyer'd have to be, and that's what you are, right? A lawyer?"

"A good one," Dex said without batting an eye.

AJ continued polishing, keeping his opinion on that to himself. Dex should have grinned over the ploy, but it was working. He wanted to know what was going through AJ's mind. Worse, he realized he'd underestimated the man; he'd underestimated every man, woman, and child who called Windfall home.

They might be a small, isolated community, living on a quaint, historical island, but it didn't mean they were backward or easily fooled. Just the opposite. Their predecessors had had little but their wits to help them navigate through a cold, often cruel world. Those ancestors had dealt with tragedy and death on a regular basis, had seen and done the unspeakable, had walked head-on into danger to support their families, and to help others, even if rescue had been merely the means to their own survival. And only the strong, the smart, had survived.

They'd passed those qualities down to their children, and their children's children. Today's Windfallers might not put their lives on the line for strangers and profit, but they were smart, and cautious, and probably ruthless when the occasion called for it. They tolerated tourists because tourism provided, but they didn't like outsiders, no matter how friendly.

Dex wouldn't forget it again. "This place have a museum?" he asked, knowing full well there wasn't one, but hoping to angle the conversation around to Meeker and his journals.

"This place is a museum." AJ set another beer Dex hadn't ordered beside the one he hadn't finished. "Windfall is pretty much the way it was two hundred years ago, except for central heat, electricity, and indoor plumbing—and you won't even find that everywhere."

Dex picked up his first beer, tapped it lightly against the second. "I'm just grateful you have it here."

"Amen, son. You curious about anything in particular?"

"Maybe it would be faster if you give me a list of subjects you're willing to talk about."

AJ threw back his head and laughed. "I like this boy, Maggie," he shouted out. "He's got a quick mind, and a hell of a delivery. Next time you're over t'the mainland, maybe you could pick up a couple more just like him so we don't wear this poor fellow out entertaining us."

Maggie stuck her head around the end of the booth. "I barely got this one back. Who knew ego weighed so damn much?"

The whole place erupted at that, laughter and catcalls, and disparaging comments about his career choice and his origins. Apparently, taking on Windfall was like pledging a fraternity, minus the physical torture, and if he hadn't had such a thick skin, some of the commentary would have had him throwing a punch or two.

"Don't look dyspeptic, son. They wouldn't be razzing you if they didn't like you."

Dex kept the frown on his face, but inside he was pumping a fist in the air. Not an islander yet, not by a long shot, but not exactly an enemy, either.

"The antique store," AJ said when the ruckus died down.

"Meeker, Josiah Meeker, owns the place. He has some artifacts on display—that's if you can find them in that maze of flea market rejects he calls antiques." His lip curled, making his opinion of Meeker absolutely clear, even if his sense of fairness got the better of his dislike. "In all honestly, some of the furniture and knick-knacks are genuine, and he has some books that are first editions. And then there's his pride and joy."

Dex lifted his eyebrows, inviting elaboration.

"Meeker collects Island journals." AJ picked up a perfectly spot-free glass and took to polishing it. If he understood the significance of what he was saying, it didn't show.

But it was everything Dex could do to keep his expression noncommittal. Though he already knew the journals existed, he felt like he'd been buzzed by a cattle prod. He didn't dare think about what those probably innocuous-looking little books, full of the seemingly inconsequential events of someone's everyday life, could mean to his future. Or that they might give the Stanhope family the answers they'd been praying for. He still had to find a way to get his hands on them.

Without letting on how important they were.

"I'm not much into history," he said to AJ.

"Just as well. Meeker isn't what you'd call accommodating, even to paying customers. Maggie seems to be the only person on the island who can talk him into anything."

Maggie. Shit. His eyes strayed to that back corner again, and although his excitement faded somewhat, he had to smile a little. All roads, he mused. He tried to stay away from Maggie Solomon, but fate kept pushing them together. And who was he to argue with fate?

"Gift store has some souvenirs," AJ was saying, "A few books on local interest for the tourists, history of salvagers, that sort of thing. Maisie Cutshaw owns and operates.

You want to watch out there. Woman can talk the ears off a cornfield and not say two words of sense the whole time. But you'd know that, seeing as she parked herself at your table for a time tonight."

With a view toward moving into his life. He'd played hell fending her off without pissing her off. "So, what do you do around here for entertainment? Besides pick on outsiders."

"Or hit on them?" AJ boomed out a laugh. "Might not be a bad idea to keep yourself busy, at that.

"Well, son, if you're thinking to keep to your room at night, there's always the television or a good book. Maggie flies in a selection from the Portland library in the fall, kind of like one of them bookmobiles. Mostly it's for the kids, but I bet there are some mysteries in there. Or maybe you're more interested in romance?"

Dex dragged his gaze off Maggie. Again. "No man is interested in romance. It's practically hard-coded into our DNA."

"Some of us are smart enough to pretend to be interested."

"Some of us are dumb enough to get married."

AJ grinned. "Marry the right woman, it's not a bad deal."

As a private investigator who'd started off, like many did, shadowing cheating spouses, Dex had begun to think there was no such thing as the right woman. Or the right man, for that matter. Having parents who'd loved each other without reservation had kept him from getting jaded—and given him an example of what he wanted in his own life. Years off, when he settled down. Somewhere far away from Windfall, he added, keeping his eyes firmly forward.

"Books are at the school if you're interested—and if Mrs. Higgins will lend you one."

"Mrs. Higgins? She married to the guy with the antique weapon fixation?"

"Yeah, but she doesn't send him after the overdue books."

AJ picked up an order from the pass-through, stepped down the bar to set it in front of a customer who began to eat mechanically, his eyes glued to the television screen. "Mind you keep your fingers clear, Mort."

Dex took a closer look at the kid sitting a couple of stools away from him. Once he got past the hunched shoulders, stringy hair, and sullen attitude, he realized it was the same kid he'd seen at the airport when he'd arrived. A dozen questions came to mind, but even if Mort's body language had invited them, AJ plowed along in the conversation, and left Dex no choice but to tune back in.

"Boy'll probably eat clear through the bar before he realizes the food's gone," AJ said. "But then, it's just him and his mother, and she's been poorly, so he's entitled to be caught up in his own world.

"We got DVD players in the rooms, and old man Mac-Donald down at the general store keeps a couple smokers on hand, if you're into that kind of thing."

Not as a spectator, but Dex kept that to himself. AJ had already noted the way his gaze kept straying to Maggie Solomon. Bring sex into the conversation and he'd probably get firsthand knowledge of whatever illegal weapon AJ kept under the counter.

Helen Appelman came around the end of the bar, pulled herself a tall glass of water and guzzled it down like she was dying. Way she moved around the place, Dex could see how she'd work up a thirst.

"You get his life story yet?" she asked her husband.

"I was working around to it."

"Rate you move, we'll all be dead first." She pinned Dex with a look. "Why are you here?"

"Can't tell you that."

She plunked her empty glass on the bar. "Bullshit."

"Actually, it's the primary rule of my profession." Both real and pretend.

"Like I said. Bullshit."

Dex laughed. It was hard not to. "A lot of people think that about lawyers, and it's true, there's a component of bullshit in what I do. But I have a client—"

"By the name of..."

"—to consider, not to mention my reputation," Dex continued, talking over her.

"Lawyer bullshit."

Helen kept coming at him; Dex kept putting her off. AJ kept lining up longnecks he hadn't ordered, but after a half hour it stopped being amusing. He'd expected the sheriff to present a problem, but George Boatwright had nothing on the Appelmans.

Dex finally gave up on manners and got to his feet. "You can charge my room for the meal and the beers, including the ones I didn't drink," he said to AJ.

"You aren't wimping out on me."

"Yes, ma'am," Dex said to Helen, "I certainly am."

She let loose a string of curses that would have made a sailor blush, peppered with the kind of insults Dex had only ever heard in a locker room. He stared at Helen a minute, then looked at AJ.

AJ threw his head back and laughed. "There's a reason her name starts with Hell, son."

George Boatwright, former army sniper and current Sheriff of Windfall Island, sat behind his postage-stamp desk, in his tiny office, in the dollhouse-sized building that served as the island's police station. The street level also held a cell barely wide enough for a cot, and a rest room with a toilet and a sink.

The cell hadn't been used in a couple of years, but he routinely changed the sheet and blanket. Just in case. He was a man who believed in being prepared. Just one of the reasons he chose to live upstairs, in an apartment it took fewer than twenty steps to cross from one end to the other. It was a Spartan existence, but it suited him. So did the island. He'd seen the world while he'd served his country, and yeah, most of those locales had involved people shooting at him. But that wasn't the only reason he was glad to be back.

Windfall was home, and home was where he belonged.

Not long ago, the picture that formed in his mind would have included Maggie Solomon, and while Maggie wasn't exactly the Donna Reed–like fantasy he had a tendency to spin in his imagination, just about any future that included her as more than a friend would have suited him.

He'd given that up in the years since his return. Funny thing, it had been easier than he would've guessed. He still loved her, just in an easier way.

And the fantasy was still intact, he mused as he picked up the phone and dialed. He'd just...recast his leading lady.

"He's here," he said as soon as the connection went through. "Claims to be a lawyer."

"And?"

"Cover story," George continued, as economical of words as he was with everything else in his life.

"For?"

"Small-time PI, not setting the world on fire. If he's not already on the dark side, my guess is he could be pushed there without much effort."

"The dark side?"

"*Star Wars* is a classic." He grinned a little, sat back,

wrapping the phone cord around his finger as reality pushed him back to solemn. "Fact is, we know who hired him. You chose to let others do the hard work of locating Eugenia Stanhope's descendants. If any exist."

"I believe they do."

"And I'll step in if, or when, it becomes necessary." Nobody would think twice about it, George thought, pushing down the guilt. "I'm the law. I can do what needs to be done."

"Make Eugenia's descendant disappear."

"That was the agreement."

"Don't underestimate Dexter Keegan."

No, George mused, he wouldn't underestimate a man with Keegan's kind of history. He could respect the man's service to his country, but what he'd made of his life after, well, mixed emotions. "I'll handle Keegan, don't worry," he said, and hung up the phone. He had a feeling he'd enjoy it.

Chapter Eight

Hello, the ladder."

Maggie pulled her head out of the engine compartment of her Piper Mirage, automatically maintaining her balance as she marked off the items she'd verified on her checklist.

She glanced up long enough to see Dex Keegan striding across the tarmac before she stuck her head back in her engine, if only for appearances' sake. Maintaining her planes was serious work, the kind of work that took laser focus. Her safety, and the safety of her passengers, depended on it.

Dex Keegan, it seemed, was hell on her concentration.

Take her clothes, she thought, disgusted that seeing him had been followed almost instantaneously with concern over what she was wearing. Grubby work pants and tee, ratty sneakers, and probably a swipe or two of grease on her face. Stupid. She pulled her head out of the compartment again, pretending to make checkmarks on her list without the least qualm. It was better than giving in to the urge to fluff her hair, she decided, snugging her worn ball cap more firmly onto her head in defiance.

Of course, Dex had to look perfect, she mused as she

looked over at him. His jeans and work boots were as worn as hers, but clean, his leather jacket battered and only more appealing because of it. Expensive sunglasses, attractively wind-blown hair—if she'd searched high and low for a picture of the perfect man, this would have been him.

"You didn't walk all the way out here," she observed blandly when he stopped next to the ladder.

He took off his glasses, slipping one earpiece into the neck of his t-shirt. "I caught Jessi on her way in and begged a lift."

That put a bit of a smirk on her face. "How are you getting back?"

"Running," he said, hooking a thumb in the direction of the small parking lot. "My gear's in Jessi's car."

An image of Dex in running shorts and a t-shirt, arms and legs pumping, muscles flexing, popped into her mind and Maggie tried in vain to banish it. At least she wasn't drooling, she thought, hoping to hell she'd managed to keep her expression blank.

"You do the maintenance yourself?"

"What, you wouldn't have flown with me if you knew that?"

"I'd have thought twice," he admitted, "but I didn't know you then."

"You don't know me now."

"I'm looking forward to changing that."

Maggie let her lips curve. "There goes my hope you're here because you're ready to leave Windfall."

"Had an urge to get out of the village."

"Everyone seemed friendly enough last night."

"That's the problem."

"Coming out here won't put off your admirers."

"You could."

She snorted. "They're not afraid of me."

"No, but they respect you."

Maggie studied his face, not sure what he was getting at. "You don't strike me as a man who'd run away from a couple of overeager women." Or anything else, for that matter.

"Maybe I didn't want to hurt anyone's feelings. And I definitely don't want to get shot."

Maggie smiled over that, fondly, and went with her gut. "You didn't come all the way out here to avoid a close encounter with a jealous husband, either. And you aren't here to ask me to run interference for you."

He shrugged. "I was going a little stir crazy at the Horizon. What's with AJ and the manic cleaning?"

"End of tourist season. And you're not here to bitch about AJ's fall routine. What do you really want?"

He gave her a look that had her pulses hammering. Disappointment leapt just as fast when he didn't act on the heat and intent she saw in his eyes.

His jaw flexed, once, but it was enough to tell her he was fighting a war, too, and not just on the physical front. He wanted something else from her. She could have put him out of his misery, but what would be the fun in that?

"Go away, Keegan. I have this to finish, then I'm off to the mainland."

"Then I guess I'll get out of your way." And he started back the way he'd come, the rear view of him just as mouthwatering as the front.

Maggie didn't even think twice before letting her curiosity goad her into calling after him. "I didn't take you for a man who'd give up so easy."

He turned back, cocked a hip, letting the moment draw out. Damn him.

"You're busy," he said when it finally suited him.

"My ears still work, and anyone will tell you I'm a whiz at multi-tasking." She turned back to her engine, smiling privately when, after what he probably considered a reasonable pause, she heard his footsteps coming closer.

He got right to the point. "I was hoping you could find the time to go with me to Meeker's."

"No."

"That's it, just no?"

Hell, no. But Maggie was still curious, and Josiah Meeker was in the past, far enough that whatever reaction she had to hearing his name, it was no longer knee-jerk.

"Suppose you tell me what you want from him."

Dex didn't respond, still weighing his options.

Maggie worked in silence for a moment that drew out because she could feel his eyes on her. It made her angry. She'd nearly gotten used to the way her entire system seemed to short out when he was near, short out and then surge back to life so that the pounding of her heart, the singing in her blood, and the buzz along her nerve endings made her feel like she'd never really been alive before she'd laid eyes on him. And then she felt him touch her, feathering the tip of one finger across the line of skin bared just over her waistband. She jerked, the wrench in her hand slipped off the bolt she was trying to turn and barked itself across her knuckles.

"Shit," she hissed, snatching her hand out of the cramped space of the engine compartment. She stepped down the ladder and moved into the sunlight, pretending to study her knuckles so she could see how much skin she'd peeled off. But it was the distance from Dex she needed.

He didn't give it to her, crowding close behind to look over her shoulder. "Does it hurt?"

She jammed an elbow into his gut.

His breath whooshed out, and he staggered back a step.

"Does it hurt?" she asked sweetly.

"Not as much as you meant it to."

"How about I give it another try?"

"Aw, just when I was going to offer to kiss your knuckles and make them all better."

Maggie fisted her hand, held it up. "Go for it."

"Wrong knuckles."

"Well, I can think of a way to scrape them up as well. You have such a nice hard head."

He grinned over that, not exactly the reaction she'd expected.

Nor was hers, that sharp ache in her center, followed by a longer, sweeter pull. She was attracted to him, and that was all right. What she was feeling wasn't. She might be a woman who flung herself through life, but this was one area where she wanted to take slow, careful steps—if she took any at all.

She'd known Dex less than a week; she had no business going slack-jawed and hot-wired over a man who was, for all intents and purposes, a complete stranger. Sex was just sex; real intimacy came from the heart, from the mind, and he clearly intended to share neither with her.

"Meeker," he said, putting them both back on solid footing.

Maggie wasn't about to ask herself why he seemed to need it as much as she did. "Suppose you tell me what you want from him, and then I'll decide if it's worth my time and trouble." Considerable trouble, she reminded herself.

Dex hesitated, but only for a second or two. "He has some journals I'd be interested in reading."

"You'd be talking about the Windfall journals." Maggie mulled that. It didn't take long. The conclusions were so obvious. "You're not just after some reading material."

"No."

"So I have to wonder why you're interested in the private goings on of people who've been dead three centuries."

"Maggie—"

"Cut to the chase, Keegan. It has something to do with their descendants."

Dex had nothing to say to that. Or rather, he chose not to, and when she looked into his eyes, she decided she should be grateful for that. What she was was pissed off.

"Do you think my friends and neighbors are idiots?" Did he think she was an idiot? That it hadn't taken her all of two seconds to figure his interest wasn't only about descendants.

Everything came down to money. Lord knew nobody on Windfall had more than two nickels to rub together, or ever had. So, it must be about something of value instead— land, personal property—hell, it could be just about anything, big or little.

"This may be a small, out-of-the-way place, and we may be simple people, but—"

"You're not simpletons. I don't think that."

"But you have secrets to keep."

"And you and your fellow Windfallers don't?"

"Maybe so, but this is our place."

"And I'm the outsider, so that's it. Case closed, shut me out without even giving me a chance."

"I am giving you a chance." Maggie took the steps that put her in his face. "If I was going to shut you down cold, I'd have sent you packing before you dragged me into this asinine conversation."

"Meaning?"

"Meaning if you want my help, you need to convince me that what you find out isn't going to harm anyone."

"The only way to do that is tell you what I'm looking for. I can't."

"'Can't' is an interesting word, Keegan. Won't is another one. Neither will gain you my cooperation." She turned toward the Piper.

Dex caught her by the arm and spun her back.

She looked down at his hand. "You want to lose that?"

He slid his fingers down to her wrist, and she knew he felt her pulse scramble before she jerked free. And when she lifted furious eyes to his face, she saw his jaw working.

Not so cool and calm himself, she realized, though she couldn't quite manage to enjoy his discomfort, not with her heart still galloping in her chest.

Dex shoved a hand back through his hair, stalked off a few steps then spun around and stomped back. This time he kept his distance. "I need those journals. And I think you're trustworthy, but here's the thing: so am I."

"Trust needs to be earned. How do I trust someone who's keeping secrets?"

"You're a damn good judge of character."

Maggie liked to think so, but she wasn't altogether sure her judgment was unclouded where Dex Keegan was concerned. She found, with very little consideration, that she wanted to believe him. That was dangerous enough to have her treading very carefully.

"I gave my word to my client. I can't go back on it."

"You may have to without those journals."

"They could be completely useless."

"Or they could tell you exactly what you need to know. These people accepted me when..." Maggie dropped her gaze before he saw too much. "You're asking me to lie to them."

"I'm asking you not to say anything."

"It's the same thing." But she sighed. She could imagine

all too well what would happen if news got out that Dex Keegan was there to hand out so much as a twenty-dollar bill.

"If I fail, someone else will be sent, and then you won't know what's going on."

"I don't know now," Maggie pointed out.

"But at least this way you can keep an eye on me."

"I've got two eyes, and they'll both be on you."

Dex slipped his hands in his pockets, looking uncertain for the first time since he'd swaggered into her life. "So you'll let me know when you're done thinking?"

"If I go see Meeker, I go alone. Don't," she added when he opened his mouth to argue.

Even thinking about a face-to-face with Josiah Meeker... For just an instant she'd been a sixteen-year-old girl again, a sixteen-year-old girl in an impossible situation. She'd gotten herself out of it, though, and she looked Dex straight in the eye now. "My way or no way."

His gaze narrowed on hers. "You have history with Meeker."

"Hello, tiny island, small population. I have history with everyone who lives here."

"It's something more than that."

"He gave me my first part-time job when I moved here," she explained because withholding it would give Dex Keegan the idea it was more important than it was. She'd even managed to say it without a hint of the anger or, God help her, the shame she always felt when Josiah Meeker crossed her mind. Or so she thought until she saw fury light Dex's dark eyes.

"It was a long time ago, and Meeker was no real threat to me. I learned to defend myself at an early age. Not all the bases where my father was stationed were kind to spindly little American girls."

The explanation came with pride—pride that she was well entitled to. She'd taken her share of knocks before that pride had forced her to shed the meekness that had been ground into her. And in striking back, she'd learned valuable lessons about strength and self-respect, about being her own best defense without losing her self-control.

The one time she'd tried out her new philosophy on her father, she learned that there were bullies everywhere, and sometimes they were too big to take on. It had taught her how to bide her time, choose her battles, cut her losses.

To keep the past in the past.

Maggie turned back to her engine, or tried to.

Dex stepped between her and the ladder, his face like a thundercloud. "I changed my mind, Maggie. Leave Meeker to me."

"Don't trouble yourself. I can handle Meeker."

"You're not going anywhere near him on my account."

"Don't tell me what to do."

"What the hell are you arguing about? You don't want to ask him anyway."

Until he told her she couldn't. She found it touching that he wanted to protect her, and infuriating that he thought he needed to. "Meeker won't give you the journals."

He whirled around, took a dozen angry paces before he spun and stomped back until he stood nearly toe to toe with her. "Jesus, I don't understand women."

Maggie huffed out a laugh. "Typical man, blaming your problems on the female sex. And don't try to hang it around my neck. My position hasn't changed. You're the one who's waffling."

"I didn't have all the facts."

"And the facts change what, exactly? You don't want those journals anymore because I had a close call fifteen years ago?"

"Stay the hell away from him, Maggie."

"What about your case?"

"There are other ways."

Maggie snorted. "You're not going to beat him up on my account." Then she lifted her gaze from his fisted hands to his furiously cold face, and her smile faded. "I shouldn't have told you."

"But—"

"You are not going to beat him up on my account," she repeated, mortified. Bad enough that she'd had to tell him about the worst moment of her life; now he wanted her to feel even weaker? "I'm not some damsel in distress, Keegan. If you lay a hand on him, you'll get no help from me."

Dex went still, seething, but his hands opened, spread.

"And don't even think about breaking into his place," she added, because he was thinking exactly that. She'd seen the flash of calculation before he shifted his gaze from hers. "I think I'll have lunch with George," she said. "We haven't had a good talk in a long while—and there's so much to talk about these days."

Dex scrubbed both hands back through his hair. "What do you suggest?"

"That you tell me why you're here."

His lips twisted. "Quite the catch 22. I keep you out of this, I might as well leave now because the chance I'll accomplish my goal is probably nil. If I meet your condition, I get the journals, but I've broken my client's confidence. And I'll have you on my conscience."

"Don't trouble yourself, Keegan. I can handle Meeker."

Dex rubbed his ribs, smiled a little. "I don't doubt it. And Maggie?"

"Hmmm?"

"The next time you hit me, I'm going to hit back."

*   *   *

Jessi leaned against the frame of the big window in the empty lobby, the one that looked out over the tarmac, hangar, helipad and two landing strips of the Windfall Island airport. The day had started off clear and crisp, with a sky so blue it almost hurt the eyes. By midmorning clouds had begun to sock in from the south, racing up the coastline in front of a tropical storm named Dante and turning her mood a little blue. Trust a man, she thought, to bring her down.

Dex Keegan was probably no better.

Not that Maggie seemed to mind. There she was, Jessi thought, her clothes covered with grease, an old ball cap smashed on her hair, up to her elbows in an engine. Not exactly your formula for attracting a man. But Maggie was so at ease, so natural. Anyone could have seen he couldn't resist her. Even when she drove an elbow into his gut because he got too close.

Some would have said Maggie had egged him into crowding her, but they would have been wrong. Maggie was Maggie; she didn't put on airs, or primp, or play games. She didn't flirt or pretend to be something she wasn't. Heck, most of the time she was blunt to the point of rudeness, and still people weren't put off.

She didn't even realize how strong and sure of herself she was, Jessi thought with a shake of her head, how irresistible that easy self-confidence could be.

She watched Maggie walk away from Dex, who looked a little put out, even though he'd gotten the last word. Jessi grinned over it, but it gave her a pang, too, because she was so lonely. It wasn't like she chose to keep the male species at arm's length. She'd had opportunities. She just didn't take them—couldn't take them, she corrected herself. Something inside her was broken—her heart, sure, but something deeper, too. She couldn't bring herself to let another man into her life. Not after what the last one had done to her. And there was Benji to worry about. She wouldn't risk her son for anyone or anything.

Maggie racketed in the door and stopped short when she saw Jessi, one eyebrow popping up. "Enjoy the show?"

"It would be better if you kissed him instead of punching him."

Maggie shook her head. "You really have to get out more, Jess. Especially if you're living your sex life vicariously through me."

"My non-existent sex life."

"Then vicarious would only be more of the same."

"You could have dinner with Dex. I'm sure dinner would lead to sex, especially if you don't beat him up again. And then you could tell me about it. In great detail. Use measuring devices if you have to."

"Why don't you and your yardstick have dinner with him, cut out the middle man, so to speak. And don't tell me it's because of Benji. I'm pretty sure there was a man involved in order for you to have him."

"Having the right kind of plumbing doesn't make him a man."

"Jess." Maggie slung an arm around her shoulders, walked with her back to the office. "How long are you going to let him torque you up like this?"

"Forever."

"No, you're not. Some guy will come along and make you forget about Lance."

"What about Benji? Growing up without a father is bad enough, and considering the type of man his father was, it's probably for the best. But how do I let a stranger into his life? How do I take that chance with him?"

"By making sure it's the right guy. By trusting yourself enough to know you would never let someone in who'd hurt either of you."

"Love is hurt, Maggie, even the deepest, best love. Especially then, because loving that deeply means you can be hurt just as deeply."

"And closing yourself off isn't?"

Yeah, it hurt. Sometimes she was so lonely she ached with it. "You get used to it," was all Jessi said. "Don't forget where we live. Windfall isn't exactly a smorgasbord of dating prospects."

"You have a point," Maggie said with the same note of resignation in her voice. Then she shrugged it off, a purely Maggie jerk of one shoulder that said, to hell with obstacles. "There's Burt Maslow," she suggested.

"He's been through every available woman on the island. Twice."

"Except you and me."

"We have good taste."

"Okay, there's Windfall High School's senior class."

"Two of them are girls, and Seth Hogan isn't eighteen yet. George would probably arrest me."

"Mo Hancock then." Maggie grinned. "You wouldn't have to worry about legal ramifications. Or competition."

"Except from his imaginary friends."

Maggie laughed, and Jessi couldn't help but join her. It felt damn good.

"Maybe you should start popping over to the mainland with me once in a while, Jess. Broaden your horizons."

"And who'd run the office?"

"Forward your calls to your cell."

"I do more than answer the phones."

"Nobody knows that better than me."

Maggie let it go, but Jessi knew she wasn't done with it yet. Like a dog with a bone, Maggie was. When she got her teeth into a problem, she'd worry at it until she found a way to fix it.

Some things, though, couldn't be fixed. They just had to be lived through, lived down. And that took time.

"So, what was Dex after? Besides you?"

"Ha."

"Not leaving so soon, is he?"

"Unfortunately, no."

"Well, whatever he wanted, it must have been pretty important for him to come all the way out here."

"You brought him. Didn't you grill him on the drive in?"

"He wasn't talking." Jessi crossed her arms, one eyebrow inching up at Maggie's silence. "Apparently you have that in common."

"Oh, good, I was worried I wouldn't be able to find common ground with Dex Keegan."

"So you weren't getting along? Why not?"

"He asked me out, I turned him down." Maggie said it with a shrug in her voice, but she wasn't making eye contact.

And who'd buy it, anyway? Jessi thought. Dex could have called Maggie on the phone instead of dragging himself all the way across the island. For that matter, he could have hung around the Horizon at dinnertime. Maggie ate there most nights.

So what was she hiding?

"Maybe you should take your own advice," Jessi said.

Maggie made her eyes wide, her expression innocent. "What advice would that be?"

"Open up. Give the man a chance."

"That one doesn't need to be given anything."

"It's not so bad to be taken once in a while, either."

"That's quite a piece of wisdom, coming from a woman who won't even risk going on a date." But Maggie glanced off toward the tarmac, as if she was considering it.

"We're not talking about dating, are we?"

"He doesn't plan to be around that long."

"Even better, since you're in love with your airplanes."

Maggie's gaze, filled with surprise and hurt, shot to meet Jessi's.

Jessi sighed, rubbing the spot between her eyes where a headache was brewing. "I'm sorry, Maggie."

"Why? It's true."

"But you don't want to be alone with them forever. You want a home and family, right?"

"I don't know."

"Oh, Mags." Jessi reached for her, but Maggie inched away.

"What's wrong with not wanting those things?" she said. "Just because I'm female—"

"Nothing," Jessi said carefully, "Unless you don't want them because you never had a proper family yourself."

"I had a family, Jess."

"Maggie, you know what I mean. It doesn't have to be a repeat of history. Family is what you make it."

Maggie crossed her arms, going sarcastic, her weapon of choice. "Fine sentiment, Jess. Let's make a sampler and hang it on the wall."

"Like your mother did?"

"Nancy Solomon was a whiz at creating a home, hot meals every night, little handmade touches, everything spic and span. Too bad it was all show and no heart."

Maggie looked away again. Anyone else would have bought her non-expression as coldness. Jessi knew better.

"It was like standing on the wrong side of a window, Jess. I could see the warmth, but I couldn't touch it, no matter how hard I tried, how good I was. Or how bad." Her voice broke, and so did Jessi's heart.

Growing up as an outsider in her own family had made Maggie strong, self-sufficient, but at what cost when she was always alone? "It's her loss, Mags." Then, knowing humor was needed, Jessi added, "I'll make samplers with you."

Maggie smiled a little, wistfully. "I'm not much for sewing."

"Well, then, I'd better get out my thimble, because God knows I'm getting stuck with the needle work while you fly off on your next adventure."

"Picking up the mail is an adventure now?"

"It's better than sitting around here making tiny little stitches—or paying the bills, which is what I'll actually be doing."

"Then I better get to adventuring so we have enough money in the bank to keep the lights burning." Maggie headed toward her office to change, dropping a hand on Jessi's shoulder as she passed by. The gesture of comfort, so out of character from a woman who habitually shied away from the softness she'd never known, brought tears to Jessi's eyes.

"Offer still stands, Jess. Why don't you come with me? It's just a couple of hours."

"Benji," Jess said simply. "It's after two o'clock already. School gets out at four."

"Then we'll wait, take him with us."

Jessi felt everything inside her lift and brighten. And just as quickly fall again. "The post office on the mainland will be closed."

"I'll give them a call. I think I can talk someone into meeting us at the airport. We'll stow the mail and then get a bite to eat."

Jessi thought about it, and going with the oddity of the day, she threw her arms around Maggie and hugged her hard. And Maggie, who preferred sarcasm to emotion, hugged back—only for a moment, but it was the gesture that counted.

"What the hell," Jessi said as she stepped back. "I'll go spring Benji from school early."

"Great," Maggie rolled her eyes, almost her old self, "now I'll have to share my hero status with you."

"Nope, I don't get to be a hero until I learn to fly something bigger than a paper airplane. Unless I talk you into the arcade. Then I can almost compete."

Maggie grinned, full out. "I love the arcade."

"Now how," Jessi said darkly, "did I know you were going to say that?"

Chapter Nine

Jessi's house sat on one of the curved roads that were nestled behind the town's main street, a tiny house with peaked roofs and fancifully painted gingerbread trim that looked as though it could have been waiting for Hansel and Gretel to happen by. But in a good way.

Dex walked up a bricked path lined with Chrysanthemums in fall colors, smiling when he heard the sound of a child's laughter right through the front door. He knocked, and at the muffled "Come in," he turned the knob and stepped through the door, saying, "I heard you feed half the neighborhood on a nightly basis," but instead of Jessi, Maggie was on the floor, tickling a tow-headed kid six or seven years old. "Well, isn't this domestic?"

Maggie sat back on her heels, not the least bit embarrassed. The kid popped to his feet and ran over to peer up at him. "I'm Benji—Benjamin Randal. Who are you? Where do you come from? Did Auntie Maggie bring you here on one of her planes?"

"Helicopter," Dex managed to get in.

"I'm going to fly one of those, too. When I get big like Auntie Maggie."

Dex looked over at her, both his eyebrows raised.

"What's wrong with you?" Maggie said.

"Nothing. Auntie Maggie."

She got to her feet, pulling the kid against her, his back to her front, and looping her arms around his neck. "Jessi and Benji are as close as it gets to family for me. If you have a problem—"

Dex held his hands up. "It's just nice to find out you have a soft side."

"It's not a side. More like a tiny little nugget of aberration I do my best to keep hidden."

"I never would have guessed."

She shot him a humorless smile. "Jessi's the one with the soft side. I assume you were invited to dinner, just like I was, so let's call a truce while we're here."

"Auntie Maggie?"

She looked down at the kid, everything about her softening, including the tone in her voice. "This is Dexter Keegan."

"Dex," he said to Benji, but he couldn't tear his eyes off Maggie, struck by the way her face relaxed, the slight, reassuring smile that made her look so...maternal. And made him go just a little breathless.

"Mr. Keegan to you, Benj," she said, looking up at him with that bite-me expression.

It put him back on firm footing again, let him forget that little tug of *emotion* he'd felt at seeing Maggie in a new—and appealing—light.

"Now go tell your mom he's here." She gave the kid a light pat on the butt to send him on his way.

"We're not at war, Maggie," Dex said after Benji had disappeared into the sunny yellow kitchen.

"You're the one with the secret intelligence." Maggie

dropped into an overstuffed chair and crossed her long, jeans-clad legs. "If you aren't the enemy, why don't you come clean?"

Jessi saved him by breezing through the doorway with Benji skipping along ahead. "Thanks for picking up Sunshine, here," she said to Maggie. "I never would have made it home in time to make my famous pork chops. They have to brine for at least an hour."

"Auntie Maggie should let you out early enough to pick up your son and brine your chops."

"Well, Maggie's a slave driver," Maggie said, rising from her armchair and letting Benji tow her off to his bedroom to show her some new poster. She shot Dex a look over her shoulder, a look that wasn't quite bland enough to hide the edge of hurt—hurt he'd caused her.

Jessi saw it, too, and she wasn't cutting him any slack.

"Maggie tried to get me out the door early, but I was stuck with a customer," she said, "trying to carve out some time for Maggie to fly him down to D.C. Her schedule is pretty intense, but that's *her* schedule."

"And I jumped to conclusions."

"Don't let her fool you. She's not nearly as . . ."

"Hard?"

"It's not the word I was looking for, but okay." Jessi headed for the kitchen. "Maggie isn't nearly as hard as she comes off."

Dex followed her, leaning on the jamb of the wide doorway, watching as she picked up a wooden spoon and stirred something bubbling on the stove. "What is she?"

Jessi shook her head, turned to face him. "Not my place to say."

"Loyalty."

She smiled, a small wobbly smile that made Dex wonder

just what Maggie had done for Jessi to inspire that kind of complex emotion, gratitude mixed with God knew what else. Sure, women were emotional creatures, but there was something deeper than friendship between these two. Sisters, Dex decided, and not because of an accident of birth. By choice. The kind of sisters who wouldn't keep secrets from one another.

Unless they could be convinced it was the right thing to do.

"What's going on in there?" Jessi asked, pointing her spoon at his forehead.

"What goes on in any man's mind?"

"If I knew that, I wouldn't have made some of the choices I made."

"Sounds like there's an interesting story there."

"One you've probably heard a thousand times from a thousand women who let the wrong kind of man matter to them," Jessi said quietly, her eyes shifting toward the doorway where her son had disappeared.

"Now," she went to the fridge and pulled out a serving plate, pulling plastic wrap off and handing it to him. "Take this into what I laughingly refer to as the dining room, and let me get the rest of this finished up."

Dex carried the plate in to the small space off the living area where a table only big enough to seat four sat, nipping a cube of cheese as he set it down.

"You're gonna ruin your appetite," piped a voice from behind him. "And you're not supposed to eat with your fingers."

Dex turned, took in Maggie's amused expression before he concentrated on his accuser. "How about hamburgers?"

"That's not a hamburger," Benji pointed out with the bluntness and logic of the very young.

"He got you there, Keegan. Good going, Champ." Maggie held her palm up, high enough that Benji had to jump to make the high five. Which only made it more fun, judging by the peal of his laughter. "You have to watch out for guys like this, Benj. First it's cheese and then they move on to the big stuff."

Benji's eyes went wide. "What's the big stuff?"

Maggie hunkered down, her smile so open, her eyes so bright, there was no way for Dex to ignore the way his pulse lurched, especially when she slid him a teasing look as she said to Benji, "Could be just about anything, but I'd keep a close eye on your Legos if I were you."

"Great," Dex said as Benji rushed off to make sure his building blocks were still where he'd left them. "The kid thinks I'm a cat burglar now."

"Cat burglar? There's that ego again."

"If I were a thief, I wouldn't be a common one."

"No." Maggie rose to her feet. "I don't suppose you would."

Jessi came out of the kitchen, wiping her hands on a towel and looking like Betty Crocker in her cute little apron. "Did someone say cat, as in are you two fighting like cats and dogs again?"

Maggie, for once, had no quippy comeback.

Dex decided it was better to change the subject, even if he'd have liked to know what Maggie had been—and still was—thinking, as she studied him.

"No wonder every kid in the village wants to move in here," he said.

"Who told you that?"

"Everybody. Not only is Benji an irresistible kid, but you're the kind of mother everyone should've had."

Maggie smiled. "She never raises her voice at dirty footprints or spilt milk, and there are always cookies."

"Nice to know my publicist is working overtime," Jessi said, but her cheeks pinked becomingly as she returned to the kitchen.

"You should give up your life of glamour at the airport and open a daycare," Dex called after her. "You'd probably make a killing."

Maggie shook her head. "More like she'd end up baby-sitting for free half the time. She's too soft-hearted."

"That's not a little self-serving?"

"Well, it's true...and a little self-serving, since I couldn't run Solomon Charters without her."

"This is really entertaining," Jessi said, coming back with her arms laden with serving dishes and a face like a storm cloud, "but do I get a vote?"

Maggie backed off immediately, but Jessi was already swinging around to confront Dex. "For the record, Mr. Keegan, I don't need you to defend me."

"So we're back on formal footing."

"We've never been off it. I invited you to my home for dinner, despite the secrets you're clearly keeping."

"Or maybe because of them?"

"Mom," Benji said, coming over to curl an arm around her.

"It's all right, kiddo," Jessi said, "Why don't you go wash up for dinner." When he hesitated, she gave him a little nudge. "Go on."

He went, but he kept a wary eye on Dex the whole way out of the room.

"You're right," Jessi said to Dex, "but you're also a guest, and it's not very polite of you to attack my best friend."

"Jessi—"

She held up a hand. "And just so you know, I don't work for Maggie. I'm her partner. Maggie insisted on giving me a percentage of the business—"

"Jessi," Maggie said again, her face going a mortified red.

"She made me a partner," Jessi continued, "because she claims she's hopeless at the business end."

"I gave you a percentage because you work just as hard as I do."

"But we both know you could handle anything you put your mind to."

"The truth is I don't want to. I'd rather be in the air or tinkering with an engine. So this works out for both of us. And you'd only take ten percent."

"I'm sorry," Dex said, and truly meant it. "I didn't intend to cause trouble."

"Didn't you?" Maggie whipped back around, pinned him with a glare. "You waltz in here and stir the pot, then step back to see what boils up to the surface."

"What choice do I have?" Dex went toe to toe with her. "No one will answer my questions."

Maggie crossed her arms, pinned him with a look. "I have questions, too. Questions like what the hell are you doing here?"

"Having dinner, I thought."

"On Windfall," Maggie shot back. "You've been here almost a week, grilling people, wandering around, wanting favors—"

He knew by the way she broke off, by the glance she shot Jessi, that she hadn't told her best friend. Interesting.

"Why don't you cut the client-lawyer privilege crap and tell us what's going on?"

"I'd really love to hear the answer to that," Jessi said. "Just like I'd love to know what you and Dex were talking about so intently the other day."

Maggie clamped her mouth shut, going sullen.

"If you value our friendship," Jessi said.

"That's a low blow, Jess." Maggie crossed her arms. "But maybe—"

Dex took Maggie by the arm, effectively shutting her up, since she rounded on him. "Can I have a word with you?"

She tried to get loose, but he only took a firmer grip. "Now," he said, catching her enough off guard that he was able to pull her past Jessi and out the front door.

Maggie jerked free, cocking her arm back.

Dex stared her down. "I told you what would happen the next time you hit me."

She kicked him instead, stalking for the door when he bent to rub at his shin.

He snagged her around the waist, dragging her back. She didn't go easily. It was a shame, he thought as they wrestled on Jessi's front walk, that he couldn't take more time to enjoy the way she felt against him, the sleek curves, the wiry strength of her body, the way she smelled like spring, with just a hint of motor oil thrown in. And then she nearly got in a killing blow.

Dex ignored his libido, twisting sideways to keep her from making it a moot point. "If you stop—" he dodged a fist, "—for one second—" he blocked her knee with his thigh, "—and listen to me—" she tried to head butt him.

He gave up on trying not to hurt her, twisting her around to put her back to his front, and banding his arms around her so that hers were trapped under his. She tried to stomp on his feet, then kicked back, but he managed to avoid injury.

"Knock it off or you're going to take us both down, and if we go down, I'm not doing the manly thing and falling on the bottom to spare you."

She only struggled harder.

"Keep it up; you're giving Jessi and Benji a hell of a show."

"Bastard," she spat. But she stopped struggling

Dex might have been sorry to let her go, if the muscles in his arms hadn't been trembling on the verge of exhaustion. "When I asked you to get Meeker's journals, you told me you wouldn't help me without an explanation. And then you made it impossible for me to get them without you. Are you going to behave and listen to me?"

She nodded once, stiffly.

He let her go, making sure to move out of the way, just in case. He'd spent two long days arguing with his conscience, and although necessity had won, he still hated asking her to take on Meeker again. After wrestling with her, though, he figured he should pity Meeker. If the man was stupid enough to lay a hand on her, he'd deserve what he got.

"Talk," she said, all ice, "or we can go inside and talk there."

"I need your word that you'll keep what I'm about to tell you a secret. Even from Jessi."

"And if I don't agree, you won't talk." Maggie hissed out a breath. "Fine."

"You know I came here for a case," Dex began.

"As a lawyer or a private eye?"

Dex smiled grimly. He should have known she'd figure that out. And he had to give her the truth. A lie would only work against him at this point—and he found he didn't want to lie to her anymore. "Private investigator. Small-time stuff, mostly."

She crossed her arms, her mood lightening perceptibly. "Taking pictures of cheating spouses?"

"I've handled some insurance cases, too. But, yeah, mostly it was divorce work." Which it galled him to admit, almost as much as the next confession. "If not for this case I'd have to seriously think about a career change."

"I'm sorry, Dex."

His gaze shot to hers, and even in the dim light he could see she meant it. Her sympathy surprised him, but not half as much as the relief he felt. He wanted Maggie's good will, sure, but this relief felt more personal, and nothing about this case was supposed to be personal. Hell of a time, he thought, for Maggie to show her sensitive side.

"If you wanted to be a PI even half as bad as I wanted the sky, I can only imagine how terrible you must feel at the idea of giving it up."

And she'd surprised him again, or maybe this time he'd surprised himself. Somewhere in the years of chasing liars and cheats he'd forgotten how much he wanted to help people—until this case, and even then he'd been more focused on the goal and the salvation, the vindication it might bring him, than how amazing it felt to be doing what he loved.

"A couple of weeks ago," he continued, feeling like a light had been turned on inside him, "a friend in Boston gave me a call. Alec is a lawyer—a real, high-profile lawyer—and he's the only person who knows why I got into this business in the first place."

"You don't have to tell me, Dex. It's none of my business."

"It's the same reason I became a cop...and the same reason I stopped being a cop. Police departments all over the country are down-sizing, so the chance I'd get to be a detective..." He broke off, shook his head at his own foolishness. Maggie Solomon showed one iota of interest, of sympathy, and here he was baring his soul. "Long story short, I became a private investigator because I want to find people, those who've been taken against their will, those who've become lost through no fault of their own, those who don't want to be found."

"What kind are you looking for here?"

"The kind who doesn't know they're lost."

Maggie scrubbed her hands through her short hair, pacing away a few steps only to whirl back, her breath steaming on the frigid air. "Stop talking in riddles and just tell me what's going on."

"I was hired to find any possible descendants of a baby who went missing from her nursery in 1931. She was ten months old."

"Eugenia Stanhope," Maggie said. It wasn't a question.

"I should have known you'd make the connection."

"I shouldn't have had to guess," she fired back.

Dex rubbed the back of his neck, knowing it was best to let her work through her anger at her own pace.

"The *Perdition* exploded and sank right out there with Eugenia on board." Maggie pointed to the dark expanse of ocean shining in the sliver of moon beyond the pale lights of the village. "It's still the biggest thing to happen around here in a hundred years—that and Prohibition. And the two go hand in hand, since the ship was docked out there to offload illegal liquor."

"I doubt you'd find many in this country who didn't break that particular law."

Maggie wrapped her arms around herself, but not, Dex thought, to keep warm. "Running booze is worlds apart from kidnapping babies. I don't believe any Windfaller would be involved, even back then when bootlegging meant the difference between life and death to the people here."

"I didn't come to Windfall Island to point fingers. I just want to find the truth," Dex said, exhausted suddenly, tired of his contention with Maggie, tired of fighting his attraction to her, weary of pitting his will against an entire population of the most stubborn people he'd ever met.

"If your aim is to find the missing," Maggie said into the heavy silence, "you picked a doozy of a first case."

He looked over, surprised that he saw in her eyes what he'd heard in her voice. "Sympathy?"

"Understanding," she corrected, her voice warmer now. "I live here, remember?"

"Who could forget?"

"Sympathy?" she threw back at him.

"Pity," he said with a smile. "Do you know the rest of Eugenia's story?"

"I know she was kidnapped by a nursemaid."

"Some say she was kidnapped, others say that the maid only wanted to have a little fun, and when she wasn't allowed to have the night off, she took the baby with her on board the *Perdition*, not intending any harm. It's widely believed they both died when the ship exploded that night."

Maggie digested that for a second. "Whoever hired you believes Eugenia may have survived. Even if you accept that as fact, what makes you believe there's any connection to Windfall Island?"

And there, Dex thought, was the question he'd been expecting. The answer, he knew, would make or break his case. "There were sightings of the maid. Credible sightings." And he could see Maggie wasn't convinced. "A woman recently died in Boston. Her name isn't important, but before she died she told her son that Sonja Hanson, the maid, was his great grandmother. And she gave him a box of documents, letters, birth certificates, press clippings."

"Let me guess, something in that box linked Sonja with Windfall. Why didn't he go to the press?"

"Money. He didn't want to expose his family to the tabloids and credible news agencies don't pay for stories, so he went to the Stanhopes directly. They paid him for the records and his silence, paid him very well, I'd imagine."

"And now they're paying you very well."

Dex drew in a breath, let it out slowly, ignoring the sting in her words. She didn't think much of him at the moment. He understood why. "The Stanhopes are American royalty. The luck belongs to whoever is descended from them."

"There's an inheritance, I take it."

"Eugenia was never declared dead—at first because her mother wouldn't allow it. In the years since her death, it was just never dealt with. Now, well, they want to be sure someone won't show up to make claims against the family.

"But you already knew this was about money."

"I figured there was something of value, and that you wanted to keep it a secret so there wouldn't be a free-for-all. Now that I know it's a fortune, I can understand the secrecy." She pinned him with a look. "Understand, not forgive."

"Maggie—"

"Jessi and Benji, they could be descendants."

"That's why you can't tell her."

Her stare turned to incredulity, with an edge of insult. "Do you think she'd falsify records?"

In for a penny…

But Maggie's quick mind had already jumped to the suspicion he would have voiced. Her brilliant blue eyes hardened, shining eerily in the faint light. "She could use the money, right?"

"I don't—" He stopped, took a moment to remind himself of his responsibilities. "I like Jessi, but I have to be objective. If word gets out, it will be almost impossible for me to do my job. Especially if word gets off the island."

She stared at him for another second, then whirled away to pace.

He could feel the fury pumping off her, so much she should have been steaming in the chilly night air.

"If you tell Jessi why I'm here, you'll only be putting her in an awkward position."

"Like me, you mean? The awkward position I'm in now, knowing you're here to turn the life of someone on this island upside down, someone I love—or at least tolerate. And I can't say a word or all hell breaks loose."

Dex shoved a hand back through his hair. He wished she'd slugged him instead. A fist to the face wouldn't have left him feeling so slimy. He couldn't even defend himself; from the minute he'd met Maggie Solomon, he'd known her personality and her history made her the only person he'd be able to...enlist.

"What, not going to apologize?"

No, because he'd do it again to solve this case. "I wouldn't mean it, and you wouldn't accept it."

"Finally, the truth."

"I'm capable, when it suits me," Dex said, and let her think the worst. They were going to have to work together, probably closely. Better for them both that she hang on to any resentment that helped her keep him at arm's length.

"It better suit you from now on, Ace, or I will out you," she said from a safe distance, physically and emotionally. "And you can take that to the bank, along with the fat fee you've left me no choice but to help you earn."

Chapter Ten

The airport on Temptation Bay—*her* airport, Maggie thought as she walked from the hangar to the office—never failed to leave her awestruck. It wasn't just about ownership, it was about pride, the kind an architect felt in looking at a high-rise come to life from a humble drawing, or a baker felt in putting the finishing touches on a wedding cake that would not only taste like heaven, but be the crowning touch on some lucky bride's perfect day.

The runways were just concrete, the buildings just aluminum, brick, wood and glass, and there were weeds to be trimmed; she'd need to get Mort on that, she told herself, and made a mental note. The place could use some paint to brighten it up—she added another mental note—to not only give her passengers great service but provide surroundings that were nice to look at. To keep the wolves from her door.

It wasn't all about paying the bills, though there'd been plenty of months she'd wondered if she'd sail over that hurdle or catch a toe and fall into a hole she'd never be able to climb out of. But even those memories made something swell inside her chest. It was like flying, flying at the best of times, when the ground dropped away, when there was no safety net but her skill with the controls, her way with engines, the sheer willpower and refusal to fail that had burned in her gut since the day she'd realized her father saw her as a failure. The day she'd decided she'd rather die than prove him right.

And sure, from the outside it might seem that part of her success could be laid at his feet, if only because his lack of faith had put that fire in her. But she chose to believe she'd have accomplished her dreams just the same; hell, even better, if he'd been a different kind of father. The kind, for instance, who'd held her up while she learned to swim, rather than throwing her into deep water and watching her head bob under the surface before panic and instinct put her into a wobbly, frantic doggie paddle. And even then, she recalled, she'd paddled away from him, though the distance to shore had been longer. She'd refused to take the easy route; it was one of the few times she'd earned his approval.

Maggie had never forgotten it.

And although she told herself she'd grown beyond needing his approval, she couldn't lie to herself and claim she didn't want it, sad as that was. Sadder still that she knew she'd never get it, not without a price tag.

She stepped inside and crossed the lobby, then made her way back to her tiny office behind the bigger open space, where the real running of Solomon Charters took place. Jessi was taking care of business in the village for the morning, leaving her to man the phones. It had been a quiet morning; under other circumstances she'd have been ecstatic, as the business side of her pet baby always left her feeling slightly queasy.

Just now she could have used a distraction or two.

With Dex Keegan around, she wasn't likely to get one. If

he wasn't tweaking her nerve endings, he was pushing her buttons. One moment she wanted him nearby, wanted the thrill of the challenge he presented, both physical and mental. The next moment she wanted him gone, off her island, taking his case of the century with him so she never had to look at her friends and neighbors again and wonder.

She couldn't have both. So she'd decided, during a long sleepless night, that matching wits and libidos with Dex Keegan wasn't an option.

That left Eugenia Stanhope. Maggie sat back in her office chair and stared at the story of Eugenia's kidnapping on her computer screen. She'd read every word a dozen times already, compared the written account with what Dex had told her, looking for clues to Windfall's involvement. As if all the years and the hundreds of minds more suited than hers to solving mysteries hadn't already proven the search futile.

The island was never mentioned, not in any of the articles or histories she'd found. Every source, almost without exception, concluded that Eugenia had perished in the explosion that had sent the *Perdition* to the bottom of the Atlantic. The kidnapping had been big news; if Eugenia had lived there was little possibility whoever had her would be ignorant as to her identity. Yet no request for ransom had been made, no one had come forward to claim the huge reward that had been offered.

There were emotions stronger than greed, though: fear, for starters, the kind of fear that would be felt by an insular, territorial, somewhat paranoid population, a population that routinely broke the laws of the time. That fear didn't come without just cause, Maggie allowed.

If Eugenia Stanhope had been found on Windfall Island, Windfallers would have been arrested. No doubt about that. There'd been little in the way of individual protections before Miranda rights were established—she'd looked it up—and the FBI at the time had been given wide powers to deal with Prohibition violations. Add in the tremendous pressure to bring in Eugenia Stanhope's abductors, and you created steamrollers. Guilt or innocence wouldn't have mattered. The Feds would have simply flattened whoever they arrested in order to get confessions.

But did she have a right to decide for the whole island now? If Eugenia's fate was linked to Windfall Island, there'd be a rise in tourism, no doubt about it. Others would see that as a good thing, and even if there was no statute of limitations on murder, who remained alive to be punished? And the inheritance? Who was she to measure the price of it—and there would be a price; that kind of money changed people, and not always for the better.

What she did know was that just the possibility of it would rip the community apart, and while she didn't have the right to deny anyone their own history, she could at least try to contain the damage—especially if that damage might be to someone she loved like a sister.

Maggie had to admit she wasn't only worried about Jessi and Benji, though. Her life was on the line, too, not in a six-foot-under way, but everything she'd built, everything she'd made herself could be taken from her. Because, while she hadn't been born on Windfall, her mother had.

And sure, she hadn't told Dex that. Life with Daddy had made her cautious with her personal business, especially with strangers, and Dex's secrecy hadn't exactly inspired her trust. Worse yet, he'd been manipulating her—still was. It made her vision go red at the edges—because of her own history, she allowed, but it didn't make the feelings any less valid. Even if she had no right to feel...anything.

And there, she admitted, was the thing that had forced her to walk away from Jessi's house without revealing a word of her conversation with Dex. It was the burn that had kept her up all night and prevented her from concentrating on the mile-long list of chores that always needed doing at the airport.

Betrayal.

Dex Keegan was nothing to her. She didn't trust him; hell, she didn't even like him. Problem was, she shouldn't be feeling so raw and hurt that he hadn't confided in her sooner. Especially since she'd already examined the case from every angle and been forced to admire his approach. That made her magnanimous, even if she had to say so herself. Being an emotional mess over Dex Keegan made her a fool.

Still, she couldn't deny that he stirred her up on every level—physical, mental, and yeah, he pissed her off. He was glib, overconfident and confusing, but that grin of his was so damn appealing she found herself smiling over it. And just to make it impossible to forget him, he had a sharp mind and a hell of a body. Total package. If only he didn't feel a need to keep secrets and tell lies.

The phone rang and, still stewing, she picked it up without checking caller ID. And that, she decided when she heard the voice that greeted her, was another transgression she could lay at Dex's feet.

"Margaret." It was her father.

She hung up. The phone rang again and she ignored it. For a half hour. She had to give the man credit for being persistent.

Jessi rushed in and grabbed the receiver off her ancient desk phone. "Solomon Charters," she said, then promptly hung up.

She dropped her purse in her bottom desk drawer, plopped her ass in her chair, and pulled over a stack of paperwork. She didn't say hello, she didn't look in Maggie's directions, and she was slapping the papers, just hard enough as she sorted them into piles, to get her attitude across loud and clear. Hurt feelings with a side of sulkiness.

Maggie knew all about it. The difference being, after a decade of history, Jessi was entitled to be upset.

But after a decade of history, Maggie knew how to get around her. She strolled out and perched on the edge of Jessi's desk.

Jessi stared pointedly at her butt until Maggie lifted her cheek, pulled the papers out from under it, and handed them over. Jessi took them with two fingers and continued her sorting.

Maggie managed not to smile. "Not talking to me yet?"

"Don't you have that backward?"

"Still don't trust me?"

Jessi huffed out a breath. "We went over this last night. *You* don't trust *me*."

"You're my family, Jess; do you think I'd keep something from you if I didn't think it was the right thing to do?"

Jessi shot to her feet, her pixie face like a thundercloud. "It's not your decision to make, Maggie."

"You're right about that. It's Dex's, and I gave him my word."

"To hell with your word."

"Without it, we'd all be in the dark."

Jessi crossed her arms, but her expression toned down from outrage to sullen. "I hate it when you force me to be logical."

"I promise I'll tell you what I can when I can, Jess. But just now, you have to trust me to do what's best for us. And for Windfall."

"I don't have much choice, do I?" Jessi sighed, sinking

back down onto her chair. "All I can do is sit back and let you handle it. I hate being helpless."

"There is one thing you can do. Forgive me?"

"Oh, Maggie."

"Anyone gets a whiff you and I disagree on something, they'll know it's big."

"Well, we wouldn't argue about something stupid."

"Exactly. People will be on you like foam on the ocean trying to find out what's going on. And you know somebody will find a way to get around you."

"Now who's lacking in faith?"

"It has nothing to do with faith. It's your soft heart that worries me."

"How about Mort?"

"Mort?"

"It's pretty obvious Dex has taken an interest in you, and I'm not the only one who might have witnessed that conversation you had on the tarmac. Mort was here, too, remember?"

Remember? She could still feel Dex behind her, that big, solid body warm against her back, his breath—

"Mags?"

She took a deep breath, then another, biting the inside of her lip so she could concentrate on the pain instead of the need fluttering low in her belly. "Mort barely talks to you and me, Jess."

"True. And if he does happen to mention it, no one will think it was more than Dex trying to get in your pants. What? It's not like he hasn't tried before, in plain view of half the island." Jessi put a hand on her knee, looked up at her. "Maybe you should let him."

Maybe you should mind your own business. Though the words flew to her lips, Maggie bit them back. She might have said them any other time, in jest or otherwise, without

Jessi taking the least offense. Just now, though, she and Jessi were searching for calm waters again; she didn't want to shove them back onto the rocks. "We're talking about you, Jess. At some point, you're going to have to lie. Look a friend straight in the eyes and lie."

"Maggie—" she held up a hand. "I know, close my eyes and think of England."

This time Maggie did smile. "Well, that's not the island I had in mind, but you've got the right idea."

"And what are you going to be doing while I'm practicing how to mislead my friends and neighbors?"

Something even worse, Maggie thought, losing every shred of good humor. "Errands."

Okay, it was a cop out, going to Ma Appelman's before she faced off with Meeker. Still, nobody had to know about it but her, Maggie figured. She always felt better after she'd spent time with Ma. She always felt stronger. Ma wouldn't accept anything less.

She pulled up in front of the saltbox Ma called home, a three-story, white clapboard rectangle situated at the extreme landward point of the island. The widow's walk circling its roof had not been employed to watch for sailors and their ships making safely into port, but to keep an eye out for anyone arriving from the mainland unannounced. Unannounced went hand in hand with untrustworthy, and untrustworthy meant enemy.

The days when that widow's walk had been routinely manned were over, but the mind-set lived on.

Ma opened the door at Maggie's knock, to all appearances a frail, white-haired old woman with nothing more pressing on her mind than greeting a friend, considering the wide smile that lit her seamed face and brightened her blackbird eyes. Behind those eyes, Maggie knew, was a mind as keen as a blade, and behind her smile a tongue sharp enough to leave wounds.

For Maggie, she reined it in. Somewhat. "About damn time you showed up," she snapped, stepping back enough for Maggie to slip by her.

"I didn't know I was late."

Ma hooted with laughter as she shut the door and clumped her way across the room, the thumping of her cane more a commentary than a walking aid. She eased herself down in an ancient armchair that sat in front of an even older television, equipped with rabbit ears studded with wads of tin foil. None of that newfangled cable for Ma.

"What are you doing here, girl?"

"I wish you wouldn't call me that." It was what her father had called her, always with the sting of dissatisfaction in his voice.

"Your father was a shortsighted fool. Thank the good Lord the rest of the military has more sense, else we'd be eating with chopsticks."

"Makes me wonder why you'd behave like him."

Ma's eyes went hard. "Watch your mouth. Girl."

Maggie met those obsidian eyes, tried not to grin. "I have to keep reminding you that you can't steamroll over me."

"Doesn't stop me from trying."

"You have everyone else on this island cowed; you ought to be satisfied with that."

"No satisfaction in wiping your feet on a doormat."

Maggie bumped up a shoulder. "Keeps the floor clean."

Ma hooted again. "You know what I'm talking about."

"Yes, I do." Maggie leaned over and kissed her cheek.

"Hmph." Ma blinked hard, folding her face into a frown.

"You haven't answered my question. What brings you to my end of Windfall?"

Love, Maggie thought, but neither of them would be comfortable with that answer. "I had some extra supplies. You'll be doing me a favor if you take them off my hands, so I don't have to find a place to store them."

"Anything I can do to help you out, child."

Maggie just smiled. It was a dance they'd done countless times. She never showed up empty-handed. Ma never took offense. "Besides," she said, "I haven't seen you in a while. I thought I'd better make sure the cats weren't having you for dinner because you dropped dead and everyone else was too scared to check on you."

"Probably give them indigestion."

"You'd probably kill them."

"Serve them right," Ma said with a chuckle.

Maggie picked up a dog-eared copy of *Poor Richard's Almanack*, riffling the pages.

"We're in for a hard winter," Ma said, "If it's half as bad as the signs portend."

"That's a first, you giving up before the first snow."

Ma made a dismissive sound, but she was rubbing her hands, and Maggie saw the slight palsy. "You young people don't know what hardship means. Why, when I was a girl—"

"You had to walk barefoot to school through waist-high drifts, uphill both ways."

"Just so you know I can handle a little bluster and blow."

"Maybe a century ago."

Ma swatted at her half-heartedly.

"When were you born, exactly?" Maggie asked. She'd tried for offhand and failed miserably, considering the way Ma was studying her face. "It's important."

Ma thought about that for a minute, then she pointed across the room to an alcove where a thick, leather-bound book lay on a carved bookstand. "Fetch me the Bible."

Maggie did as she was told, carefully. The binding was cracked, the pages buckled from the perpetual damp of the island, but it was obviously a cherished family heirloom.

"Meeker's been trying to get his hands on this for years," Ma said when she took the book from Maggie. "Offered me a thousand dollars a few months back."

Maggie hummed in the back of her throat.

"He's cheap, all right. This book is priceless, and I'll be dead and in my grave a month of Sundays before that sour-faced jackass lays a hand on it."

"I can't imagine AJ selling the family Bible."

"I'll haunt him if he does, then I'll haunt you for letting him."

"How did I get roped into this?"

Ma sniffed. "Think of you as a daughter."

Touched, Maggie kissed Ma's cheek again, then went around behind her chair, as much to hide the mist in her eyes as to look over Ma's shoulder.

"No, you don't." Ma snapped the Bible closed.

"Spoilsport."

"It's AJ's sport I'd be spoiling, and he'd have my hide."

Maggie huffed out a breath, mostly for effect, although she could already imagine AJ's expression when she called him by his actual name. Then again, where would be the fun in that?

"Here I am," Ma said, turning to a set of gold-edged pages.

From what little Maggie could see from her frustratingly safe distance, each page held two columns of lines, one for name and one for birth dates.

Ma pointed to an entry and read, "1 May, Nineteen Hundred Thirty-three."

Maggie closed her eyes for a moment, silently grateful.

"Now I wonder why my birth date should be such a thing of interest to you," Ma said, "and such a matter of relief."

Maggie grinned at her. "Somebody ornery as you could live this long, it gives me hope."

"Don't fool yourself, child. Ornery is what got me here."

Mother Appelman's house was hard to miss. So was Maggie's car sitting in the driveway. Dex leaned against the driver's side door. He didn't have to wait long before Maggie came out, his heart giving an odd little thump when he finally saw her. She wasn't quite so happy to see him, her steps faltering before she crossed her arms and frowned. "What are you doing here?"

"Same as you, I'd imagine."

"She's not Eugenia," Maggie said. "She was born in thirty-three."

"That's one question answered. I have a few dozen more." He started past her, but Maggie surprised him by laying a hand on his arm.

He studied her face for a moment. "You don't want me talking to her."

"You really think Eugenia might still be alive?"

"It's not likely."

"If she is alive, she's not on the island. Ma is the oldest woman living on Windfall."

"Which means she may have known Eugenia Stanhope, and if she moved, Mrs. Appelman may remember where she went."

"And how are you going to ask her without giving yourself away?" When Dex had no answer, she said, "Whatever you decide, you'll have to ask her another time. She may not be eighty years old, but she's close, and right now she needs her rest."

"I can't argue with that, especially if you agree to have a drink with me."

"Deal," she said, surprising him again.

And then she walked around to the back of the car, opened the trunk, and took out two bottles of water, flipping one to him.

"Not exactly what I had in mind."

"If you were a lawyer, you'd know better than to leave loopholes a mile wide."

Dex opened the water and took a swig. It was lukewarm and tasted like plastic, but it gave him something to focus on, kept his eyes from straying to her subtle curves, and stopped his mind from fogging. Maggie had put him off his stride from the minute she'd walked out of Ma's house. He didn't know how, but he had to get his balance back again.

"I'll have to talk to her at some point," he said.

"Yes, you will. She knows everything about Windfall, kind of the keeper of the spoken lore, which is a good thing when a jackass like Meeker controls the written."

"You, uh, haven't been to see him yet?"

"I'll get to him in my own time."

"Maggie. I'm sorry. If there was another way..." He stepped closer to her.

"You're crowding me again."

"It doesn't seem to be bothering you this time."

"Oh, it's bothering me. I'm just trying to figure your angle."

"Ouch." Dex stepped back, kept it good-natured, but there was a definite sting that she'd think he would use that kind of weapon.

"Don't beat yourself up, Keegan," she said. "You can't manipulate everyone in the world."

"You think you're such a hard nut to crack?" He grabbed her by the upper arms and jerked her against him, taking her mouth.

He'd expected her to fight, so it caught him off guard when she fisted her hands in his jacket. She'd had some self-defense training, he remembered, as she used her weight to pull him off balance, twist them both around, and shove him against the car.

Then he stopped thinking because she poured herself into the kiss, tilted her head, and pulled him into a dark, sweet world filled with heat and intensity and promise. She made a breathless little sound that seemed to arrow straight through him, and even as his blood took fire she slipped her arms around his waist and laid that long, lean body against his, collarbone to knees, and gave him everything she had to give. At least he hoped she hadn't held anything back, or he'd be in real trouble when they finally got together.

And they would be getting together.

If this kiss taught him anything, he thought in the last rational part of his brain, it was to stop deluding himself that he could keep his hands off her for much longer. But just to prove he wasn't completely helpless, to let her know she wasn't the one in charge, he broke the kiss.

He didn't push her away, wrapping his arms around her and staying all but mouth to mouth with her. And although he could feel her muscles tense, she didn't test his strength. Or her own.

"The next time we do this," he said, "we won't be outside, where half the village gets a free show. We'll be somewhere we can finish it."

"You keep making threats—"

"Not a threat, a promise." This time, when he felt her muscles bunch, when those brilliant blue eyes narrowed on his, he turned her loose. Not because he was afraid his strength wouldn't be enough. But because he might not let her go.

She climbed into her car, fired it up, and sped off, but not before she shot him a long stare through her window— not so sure of herself now.

Dex was still grinning when he pulled out his cell phone and dialed, setting off on foot through the village. "I thought you'd be brow-beating some poor schmuck for one of your high-powered clients," he said when the call went through.

"That's your M.O.," Alec Barclay said. "I work for the little guy."

"Well, I work for you, and since I'm barely getting paid, you can trot your ass up from Boston to help me."

"First," Alec said, "I can't just drop everything. Those high-powered clients get cranky when I don't show up for depositions and court appearances.

"Second, you solve this case and there's a hefty finder's fee coming your way, not to mention you'll have made a name for yourself no amount of money can buy—which is the real reason you agreed to take this on."

"It's not going to get solved at this rate."

"Going that well, huh?"

Dex filled him in—with a little careful editing. It sounded whiny, even to him, that he was raising the white flag after such a short and relatively uneventful time, but his gut was talking, and it was telling him he needed help—outside help.

"Outnumbered, huh?"

"Yeah," Dex said sheepishly.

"And you're going to throw me to the she-wolves as a distraction?"

"I'd date you."

Alec laughed, long and hard. "Never thought I'd see the day when you cried Uncle because a few women wanted in your pants."

"Paige Walker is one of those she-wolves," he lied without hesitation.

"The movie star?" It sounded like Alec had swallowed his tongue. "You're making that up."

"Turns out she grew up here."

"And now she's hiding out there."

Not yet, Dex allowed, but she might show up, seeing as the rest of the world was so unfriendly just now. "Why wouldn't she, considering how well these people keep secrets from the outside world? So..."

"She's off my list," Alec said darkly, referring to the list every guy had of his fantasy women.

"Hell, she is the list in your case."

"Not anymore."

"Since the sex tape."

"Since she's an illusion, and the family is firmly rooted in reality. As long as reality comes with a Mayflower pedigree."

Dex just shook his head over the foibles of the wealthy. "Fascinating as I find your family's pursuit of dynasty, Alec, I have a real problem here."

"Kiss my ass, Keegan," Alec said good-naturedly, adding, "I really do have a heavy caseload at the moment, but I'll clear some time and come as soon as I can. And in the meanwhile, I'll do the next best thing."

Chapter Eleven

When Maggie left Ma's, she kept to the village's winding back streets, but it wasn't Dex she couldn't face. It was herself—weak, filled with needs she couldn't corral, and cravings she didn't want to. And now Dex knew it. Hell, the cat wasn't just out of the bag, it had clawed its way free and was on the prowl.

She could still feel the heat of Dex's mouth on hers, still taste him, dark and intoxicating, on her tongue. She knew how his body fit to hers, the way his arms banded around her, and how all of it combined to incinerate her from the inside out. The sound of his deep voice, promising they'd finish what they'd started, seemed to ring in her ears and steal her breath.

The only defense in her arsenal was anger. So she embraced it.

She embraced the anger when she parked on the side street where her Mustang wouldn't be as noticeable. She embraced the anger when she slammed out of her car and strode along the boardwalk to the antique store. And she sure as hell embraced the anger when she shoved her way through the front door and came face to face with Josiah

Meeker—and then she didn't need Dex to put her in a fighting mood.

Just the look on Meeker's face was enough.

"Well, now," he said with the kind of smile that made her skin crawl and her hands fist, "look what the wind blew in."

"The wind had nothing to do with it."

He stared at her some more, and this time his lips pursed consideringly before he concluded, "You want something."

"So do you," Maggie shot back. "The status quo. And you're willing to do just about anything to keep it."

"Blackmail, Maggie?"

"I'm not above blackmail, and it still puts me so far out of your league you have to look up to see the soles of my boots."

Meeker lost his sneer. "What do you want?"

"The Windfall journals."

"What—oh, for Keegan." Which brought back the sneer. "I wonder what all your so-called friends would think if they find out you're helping him? Working with an outsider."

"I'm not doing this for Keegan. But if I were, and it became public knowledge, I imagine it would be almost as bad as everyone learning my father paid you to keep tabs on me for him. An outsider."

Meeker spread his hands, pasted on what he must've thought was a smile of innocence. "Now, Maggie, you misunderstood—"

"I knew exactly what you meant when you started unzipping your fly."

"I cared for you."

"Bullshit. Sex is about power to you. You saw an opportunity and you took it. You thought you could get me to sleep with you by threatening to tell my father lies about me."

"He knew how you were. Why else would he have you watched?"

To safeguard his precious reputation, Maggie answered in the aching silence of her own mind. If she'd believed her safety had meant anything to him, she'd have told Admiral Solomon. But then, she hadn't needed him, had she? Then or now. "I was sixteen. I doubt the law would have any trouble labeling your intentions."

"I'm fairly certain the statute of limitations has run out."

"There are many kinds of laws, Meeker. You've lived here all your life; you ought to know that." And since she'd had as much of him as she could take, she held out her hand, palm up.

"And if I refuse?"

Maggie stepped sideways and flicked a little glass trinket off the edge of a nearby shelf.

Meeker lunged forward, just managing to catch it. "Jesus, that's crystal, about a thousand years old, and nearly priceless."

"So is my time."

She could hear him grinding his teeth, but he turned on the heel of his Italian loafers and threaded his way through the maze until he arrived at the little, climate-controlled room behind the counter where he kept the most precious of his merchandise.

The farther she got from the door, the more claustrophobic Maggie felt. She followed him to make sure he handed over all the journals. She stayed in the doorway, though. She'd learned the hard way not to let herself get cornered.

"They don't leave your sight," he said as he gave them to her. "Or you'll answer to me."

"You have my word that I'll take care of them. And my word actually means something."

"I never thought you'd be such a vindictive—"

"Be careful, Joe. I kept my mouth shut for the sake of your family."

"You told Boatwright."

"He was my boyfriend, not the sheriff. And he's kept it to himself all these years because I asked him to." Maggie kept her eyes on his so she knew he was listening and believing. "But you can bet everything you hold dear that if he ever hears of you putting one finger out of line, he'll deal with you. And if he doesn't, I will. I'm a lot stronger and faster than I was at sixteen." She took a step forward. "Touch me ever again, and it'll be the last time."

"I don't have to touch you, Maggie. I know you remember me every night when the light goes off and you're alone in the dark. Alone and afraid."

Maggie snorted. "You were just one of the *tools* my father used in his attempts to bring me to heel, Joe, a far from effective one. On the rare occasion you cross my mind, it's the picture of you curled into a fetal position on the floor, wheezing and moaning in pain." She smiled coolly. "Fear is not exactly what I'm feeling in those moments."

"Fine words," Meeker spat. "But you have one fatal flaw, Maggie. You fight fair."

After leaving Meeker's, Maggie picked up burgers and fries from the Horizon and took them to George's office—part apology to him, part soother for herself. After her previous two run-ins she badly needed to see a friendly face. And, she admitted, she wanted to tell George why Dex Keegan was there. She wanted to dump the whole sorry mess into his lap and pretend she'd never heard Dex Keegan connect Eugenia Stanhope's kidnapping with Windfall Island.

It wasn't, however, something she could scrub from her

mind like muddy footprints tracked onto a clean kitchen floor—and not just because she'd given her word. This was her place, her world; she couldn't protect it with her head in the sand. She didn't believe Eugenia had survived all these years without the world finding out, but on the off chance she was wrong, she had to know where this thing might lead. Or to whom.

So when George asked, "What's new," she said, "Not a thing, how about you?"

"Dex Keegan."

So much for keeping the conversation neutral. She dropped into the lone chair beside George's desk. "What's he up to now?"

"Causing chaos wherever he goes."

Maggie couldn't have agreed more.

"He runs five miles every day. You'd think it was the Boston Marathon, the way half the women in town line the streets waiting for him to happen by."

Maggie laughed at the disgruntled expression on George's face.

"Enjoy yourself now, Chuckles. The next time the Maslow twins start kicking and scratching, I'm sending you in to sort it out."

Just the notion of Cindy and Mindy Maslow, forty-something and as round as they were tall, in a catfight made her smile.

"Why didn't you just throw Dex to them?"

George smiled a little, reluctantly. "The thought crossed my mind, but he can run faster than all three of us."

"George, you have a gun."

"Any particular reason you want me to shoot him?"

"I barely know he's still around," she said, but she didn't meet George's eyes.

"Not for lack of trying on his part, or so I hear. He was out to the airport the other day."

"And the whole island is talking about it. Since everybody is busy trying to make a couple of me and Keegan, you might as well know I just ran into him at Ma's."

George sat forward. He didn't say anything, but unlike when she was with Dex, Maggie felt compelled to fill this silence because George was her friend. That didn't entitle him to know everything. "I was coming out as he was going in, but I asked him not to bother her because I left her resting."

"It's no wonder what he wants with Ma. She knows everything about Windfall." George sat back again, steepled his hands. "You're pretty knowledgeable yourself."

"And?"

"And you've made it clear you don't want anything to do with him."

Maggie waited him out, let the silence work for her this time.

"He came here for a reason, Maggie. If I were in his shoes, with half the population hot to trot and the other half freezing him out, I'd look for somebody like you, tough but fair, somebody fiercely protective of her home."

"Somebody you could manipulate?"

"Nobody gets one over on you, Maggie."

That was exactly what she'd told Dex. And she hadn't completely believed it then. "You getting at something, George?"

"He had dinner at Jessi's the other night."

"Right. Me, Jessi, and Benji. Just in case your sources didn't give you the whole picture."

George wasn't fazed by her frosty tone. "One of the neighbors said the two of you had a fairly passionate discussion standing on Jessi's front walk."

"Passionate?"

"Her word. She said it looked like you might do him bodily harm, and not in a good way. He giving you trouble?"

Maggie crossed her arms. "I wouldn't call it trouble, exactly."

"What would you call it?"

"Nothing I can't handle."

"Maggie—"

"If I need help, George, you know you're the first person I'll call."

"Is that supposed to make me feel better?"

"I didn't know that was my job."

George scrubbed a hand over his face.

"I'm sorry, George, you know how I am..." She broke off, feeling as discouraged as he looked. "My history."

"Yeah," he said on a heavy sigh.

He understood, Maggie knew, but he didn't like being lumped in with her father, even if it was just a chromosomal similarity. She didn't much like it herself, but she'd likely always have a hard time relinquishing control to a man—any man.

"So altogether that accounts for about ten hours of his time," she said casually. Even if her latest...interaction with Dex Keegan had gone unwitnessed, it would be nice to know what else he'd been up to, besides whipping the female population into a sexual frenzy. "What about the other couple hundred?"

"Nothing remarkable," George said. "He's been to just about every business in town, asks different questions every time. Can't make heads or tails out of what he's up to.

"He said anything to you?"

She only shook her head because the lie stuck in her throat.

"Well, he seems to have a special interest in you, so if you find out what he's after, I'd appreciate it if you'd let me know."

Maggie nodded, too grateful that he was dropping the whole matter, including any questions that might lead to her involvement, to wonder why he wasn't pushing harder for answers.

Chapter Twelve

If he'd had every style of house in the world to choose from, Dex would have picked the Arts and Crafts bungalow sitting behind the airport's office and hangar. Painted in muted shades of green and brown, the lines of the house were spare, simple, utilitarian. No-nonsense, like its owner. The lawn was neat; the landscaping tended toward shrubs and flowering bushes that didn't need much care, and were low enough so they didn't obscure her view of the rocky, tree-lined curve of Temptation Bay.

Even the wider backdrop of the ocean spoke to its owner's temperament, Dex mused; Maggie Solomon was the kind of woman who'd walk face-first into Hell if the devil issued a challenge. And the Atlantic, its deceptively placid surface hiding such dark moods and dangerous depths, suited her.

Dex climbed the wide steps to the deep, roofed front porch. He knocked on the carved front door, with its stained glass window in squares of color. No answer. So, first rule of PIs everywhere, he tried the knob. And found it unlocked.

In all fairness to himself, he thought about it before he just walked in, but the chance to see how Maggie lived was irresistible. He'd expected the inside to be as neat, beautiful and as practical as the woman who lived there, and it was. The floor plan was open and unhindered. One room flowed into the next through wide doorways. The floors were wood, the ceilings were high, and the windows were uncurtained, making the space feel even airier and more expansive.

But whatever else Dex expected to find, it wasn't Maggie at the dining room table, her head pillowed on her arms, asleep in a sea of papers.

He felt a tug, something that might have been tenderness if he'd dared to name it. And then he got a better look at the papers. Even from the doorway he could tell they were copies of handwritten documents. In the space of a heartbeat he forgot everything else.

Before he could get farther than the doorway, his footsteps woke Maggie. She blinked groggily, then jumped to her feet and moved between him and table.

Dex crossed his arms, battling anger now instead of attraction. "Trying to beat my time?"

Maggie mirrored his stance. "Do you always walk uninvited into other people's houses?"

"The door wasn't locked."

"Because I live in a place where privacy is respected."

"But not promises?"

"What promise have I broken?"

Dex held her gaze for a moment, but he had to admit he'd only assumed she'd hand over the journals as soon as she obtained them from Meeker. He knew how personally she was taking the matter of Windfall Island's possible involvement in Eugenia Stanhope's kidnapping. Now he realized that in telling her about the journals he'd handed her an irresistible opportunity to find the truth on her own. Even if it cut him out.

"I thought you were too straightforward to go behind my back."

"Your mistake," she said, but her gaze dropped, then narrowed in on his sweat pants before lifting again as far as his sweat-soaked t-shirt. She drew the obvious conclusion, that he'd run all the way from the village. "Didn't want anyone to know where you were going?"

"I figured you'd appreciate not being the talk of the town."

She nodded once, grudgingly.

He indicated the papers. "You don't trust me."

Maggie braced her backside on the table, crossed her booted feet. "This is my place, these are my people."

"But you didn't grow up here."

"Doesn't make it any less true."

And Dex thought he knew why. Maggie was every bit as rabid about her privacy as the rest of the islanders. And even more suspicious of outsiders.

"Why should I trust you?" she continued. "You haven't told me the whole truth. In my book that gives me the right—hell—that means I have an obligation to make sure nobody gets hurt while you're doing your job."

Dex counted to ten, then counted again, trying to see past the hard wall of anger inside him, the betrayal he knew he had no right to feel. Maggie and he certainly weren't friends, and they had no other relationship, by his choice as much as hers. True, she'd agreed to get the journals for him, but he understood why she hadn't handed them over right away. If his family had been threatened, he'd do more than go behind her back. "I told you exactly why I'm here."

"Not until I left you no choice."

He blew out a breath. It didn't help. The heat still rose in him, high and hot and fast. He didn't know if he wanted to kiss Maggie or throttle her, but either way he knew putting his hands on her would be a mistake.

"You know, I understood that finding Eugenia Stanhope

would be a hell of a long shot. If I'd known I'd need your help to solve this case, I would have turned it down flat."

Maggie smiled slightly, ignoring the insult. "You don't think she survived the kidnapping, either."

"I think there's a high probability this is a waste of time."

"But you came anyway. Why?"

"The family deserves to know the truth. It's been more than eighty years. They could have had her declared dead, and moved on, but they've been holding out hope."

"And you want to give them an answer. And the friend who asked you to take the case?"

He gave her one of the one-shouldered shrugs she used as a pillar of her conversational style.

"Putting your life on hold for a wild goose chase is a pretty big favor."

"He's a pretty good friend."

"With a connection to the Stanhope family?"

It was Dex's turn to smile. "He's their lawyer."

Maggie studied on that for half a minute, the way she did when she was turning a puzzle over in her mind. "What does he know that he didn't tell you?"

That stopped Dex. He'd never considered the possibility that Alec hadn't told him everything.

"It's no fun when the shoe is on the other foot, is it?"

"He told me everything I need to know," Dex said. "The rest is up to me." He looked past her, at the papers stacked and scattered on the table.

Maggie stepped aside. "Be my guest."

He thought about taking the journals and going off on his own, but without the assistance of a local, he'd be lost. Like it or not, Maggie was the only one he could confide in. "What do you want, Maggie?"

"The truth."

"I won't lie to you again unless I have to. I can't promise I won't have to."

She looked away, then back. "Thank you."

He smiled. "You're welcome. What else?"

"Your friend, the one who convinced you to take a job you didn't want—"

"I already called him."

She straightened, tucked her hands in the pockets of her jeans. "Then let's get started."

I won't lie to you again unless I have to.

Maggie sent Dex upstairs to take a shower—not because she found his scent objectionable. Because she didn't, and she needed to focus on something other than Dex. Something other than having sex with Dex. Because that would be bad. Right? Their relationship already had more wrinkles than she could hope to iron out if they spent a lifetime together. Not that she would spend a lifetime with a man who couldn't be honest with her.

I won't lie to you again unless I have to. She wanted to believe him—foolish when he'd qualified that promise in a way that all but left the door wide open for him to dish up whatever bullshit he chose.

She took a seat at the head of the table again, and turned her attention to the task at hand. It did her no good to second-guess a choice she'd already made, a choice she knew was right. Even if it meant working with Dex Keegan. She couldn't protect Windfall Island if she wasn't on the front line.

Dex walked in, hair wet and tousled, wearing a t-shirt that was baggy on Mort, but stretched tight across Dex's chest. Same with the work pants, which he'd had to leave unbuttoned.

When her mouth went dry, she forced a laugh. "Mort has the height, anyway."

"He doesn't have the height, either." He grimaced a little, shifted his hips, and Maggie's gaze arrowed down.

She lost her breath as the heat rose in her, from her toes all the way up to the crown of her head, settling in her belly and breasts on the way. She closed her eyes and turned forward, trying to think of anything but Dex, how much she wanted him, and how hard it would be to work with him just a few feet away, day after day, without losing control and taking him up on the offer that was hot in his eyes nearly all the time.

Somehow she needed to stop this…this assault of need whenever Dex was around, this yearning for something she'd never known. And had never wanted, she reminded herself. Letting him in—letting any man in—would be a mistake.

She knew what it was to love—not the romantic kind of love, sure, but wasn't a father the first man every little girl loved? And when that first love went wrong, when that love was thrown back in her face, how could she help but end up scarred? She wouldn't survive that kind of rejection a second time.

"Earth to Maggie."

"I threw your clothes in the washer when the shower stopped running, then the dryer." She slanted him a look, managed a slight, sarcastic smile to go with it. "You were in the bathroom a long time."

Dex eased into the chair closest to her, his face twisting into another of those grimaces she thought, at least in part, was meant to defuse the tension in the air. "I was trying to figure out a way to protect my manhood without losing my life."

She arched a brow.

"Coming down here naked wasn't an option, was it?"

"Only if you wanted to keep walking right out the front door."

"Weather's taken a turn toward winter, in case you haven't noticed."

"Oh, I noticed."

"There, you see? Freeze my, uh, body parts off, or..." He shifted again.

"I get the picture."

He leaned toward her, grinned. "The real thing is right here."

And there she went again. She couldn't even meet his eyes for fear he'd see what he did to her with his big, fit body and his easy good humor. As if he didn't already know, she amended, lifting her gaze to his, letting the frustration she felt show. "You came here to work."

"The work will still be there in, say, an hour."

"There's that ego again."

"Maybe I've earned it."

The way he delivered that line irritated her just enough to take it as a challenge, and call him on it. "Put your money where your mouth is."

"I—Huh?"

She shoved her chair back, fisted her hand in his t-shirt, and when they both came to their feet, dragged him against her. "You heard me," she said, crushing her mouth to his.

He froze for a second, then he kissed her back, his mouth hot and amazing as it moved over hers, and then his hands were on her, too, one settling at her waist, the other continuing down to her backside, both pressing her against him. Her head spun as the heat rose in her blood, became an inferno raging through her with every beat of her heart. She arched against him, twisting slowly to feel the friction of her body moving against his.

She wanted the burn, the slide, the scent, the feel of him inside her. Taking her.

When his hands fumbled at the snap on her jeans, she undid them herself, shoved them off, then dealt with his pants and boxers, measuring the hard length of him with her hand. A groan rumbled from the back of his throat, and the need inside her turned up another impossible degree.

"Now," she said as the hunger inside her took on a life of its own.

His hands rushed over her, heating her skin, igniting her nerve endings. He trailed his mouth down her neck, stopping to flip her hoodie up by the hem and straight over her head. "You wear too damn much," he grumbled when he saw the tank beneath.

Hands shaking, Maggie sent the tank after the hoodie and reached for the hooks on her bra.

Dex stopped her, reaching out to run a finger across the top edge of the plain white cotton cup over her left breast. "Wings?"

She didn't look down at the pale gold tattoo that dusted the skin over her heart. Instead, she held Dex's eyes. "My one true love."

"Neither of us is interested in love," he said, putting his mouth where his hand had been.

It was like falling into an active volcano, a long descent into heat while nerves twisted and muscles tightened, and then the world erupted, fire and pleasure so intense it rivaled pain. She went blind and deaf, lost to the feel of his mouth sucking hard at her nipple, to his fingers slipping beneath the elastic of her panties and inside to stroke her mindless. Her body bowed back, the orgasm ripping through her, wave after wave of pleasure that tore the breath from her and left her wrung out, weak with pleasure.

Before she could even hope to recover, Dex took her by the hand, and when she stumbled on legs gone to rubber, he boosted her up, urged her to wrap her trembling legs around his waist, and bore them both up the stairs.

He hesitated at the top, and she said, "there," pointing to her bedroom before she sucked his earlobe into her mouth, nipping it then soothing with her tongue. He ran them both into the wall.

Maggie barely noticed because finally, finally he was lowering her to the bed, and she could appreciate the clean scent of his skin, take her time discovering the ridges of muscle along his back, enjoy the way his muscles quivered when she ran her fingers down his belly.

"Let me," she said in the voice of a stranger, thick with need, unsteady from the power of what he was doing to her. What they were together. She took the condom he'd found in her bedside drawer, ripped it open and smoothed it over him. Slowly, breathless at the way he watched her, his eyes black with desire and narrowed with promise.

"Bring it on," she dared him.

He caught her wrists and staked them to the bed, driving himself into her in a single powerful thrust that jerked her back to the edge of that shattering precipice. He kept his eyes on hers as he began to move. She met him, stroke for stroke, and when he released her hands, she reared up to run her tongue over his chest, tasting the salt of his skin before he lifted her knees and drove even deeper.

She cried out, then gasped "don't stop," when he almost did.

Dex hooked her knee again, planted his other hand on the mattress, and stroked into her, again and again. All Maggie could do was brace herself and take it, heat and hardness and friction, pressure and need coiling inside her, tighter and tighter until she twisted beneath him, straining and begging wordlessly until she broke, coming in a rush as Dex thrust into her one last time.

He locked himself inside her, his breath tearing in and out as she felt his climax shudder through him. "I think I'm dead," he said, collapsing beside her.

But when he would have gathered her against him, Maggie sat up instead. She refused to interpret the emotion that flashed across his face as hurt. But her heart felt like lead in her chest.

"If you're getting water," he began, then his voice, scrupulously even, turned into a whip, "No, fuck that, Maggie. Why are we here, in your bed?"

"Because I wanted to be here. Because I thought..." She settled back against the headboard. She did not, much as she wanted to, fist her hands in her hair. It was too telling a gesture, too evocative of the nerves crawling like caterpillars under her skin. Too indicative of the emotional connection she didn't want to make with Dex. Couldn't make, even if it hurt them both. Better to be hurt now than when he left, especially if she was foolish enough to let her feelings get away from her.

She made herself face him, kept her eyes on his in the dim afternoon light, though it was harder than she'd ever have believed possible. "We needed to get it out of our systems," she said, and when her voice tried to waver, she steadied it, ruthlessly. "We'll be working together, very closely together."

He grinned, infuriatingly. "And you don't think I can keep my hands to myself?"

"You seem to have some trouble in that area, yes."

"You attacked me."

Her mouth dropped open, and for a second she was at a complete loss for words. Until he pillowed his head on his hands and grinned even wider.

"Your clothes must be dry by now," she said curtly. "Have a nice run back to the village." She started from the room, but he bounded up, catching her around the waist, lifting her feet off the floor, and bearing her back to the bed.

Before she could catch her breath she was on her back with Dex on top of her, her arms and legs imprisoned under his bulk. She didn't give him the satisfaction of struggling.

"We're not nearly done with one another," Dex said, and kissed her, so slowly and thoroughly she felt real panic.

Because she wanted to kiss him back, just as slowly, just as thoroughly, and without any walls. It scared the hell out of her, how badly she wanted to simply surrender. "Stop," she said, when he gave her a second. "Please."

Dex leaned back, studied her face, then eased off her completely. "I'm sorry, Maggie—"

"Don't." She rolled to her side, took a moment to deal with the mortification that she'd shown him that kind of weakness.

"It doesn't have to be war between us," he said quietly.

"Dex, I . . . I don't know any other way."

"How about friendship, or partnership, if that's easier."

She shifted back to face him, still feeling uncertain. "How can we be friends, or partners, without trust?"

"I trust you, Maggie, and I'd say you trust me more than you believe. Otherwise, we wouldn't be here together, like this."

And that troubled her, too. Because she knew, deep down, he was right.

Chapter Thirteen

A hot shower, Maggie decided, was just what she needed. Time to remind herself what was at stake, both personally and for Windfall Island as a whole.

When Dex stepped into the tub, she looked over her shoulder, irritated at having her peace interrupted. The sight of him naked didn't do much for her self-control, either. "You just had a shower," she pointed out.

"There wasn't anyone to wash my back," Dex said, infuriatingly chipper. "I couldn't bear the thought of you suffering the same fate."

"I never have anyone to wash my back. I manage."

"Why should you have to today?" he said, soaping his hands and rubbing them over her back.

It felt good, she had to admit, moaning just a little as the heels of his hands worked her well-used muscles, hard enough to make it a massage as much as a cleansing. And when his hands slipped around, when he ran those hard palms and clever fingers over her breasts, she had to brace her hands on the cool tile of the shower.

Dex pulled her back against him, nudged her legs apart, and she felt him, gloriously aroused, as he slipped inside her.

"Shhhh," he said when she tried to turn.

His mouth dropped to her shoulder, biting lightly. One of his hands covered her breast, the other slipped down between her legs, and she was surrounded by him, overwhelmed. The hot water beat down on her, and the feel of Dex strong against her, hard inside her, of his hands driving her higher and tighter, simply destroyed her so that when she came, when Dex found his own release and let her go to brace himself against the shower walls, she slid down into a heap, barely feeling the cold ceramic of the tub against her heated skin.

Dex slumped down beside her. They looked at each other and just laughed.

"If we keep this up," he said, "I'm not going to live to the end of the week.

"I was only trying to take a shower," Maggie reminded him.

"And I was trying to help you. It's not my fault you're so appealing when you're naked. And you started it, remember?"

"Well, I'm finishing it," she said, making a feeble attempt to climb to her feet.

Dex took her by the hands, and they pulled each other up, swaying like drunks on legs still weak and trembling.

"You owe me a back washing," Dex said when they let each other go and neither of them fell down.

"Yeah, not a good idea." Maggie stepped out, handing him a washcloth. "Better hurry," she added, "the water's getting cold," and she went into the bedroom, throwing on the first clothes she could find before he came into the room and tested her willpower.

Two hours later, they were back in the dining room, with Dex sitting beside her at the paper-covered table. He claimed it would be easier for them to work together if they didn't have to pass papers back and forth across the table. She thought he was trying to drive her insane.

"Are you kidding me?" she said when he leaned in for the dozenth time, close enough to brush his body against hers from thigh to shoulder. Her heart galloped, her breath came short, and sweat popped out on her upper lip. For a woman who prided herself on her rigid self-control, it was embarrassing that he could, with nothing more than a simple touch, turn her inside out.

"I need those pages over there," he said, pointing to the pile farthest away from him.

Maggie picked up the stack and slapped it down in front of him. Then she picked herself up and moved around the corner of the table.

Dex slid into the chair she'd vacated, his knee bumping hers.

"What are you, five?"

"I'm surprised you have to ask that question, considering."

"Ego," she snapped.

Dex lost some of his humor—at least his mouth stopped twitching. "What are you so worked up about?"

"Who's worked up?" She pulled some papers over in front of her, then shoved them away again. "Having sex with you was supposed to make the craving go away."

"I'm not a grilled cheese sandwich."

She snorted. "You're more like a bottle of booze at an AA meeting. You know you can't have a drink, you know it's the worst thing in the world for you, but that's just logic." And logic was no match for a need this big.

"The worst thing in the world?"

"The situation. You know what I mean."

He ran a finger down the little line between her brows.

"Stop thinking," he murmured, "Stop figuring angles and worrying about what happens down the line."

She already knew what would happen if she was foolish enough to let herself fall for him. Ignoring it wouldn't change it. "I can't put my head in the sand."

He kissed her, another of those slow, gentle kisses that left her utterly undone.

She put her hand on his cheek, eased back before he could take her under, make her forget there would even be a tomorrow. "Let's work."

Dex rested his forehead on hers for a second before he shifted back into his chair. He took a deep breath as he surveyed the piles of papers scattered across the table. "Give me the high points," he said.

"I copied the journals," she began, and at his questioning look, added, "I waited until after Jessi left for the day, so she doesn't know. Some of them are really fragile, so I thought it best if we didn't work directly with them. Besides, Meeker wasn't going to let me keep them long before he started making noise. To me," she added hastily when Dex's eyebrows shot up. "He wouldn't go public."

"You threatened him."

"Bet your ass," Maggie said, "but there's his pride, too. He wouldn't admit he lent them to me, let alone why. But he's a pain in the ass when he doesn't get what he wants. I figured once we had the copies, I could give them back, even if we haven't had time to go through them all."

"You told him they weren't helpful?"

"I didn't tell him anything. I let him infer."

"Denial, especially when volunteered, often means just the opposite," Dex said with a slight smile. "You'd make a pretty good PI."

She shook her head. "What goes around."

"How much have you looked at already?"

"Not much before I fell asleep. It's pretty dull reading, and I was up half the night manning the copier," she added in her own defense.

"Some trusty assistant you are."

"I obtained the journals. That makes you the assistant."

"I'm the PI."

Maggie laughed. "Sam Spade you're not, and I'm no Effie Perine."

"You have the attitude, you just need the wardrobe."

"Effie didn't wear flight suits?"

Dex grinned. "No, but I bet she had lace on under her sensible clothes, just like you. Now, if you could scare up some garters..."

Maggie just shot him a sidelong look.

"I'd be willing to accommodate your fantasies," he offered.

"At the moment my fantasies consist of staying awake long enough to make it through one of these journals."

They worked in silence for a little while, not making much progress. Partly, Dex admitted, because it was damned hard to keep his mind on what he was reading. And since he couldn't seem to keep her off his mind, he didn't see why he couldn't put his hands on her as well. At least he'd start with his hands. With a slight, speculative smile, he sent Maggie a sidelong look.

She scowled back at him. It only made his smile widen.

"Get your mind out of the gutter."

"It wasn't in the gutter." It was in her flight suit, and she wasn't wearing anything beneath it but garters and hose. Sheer black hose—

"*Hey.*"

He jerked a little, tore his eyes off her. "We need some kind of system here."

"I'd suggest a blindfold, but that might be problematic under the circumstances."

"A blindfold wouldn't solve the problem," he said, grinning again.

"Maybe I should move to another room."

"I used your soap and shampoo." He drew her in with every breath he took, and wasn't that part of the problem? Even when he managed to keep his eyes on the documents in front of him, it felt as though she was leaning over his shoulder, those long, strong arms of hers wrapped around him, the warmth of her breath at his neck and the heat of her body burning through him so all that was missing was the taste of her, like dark sweet cherries, tangy and edged with—

She sighed hugely. "I repeat, get your mind out of the gutter, Keegan."

"Am I that obvious?"

She shook her head and shoved the pile of journals over in front of him. "You said we need a system, come up with one."

He echoed her sigh, and, with an effort he thought heroic, put her out of his mind long enough to remember that he'd come to Windfall Island with a goal, and even if the side benefits were amazing and irresistible, there'd be time for that later.

"Okay," he said. "Eugenia was kidnapped in 1931, but since that event is closely linked to Prohibition, we should widen the scope to include anything from that era. The 18th Amendment was passed in 1919, and repealed by the 22nd Amendment in 1933. Anyone involved in running illegal booze could have been in a position to stumble across the nurse, Sonja Hanson, and the baby.

"And even if there aren't any references here," he

concluded, laying his palm on the journals, "it may be there were stories told in the family."

"I don't know. I think if there were stories, they'd have come out by now. If a Windfaller, any Windfaller, took in a baby, how would it be kept secret? This place is gossip central, and it would only have been more so eighty years ago. Phones weren't even that common back then. There would have been more community gatherings, more face to face."

"Eugenia went missing in mid October, just in time for people to hibernate for the winter."

"She was eight months old. She'd have been fourteen, fifteen months by the time spring came around. Somebody would have noticed."

"Maybe she was small for her age."

Maggie bumped up a shoulder. "I guess it's possible, but there would have been rumors, suspicions."

"Which brings us back to where we started, but now we can't limit our search to those involved in bootlegging. Anyone could have written down an idle suspicion."

"Why don't we start with trying to date the journals, so we can at least eliminate the ones that are too early."

Dex scrubbed a hand over his face. "Got any coffee?"

"Sure, it's in the refrigerator. There's a grinder on the counter, right next to the coffeemaker."

Meaning she wasn't about to wait on him, just because she was a woman. He could have pointed out they were in her home and her gender had nothing to do with it. But he decided to pick his battles. "I could use something to eat," he said instead.

She only waved a hand absently and told him he was welcome to whatever he could find.

A half hour later, Dex returned to the dining room, carrying a tray holding two mugs of coffee and one plate full of food. He set one of the cups next to Maggie, said, "I figured you take it black."

"Right the first time," she said, but when she caught sight of the plate, she lifted her eyes to his, one brow piqued.

"You're an energetic woman, Maggie," he said as he took his seat around the corner from her. "I'm going to need fuel to keep up with you."

He expected her to scowl at him again. Instead, she smiled, slow and sexy. "Where's mine?"

Dex laughed, scooted the plate to the corner between them, and picked up half a sandwich piled high with cold cuts, cheese, lettuce and tomatoes.

Maggie did the same, saying around a mouthful, "While you were eating me out of house and home, I pulled together some reference materials."

Dex flipped through the short stack of books she shoved his way, choosing one that contained references to Prohibition along the east coast of the United States. In addition, there was a laptop computer open beside her.

"Don't look so surprised. I read on occasion."

"History?"

"Okay, so that was research for my tourist flights. So what?"

He just grinned. But in the back of his mind, he couldn't say it surprised him that, even here, her life was all about her business. And how could he fault her for it when it was the same for him?

That didn't mean he couldn't take a detour once in a while, especially when that side road led somewhere so interesting.

"I prefer mustard over mayo, just so you're aware," she said evenly. She hit the power switch on her laptop, then looked up at him. "For next time." She took a huge bite of her sandwich, absolutely straight-faced.

Until Dex reached over and rubbed his thumb across her bottom lip before he nipped away a bit of mayo at the corner of her mouth. "I'll remember that," he said, keeping his gaze level despite the thrill it gave him to watch hers glaze over. "For next time."

Dex's idea of organization began with trying to date the journals, then put them in chronological order. For the life of her Maggie couldn't begin to know where he got his patience.

She sat for hours at a time in a pilot's chair, didn't she? She spent long periods buried in one of her engines without losing focus. She even managed to handle the paperwork it took to operate an enterprise regulated by the government. And nobody could generate tedium like the government.

Yet she couldn't go five minutes without fidgeting. Even now, her leg was pistoning so madly the table was shaking.

"Maggie," Dex said mildly.

"This is so boring."

"We'll find something. We just need to stick with it."

She surveyed the stack of copies still waiting to be read. There wasn't that much patience in the world. "We're going to need help, Dex. Jessi actually likes paperwork. I don't see why we can't include her."

"Yes, you do, or you'd have told her already, no matter what I want."

She ground her teeth, pissed that he was right, and pissed that he sat there plowing through documents like some stodgy old historian while she felt like a sulky kid sentenced to an interminable load of homework.

"You ought to be wearing a cardigan, you know; one of those ones with the patches on the elbows, and a pair of horn rims."

"You ought to be reading."

Shit, she couldn't even get him to snipe at her. At least a bout of snark would take the edge off the torture she'd brought down on herself. "I've never seen a group of people so averse to using dates in my life."

Dex merely laid a hand on a stack of papers off to his left. "These seem to be more ledgers than journals. There are counts of everything: people, supplies, ships that were salvaged and how the spoils were divided. They have to predate the twentieth century."

Maggie shoved her hands through her short cap of hair, tried to remember what was at stake. "I don't think we're going to find anything helpful until we get some more information." She held up a hand before he could respond. "But we can read and index, and when your friend arrives with the rest of the story, the search shouldn't take long."

Dex put down the papers he'd been holding. "Maggie, Alec doesn't have any more information than I do."

"What about the papers Stanhope bought from the nanny's grandson?"

"They're mostly about Sonja Hanson's life after Eugenia went missing, claims that she'd been persecuted unfairly, without offering any real proof. Once the furor died down she got married, changed her name, had kids, and never told anyone she'd worked for the Stanhopes. But she kept this shoebox full of newspaper clippings, and when she knew she was dying, she told her daughter the truth."

"Her truth."

"It's the only starting point we have. Some of the details are vague. Maybe her memory was going, or maybe she glossed over the details to make herself look better. The truth is she was young, barely twenty at the time, and single. And there's no doubt she would have known of the nightly party that took place on the Rum Runners anchored off shore.

"She claimed she'd asked for the night off, but the Stanhopes were attending a charity ball, and a couple of the other servants were already off duty, so she was refused."

"Why not just go another night?"

"A man would be my guess."

Maggie rolled her eyes. "The root of all evil."

"Not to a young woman in the twenties."

Maggie had to agree with Dex there. As a nanny in the Stanhope household, Sonja would have been fairly well paid, but she'd have been at the beck and call of the family, nearly around the clock. Getting married wouldn't have relieved her of the hard work, but at least it would be her house and her children.

That didn't excuse what she'd done out of spite and selfishness.

"She just wanted to have a little fun," Dex said, as if he'd read her mind. "Being new to the household, she probably got stuck with all the weekends and the worst of the chores. Missing her date was probably the last straw."

"So she kidnapped an eight-month-old baby?"

"She claimed that wasn't her intention. She wanted to go to the party so badly she convinced herself she could take Eugenia with her and nothing would go wrong."

"Easy to say that all these years later." Maggie got to her feet and stretched, trying to ease the kinks out of her back. "How much of the story do you think is whitewash?"

"She's not around to ask, so we'll never know what her actual intentions were. What we do know is that she boarded the *Perdition* with Eugenia, then at some point during the evening she moved from the *Perdition* to one of the other ships moored alongside."

"And she left Eugenia behind?"

"This is where it gets interesting."

Dex rose, too, stretched much as Maggie had done, and brought that simmering lust she'd only managed to bury back to buzzing life. Maggie turned her back, wandered to the window, trying not to remember how it felt to have his hands on her. Dex, however, didn't seem to be having any trouble focusing on Eugenia's mystery, and that made it easier for her to put it aside. Keeping her distance from him helped.

"Sonja claimed to have met a man named Giff from a nearby island," Dex continued.

"Windfall isn't the only island hereabouts."

"But you know the name."

Maggie rubbed at the gooseflesh on her arms. "I don't want to jump to conclusions."

"He was the one who shuttled her from the *Perdition* to the other ship. He told her he wanted to dance with her, so, thinking they were going to be around for a while, she left Eugenia on their smaller boat because she thought the baby would be safe there until she could come back for her."

"Meaning Eugenia wouldn't have been on board when the *Perdition* blew up."

"Meaning."

Maggie thought about that for a second. "Just Giff, huh? There are Giffords on Windfall Island, but it's a pretty common name."

"How many of them ran liquor during Prohibition?"

"Don't know," Maggie said, turning to face Dex now. "It wouldn't have been that unusual along the coast."

Dex sat, pulled the papers he'd been reading back in front of him. "I don't know about you, but a guy named Giff doesn't sound like a journal-keeper."

"We won't know until we go through them all, but at this rate it's going to take a lot of time, and even if we find something from the right year, I wouldn't believe everything you read in these. But you already knew that, even with the nanny's story."

"It's just a story, and you pointed out yourself she probably adjusted it to make herself look innocent."

Maggie sat down, huffed out a breath. "So what else do you want from me?"

"I need to talk to people on the island, see what kind of oral lore there is."

Oral lore. Jesus, how he talked. It was just one more thing that set him off from everything and everyone she knew. "I wouldn't believe everything you hear, either. Folks around here have been embellishing the truth longer than status has been a symbol."

"That's a long time," Dex agreed. "It's always tricky to separate truth from fiction, but there will be truth in there somewhere."

She sighed. "I'd tell you to have fun."

"But you know I won't get anything asking questions by myself."

She wanted to refuse, but she knew he was right. People would relax with her around. She'd get information they'd never give to Dex; as much as he might have wormed his way into some level of acceptance, he was still an outsider.

"Have dinner with me tonight, Maggie."

"No."

"If they think we're dating—"

"If they think we're dating the only stories you'll hear will be about me, and that won't get you anywhere." But the real problem wasn't what other people would think; it was how it would feel to her.

"It would be entertaining. And enlightening."

And she had her own secrets to keep. "I'll help you pick brains. I won't lie any more than I have to."

Dex leaned forward, cupped the back of her neck, and laid his lips on hers. He wasn't gentle this time, but gentle wasn't what Maggie wanted. So, when he nipped at her bottom lip, she dove into the kiss, fisted her hand in his shirt and gave in to the desire that had only grown since she'd discovered the incredible heat and amazing pleasure they could find in each other's bodies.

This time it was Dex who pulled back, Dex who was breathing hard and looking shell-shocked. His eyes met hers, clearing enough for speculation to light his gaze.

"You'll sleep with me, but you won't date me."

"That's just chemistry, Dex."

"Chemistry isn't a bad foundation."

Maggie bumped up a shoulder, the gesture far too casual for what she felt. "We're not building a house."

"We're building a case."

"That has nothing to do with me," she reminded him—and herself, the truth of it bleak enough to help her settle the rest of the way. Dex wanted to solve his case; if she meant anything to him apart from the physical, it was as a means to an end.

"So . . . no to dinner."

"No to dating. But if you happen to be having dinner at the Horizon tomorrow night, you just might run into me there." She went into the kitchen, came back with a key ring she'd taken from the pegs by the back door, and flipped it to him.

Dex snagged the ring out of the air and looked at the fob. "These keys belong to a Jaguar."

"XK120 Roadster, to be exact. '54."

His eyes shot to hers, and Maggie had the pleasure of knowing she'd truly surprised him.

"I'm restoring it. The mechanical work is done. The car runs like a top, but it's not all that pretty to look at right now."

"And you're just going to let me borrow it," he said, still staring at the keys as if he thought they'd disappear like smoke if he took his eyes off them.

Maggie arched a brow, leaned against the doorjamb. "I'll give you a good rental price, anyway."

That made him grin—like a fool, sure—but at least he was himself again. "Kind of mercenary, aren't you?"

She bumped up that shoulder. "I'm not the one who's getting paid a daily rate."

"Touché. I guess I should be grateful you're not charging me for the help."

"Well," she said, "I can think of a way for you to repay me." She pushed away from the doorjamb. "If you're not in a hurry."

"I'm in a big hurry, all of a sudden, but it has nothing to do with trying out the Jag."

Dex reached for her, but she stepped back. He'd been in control before, and she'd been helpless under his hands, his mouth, to do anything but surrender. There'd been no complaints; how could there have been considering the outcome? But it had left her feeling vaguely concerned, and while Dex had done and said nothing to make her think he considered her surrender a weakness, it didn't take words and actions to make her worry.

She was testing him—testing them both—but she needed to put her fears to rest.

Dex saw the intent in Maggie's eyes, the heat and need. The aggression. She wanted control, and he was a man who, under certain circumstances, could go with the flow. All of those circumstances involved him getting what he wanted. The occasion certainly fit the bill.

Maggie surprised him, though. He expected her to go for the fast, sweaty thrill, an encore to what they'd brought each other before. He wanted that, wanted a steep, insane roller coaster ride with dizzying ups and downs that left no room for thoughts or concerns. He wanted to feel her pulse scramble when he put his hands on her, feel his mind fuzz when she put hers on him. He wanted that mindless, breathless second in time where pleasure was all that mattered, and the pleasure they brought to each other was nearly too intense to bear.

Instead, she stepped forward, almost hesitantly, and kissed him. Just a touch of her lips to his, all it took to blur his mind and make him want to take it slowly, to savor and enjoy every second of the time she spent in his arms.

And then she speared her hands into his hair, lifted onto her toes, and took. Took his mouth, stole his mind, and shot his body into a need so great it nearly buckled his knees. She took his shirt by the hem and whipped it over his head, then put her mouth on him again while her hands slipped down over his stomach.

She popped the snap at his waist, unzipped his pants, and shoved them down, then took him, hard and aching, into her hand. Her mouth slid down to his neck, then lower, nibbling, nipping down his ribs.

"Don't, God, Maggie," he groaned, and when she didn't stop, he jammed his hands under her armpits and hauled her upright.

She laughed, a sound of pure, feminine power, and stepped back, stripping off her shirt and pants. She wore serviceable white cotton beneath her clothes, the bra skimming across the swell of her breasts, the panties riding low across her belly, high on her hips.

He reached for her, but she stepped back, just one step while she reached behind her back and undid the bra, slipping it off without a hint of self-consciousness. Her panties went the same way and were set carefully aside with the bra before she turned back to him. "I'm afraid we're not going to make it to the bedroom," she said.

Dex was afraid he wouldn't make it to the floor. All he could do was stand there, mouth dry, pulse hammering, holding onto control with a death grip as Maggie pulled him down, straddled him, took him in. Her body clamped around him, a wet, velvet fist. She rose over him, slim as a willow branch, strong as steel. She began to move and the world narrowed down with her at the center, her eyes blue flames that trapped him in a prison of heat and friction, of pleasure rising, building, coalescing to a hot, aching ball of desperation.

He lifted, took her breast into his mouth and heard her breath catch, felt her heart stutter then race. She slowed, lifting and then grinding down on him in measured strokes, every slide of her body around him a study in torture he didn't want to end. He wrapped his hands around her narrow ribcage and feasted, loving the taste of her skin, the texture and firmness of her flesh. Her every sigh spurred him, her breathless moans were like music. And her pace was driving him mad.

He slid his hands down to take her hips, met her thrust for thrust as she rose over him again, slim and lovely in the pale lamplight. He felt control slipping away again, felt his body tightening, and decided he'd be damned if she shoved him over the edge without her.

He used his hands, his mouth, ruthlessly, just as ruthlessly holding himself back until he heard her breath sob in and out, felt her tighten around him like a vise. Until her body bowed back and he felt that first wave of pleasure rip through her.

Then he let go, let ecstasy blast through him, cradling her as they fell, endlessly, shattered. And held her as they came back again, whole, but changed, irrevocably. For the better? he wondered as his breath tore in and out of his lungs, as his heart raced and stuttered in his chest.

Maggie, slumped into a heap over him, stirred, mumbling grumpily when Dex tried to shift her aside. "You're so warm and comfortable."

"The floor is cold and hard," he said. "Much as I'm enjoying the cuddle, Maggie—"

She shot upright and slipped away from him. The look on her face would have pissed him off if he hadn't been so damned tired of seeing her shy away from any soft emotion where he was concerned.

Dex rolled to his side, hissing a bit on the cold floor. It took a couple minutes before he could find the energy to climb to his feet, and then he just stood there, waiting until his breathing and heartbeat calmed, before he pulled Maggie to her feet.

She stumbled a bit; it gave him back a little of the self-respect he'd lost at being so destroyed by her. Sweeping her into his arms took him the rest of the way—he was even able to laugh a little when his legs weren't as steady as he wanted them to be. But he had enough strength to hold her tight when she tried to push out of his arms.

"Don't be a coward," he said rustily, nipping the side of her neck because it was right there, handy.

Maggie huffed out a laugh, braced her hand on the wall as he carried her up the stairs. "My legs work perfectly well," she said, although she wasn't trying to use them, he noticed. "And why in the world would I be afraid of you?"

"Not me—well, not directly. Your feelings for me."

She slanted him a look. "I have no feelings for you—okay, at the moment there's gratitude, but not the kind of feelings you're talking about."

Dex dropped her unceremoniously on the bed. "But you could have."

Maggie rolled to her back and looked him straight in the eye. "What about you?"

"You're afraid of my feelings? You think I'm going to fall in love with you." It wasn't a question, any more than he asked her opinion when he slid into bed with her. "Now whose ego is kicking up?"

She didn't laugh. "I'll only hurt you."

She could, he thought, so it was a good thing he'd decided not to fall in love with her. "We both know the score here, Maggie. Spending a night in the same bed won't change it. But I'll leave if you want me to."

She gave it a beat, that split second feeling like a lifetime before she shrugged and settled onto her side. She pulled his arm around her waist and relaxed back against him with a little sigh.

Her breath evened out almost immediately, her body going lax and pliant as she fell into sleep—and left Dex awake and wondering who she was really warning, and what it meant that the idea of Maggie having feelings for him—soft feelings—should leave him so . . .

Lost in the confusing and unfamiliar maze of his own emotions, Dex drifted off, warm and content.

Chapter Fourteen

Maggie was gone when Dex got downstairs and wandered into a kitchen scented with coffee, although the pot was empty and clean. The keys he'd dropped in the dining room were on the counter, along with a note written in bold, slashing strokes that read, *I figure you for a late riser. All those long nights doing cheating spouse work. There's coffee in the thermos, pop tarts in the cupboard, and gas in the car. Help yourself to all of the above. No charge for the lodging or the continental breakfast.*

She was kicking him out, Dex decided, but the way she handled it was so quintessentially Maggie it brought a smile to his face. He pocketed the keys, hooked the thermos, grabbed a foil packet, and, still grinning, headed into the dining room.

He'd intended to work a few hours, cut his way through some of the paperwork he'd already decided would yield little usable information. But if having Maggie close by was a distraction, not having her there was an even bigger one. Her absence made it nearly impossible for him to think of anything else.

Maggie shooting him daggers every time he brushed

against her. Maggie with the quick wit and the smart mouth. Maggie with that sulky expression and irresistibly sexy body. Maggie taking him, emptying him out, then filling him back up. With her.

He looked at his watch again for what had to be the dozenth time. And then he realized he was waiting for her to get home.

Home.

It was a like a fist to the gut—not the word, the feeling behind it. He'd grown up with parents who loved him and his brother and sister, and who had so much love between them it had always been clear they were the center of each other's world. His parents had built a life based on that love, brought their children into that world, and made it clear that they were meant to go out, someday, and make a world of their own with someone they loved.

They'd set a damned high bar, Dex could see now. They'd given him a foundation that demanded one hell of a structure be built on it. And he would, someday, when he could ask a woman to build a home with him without having to worry about the day he might be carried back to that home in a coffin. His sister had faced that day, lost the man she loved, the father of her two small children, to a drug dealer's bullet. Dex had watched in awe as she bore the heartache and fought to rebuild her little family from that kind of staggering loss.

The search for Eugenia Stanhope might not be dangerous, but the next job could be, or the one after that. There'd be no home for him, he'd vowed, until he could walk through the door with a clear conscience and an open heart.

He looked around this house where he'd spent a single night of his life, and understood how easy it would be to second-guess that vow.

But Jesus, he thought, he'd be a fool to fall in love with a solitary, contrary woman like Maggie Solomon. There were a million small reasons, and one huge one: she'd never love him back.

Those gold wings were tattooed over her heart for a reason, and only an idiot could have seen her with her father and not understood that reason. Phillip Ashworth Solomon had used love as a hammer against his only daughter, and the blows she'd taken had left her closed off, damaged.

Afraid.

He pushed to his feet, walked out of that house with the banister made for sliding, the wide-open spaces he could so easily see strewn with toys, those big windows overlooking the generous back yard with its little beach off to one side and the dock perfect for a sailboat. The whole place was kid paradise.

It made him itchy—hell, it made him sad to know Maggie would have laughed her ass off over the notion of committing to anyone long enough for even the idea of children to become a part of the relationship landscape. But he could see it all. More, he could feel it, the way it would be to make a life here, to make a family. To go to bed each night and wake up each morning on the shores of Temptation Bay...

Jesus, he thought, clattering down the wide steps and heading straight for the small parking lot next to the office. If he hadn't completely lost his mind, he would have remembered Maggie's house wasn't the only building with wide windows. He'd have waited until a time when he could avoid any uncomfortable run-ins. Like the one he was about to have with Jessi Randal, who chose that moment to appear through the back door of the office and set out on an interception course. Since it would be rude, not to mention telling, to turn away, he kept walking. He added the easy smile just to prove he could.

"Well, that's some Cheshire grin, Mr. Keegan," Jessi said. "I'd ask why, but I'm too much a lady."

"You don't really need to ask, do you?"

She shot him a look from under her lashes, the smile on her face going smug. "Jumping to conclusions is never a good idea."

Not much of a leap in this case, Dex thought. He considered asking her to keep it to herself, but he'd learned the hard way that would be insulting. Jessi had Maggie's back; she wouldn't blab because she understood the importance of privacy to her best friend. "When's Maggie due in?"

As Dex had figured, Jessi let the subject of his sleeping arrangements go. "She'll be gone most of the day."

"Delivery or pick up?"

"All of the above. Maggie's a whiz at scheduling, saving up off-island errands until she has a charter, so she can make a daisy chain of the stops and save on fuel."

The woman was efficient, Dex mused, another little facet of her character he found irresistible. "Can you give her a message for me?"

"Sure."

"Tell her thanks for breakfast," he held up the pop tarts, "and since she bought, I owe her. Let her know I'll be at the Horizon, seven o'clock, to pay my debt."

"She won't show."

"She'd better. It was her idea."

"Uh...let me go inside and forward the phones to my cell, and I'll drive you into town. You can tell me the rest of that story on the way."

Dex pulled the keys to the Jag out of his pocket, held them up. "I appreciate the offer, but Maggie loaned me a car."

"She—" Jessi grabbed the ring out of his hand, stared at it for a second. "The Jaguar? Her Roadster? She barely lets anyone look at it, let alone drive it."

"Yeah," Dex didn't ruin his nonchalant attitude with a grin. "She's a hard one to anticipate."

"Isn't she just? I think I should go inside now, and check the weather."

"What?" Dex swung around, caught Jessi by the arm as she'd already started for the office. "Maggie flew in bad weather?"

Jessi simply smiled, the one brow she lifted taking it smug. "It's not the weather up there I'm worried about, Dex, but I think it might be snowing in Hell."

Maggie's Jaguar Roadster looked like hell, but it zipped nimbly through the curves and stretched out on the straight-aways, as sleek and muscular as its namesake prowled the jungle. The woman definitely had a way with an engine, and having his hands on the wheel, hearing it purr, put the finishing touch on the amazing night past and a morning that had dawned in clear-skied, autumn-painted perfection.

He slowed for the turn into Windfall village, fielded the first open-mouthed stare from Maisie Cutshaw, and his mood plummeted, hitting rock-bottom between one thud-ding heartbeat and the next. The Jaguar, he thought darkly, the same car that had buoyed his morning now weighed like an anchor, made heavier by every long, assessing look that came his way.

Well, he thought as he parked in front of the Horizon and stepped out of the car, he'd wanted everyone to think he and Maggie were involved. Mission accomplished. He walked inside, waved through the big doorway to AJ, man-ning the bar, and stopped short when Helen snagged him

by the arm, cut off whoever she had on her cell, and asked
him about the Jag.

"Maisie, right?"

"She was taping up the gift shop windows and saw you
drive by."

"Why was she taping up the windows?" he asked.

"For the winter storms," Helen said, sounding put-upon.
"We get a fair bit of wind, sometimes more than a fair bit."
Her eyes narrowed. "And you're changing the subject."

"Sure, but how much is a fair bit? And what's blowing
around that breaks windows?"

"Hail sometimes, or tree branches. There's a big old
oak behind Maisie's place, and you know how those things
shed if they're not trimmed regular. One good blow and . . ."
Helen jammed her hands on her hips. Her foot was tapping,
too. "The car?"

Dex had to work hard not to laugh.

"Where were you last night?" Helen persisted. "As if I
didn't know."

"I'd love to talk about it, really, but I have to make a
phone call. Feel free to listen in."

Helen's irritation took on an edge of insult. "I don't listen in on the guests' phone calls. And don't think this conversation is over. Everybody in town knows you're driving
Maggie's car and they're all wondering what else Maggie is
sharing with you. Just remember, I asked first."

"Okay, you can grill me about it later."

"And not get any damned answers," Dex heard her mut-
ter as he hightailed it up the stairs, fishing his room key
out of his pocket so he could get inside before he ran into
anyone else bursting with quest—

He stopped mid-thought, took one good look through a
door he could only half open because it was jammed up

against something which, on further investigation, turned out to be his mattress. Drawers hung out of the low dresser and nightstand, the closet gaped open, and the bedclothes were in a heap in the corner. He leaned around the door, saw the mattress had been slashed. It appeared even the edges of the carpet had been ripped from the tack strips.

Not trashed, Dex concluded, but the room had been thoroughly searched. He only thought about it for a minute before he dug his phone out of his back pocket, flipped it open. Under other circumstances, he would have put the room to rights and kept it to himself. But there was no way to hide a slashed mattress, and no point inviting questions by not reporting the break-in. Ten minutes later the sheriff of Windfall Island turned the corner and strode, in his measured, deliberate way, to Dex's door. AJ was right behind him.

The two men took the same sort of slow perusal Dex had made. AJ just shook his head, looking grim.

"Did you go in?" George asked him.

"No."

"Not curious about what's missing?"

"Nothing in there to steal," Dex said in the same flat tone. "Nothing of mine, anyway. My money's on me, and my files are in the..."

"Jaguar," George finished for him, his voice a notch tighter and just a little rough at the edges. "Word travels."

Dex closed his eyes, tried to hold the words back, but they came out anyway. "Maggie rented it to me." And yeah, that sounded defensive, and judging by George's expression, the fact that he was paying for the privilege of driving Maggie's car didn't mitigate anything. Since the man wore a gun, Dex figured he ought to be concerned. Instead, he felt sympathy. He swallowed it back, let it ice over, put emotion away, and set his mind on the situation at hand.

"How long has the room been vacant?" George asked.

"Don't remember seeing you come in last night," AJ said helpfully.

George's eyes cut to Dex's.

Dex stared back coolly. "The lock is still intact, the window is closed and latched from the inside. Whoever did it must have had the key."

"Yeah, that might narrow things down in the big city."

"So let me get this straight. I've been sleeping in a room anyone on the island could get into?"

George's mouth twisted. "Not at night, or you'd have called me before this."

Dex thought about it, nodded. "The Maslow twins," he said for George's and AJ's benefit.

"Yeah," AJ said, grinning outright this time, "except the call would've come when their old man showed up with his twelve gauge."

Dex pretended to squirm at that idea, and his mind was on weapons. But they weren't trained on him. Despite the ego Maggie liked to tease him about, he didn't think for a second any woman on the island would break into his room simply to get to him. Why rip up the carpet and trash the room when they found it empty? Why slice open the mattress if they were only after a roll on it? No, whoever had done this had been looking for something...and there was only one thing Dex might have had of any value: information about Eugenia's descendant.

The violence of the search left Dex with some real concerns about what might happen to that descendant—if there was one, and he was incompetent enough to let the information get out.

George spent the same silent minute coming to some conclusions of his own, it seemed. "Thing is," he said to

Dex, "you were gone during the day. Just about anyone could be responsible for redecorating your room. AJ locks up at night, but everyone on the island knows where he keeps the master key."

"And there's nobody at the front desk most of the time," AJ put in. "Not once tourist season is over."

"Nice secure place you're running here," Dex said to George.

"First," George shot back, "I don't run Windfall Island. If I did—"

"Yeah, I'd be gone. Got it."

"Second, I'm not the one with all the tempting secrets."

"So it was just somebody trying to find out why I'm here?"

George shrugged. "What else could it be?"

Right, what else? Dex took a deep breath, exhaled, letting go of the darker possibilities swirling in his brain at the same time.

"You've become quite the mystery, Keegan. Whoever it was came when they knew you'd be out, then probably got a little angry and a lot carried away when it turned out to be a wild goose chase."

"You'd know the people here," Dex said by way of agreement. "But you're not going to dedicate a lot of time to finding out who's behind this."

"Who do you want me to question?"

"Start with everybody, then narrow it down from there."

George rocked back on his heels. "I'll ask around, but I can tell you now, nobody will own up to this, and if anyone else knows who did it, they won't snitch."

"Not for an outsider, you mean."

"Not for anybody," George said evenly. "It's not our way."

"So I've noticed," Dex said sourly. These were the damnedest people, gossiping about everybody and everything as long as it was something inconsequential. The important stuff they took to their graves. And he couldn't insist George take the break-in seriously without giving him a damn good reason.

"You can come down to the station house later, fill out a report," George offered.

"I'll leave that to you," Dex said to AJ. "It doesn't appear anything of mine was stolen." Except his sense of security.

And he was better off without it.

Maggie radioed in just after four o'clock, and Jessi took her first easy breath of the day. Contrary to what she'd told Dex, she always worried when Maggie was in the air. Added to that, the weather service had predicted the first serious fall storm. It was for later that night, sure, but the Atlantic rarely fit itself into the forecasters' tidy little schedule.

Jessi acted as air traffic controller in cases where Maggie wasn't around. Even though Maggie didn't need any assistance landing at Windfall Airport, she insisted all FAA regulations be observed. So when Maggie called in her approach, Jessi answered, cleared her for landing, and pretended to guide her in.

She was watching at the big front windows of the lobby when Maggie came around the back of her little Piper and opened the passenger door. A man stepped out—Holden Abbot, Jessi knew, as she'd taken the reservation. She could still remember his voice, a deep, languorous drawl, dripping with Southern honey.

He had the body to go with it, too: tall, lanky, and boy did he know how to wear a suit. Or maybe the suit was worthy of the body, so perfectly tailored she could tell there were muscles on his long, lean frame. And that face—well, he was definitely attractive.

He had a killer smile, too; easy, cheerful. Holden

Abbot's smile lit up his face, made what might have been far too cover model into something more approachable, engaging and inviting.

Even from where she stood, Jessi could see that his smile made it all the way to his eyes. And because she found it so appealing, she walked away from the window.

By the time Maggie swung through the door with Holden Abbot behind her, Jessi was back behind her desk, buried in paperwork up to her elbows. The task was real; her portrayal of unbreakable concentration should have won her an Oscar. The iPod earbuds she'd shoved in her ears added to the illusion, even if she hadn't had time to turn the damned thing on—which made it easier to hear Maggie when she yelled, "Jessi!"

She tugged on the wire, the earbuds popping free as she looked up. And her breath stuttered. That smile, she thought, catching herself before her mouth dropped open. From a distance that smile had been inviting; up close it was lethal.

"Jess!" Maggie said loudly enough to tell Jessi she'd said it at least once already, and when Jessi glanced over she was smiling smugly. "I said, this is Holden Abbot."

"Call me Hold," he said, offering his hand. "Everyone does."

Jessi rose, took it, and immediately wished she hadn't. His hand was warm, his grip strong but gentle. And his scent, just soap and man, was tempting enough that she almost leaned in for a better sample. She didn't, and let go of his hand before he could feel her tremble. And because his smile never wavered, because he seemed not one bit affected, the trembling went away, and was replaced by annoyance.

"Welcome to Windfall Island," she said, ever-cognizant

of her duty as representative and part owner of Solomon Charters. "If you'll excuse me, I have work." She looked at Maggie. "Unless you need me to take Mr. Abbot into the village."

"No need," Maggie said, frowning just enough to tell Jessi she'd seen the wintry attitude even if Holden Abbot hadn't. "He's staying here, for the time being. At my house."

Jessi's mouth did drop open this time.

"I'm not sure what Dex has in mind," Hold said, that honey-dripping voice not helping Jessi's presence of mind. "We—Maggie and I—thought it might be a good idea if I lay low until we can talk to him."

Jessi snapped her mouth shut, took a second to establish some control, just a little self-control so she didn't appear to be a complete idiot. "Well, you can talk to him tonight, since you're dating."

Maggie shot Holden Abbot a look. "We're not dating, I—"

"Loaned him a car," Jessi said, relaxing now that the focus was off her. "And not just any car, a Jaguar XK... something Roadster."

"An XK120? Year?"

"Fifty-four," Maggie supplied.

Hold whistled between his teeth. "Completely restored?"

"Mechanically. He still looks like sixty years of bad luck."

"He?"

Maggie crossed her arms. "No woman could possibly put me through what that car did."

Hold laughed, long and loud, and if his smile wreaked havoc, his laugh seemed to twine around inside Jessi, bright and irresistible.

She put a frown on her face and a bite into her voice.

"You have a date, remember?" she said to Maggie. And those words—not the ones she'd intended to say—let her know the bitchiness had a root in something other than a desire to put Holden Abbot off.

Maggie caught it, too. She leaned back against a file cabinet, crossed one booted foot over the other, and popped up one perfectly arched eyebrow.

Jessi crossed her arms as well, braced a hip on her desk, and met Maggie's bland stare head on. "Your date?" she prompted, not about to give in to Maggie's snotty non-verbal comeback. "I'm all ears."

"That's a change; usually you're all mouth."

Jessi laughed. She never could out-snark Maggie, and she had to admit it was her fault. This time. "I do like to talk."

"Maybe you could keep Mr. Abbot company while I fill out my logs."

"Of course." Not like she had a choice, with Maggie already halfway out the back door. She sat again, gestured Hold to one of the worn metal-framed chairs against the far wall.

Instead of sitting at what she'd have considered a safe distance, he brought the chair to her, placing it at an angle to her desk and lounging—it was the only way she could describe the way he draped his lanky body over the small chair. All that was missing were the arms crossed behind his head.

Annoyance roared through her again, that he could be so damned relaxed while she felt so...itchy.

"What brings you to Windfall, Mr. Abbot?"

"Hold," he said with a tone of slight rebuke. "If you keep calling me Mr. Abbot, sugar, I'm going to take it as an insult."

Jessi looked up from the invoices she'd gone back to sorting. "If you evade my questions, I'm going to wonder why you're keeping secrets. And don't call me sugar."

He grinned. It killed her. She smiled back, nothing else she could do. While she understood that he'd completely defused her temper, she couldn't help herself.

"I was asked to help Dex Keegan with a little case he's working on here."

"Oh?" She forgot the invoices completely. "Why?"

"I'm not sure, exactly," he said in a calm, measured way that told her he didn't so much weigh his words as enjoy saying them. "I haven't talked to him directly. A friend of his asked me to come along, see what I could do."

"What do you do for a living?"

"Lots of things. Research, fact-finding, and I have a specific interest in genealogy."

"Really?" Jessi sat forward. "Why does Dex need a genealogist?"

"Well, now, maybe you should ask him."

Jessi sat back again, crossed her arms. "Maybe I should ask Maggie."

Chapter Fifteen

About time you showed up."

Maggie crossed the Horizon's lobby, saying nothing because she was nearly an hour late, and she'd be damned if she told him it was because she'd changed her clothes three times before she'd settled on a pair of slim jeans and a white, man-cut shirt, open with a white stretchy tank beneath. Blue jeans and a t-shirt ought to be good enough for Dex Keegan—hell, her flight suit would have done, but she'd felt an urge to primp, and while she didn't practice self-delusion on a regular basis, it didn't pay to examine her reasons too closely.

"It was worth the wait," he said, but without the flattering up and down that would have been her rightful payoff for taking an hour to dress for him. "Where's my genealogist?"

Maggie absorbed a little sting, told herself he was doing her a favor, establishing the emotional distance she needed. And if she didn't quite buy it, she sure as hell wasn't going to let him see he'd hurt her feelings. "I wasn't sure you wanted everyone to know you ordered one."

"They'll hear about him sooner or later. I found that out the hard way this morning."

"Took some heat over the Jag, huh?"

"You knew I would."

Maggie couldn't quite hide her grin. Not that she tried very hard. "You want everyone to think we're dating."

"And you don't."

She shrugged. "If people stick their nose into my private business and get the wrong impression, why should I care?"

It was Dex's turn to smile. "So you have a personal objection to being my girlfriend. I wonder why?"

"Maybe it's the way you call me your girlfriend."

"Would you prefer lady friend? Private flight attendant? Friend with benefits?"

"Don't flatter yourself; we're not all that friendly." Especially at the moment. But she forced herself to keep the smile on her face—even if it galled her to put on a show. "Abbot is at my house."

"With Mort and Jessi? And if he tells them why he's here?"

"He's your genealogist. I don't know what he was told to say or not say, but I can tell you he was pretty forthcoming with me."

Dex shoved his hands through his hair, and while his upset might have entertained her any other time she knew what was at stake. "I left him in the office with Jess, but I don't imagine he's had any interaction with Mort."

"But Mort knows you brought another outsider to Windfall. Sooner or later he'll tell someone."

"Better plan on sooner. He's not much of a talker, but he's been pretty popular lately, seeing as he's on the front line, so to speak."

Dex chewed on that a moment, seeming more resigned than angry. "Mort coming into the village tonight?"

"He lives in the village," Maggie said, waging only a brief war with herself before she gave Dex as much of Mort's story as she was comfortable with.

"His mother hasn't been well for a long time. She's supposed to be having surgery. Cancer." Or so Mort had been telling her for a while, she thought, kicking herself for getting so wound up in her own life she forgot to check in with a friend who was going through something so terrible. "He spends most of his time either at the airport or at home taking care of her."

"I've seen him in here before."

"He gets away for a meal or a beer now and again." And that was all Maggie was willing to say about anyone else's affairs. "I could use both myself."

Dex reached for her arm, and when she shifted away, turned it smoothly into a gesture toward the inn's dining room. His eyes, hot and narrowed, told a different story, even if he managed to keep his tone casual. "Weather was dicey for flying today."

"Which is why I didn't take time out for lunch," Maggie said with the same tense undercurrent beneath the same casual tone, "so I could get back before things turned ugly."

"Maybe you shouldn't have gone up in the first place."

"I've flown in worse."

"Stupid."

Her gaze shifted to his. "If this was a date, I'd be leaving about now."

Dex blew out his breath.

Maggie could see him pulling back on his temper and did the same with her own. "We both have well-established lives, Dex. I'm not about to consult you before I fly, and you're not going to check in with me before you decide how you spend your day."

He gave her a slight smile and said, "Neither of us are used to making concessions."

And both of them were steering clear of any emotional attachment. "So where's your friend?" Maggie asked as they entered the Horizon's big dining room. "The one with the answers."

"Alec couldn't clear his schedule. Said he'd do the next best thing to coming himself, and I'm glad he did. I should have thought about bringing Hold in," he added, choosing his words carefully in the room crowded with big ears. "He's thorough, even if his way takes more time."

Dex stopped at a table for four, pulled out a chair, and left her no choice but to take it.

"Do we have to sit in the middle of the damn room?"

"Yes." Dex took the chair next to hers.

"I feel like I'm on display."

"You're not the outsider."

"No, I'm the one who has to live here after you drop your bomb and leave the island." And sniping at him all night would only make them both unhappy. Best not to think about the day Dex left Windfall for good, not to wonder how much it was going to hurt. "Look, Dex, we both want the same thing, right? Why don't we call a truce?"

"I didn't realize we were at war. Especially after last night."

And wasn't it telling, Maggie thought, that she was the only one admitting they weren't comfortable with one another on this so-called date, in this very public setting.

She spotted AJ heading for their table and said, "Here we go," smiling easily for the first time since she'd walked in the door. "Hey, Alphonse."

"Maggie. Dex, are you settled in your new room?"

"What's that supposed to mean?"

"No, Maggie, I didn't mean he was moving in with you. Not that Dex wouldn't want to, but we all know your place is off limits. Not that you aren't…friendly sometimes, but—"

"Men are okay to sleep with, but I don't exactly welcome them into my life."

AJ's eyes shot to hers, red creeping up from his neck.

Maggie was more than a little embarrassed herself, even if she refused to show it. "Since I won't let you move in with me," she said to Dex, "I'll assume you're getting a new room here. Having the old one steam-cleaned?" she said sweetly to AJ. "We all know what a clean freak you are."

"Somebody tore up my room," Dex said, his expression carefully blank. "I'm in the mood for a burger, Maggie, how about you?"

"You'll have my chicken and dumplings," AJ said, and fled into the kitchen.

Maggie sat back in her chair, shifted a little so she could watch Dex's face. "Still keeping secrets?"

"It was no big deal, probably someone trying to find out why I'm here." He shrugged, keeping the nagging worry he felt to himself. No need to alarm anyone just because it set off warning bells for him. "Just got a little carried away."

"Oh, well, sure, it must have been one of Windfall Island's crazies on a quest for gossip."

Dex shot her a look, but he let the insult pass. "Nobody knows why I'm here, except you and Hold. He doesn't know anyone on the island, and you haven't talked. What else could it be?"

"What else?" She sat back, huffed out a breath, admitting that for all her grand speeches about the two of them being independent adults, she still would have liked a phone call. "I guess I should apologize."

Dex grinned, slapped a hand over his heart. "I don't think I could survive it."

"If we didn't kill each other last night, I think we can make it through a couple of I'm sorrys."

"A couple?"

"If I'm going to apologize, I think it's only fair you do the same. I'd say you owe me at least one apology by now."

"Why don't I buy you dinner and call it even?"

"You ought to buy me dinner anyway, seeing as you ate me out of house and home the last two days."

He grinned. "You're the reason I worked up such an appetite."

She smiled back before she could stop herself, but her smile faded at the way his eyes darkened, heated, the way he leaned toward her. The way her breath caught in the back of her throat as everything in her yearned. "Be careful," she murmured, as much a warning to herself as to Dex, "or everyone will think we're sleeping together."

"We are sleeping together."

She arched her brows, looked around the room.

So did Dex. More than one of the faces turned their way looked pissed. "I see what you mean," he said, "but it's not all bad. Knowing you're doing something...illegal adds an extra thrill."

Maggie leaned toward him. "Didn't seem like you needed an extra thrill last night."

Dex met her halfway, ran a finger across the back of her hand and sent shivers racing through her. "I don't know. I'd probably need to try it again to be sure."

"Am I interrupting?"

They jerked apart, looked up, and there stood Maisie Cutshaw, very much hoping she was right. After all, she'd timed it that way, the better to have something to gossip about.

"So," Maisie said to Dex, wasting no time. "Did you ever find out who broke into your room?"

He shifted his eyes to Maggie. "I've been busy, but I'll make a point to stop in and ask the sheriff."

"George is so close-mouthed. Nobody's been able to get a word out of him."

"Maybe you're using the wrong inducement," Dex said. "He's single, you're single."

Maisie giggled—until Helen hip checked her out of the way. "It was our break-in," she told Maisie as she set down wide bowls filled with light-as-air dumplings swimming in a thick stew chock full of chicken and vegetables. "If anyone gets the scoop, it's going to be me."

Maggie closed her eyes and took a deep breath of the steam wafting off her bowl.

Dex reached over and tapped her wrist. "You might want to do something about that," he said, indicating Helen and Maisie on the verge of coming to blows.

Maggie picked up her spoon and took a bite, sucking in air because it was piping hot. Dex got to his feet while she was taking her second cautious bite.

"Um . . ." she began, then simply watched as he waded in between Helen and Maisie, who both turned on him.

Helen wagged a finger in his face; Maisie poked him in the shoulder. Maggie sat back, grinning, and watched as AJ loomed up behind the two women, took them each by the collar with one huge hand, and towed them away from the table.

Dex dropped back into his chair, and Maggie burst into laughter, along with nearly everyone else in the place.

"You look like somebody threw a grenade into your foxhole and it blew up right next to you."

Dex scrubbed a hand over his face. "Why the hell didn't you stop me?"

"I said 'um.' "

"Yeah, that was a lot of help."

"Maybe I should have tripped you instead, or tackled you."

"Ha, ha." But his lips curved into the slightest of smiles. "Maybe you could tackle me later, make up for nearly getting me killed."

"You nearly got yourself killed. It was very entertaining."

"You should be safe now," AJ said, having dispatched Helen to the kitchen and Maisie back to her table. "I hope you learned a lesson from this."

"Thanks, Dad," Dex said.

"Eat up, kid. If you're dumb enough to put yourself in the middle of a Windfall catfight, you'll need your strength."

The Horizon was hopping, Dex noted. It hopped near every night, as he'd seen firsthand since he'd spent most of his evenings since he'd come to Windfall in the big, homely dining room/bar. Unfortunately, it wasn't hopping in his direction.

For the first time in nearly two weeks, the downright nosy citizens of Windfall Island were giving him a wide berth, and he was torn between enjoying the chance to have a quiet conversation with Maggie and missing an opportunity to further his mission. Then again, Maggie wasn't exactly giving his ears a workout.

"It's no wonder nobody else in this place will talk to me with you giving me the cold shoulder."

"I didn't have lunch." She glanced up from her meal, her brilliant blue eyes skimming over his before she looked past him.

"Working around the perimeter of the room from the door, counter-clockwise," she said between bites. "First booth is the Napleton family, Steve, Mary, Kelly and Nick, in order of age—last set of tourists I'm flying out on the weekend, so they won't be helpful.

"Next booth, Jed and Martha Morgenstern, still channeling ancient Romans. Martha's a Hallett, her family is from the island, but she met Jed on the mainland. The Halletts were upstanding citizens, notwithstanding Martha's penchant for kinky sex. I doubt her grandfather was involved in running booze, aside from buying a bottle now and then for personal use.

"Then you have Maureen Lipshutz, or Madam Magda, as she likes to be known." Maggie's laughing eyes met his. "She might actually be of some help, since she claims she can channel the spirits. Of course, she's never come up with any convincing proof of that, but the tourists eat it up.

"Morris Hancock is at the table next to Magda's. Conspiracy theorist, blames everything on the government, thinks there are aliens living among us. Next..."

She kept going, listing off the occupants of each booth or table and adding a touch of their background as an indicator of potential usefulness to the kidnapping. Although Dex admired her ability to size up her surroundings with just a glance, the names were meaningless to him. And he found her ability to ignore him for a plate of chicken and dumplings lowering. "We don't have to talk about the case."

That brought her head up, her gaze streaking to clash with his. "That's why we're here."

"We could talk about last night. And this morning, and yesterday afternoon."

"Why?"

She looked so baffled he had to grin. "I'm a guy."

"I've had firsthand proof," Maggie said, still serious, but

with a devilish glint in her eyes. "And if you keep looking at me like that, the whole place is going to know it."

"Does it embarrass you?"

"It's not embarrassing, it's private."

"Maybe my huge ego needs feeding again."

"Well, then, your ego will be the only thing getting anywhere near me."

His grin widened. "Are you using sex as a weapon?"

"I'm putting it on the back burner."

Where it belongs, Dex reminded himself and vowed not to forget it.

"The table in the back, at the edge of the dance floor," Maggie said, picking up the tour where she'd left off.

"Dance floor?"

"What passes for one in here."

Dex made a casual and leisurely survey of the tiny rectangle of parquet flooring, filled to capacity by three middle-aged men playing darts.

"Those three guys you're staring at are Sam Norris, Han Finley, and Zeke Gifford."

"Giff." Dex's gaze shifted to Maggie's face, but she'd gone back to her meal, so he turned his attention to the trio of men winging darts at the board on the wall that edged one side of the dance floor. "They look like they know their way around a shady situation."

"They wouldn't be Windfallers if they didn't."

"And I'll bet they take after their fathers. And their grandfathers."

"Worth a conversation," Maggie said, pushing her empty plate away. "How about a game of darts?"

"My thought exactly."

"I could take you," she said, grinning.

"Want to put money on it?"

Maggie popped up an eyebrow, got to her feet. "You're already paying for dinner. I don't want to take any more of your money."

"Big words," Dex said, following her as she threaded her way through tables, returning greetings as she went.

"Hey, Maggie," one of the men called out as she stopped beside them. "Wanna dance?"

"Made that mistake at the New Year's Eve party, Zeke. My feet haven't recovered yet."

"What are you doing with the mainlander?" Zeke yelled out over the laughter.

"A girl's gotta eat. I'm not above taking a free meal when I can get it." She slanted Dex a look. "Even from a mainlander."

"Keep it up," Dex said under his breath. "If you gentlemen are finished, Maggie is going to stand me to a game."

There was more laughter, longer and louder, and Zeke yelled out, "She'll wipe the floor with you."

Dex held his eyes. "Winner buys a round."

"Clever, Keegan," she said for his benefit only. "Win or lose, they have a drink with you."

He smiled. "Side bet?"

She shrugged.

"Afraid, huh?"

"Of you?" She picked up a dart, glanced at the board like she had at the room earlier, then let it wing as her gaze shifted back to his. Not a bull's eye, but not far off.

"Maybe we should keep it to a drink."

"Afraid?" she asked with a laughing toss of her head.

"Terrified."

That stopped her, that drawl in his voice, the quiet confidence in his dark eyes. She didn't know why it made her pause; she could beat him at darts, right? But there was just enough doubt mixed in with what she knew about Dex and his tendency to hold back when it suited his purposes.

"Not having second thoughts."

"Not hardly." She handed him a set of darts, stepped sideways until she stood next to Han Finley. "Maybe you should take a couple of practice throws," she said to Dex, "so you can't claim I had home field advantage."

"How about we just get on with it." Dex glanced over, winged a dart at the board as his gaze shifted to her.

Not a bull's eye, triple twenty, the dart thunking into the narrow green strip on the twenty-point section, scoring Dex the largest possible amount of points for a single throw, since even a Bull's Eye was only fifty.

The small crowd that had formed roared, a couple of the men, including Zeke, shooting fists into the air.

"So much for island loyalty," Maggie said, and while Dex was setting up for his next shot, she grabbed Han's arm and yanked. "Do not call me Cousin," she said when his head dropped down next to hers.

He rubbed his arm, grinned. "Sure thing, Cousin," he said, just as the crowd roared again at Dex's second triple twenty.

Maggie met Dex's triumphant grin with an appropriately snotty look, but as soon as he turned away, she glared up at Han. "I mean it, Han."

"I'll hold my tongue, Maggie, but if my dad shows up—"

She stopped listening, turned away from Dex because she knew her face had gone white. Asking Han to cover for her was one thing. Asking Emmett Finley—her Uncle Emmett— to pretend they weren't related—well, she couldn't hurt him like that. So, she'd have to find another way to keep Dex from finding out her mother had been born on Windfall Island, and that she'd kept it from him. At least until she could work up the nerve to tell him herself.

Thankfully, Dex was busy winging his third dart home, and Maggie put some distance between herself and her cousin just as the dart thunked home. Triple twenty.

"Hustler," Maggie said, accompanied by catcalls and shouts of encouragement from the women gathered around. "I should have figured."

"So why didn't you back out?"

"It's all for the cause, right? And there was only a drink on the line."

"Partly for the cause," he corrected her. "You wouldn't respect a man you could beat—at anything."

"I just recently learned the value of surrender," she said, even as she threw her last two darts, both bull's eyes, and lost. "Sometimes it's the only way to really win."

"Uh," Dex said, so delightfully flustered Maggie had to laugh.

"We can discuss it later."

"We don't have to talk," Dex said. "You can just show me."

Maggie smiled, enjoying this new power she'd discovered. "So what are we drinking?"

"Nothing."

"You won, I buy."

"But I pick the time." Dex looked straight into her eyes. "And the place."

Chapter Sixteen

Maggie was keeping her distance, Dex decided, and giving him a clear field to pick the brains of his newfound friends. He held up a hand to signal AJ for a round, figuring a beer would melt whatever ice he hadn't already broken.

"Ingratiating yourself, Mr. Keegan?"

Dex jerked around, came face to face with Josiah Meeker, wearing his usual black suit and sour expression, but this time with a hard light in his eyes. "Just having dinner and a little entertainment," Dex said, trying to figure out why Meeker was baiting him. He offered the darts. "You up for a game?"

"Not with those."

Dex eased back a step, considered Meeker long enough to have the other man fidgeting before he said, "Care to enlighten me?"

"Right after you give me the same consideration. Me and everyone else. Except Maggie, of course."

Dex went cold, every muscle in his body poised to attack. "She'd better not be a part of whatever game you're talking about."

"You brought her into it by getting her to blackmail me—"

"Careful," Dex said softly.

Meeker backed up until he ran into the wall. Dex followed him, staying right in his face. "If I'd had my way she wouldn't have been the one coming to see you."

Meeker gave a rude snort. "You were perfectly happy to use her."

"Nobody uses Maggie," Dex said. "But then, she made that clear to you, didn't she?" He started to turn away, then it occurred to him that he was letting anger blind him to an opportunity. "This isn't about Maggie, though. This is about the journals."

Meeker held up both hands. "I'm just curious, like everyone else," he said with a grimace of a smile. "Including the Maslow Twins. If you'd come clean about why you're here, they wouldn't't've trashed your room trying to find out."

"The Maslow twins. Is that the general opinion?"

"They haven't denied it. You're probably lucky they didn't find you in residence," Meeker said, sounding like he'd have paid to watch.

Dex would have preferred to be there himself. It would have been nice to put a name to the vandal—not to mention a motive. But asking questions never got him anywhere.

He held up the darts. "Who's next?"

Helen elbowed her way through the throng, expertly balancing a tray crammed with long necks. "I'd think twice before I took him up on the invitation," she said as she handed out bottles. "Maggie can and has kicked each of your asses at darts. Dex just kicked hers. No offense, Maggie."

Maggie toasted her with her beer, but her eyes moved from Dex to Meeker. Dex shook his head slightly at the question he saw there.

"Even you boys can do the math. Besides, Dex already bought the round."

"In that case, let's just play for fun." Maggie took the darts, gave Dex one long, enigmatic look, then threw one. Triple twenty. The place erupted.

Trust Maggie, Dex thought. She'd probably let him win.

The rest of the crowd was already placing bets, turning the friendly game on its ear. Dex took his beer to the high table where one of the smugglers' descendants sat, and held out his hand. "Dex Keegan."

"So I've heard," Han Finley said in a broad New England accent. He kept his eyes on the game.

Dex's hopes took a sharp dive, then Han took his hand, introduced himself, and took the beer Dex handed him.

"Folks around here call me Han," he said.

"Like *Star Wars*?"

Han smiled slightly. "Yeah, never heard that one before. I'd expect a mainlander to be more creative."

"Should I ask if the force is with you? Where's Chewie? Although a couple of these guys could qualify."

It took a second or two, then Han snorted out a laugh.

Dex took a long pull from his beer, without really drinking. The point was to loosen up everyone else, not himself.

Han, however, didn't seem to be much of a talker. Dex's eyes stayed on the dart game, which a quick glance showed him Maggie was winning. Then Han lifted his beer, the label flashing in the lights from the Wurlitzer.

Dex looked at his own bottle and grinned. "This is a local brew, right? Windfall Gold."

"AJ likes to support island business. We all do."

"Nothing wrong with that, or this beer. I don't imagine I could get it in Boston."

"Doubtful."

"Maybe I could smuggle some in."

"Wouldn't be a first." Han's mouth quirked up. "You

could say Windfall has a rich history in exporting alcohol to the mainland."

Dex allowed himself a grin, but he kept it short of triumphant. "There's a story there."

Han shook his head. "If you want the story, you have to talk to my granddad. He was just a kid during Prohibition, but he spent some time on the smuggler's run with his old man, my great grandfather. He'd likely be here tonight, if he hadn't been feeling poorly the last little while."

"I'm sorry to hear that," Dex murmured, and although he wanted to press Han for more information, he let it go. It wouldn't do to tip his hand now that he'd finally gotten a lead.

"Maggie kicked Zeke's ass," Han said, "Like usual."

But when she would have settled at the high-top, Dex told Han it was nice shooting the breeze. Han lifted his beer in salute as Dex took Maggie's elbow and steered her back to their table.

And because he could feel her getting ready to wrench herself away, he leaned close and said, "Did Han Finley ever tell you about his grandfather running booze with his great grandfather?"

"Emmett?" Maggie slid onto her chair. "He's mentioned it."

"And you didn't."

"I…He was just a kid. And he never finishes the story. I don't think he can. I don't think he remembers it anymore."

"But there's nothing wrong with your memory."

"There is when you're around," she snapped, head down, picking at a rough spot on the table top with her fingernail.

Dex hadn't expected anger from her. And she wasn't meeting his eyes. "What's going on?"

"I guess I owe you another apology," she said, her gaze bouncing off his. "Although if you think about it, it's really your fault, since you're the distraction.

"And see?" she said before he could unglue his tongue from the roof of his mouth. "You want to talk to Emmett Finley, he just walked in the door." She lifted a hand in greeting to an old man, stooped and wrinkled, the same old man Dex had seen her talking to before, in the corner booth in the back.

Emmett returned her wave, but he took his sweet time making his way to their table.

"Does he know everyone on the damn island?"

"Yes, and he's going to greet them all. He doesn't know you're in a hurry to close your case and get back to your life."

"Don't sell yourself short," Dex said.

"I never sell myself short," Maggie shot back. "I'm a realist."

"And I'm not around for the long haul. But you don't want me for the long haul. All you're after is a nice meal and passable conversation."

"Passable?"

Dex shrugged. "You're not a talker. I get that."

Maggie sat back, the belligerent look on her face telling him she was spoiling for a fight. He didn't know why, but he wasn't going to give her one if he could help it.

"You didn't come here to talk to me," she said. "I'm a means to an end."

"There's no reason we can't enjoy each other's company in the meantime."

"Why, because we're having a relationship?" She glared at him, brilliant blue eyes narrowed, angry, and just a little...*panicked?* "We're having sex. Sex is not a relationship. Being manipulated into helping you is not a relationship."

Sex? They'd been as intimate, physically, as two people could be, but the notion there might, even jokingly, be emotion involved sent her into a tailspin.

Would it be so bad, Dex wanted to ask her, if they did more than scratch a mutual sexual itch together?

The trouble was, he didn't know the answer to that question. He just wished they could both just let go and enjoy it. And damn it, they ought to be able to hold a conversation, exchange small talk, share their day. But the only subject that felt comfortable was the case. He damn well wasn't going to let her club him to death with it.

"Fine," he said, "Go ahead and tell everyone why I'm here."

Maggie sat back, clamped her mouth shut.

"Yeah, that's what I thought. And as for the sex, it's nice to know you think I'm the kind of man who just jumps in the sack with every willing female I run across."

"So you're having deep feelings for me?"

Dex ran a hand back through his hair. "I thought we were getting to be friends, at least. Where it's going is as much a puzzle to me as it is to you, but at least I'm willing to see the possibilities. And that scares the hell out of you. Why is that?"

"There are no possibilities. You're not staying."

"And if I did?" He gave it a beat, but she only looked away. "Yeah, that's what I thought. You can't trust. And don't hang it on me again."

"Right, you didn't start out by lying to me, and to everyone I know and love?"

He blew out a breath, reaching for just a little more patience. All he found was weariness. "I'd suggest we take a step back, but you've never stepped forward."

"Until last night."

"But that was just sex."

Her gaze dropped, and when she looked up again what he saw there staggered him. Vulnerability, and misery. She was hurting, and he knew he bore some of the blame.

Her name trembled on his lips, but his voice wasn't the one that said her name.

"Maggie!" Emmett Finley tottered his way to their table, finally, and when he stooped to kiss Maggie on the cheek, Dex swore he heard the man's joints creak.

"Emmett Finley, meet Dex Keegan," Maggie said, her eyes, and the joy lighting them, all for Emmett.

Emmett took the hand Dex offered him, but instead of shaking it, he steadied himself as he lowered slowly into the chair next to Dex's.

He sighed with gusto when his butt hit the seat. "It's a hell of a thing," he said, "when sitting takes as much out of you as standing."

"I was going to stop by tomorrow," Maggie said, "but here you are. Have you eaten?"

"I have," he said. "Thank you."

"And you're set for supplies, heating oil?"

"For a time. Could use to have you look at my furnace. Don't seem to be working quite right. Or maybe it's just the cold settling into my old bones."

"I'll send Mort over. He's better at that sort of thing than I am."

"Appreciate it. So, Mr. Keegan—"

"Dex."

"Dex, you sparking my girl?"

The direct, mildly threatening expression on Emmett's face had Dex leaning back in his chair, considering his answer carefully.

"Don't you dare talk about me like I'm not here," Maggie said. "I take care of myself."

"It may be old-fashioned, but it's the responsibility of your closest male relative to look after you, Maggie. Your father is a total failure, and since I think of you like a granddaughter—"

AJ came over and set a thick slab of chocolate cake in front of each of them. Dex didn't miss the look that passed between him and Maggie—or the way she changed the subject. But then, her father was a sore subject for Maggie, and AJ always seemed to have her back.

"Nobody bakes like AJ," she said, forking up a huge mouthful of cake and closing her eyes in bliss as it hit her taste buds.

"Reminds me of my mother's," Emmett said. He took a bite with a palsied hand. "She loved to bake, and she had a way with cakes especially. Light as a feather they were." He looked at Maggie, winked. "But AJ, you run a close second, son."

"I'm proud to run a close second to your mama, Emmett. She was one of a kind, that's for sure." And AJ took himself off to the bar.

Emmett sighed wistfully. "She surely was, but my sister came close, God rest both their souls. You remember, Maggie."

"I didn't have the good fortune to meet either one of them," Maggie said. She reached over and covered Emmett's hand. "Dex wants to hear about Prohibition."

Emmett seemed confused, his gaze shifting to Dex's face.

"Han said you used to help your father run illegal liquor to the mainland."

Emmett waved it off. "I was nothing but a kid then."

But kids heard and saw all sorts of things their parents thought they were oblivious to, and a boy with a strong back would have come in handy in situations where speed was invaluable and the more hands pressed into service the better.

He could have sworn Emmett's expression sharpened, but when he looked closer the old man's eyes were rheumy, focused on the past.

"My da had a hand in lots of pies back then. Times were hard. Man has a family to support, he does what's necessary." He smiled cannily. "Can't say I ever knew of anything strictly illegal, but I recollect the big ships moored off the coast, twelve miles out where the stupidity of the U of S government couldn't touch them."

"Do you remember the night the *Perdition* exploded?"

"Oh, aye." He sighed. "Hell of a thing, it was. The ground fair shook with the explosion, flames and debris shot hundreds of feet into the air when that hold full of booze went up. You could smell the pitch all the way to shore, hear the crackle of the flames, the hiss of burning timbers hitting the water as they fell back down. Musta been what hell is like." He trailed off, seemed to jolt back to the present. "Reminds me of the time we had a bonfire on the beach. You remember, Maggie."

"There've been lots of bonfires," Maggie said. "Only one ship explosion."

But although Maggie tried, she never managed to steer Emmett back around to the story of the *Perdition*. If he'd joined in on any of those dead-of-night rum-running operations, he was keeping it to himself, or, more likely, the memories were long gone.

Dex would have bet on the latter as he was regaled with the same story more than once over the next hour, and there were moments where Emmett simply trailed off into silence. Age, Dex figured, had taken as high a toll on Emmett's mind as it had on his body. He listened carefully, though, asked questions, and filed the answers away. And he made a note to talk to Emmett again, earlier in the day when he'd be fresher.

"Well," Emmett said at last with a voice that had gone thin and wavery, "I'm for home."

"I'll take you," Maggie said, getting up so she could steady Emmett. But once he was on his feet, he shook off her attempts to take his arm.

"Got to make a pit stop."

"Yeah, you're on your own there." Still, Maggie walked slowly behind him as he shuffled into the lobby. When Emmett detoured into the men's room, Maggie pulled her jacket out of the little cloak room.

"You want company?"

"I was up before dawn."

"On very little sleep," Dex allowed.

She held his gaze, but hers was inscrutable. "Nothing stopping you from going back in there and picking more brains."

"Being picked up myself, more like." He dipped his hands into his pockets because he wanted to put them on her. It baffled him, as always, that he should be so drawn to such a prickly, irritating woman, but there it was. "I guess I'll go back in there."

"You do that," she said. Her expression was placid, but there was enough heat in her tone to tell him she wasn't all that happy with his decision.

He nearly grinned over it. She didn't want him to take it for granted they'd spend every night together, but she didn't like it when he accepted it. "I'll see you tomorrow."

"Oh, goody."

He did laugh at that. Her snotty tone put him at ease, but then her contrariness had attracted him from the first.

Most nights, George Boatwright wandered through the Horizon, keeping a weather eye on the citizens of Windfall Island. He knew who liked to indulge a little too freely, who'd hooked up, who'd broken up, and who was bent over it. Booze, fighting, and sex, the Windfall Island trifecta. And he wouldn't trade a single one of the drunks, scrappers or lovers for a suburb full of law-abiding nuclear families who tucked themselves in sharply at ten p.m.

He didn't often sit down for a meal, not because AJ's cooking failed to appeal to him, but because he was just as happy with a can of soup or a grilled cheese sandwich thrown together in the comfort of his own tiny kitchen. When he was on duty, he was on duty. And he was always on duty.

Every now and again, though, he joined Maggie, and shared a meal and a quiet hour or two. Seeing her with Dex Keegan brought him up short.

They sat in the middle of the room, but they were an island of intimacy in the big, boisterous crowd. Maggie didn't even notice him, and anybody looking at them could tell they'd been together, even if they didn't know Keegan had been spending a lot of time out at the airport.

George moved on, forced himself to put one foot in front of the other. It wasn't like she hadn't taken lovers before, he reminded himself. So had he, George allowed. It was that this time she might get hurt.

Maggie liked to convince herself she had a heart of stone, but George knew better. He'd broken her heart in high school, and sure, that was a long time ago. But he could still remember how it had felt when she'd looked at him, her eyes dry and devastated. He'd never stopped regretting that he'd lost her love.

In the end, though, he'd gained her friendship, and he'd be damned if he stood by and watched her get hurt.

She'd slept with Keegan. She'd loaned him a car. The Jag, George thought, his jaw clenching. Even though Maggie would have denied it meant anything, George knew better. She didn't give herself casually, and she never played fast and loose with her machinery.

Somehow Keegan had worked his way around her walls. But George had a trick or two up his sleeve.

He found a quiet corner at the end of the bar farthest from the tables and juke box and pulled out his cell phone, waiting impatiently as it rang a half dozen times before the call connected.

"He's been here a couple weeks already," George said. "Made no progress." Well, he amended privately, Dex had gotten his hands on Meeker's journals—or rather Maggie had. But that was immaterial—the journals wouldn't help Keegan. If there'd been anything useful to be found there, Meeker would have made something out of them. God knew he'd tried hard enough. "It's time to call this off. Eugenia couldn't possibly have survived the explosion."

The voice on the other end of the call sounded groggy and testy. "I need to be sure."

George clenched his jaw once, relaxed it. "The cops and Feds couldn't find her eighty years ago."

He heard a soft, derisive puff of laughter. "The local police botched the investigation, probably on purpose because they were on the payroll of those disgusting rum-runners. And the Federal Agents were no better."

"Then send someone else, someone with more experience."

"No."

"What makes you think Keegan is the right man for this?"

"He's gotten under your skin, hasn't he?"

Again, George had to take few seconds. "I just don't like the way he's doing his job," he said when he could keep his voice cool and even. "It seems to me he's stirring the pot more than anything else."

"Well, this pot is big and old, and I imagine if it's stirred long enough all sorts of interesting things will rise to the top."

"Someone rifled his room," George allowed.

"There you go. Any idea who did it?"

"Could be just about anybody. And there's no saying it was connected with Eugenia."

"So find the culprit and you'll have your answer."

Maybe so, George thought as he ended the call, but he'd see to it that Keegan didn't do any more damage than necessary. To any islander.

He stepped back into the noise and activity, took a long, slow look around, then made his way to the other end of the bar. "Hey, Mort," he said, taking the stool next to Maggie's handyman.

"What?" Mort said sullenly.

"Let's talk about Dex Keegan."

Chapter Seventeen

Relationship, huh.

Relations, yes, Maggie mused; relationship, no. That word scared the hell out of her, but nobody in their right mind would call one night in the sack—no matter how good it might have been—a relationship, especially when the rest of her interactions with Dex Keegan consisted of one kind of disagreement or another. So why did she still feel like jumping in her Piper or Twinstar and soaring to a place where there was just her and empty blue sky?

She hadn't known how to act around Dex, and that was new to her. It wasn't like he was her first lover; why the hell did she feel so . . . shy? She was never shy. And why had she watched him so closely, at least when he wasn't looking; why had she studied his expressions, parsed his words? What the hell had she been looking for?

The questions swirled in her mind, spinning around until she realized she didn't actually want the answers. Best, she decided, to put an end to that part of their—ha, ha—relationship, and go on like nothing had ever happened, or rather like it had meant nothing. Absolutely nothing. He was a man, she was a woman; they'd had sex, end of story.

But she very much worried it wasn't the end of the story. And when she wondered just what kind of a story she might be spinning in her head, it gave her a sick feeling in her stomach. She didn't think there was any outrunning that feeling, but she had to try.

She pulled open her front door and found Jessi, fist raised to knock.

"Jeez," she said, slapping a hand over her heart.

"Why are you so edgy?"

Maggie tried to give Jessi a shrug, felt both shoulders go up. And stay up. Edgy was a good word for what she felt—not that she'd admit it. "What are you doing here?"

"I, uh," she edged to one side to look past Maggie, into the house. "Where's Dex's genealogist?"

"Sleeping, as far as I know."

"What's the deal with him, anyway?"

Maggie stepped outside, pulled the door shut behind herself. "Dex hasn't told me anything about him."

Jessi sighed.

The very fact that she wouldn't push or pry made Maggie's mind up for her. She walked over, rested her butt against the railing of her front porch. "Dex is here to solve the Stanhope kidnapping," she said before she could talk herself down. She felt immediately as if a weight had been lifted from her chest.

It took a minute to sink in, then Jessi looked over at her. "That's why he called in a genealogist. You'd better tell me the whole story, Mags."

Maggie smiled, gave Jessi a come-along tip of the head and waited for her to settle on the bench close by. "I shouldn't have kept it from you."

"You had to promise Dex you wouldn't tell anyone, right?" She nodded a heartbeat after Maggie did. "What choice did you have?"

"Dex isn't going to be happy I told you now."

"His happiness isn't the point, is it? I mean, he came here looking for evidence of that poor baby…Jesus." She reached out, caught Maggie's wrist in a bruising grip. "I just got the rest of the picture. He thinks the kidnappers came from Windfall Island."

"No, Jess, he doesn't think that. At least he didn't say that to me. He found a clue that could mean Eugenia Stanhope ended up here somehow."

"I thought…Wasn't she killed when that ship blew up?"

"There's no proof of that."

"She might have lived." Jessi sank forward, resting her head on her knees for a moment before lifting it again, eyes wide and swimming with a host of emotions. "There could be someone on Windfall who doesn't know they're a member of one of the wealthiest and most important families on the east coast."

"It might be you," Maggie said.

Jessi covered her mouth, laughing a little. "I could be a millionaire and not even know it. Just think what you could do with that kind of money. Just think what any one of us could do."

"You can have it."

"Are you saying you'd turn it down?"

"I'm saying I'm happy with the way things are." Maggie looked out over the airport, loving every one of its weathered buildings, its landing strips in need of a good repaving, its rocky shores and the choppy gray-blue water of Temptation Bay. A storm had passed through during the night, thunder and lightning and rain that seemed to have washed the sun and the sky clean. "I've been thinking of turning over another five percent to you. You deserve it, Jess."

"Maggie, no. I just answer the phones and keep the books, and you already pay me too much as it is. Solomon Charters is what it is because of your hard work."

"Not entirely." But she'd started with nothing, and built this place. It might not look like much, but it was hers. She didn't want some big city folks galloping in on what they'd see as white chargers, thinking they could buy her life away from her just because she had their blood and they had half the money on the planet.

"Maybe..." Jessi stood, paced a little away, then turned back. "Maybe I could work with this Abbot guy. He won't be able to do a genealogy of the island without a local's help, right?"

Maggie smiled. "That's a hell of an idea, Jess."

"Good." Jessi exhaled explosively. "That's good. It won't seem so, I don't know, like my life is about to explode, if I can be part of the investigation."

"Explode is a good way to put it." Maggie scrubbed both hands over her face and back through her hair. She considered, seriously considered, telling Jessi to keep her name off the damned thing. Which wouldn't be fair to Jessi, she decided almost immediately, asking her to lie. "A genealogy will be a big help, and you're right about Abbot. He won't accomplish anything on his own."

She'd just have to keep an eye on the thing, Maggie told herself, decide how to deal with it when it became necessary. And yeah, that was procrastination at its finest, but hopefully, before then she'd find a way to tell Dex the truth about her own origins. And if not, well, he could hardly have expected her to confide in a stranger who'd been keeping his own secrets.

"I imagine Dex will be here sometime this morning. We'll tell him then."

"You two have been spending a lot of time together."

"Yeah, well, we've been working."

"All night?"

"Look, the only reason Dex told me the truth about Eugenia Stanhope is that he needed me to get the island journals from Meeker."

That wiped the smirk off Jessi's face, replaced it with sympathy. "He wouldn't have asked you if he knew, Maggie."

"Yeah." She shrugged it off. Dealing with Meeker was never pleasant, but she knew how to handle it. "We've been going through them, trying to find any hint of Eugenia."

"And?"

"I can tell you how many ships were salvaged in 1892, what the cargo was, and how it was awarded, right down to the last ballast stone. We haven't found a trace of Eugenia yet. Hell, we haven't even found a journal that dates from the 1930s."

"You might not," Jessi said.

"We know that, too, but we have to try."

And that meant hours spent in very close quarters with Dex Keegan. And this desire for him that she couldn't seem to shake.

As soon as Dex saw the last of the village in his rearview, he punched it, screaming down the first straightaway, then working the gears and the clutch as the road climbed and curved around the rocky shoreline. The sky overhead was as brilliant a blue as Maggie's eyes, the Atlantic to his left a deeper blue, restless as it dashed itself against the shore, foaming over the smooth stones or shooting high in spumes of white.

Maggie would probably be pissed as hell if she knew he

was driving so recklessly, but what Maggie didn't know, he thought as he came around a low hill—

And saw the road completely blocked by a jagged pile of rocks.

He swerved by reflex, fought the wheel, the car going into a spin and slide that left him pointing at the wide ocean, fronted by the jagged rocks that studded practically every inch of the island's coastline.

Dex had a split second to make a decision, punch the gas and fly, if he was lucky, over those lethal points of stone. And hope like hell he could get out of the car before it sank. Or he could try to keep the car on the road, and away from yet more lethal rock that would end him just as surely in a vehicle built before airbags were even dreamed of.

Before he'd finished the thought, he'd already punched the gas and spun the wheel, taking the car out of the spin. Then he jammed on the brakes, all but stood on them, praying Maggie had been as fastidious there as she'd been with the engine. The tires bit into the road's surface with the shriek and smoke of burning rubber, the car sliding, sliding, and shuddering to a stop barely inches from catastrophe.

He sat there a second, heart pounding, replaying that split-second, and realizing he'd actually missed the rocks. It wasn't just wishful thinking. He blew out a breath, felt his mouth curve.

And then he thought about Maggie. "Shit," he said, pulling out his cell, hitting speed dial before he could let a single one of the dozen voices crowding his mind—each with a valid excuse—talk him out of the inevitable.

"Solomon Charters," the voice—Maggie's voice—said, sounding just irritated enough to tell him she knew who was calling, even before she added, "You're late."

"Yeah? Well, I'm not getting there any time soon," Dex

said, relaying his predicament. The line went dead before he finished, without Maggie having said a word. Dex figured she'd make up for it when they were face to face.

"You think that was a ride?" he muttered to himself as he climbed out of the Jag. "Just wait until Maggie gets here."

Sure enough, barely five minutes passed before he caught the sound of an engine approaching, heard rubber squeal from the other side of the rocks tumbled across the road. Maggie appeared at the lowest point of the rock slide, slipping as she clambered over, but not stopping to see what kind of damage she'd done to the shin she barked on the rocks.

Her feet hit the pavement, her eyes met his, and for a minute, for one incredible, heart-stopping minute, he thought she was going to throw herself into his arms. Her feet took her to the car instead. And Dex called himself a fool.

She took a long, hard look at the tiny space between the Jag and the rocks, then bent to run her hands over the front of the hood, down to the bumper.

She got on her hands and knees, then her belly, swearing long and loud as she stared under the car. "Oil pan's toast." She shoved herself up to her knees, sat back on her heels, and glared at him.

"I was there, too," Dex reminded her, stung.

"Any fool can see you're all right."

He pretended to wipe away a tear. "Your concern is touching."

"Do you know how many hours I've put into this car?"

"A hell of a lot more than you've spent with me," he said, telling himself it was stupid to be jealous of an automobile, even one as amazing as a '54 Jag Roadster. Then she stroked her hand over the hood again and every muscle in him clenched. "You and the car want to be alone?"

She rose to her feet, and this time, her focus was all for him. And not in a good way. The heat from that fulminating look was enough to rock him back. He stepped forward instead, moved in on her.

Maggie slapped both hands on his chest, shoved him back a step. And he let her, because he saw more than anger in her brilliant blue eyes.

"What the hell were you thinking?"

Dex stuffed his hands in his pockets because he didn't know what to do with them, except he was pretty sure putting them on her was a bad idea. She didn't want to admit she was feeling even a little concern for him, and if he did push her to say it, what the hell was he supposed to say back when he wasn't exactly sure how he felt about her? Thank you?

"I rebuilt that engine," she said. "I know what it can do. Tell me you weren't trying to find out."

She whirled and paced off, not waiting for an answer. She stopped with her eyes on the roadblock, and when she turned back she seemed calmer, marginally. "This happens once in a while. Anyone with half a brain is careful coming around the curves."

"You mean like you were the other day when you took this road about ninety miles an hour?"

"I know where the most likely trouble spots are. We were heading into town, and I didn't take this road. I took the one on the sheltered side of the island."

"It's straighter," Dex allowed. And if memory served there weren't as many outcroppings high enough to spill into the roadway when Mother Nature decided they'd stood long enough. Or maybe Mother Nature was being falsely accused in this particular instance. Maybe Mother Nature had gotten some help.

"What?"

He looked up, thought about putting Maggie off, just until he could give the situation more thought.

"You're wondering if this was an accident," she said, before he had to decide whether or not to lie to her. "I'm the only person on Windfall who knows why you're here. Me and your genealogist. And your employer."

"None of them want me dead."

"Hell, I've wanted you dead a couple of times, and I barely know you."

"There's a lot of money at stake, Maggie. One of the Stanhopes might think it's a better idea to leave the past alone in order to secure a brighter future for themselves."

Maggie's hands fisted, then opened before she shoved them into pockets. "It has to be an accident. No matter what the people here think of you, nobody on Windfall would do this where Mort or Jessi or I could happen along and get hurt. And if they did, the only way to create this kind of mess is dynamite.

"And even if the village is too far away to hear a small blast, there's always someone at the airport—Jessi during the day, but I live there—and Mort has a room at the hangar for when there are early-morning or late-night flights."

"There was a storm last night. It could've been done under the cover of thunder."

She shook her head. "I think I'd have noticed."

"All it would have taken is a small charge. Just enough to shift the supporting rocks at the bottom of the pile." Dex walked around the rockslide, studying it with new eyes. If there'd been any sort of charge, there'd be smaller rocks and dirt blown all over the damn place. Except, he reminded himself, it had rained hard last night. The roadway would have been washed clean of dirt and small rocks, made it look more like a natural occurrence. His gut didn't buy it. Too much of a coincidence that it had happened at that particular spot on a road only he or Maggie would be likely to use. "A couple of M-80s would have done the trick. Those are big firecrackers."

"I know what M-80s are," Maggie shot back. She crossed her arms, clearly troubled. "Your room was searched and now this. You think it was deliberate?"

The itch between his shoulder blades sure as hell did. "I don't believe in coincidences."

"So what do you think was the point?"

"I don't know. It feels more like a warning than an attempt to cause harm."

"Tell that to my car."

Chapter Eighteen

The short ride to the airport was quiet and tense. When they arrived, Maggie slammed out of the car and stomped off without giving Dex so much as a backward glance.

Best to let her cool down, he decided, aiming himself toward her house and the mound of paperwork that waited inside. Just as he was climbing the steps Holden Abbot, complete with his trademark smart-aleck smile, stepped out onto the porch.

"Good to see you, Dex," he said in his lazy Southern drawl. "Alec tells me you've got yourself some trouble here."

Dex shook the hand Hold offered, but his eyes strayed to Maggie, disappearing into a small building that looked like a tool shed. "That's putting it mildly."

"You're not going after the lady pilot?"

"I've grown attached to my head. I'm afraid she's looking for something to take it off with." As if her temper wasn't enough.

"What did you do?"

Dex pulled his gaze back, smiled a little. "I'm wondering that myself. She loaned me a car—"

"'54 Jag Roadster. I heard. That's a lady takes her machinery seriously."

"There was a rockslide on the road in from town, around a blind curve."

"And you had her opened up, right?"

Now Dex grinned. He couldn't help himself. "Point is, I managed to miss the rocks and the ocean."

"So, is she upset about her car, or about you?"

Dex stared after her again. "If she was concerned about me, she did a good job of hiding it."

"Well now, she would, wouldn't she? A woman never likes to tip her hand on her feelings. 'Least not before the man she has feelings for does."

Now there was a concept that had never crossed his mind. Maggie had made it clear she wasn't in this thing for the long haul. Hell, she couldn't wait to see the back of him. It occurred to him now, though, that perhaps she was protesting a little too much. And now that it had, it didn't mean the subject was open for discussion. "I'm not here for romance."

Hold took a seat in a rattan chair, crossed one ankle over the opposite knee. The expression on his face was... skeptical.

"Do you want to invent a love life for me, or talk about why you're here?"

"Why can't I do both?"

Because, Dex thought, Hold couldn't begin to imagine what was going on between him and Maggie. Hell, Dex couldn't figure it out himself. "I'm working on the Stanhope kidnapping," was what he said. "Still want to talk about romance?"

But he already had his answer, because Hold surged to his feet, grabbing his head with both hands.

"I thought that would get your attention." Dex had known Hold Abbot for a handful of years. They'd never worked together, but a case like this had to be the Holy Grail to a genealogist.

"The family thinks Eugenia survived the kidnapping?"

"They'd like an answer once and for all," Dex said.

Hold whistled between his teeth. "The Stanhopes could be running on hope. But you don't think so."

"I think it's possible she lived, but not likely."

"And yet here you are," Hold said. "If Eugenia is alive, it'll make your career."

"It will make my career either way."

"Only if you solve it."

"We," Dex said. "If we solve it."

Hold tipped his head, gave the idea some thought. "I can do a genealogy," he said at length. "Shouldn't be too difficult, seeing as I only have to go back a couple of generations."

"You don't know these people. First off, they don't keep records, and even if they did, they won't share them with you."

"But I'm so damned charming," Hold said with a grin.

"Yeah, the women will appreciate that, the men will want to shoot you."

"Damn, son, how do you expect me to accomplish such a Herculean task?"

"Jessi Randal, Maggie's partner. She doesn't know anything about this yet, but I know she'll be willing to help. And Maggie trusts her, so that's good enough for me."

Hold pursed his lips in a way that told Dex he was considering his next words carefully.

"Spit it out."

"I told Jessi I'm a genealogist."

"You told—" Dex ran a hand back through his hair.

"Could you keep your profession—hell, keep everything to yourself except your name."

"Sure," Hold said in the same good-natured drawl. His eyes told a different story about his mood. "I'll hold my conversations to my companion's health and the weather."

Dex sucked in a breath, let it out. "I know you think I'm crazy, but Windfall Island is . . . unique. And there's a lot of money involved. If the islanders get wind of it—"

"I get the picture." Hold smiled, at ease again. "Don't reveal my profession to the locals."

"This local already knows," Maggie said, coming up the steps. "And since I'm a definite minority, you might want to think about that before you discuss it out in the wide open where anyone can sneak up on you."

Hold gave a little shake of his head. "I wasn't prepared for this to be a . . . situation."

"That's one way to put it," Dex muttered. He turned to Maggie. "What about Jessi?"

"If you want to know if she can be trusted, the answer is yes. If you're asking how much she knows, she knows everything because I told her. And before you say something you'll regret, I just heard you say you were going to tell her anyway."

"You didn't know that when you went back on your word."

She met his gaze, hers hardening. "Keeping it from her is one thing, lying when she asks me point blank? Never going to happen." Her eyes shifted to Hold, who, for the first time, looked a little shamefaced. "If you didn't want her to know, you should have muzzled Southern Comfort here."

"You could have said something to him on the trip in from the mainland."

"I could have. But you made it crystal clear you were running the show, so I figured you'd gagged him already."

Yeah, she was pissed off at him, Dex thought. He wasn't feeling too forgiving himself at the moment. "I hope you asked her to keep it quiet."

"I didn't have to. She knew without being told what kind of fallout there'd be if your purpose got out, not to mention she's been on the wrong side of island gossip enough to steer clear of it."

"Now," Hold said, "There's a story there."

"It's Jessi's story," Maggie said coolly before she turned back to Dex. "You really ought to stop underestimating people."

"Knee-jerk," Dex said. "The last few years haven't exposed me to the nobler side of humanity."

Maggie shook her head, seemed to relent a little. "Windfall hasn't raised your opinion much, what with our penchant for gossip."

"I take it you don't indulge," Hold said. "Else Dex wouldn't have confided in you."

Maggie sent Dex an arch look. "I didn't give him much of a choice."

"I do love a woman who knows her own mind." Hold took her hand, lifted it to his lips.

Dex's irritation notched up a couple more degrees, especially when Maggie laughed, a low, flirtatious sound that grated along the nerves she'd already scraped to hell and back.

"I have a feeling I'm going to like you," Maggie said to Hold.

"That's good, because I already like you."

"If you two are done bonding," Dex scowled, "maybe we can get back to the reason Don Juan here showed up in the first place."

"Absolutely," Maggie said. "Right after I deal with business."

*   *   *

She'd spied Mort crossing the wide expanse of open area between the office and her house, a weed whacker in his hands. Maggie clattered down the steps, her stomach still tied in knots so tight it was a wonder she could stand upright, let alone keep it from showing on her face. Hold's easy humor and friendly manner had helped, but she could still remember her first glimpse of the Roadster, sideways across the road, its front bumper mere inches from the rocks, its front tires a hairsbreadth from the edge of the sheer drop-off into the ocean.

It wasn't the car she'd been worried about.

Sure, she'd checked the Jag for dents and scratches, but only to keep from throwing herself into Dex's arms, running her hands over him instead. And giving her feelings away to him. It was more than she could stand just to admit to herself she'd done anything as stupid as fall—as develop feelings for Dex Keegan.

What she could do, all she could do, was to get through this insanity Dex had brought with him to Windfall, and remember that Solomon Charters would be her life long after Dex Keegan had left the island—and her—behind.

"Saw you come out of the tool shed," Mort said in his economical way. "Figured you were looking for me." He gave Dex and Hold a passing glance, then seemed to put them out of mind.

Mort wasn't what Maggie would have called a sociable person. Hell, he made her look like the life of the party. But he was dependable. "There's a rockslide about five miles out on the east road."

Mort slipped his hands into his pockets, his plain face placid as he mulled that over. "Wasn't there this morning."

"What time did you come in?"

"'Bout five, give or take."

"That's pretty early," Dex observed.

He could have been the wind for all Mort noticed, so Maggie answered instead. "He arranged it a couple of days ago because he wanted to get off early today."

"Why?"

"Dex," Maggie murmured, but her eyes were on Mort's face, and she could see he'd taken offense. "Get the little tractor and go shift those rocks off the road," she said to him.

He sent Dex a final dark look then took himself away.

"He's taking his mother to the mainland this afternoon," Maggie said to Dex, "She's starting chemotherapy in the morning. And I'm only telling you this to shut you up."

"And make me feel like a heel."

"Don't beat yourself up. You didn't know." She swung around and clattered back up the stairs, giving Dex a wide berth. She would have preferred to send him packing; she could have used some time alone to deal with… everything.

Instead, she walked straight through the house and back to the dining room, figuring to put Dex and Hold to work on the journals.

And caught Jessi elbow deep in paper.

Maggie sighed; she wasn't going to get so much as a moment to herself, at least not in the next little while. And if she ever got that moment, she was really, really going to need it.

"Find anything interesting?" Dex said to Jessi.

Her gaze shot to Maggie. "I, um…" She flicked a glance at Hold, then turned to face Dex, squaring her shoulders. "Maggie told me why you're here, and I'm going to help. Whether you like it or not."

"Okay."

"Okay?" Maggie took a couple of deep breaths, working hard to rein in the temper that had nowhere to go. "You were mad five minutes ago. Now it's okay?"

"I wasn't mad; you jumped to conclusions."

He just stood there, a slight smile on his face, and here she was, spoiling for a fight. "I went back on my word, you said. It was stupid of me to give you my word, at least where Jessi is concerned, which is why I didn't keep it. We'd be even stupider not to let Jessi help with the genealogy because we all know that nobody is going to willingly talk to Hold—no offense, it's just that you're an outsider, and why are you grinning like an idiot," she finished, her eyes narrowing on Dex's outrageously amused face.

"I think that's more words than you've spoken to me in all the time since we met."

"So?"

"So, I think it's cute that I make you nervous."

"You don't make me nervous."

"Yes, I do. You don't like making me mad."

Maggie threw her hands up. "You are mad, crazy as a loon."

"Maybe, but you broke your promise."

"You conned me into making it in the first place," she grumbled.

"I used logic."

"You used manipulation."

"Maybe a little." He grinned even wider. It was infuriating.

Maggie punched him in the arm.

He grabbed her. "I told you what would happen the next time you hit me."

"Then let me make it worthwhile."

But Dex was already wrapped around her, his arms banding hers to her sides, his legs bracketing hers... and he was aroused as she was. She'd be damned if she let him know it. "I still have teeth," she said, and tried to sink them into his biceps.

"Ouch. Damn it, Maggie." He overbalanced her, took them both to the floor. But she fought like hell to keep him from incapacitating her again.

"Maybe we should leave," Hold said, his voice cutting through Maggie's anger.

There was still a red haze crowding her vision, but it was embarrassment now.

"Man, it was just getting good," Jessi said. "Why did you have to open your mouth and ruin it?"

Because Dex had gone as still as she had, and because he was draped over her like a hundred and eighty pounds of sandbag, she shoved at him with every ounce of strength she possessed. "Get off me."

He did, climbing to his feet then holding a hand down to her. She took it, let him help her up, and stared back at her audience, one eyebrow lifted, daring them to comment.

Hold just stood there, grinning hugely.

Jessi huffed out a breath. "Great, the first interesting thing that's happened around here in years and Charm Boy with his pretty southern manners has to go and ruin it."

"Sugar," Hold said to Jessi, "if you want exciting, stick with me."

"I'd rather eat a cake of soap. Lye soap. The whole thing."

"Well, now, I hope you get to like the taste of it, because from the sound of things, we're going to be spending a lot of time with one another. You and I. Together."

Still grinning like a lunatic, Hold slipped his hands in his pockets and rocked back on his heels.

Maggie worked hard not to smile, especially when Jessi, irritated and more than a little frantic, appealed to her.

"Do we really need him, Maggie? I mean, it can't be that complicated to draw a bunch of squares and circles and write names inside them."

"There's more to a genealogy than that. Especially when you're tracing a whole community."

"Windfall isn't that big," Jessi insisted. "Maggie, tell him. There can't be a hundred families, if you go right back to the salvaging times."

"We don't have to go back that far," Dex said, "but time is an issue. The longer it takes to solve this, the more likely my reason for being here will get out, especially with Kentucky Joe and his big mouth. And then we'll have a problem on our hands."

"Now, I'm about done with all the name-calling and insults," Hold said. "If Dex'd made secrecy a matter of record, I'd've taken more care with what I said." He looked at Jessi. "And who I said it to."

"And I'd still be in the dark," Jessi said.

"Truth is," Dex said to her, "I'd already decided to ask for your help with the genealogy. It'll be much easier for you to gather information than Hold."

"In other words, I was right," Maggie said.

"Sure, we can use those words, if that's what's important to you."

Maggie shot Dex a cocky smile. "Right at this moment? Yeah. And you haven't actually said the words yet."

Dex grinned back. "Make me."

"Jeez," Jessi groaned. "Can't the two of you put your hormones on hold for five minutes? Have some pity for the celibate in the room."

Hold swung around and gave her a long, intent study.

"Oh, don't be such a...a man," she snapped at him. "Won't it create suspicion if I go around asking everyone for their family lineage?"

"She's got a point," Maggie said. "Suspicion is kind of a way of life around here."

"Then don't ask," Dex said. "I'm sure you can go back at least a generation on your own, and Maggie and I will keep working on the journals."

Jessi looked over at Hold, her eyes narrowing when she caught him grinning at her. "Fine," she bit off. "What do we do if we find anyone likely?"

"We'll cross that bridge when we have to."

"There are no bridges on Windfall," Jessi pointed out. "We won't have anywhere to run when everyone finds out what we've been up to."

"We don't need a bridge," Maggie said coolly. "I can fly."

Chapter Nineteen

Hold took himself off to sweet-talk Jessi into working with him on the genealogy. Maggie stood there for a moment, staring at Dex, daring him to say a word.

Wisely, he turned toward the table, with its stacks of papers. His expression could best be described as resignation.

"Unfortunately, they're not going anywhere," Maggie said.

Dex took his customary seat. "Neither am I."

"Unfortunately." She said it with a slight smile and enough sarcasm to let him know she was kidding. Mostly. When she slid into the chair opposite his, she knew her need for distance wasn't lost on him.

But he let it go.

She chose a stack of papers at random. Dex pulled over the yellow legal pad they were using to classify the journals and assigned it a number. Maggie wrote the number on the top page and, with a bolstering sigh, began to leaf through the pages, skimming for meaningful words or phrases.

She didn't get far.

"What?"

She realized she'd gone still, but all she could seem to

do was stare, dumbstruck, just her eyes flying back and forth across the page.

"Out loud," Dex ordered.

She held up a hand, and when her eyes lifted to his, she could see he'd caught her excitement. " 'They anchor off shore out of the reach of the Coast Guard, filled with liquid gold, for that's what the mainlanders will pay when someone else is willing to take the risk.' "

Maggie flipped backward, scanning the pages until she found the beginning of the passage, then reading so fast the words blurred together. "It talks about the ships sailing down from Canada or up from the Indies," she paraphrased.

"All that money was sliding right by Windfall Island and into Portland, while the people here could barely afford to feed their children. Ironic that running booze provided what the government couldn't."

"The 18th Amendment was passed in October of 1919," Dex said, staying on point. "Eugenia went missing in thirty-one. Any idea when that was written?"

"The passages are only dated with month and day, but I'd say this takes place a good ways into Prohibition. From what I can tell the crews were fairly well established." The room went silent but for the whisper of paper as Maggie leafed through the pages, looking for a date. "Here," she said about halfway through the stack of copies, "January, 1928. This ends in the spring of that year."

Dex reached across the table, pulling the top sheet from her discard pile. When she saw him sorting through the journal copies, comparing the handwriting with the other journal copies, she did the same. By the time they were finished, they'd come up with five more possibilities.

Maggie took the copies and placed them side by side. Dex came around the table to look over her shoulder, but she barely noticed, caught up in the puzzle. She flipped through the pages, finding enough dates to put them in what she thought was the correct order.

"This one," she placed her right hand on the copy second from the end, "should include the time of the kidnapping."

She handed Dex the copies. "You read, I'll take notes."

He held her eyes for a few, humming seconds.

"It's your case."

Dex nodded, then handed her a legal pad before seating himself in the chair next to hers. It didn't take him long.

"There was a measles epidemic," he said somberly, reading a list of names, children who'd died in the summer and fall of 1931, when Eugenia had been taken from her nursery in Boston.

"You're not writing. You okay? Maggie?"

She rubbed her aching eyes, said, "Give me the names again." But she put her pen down before he could. "You know, the genealogy isn't just a tool for you to solve the kidnapping, it's for the island, too. These children are gone, but they had families."

"You're right. But hiding the truth from them doesn't solve anything."

"I just... You need to be really sure before you open the door to this kind of pain." She took the pages from him and began to write, the scratch of her pen disturbing the tense silence.

"Can you tell who wrote it?" Dex asked when she was finished.

Maggie started a little. She'd forgotten he was there, but now all she could seem to think about was the heat of him so close beside her, the scent of his skin, the way it made her nerves tremble to know his eyes were on her.

She got to her feet, taking the excuse to put a little distance between them as she began to check the first and last pages of the journals they were working with. "I don't see a name, and I made sure to copy everything with writing on it, even the front and back covers."

"And she's back behind her walls."

She rounded on him, but made sure to stay a safe distance away. "Excuse me?"

"Where's the woman who was nearly in tears reading about a bunch of dead kids you didn't even know?"

"What good do my tears do them and their families?"

"I'm not letting you freeze me out."

Maggie backed away from him. It mortified her, but it would be even more embarrassing to throw herself at him. "You just want to have sex."

He grinned. "I wouldn't mind seeing that tattoo again. I don't think I took the time to properly appreciate it before."

"That's where my heart is."

He kept coming, taking his time as he circled her around the table. "Warning me or reminding yourself?"

"You don't need warning and I don't need reminding."

"Are you sure?"

She didn't bother to ask him if he referred to himself or to her or to both of them. She just wanted him to go away and stop asking questions that made her think about things she didn't want to think about. Like her feelings for him. "We should take the list over to the office. Hold and Jessi can start with these families."

That stopped him. He held her gaze another minute, but he quit stalking her. The case, she thought, took precedence over everything else.

She probably should have been more grateful.

*   *   *

Hold looked at the list briefly, then handed it over to Jessi. "You're thinking it's possible, if Eugenia was brought to Windfall, that she might have replaced one of the kids who died from the measles," Hold said.

"Insensitive jerk," Jessi sniffled.

"Jess."

Hold put up a hand. "It's not that I don't feel for these people, Jessi. I don't know them personally like you do."

Jessi sniffed again, but she relented enough to glance over at Hold. "If Eugenia took the place of a baby that died, wouldn't the family have hidden it completely? What I mean is, maybe the name isn't on this list at all."

Dex crossed his arms and leaned back against the wall. "I can see it being kept from the mainland, but do you really think nobody in the Windfall community would know, or at least figure it out?"

"It was coming onto winter," Hold said. "With an epidemic like measles, people would have been keeping to themselves even more than usual."

"To prevent the sick and recovering children from being exposed to more illness," Maggie said, "Flu, bronchitis, even a common cold would have been devastating to an already weakened system. By the time spring came around six, seven months later, if Eugenia was switched with a baby close to her own age, it's likely no one would have noticed a difference."

"We can't know until we rule out the names on this list," Hold put in.

"So we'll start there," Jessi said, raising her voice as the radio squawked. She looked over at Maggie. "Are you expecting anyone?"

"No." Maggie crossed the room, picked up the mouthpiece,

and answered with Windfall Island's code, feeling her heart stop at the response.

"Maggie?" Jessi laid a hand on her shoulder.

"It's a military helicopter, ten minutes out."

"Tell the pilot he can't land here."

"I can't refuse privileges, Jess. I won't."

"But—"

"He's not the entire military." She picked up the radio and gave them the go-ahead to land.

"I can tell him you're not here."

"Your father?" Dex asked.

Maggie ignored him, sharing a long look with Jessi. She was tempted, truly tempted. "I won't let him make a liar out of you, Jess," she finally said, starting for the door. "Or a coward out of me."

Dex stepped in front of her, took her by the arm. "Talk to me, Maggie."

She shook him off, and after a speaking look to Jessi, she kept walking. Jessi stayed where she was and kept Hold with her. Dex Keegan, on the other hand, couldn't have cared less for her preferences.

He fell into step with her, forced her to stop in the empty lobby and deal with him. "Take a hint, Keegan."

"You won't tell me what's going on, and I won't find out by staying inside."

"Not everything that happens on this island is your business."

"You're my business, Maggie."

She snorted softly. "Typical man. Give him a little affection, spend a night in his bed, and he thinks he can tell you what to do."

"I spent the night in your bed," Dex shot back. "I can't say I recall there being a lot of affection involved."

"On either side."

Her famous temper was in full bloom, but so was his. "Damn it, Maggie, why can't you, just once, open up? Tell me what's wrong."

"You think barking at me is going to get you what you want?" She made a disgusted sound in the back of her throat. "I grew up being intimidated by the best."

"My old man was military, too. They can be tough on their kids."

She paced away, wrapped her arms around her waist, so cold and empty she felt like she'd collapse into the void where her heart should be if she didn't hold on tight.

"What about your mother?"

"What about her? She was so beaten down—"

"He hit her?" Dex started for the door, realized there was no one to take his temper out on yet, and came back. "He hit you?"

"No, he didn't hit my mother, and he only slapped me once when I was sixteen. I ran away."

Dex moved in, silent and cold, furiously cold. She couldn't worry about his anger now. She needed all her strength for the confrontation to come, and she wouldn't be doing any of them a favor—especially not Dex—by letting him go off on her father.

Phillip Solomon was nothing more than hot air and bluster when it came to his lone offspring, if only because he knew it would reflect badly on him. He'd have no selfish reasons to pull his punches toward a man foolish enough to defend her. No matter what she felt for Dex, she wouldn't have him on her conscience because he felt sorry for her.

"If you could step off," she began.

Dex blinked once, only just seeming to realize he'd backed her up against the wall. He took one step away, then another, woodenly because, she decided, he was still angry. But not with her.

"I'm sorry."

"What for? You're right about military men being hard on their children, but you were a boy."

"I have a sister," Dex said, his smile slight and fleeting. "He was easier on her."

She swallowed against the tightness in her throat. "Before I even understood what the word 'disappointment' meant, I knew I was one to my father. For starters, I was born a girl. When he noticed me at all, it was to let me know I was nothing, and would be nothing. The most I could aspire to was wife. I saw how well that worked out for my mother." She turned away, staring out the window. "She could never please him, either."

"She gave up," Dex said. "You never did."

"I don't know if she gave up. Sometimes I wish I'd known her before she met him. I wonder if maybe..." She broke off, shook herself out of the dream she'd had so often as a child. It came less and less now, and Maggie realized she'd given up—on her mother. Another sorrow she could have laid at her father's door. If she'd bothered to keep a tally.

"He tore her down, year after year, until she thought even less of herself than he did. She didn't think of me much at all. I was her failure, you see. She didn't give him a son. He never let her forget it. It was just too bad for him that I had more of him in me than was good for either of us.

"After I ran away, he found me and sent my mother and me here. For her it was exile, for me it was coming home."

"The tattoo was your way of rebelling."

She looked at him for the first time since he'd let her go. "I've always wanted the sky. I made the mistake of telling him about it once." Her smile turned sad. "I was young, young and hopeful enough to think what I wanted mattered to him. He laughed. So I set out to prove I could do it. It wasn't that difficult. He'd never cared enough to look at my report cards, or take an interest in me. It was only in public he made sure we appeared to be a real family."

She looked over at him. "You saw it the other day. He's a master at putting on a good show."

"It wasn't that good a show, Maggie."

"Not to anyone who looked closely." And Dex would have looked closely, even if it hadn't been her. He was that kind of man, the kind who looked beneath the surface. And when he found a wrong, he'd want to right it.

But there were just some wrongs that had to be fixed by the author, and Phillip Ashworth Solomon would no sooner admit he'd made a mistake than turn in his stars. "I talked a couple of the navy pilots into teaching me how to fly, and before I knew it I was a sort of mascot to them, the little girl who wanted the sky."

"They took you under their wings."

"Yes." The memory brought tears to her eyes. "It was the first time I understood... They were my fathers, Dex. Until Phillip got wind of what was going on."

"He wasn't happy about it."

"He was, actually. I had wings of my own by then, and a piece of paper that gave me the right to use them. The navy was pushing for female pilots at that time. Having a daughter in the program would have reflected well on him, and that would have furthered his career. But he wasn't about to share credit for it. He transferred every one of those pilots away."

"And you refused to go into the navy."

She banished the faces of those selfless young men

who'd rescued her, even if they'd never known it, all those years ago. "I told you I was like him. Spiteful, vindictive, I knew just how to hurt him and I didn't hesitate."

"Maggie—"

"I got the tattoo of wings just about where they'd be on a naval uniform and told him they were the closest he'd ever get."

"I've seen you fly, Maggie. You didn't get that tattoo out of spite. I'd say those wings are right where they're supposed to be."

"I've already told you the rest," she said, trying desperately not to think about the compliment he'd given her, how he seemed to understand her so deeply. She needed to be cold now, cold and hard and heartless.

"He tracked me down and sent my mother and me to Windfall until I got with his program. If she hadn't hated me before that, she did after. When I turned eighteen she left, went back to him. I stayed. I worked my fingers to the bone to buy my first plane—not just to spite him, but that was part of it. I always wanted to be a pilot, and I'd be damned before I let him screw that up for me. I just did it my way. Without him."

Dex didn't say anything, not that she gave him the opportunity. Now that she'd opened the floodgates, she was getting the whole sorry tale of her life out. No matter how much it broke her heart to say it out loud.

"Every time he's up for a promotion, he tries to use me to his advantage. I fly everything that defies gravity, and I'm not so old I couldn't still enter military service, so I can devote my life to being of use to him and whoever he decides to marry me off to." She rubbed at her arms, even more distressed at the notion of being trapped into marriage with one of her father's protégés.

Dex reached for her, but she stepped back, feeling so brittle she knew his sympathy would break her. She tipped her head and took a deep breath. She couldn't shatter yet.

It took a minute—Dex's ears weren't trained for the sound of aircraft, but he finally heard it, too.

"It sounds like a Huey," he said.

"It is." She squared her shoulders, lifted her chin. "Daddy's here."

Chapter Twenty

Maggie stepped out of the shadow of the office, not bothering to shield her eyes from the sun and wind. As the Huey landed a couple hundred yards away, Dex ranged himself beside her. She held herself like she was braced for a blow, and judging from what she'd told him, she'd get one. It wouldn't be a physical one, but there were worse ways to be wounded.

"You'll want to back up, out of the damage path," she said to Dex.

"I can take care of myself."

"So can I." But she didn't sound so sure of it, even to her own ears. "Admiral Phillip Ashworth Solomon, United States Navy," she said as he climbed out of the Huey. "I'd call him my father, but what he really is is the uniform."

"I've met his kind a time or two," Dex said.

"You've never met his kind," Maggie murmured as Admiral Solomon strode up and stopped a few paces away. His bearing was military, his jaw was locked, his attitude was slow burn.

He gave Dex a long, fulminating stare before he turned it on his daughter.

"Dex Keegan," Dex said, shifting a little to put himself in front of Maggie.

"What's your story, son," Solomon snapped out like an order. "You strike me as a man who's done his duty by his country."

"Army, Special Forces."

Solomon smiled for the first time, the smile going smug and satisfied when he shifted his eyes to his daughter and back again. "Well, now," he said. "That's fine."

"Whatever you're thinking, you can forget it," Maggie said, swiping Dex out of the way with the back of her hand. "I don't need a man to back me up, and I don't need one to stand in front of me."

"You don't need a man at all," her father scoffed. "Not even a father."

Maggie wanted to put her hands over her ears, to shut her eyes, to walk away. But she knew he wouldn't leave her alone until he'd had his say, and by God, she'd hold her head up while he did. Phillip Solomon only respected strength, and strength was what he'd see in her.

"I can't imagine you came all this way," she said coolly, "and took time out of your busy schedule, just so you could tell me what I already know."

"I wouldn't have to take the time, travel to this armpit of an island, if you'd bothered to take my calls."

"You could have taken the hint."

"How can you give me a hint when you won't talk to me?"

"Always so literal, Phillip."

"I told you not to call me that."

"Fine. Admiral, then."

"You used to call me Daddy."

"I was five. I didn't know what a disappointment I was yet."

Solomon sighed, braced his hands on his hips and looked around, clearly searching for patience.

"You haven't bothered to deny it."

"I didn't come here to argue with you, Maggie. You know what I want."

Maggie gave up any hope that this time he would hear her. "Joint Chiefs."

Solomon smiled. It was the first genuine pleasure she'd seen on his face since he'd arrived.

She'd never let him see how deeply it cut her. "If you came looking for a family to show off," she pointed up, "the exit is that way."

"I need my daughter."

"No. What you need, what you always wanted, was a son. That's the one thing I can't give you, even if I wanted to, and I'm done with atoning for an accident of birth I couldn't control and wouldn't change if I could."

"You should be flying for the navy," Solomon shot back. "You should have been one of a special few female naval pilots—you would be if you weren't punishing me for," he spread his hands, "for whatever the hell it is you think I've done to you."

Maggie just threw her hands up. What could you say when someone refused to listen?

"Just come down to Washington for a week—"

"Mom's there, and I'm sure you'll just spend all your time apologizing for me. Here's my daughter Maggie," she parroted. "Didn't go to college, didn't join the military. I couldn't even manage to land one of the uniforms you paraded in front of me and pop out a half dozen navy brats for you to add to your résumé."

Phillip Solomon stared at his daughter, looking sincerely puzzled. "Do you really think that's my opinion of you?"

"Not just think, I know."

"I've never said any of that, Maggie."

No, she thought, of course not. But the disappointment had been there in the way he spoke down to her, the grooves that dug into his distinguished features when she didn't toe the line. It was in every gesture and every word, even in the way her mother made excuses for him, blame by elimination because if it wasn't Phillip's fault then it must be hers. Until one day, Maggie recalled, she'd had enough.

One day she'd looked him in the face and told him he couldn't treat her like she was wrong, just for being. And because she'd had the temerity to challenge him in his own home, he'd kicked her out. She'd expected that reaction, but it still hurt to remember the way her mother had stood by, wringing her hands, and let her go without a word of farewell.

"I got the message loud and clear the morning I woke up and you and Mom were gone from the island."

"You were already half out the door."

But he could have stopped her. All he would have had to do was stand aside. Her mother would have ... what? Stood up for her? That was an empty hope, even if she'd never quite gotten past it.

"I won't be a prop in your quest to run the navy," she said to her father. "I won't sabotage you, either, but if you wanted to have the perfect family to parade in front of your cronies, you should have thought about that when it might have made a difference for all of us."

Phillip scrubbed a hand over his face. "I'm tired of this game you insist on playing."

"It's no game for me." It was her life, and she'd live it so she could look herself in the mirror every morning and not see her father's low opinion of her reflected back.

"Margaret," he began, abandoning attack to wheedle instead. "I need you to come to Washington. It's important."

"No."

"Whatever I did or didn't do—"

"It's not about you anymore, Phillip. I know that's hard for you to understand, but I've been an adult for a long time now. Since I was sixteen, to be exact."

"So you're still on that," he said, sounding dejected, another weapon in his arsenal, this one designed to arouse her sympathy.

And he did, God help her. It took every ounce of strength she possessed to stop herself from caving in. "You closed the door on me, remember? You can't just open it again because it's convenient for you."

"We could be a hell of a team, Margaret. It's a shame you hate me so much."

"Hate?" She shoved her hands back through her hair, clamping down viciously on the anger that wanted to erupt, the tears that wanted to flow. "I love you." *Despite everything.*

"Love is a weak emotion."

"No, it isn't. And not admitting it makes you a coward— worse than a coward if you can't even feel it."

"You're just being contrary."

"Contrary?" This time she laughed, though there was no joy in it. "Contrary would have been living my life to spite you, denying myself what I've always wanted just because it was part of the future you mapped out for me. I got the sky, but I got it my way.

"Contrary would be allowing the way I grew up to color everything in my life. I don't." She looked over at Dex for the first time. She'd already let her walls down, might as well get it all said. "I may be slow to trust, that doesn't mean I can't, and I'm careful where I love, because I won't give it with conditions or strings. Love isn't a tool to be used to get what I want. Love is something to give, and if you're very, very lucky, love comes back to you."

"So, you won't help me," was all Phillip said.

She smiled sadly, shook her head. "But I hope you'll come back when it's just about you and me."

"I won't ask again, Maggie, and your mother won't go against me."

"I know." She lifted her chin, met his eyes.

This time, Phillip Solomon was the one who looked away. "We're the only family you have."

"No, you're not. I have a family, not because they're blood, but because they love me." She gave him a beat, and called herself a fool for still hoping he'd bend enough for there to be a middle ground for her to meet him in.

He only turned on his heel and marched himself back to the Huey. He never looked back.

It struck her like a knife in the chest, though she understood that was exactly what he wanted. Even after all the years and all the effort she'd put into growing, becoming strong and making herself into a woman she could respect, it took so little to turn her into that small, wounded child again.

But only for a moment.

She'd convinced herself she didn't need anyone. Any man. She still believed that, but it would have been nice not to feel like it was her against the world. Even if she was the one who'd started the fight.

She turned, and there was Dex Keegan, standing at her side like the fulfillment of all her wants and needs.

But he was only another fantasy.

"Maggie," Dex began.

"Don't. Not one word."

"No, words aren't what's called for here." He moved in,

put his arms around her. "Let it go," he said, and left her no choice. The warmth of his body against hers, the intimacy of his breath feathering at her temple, the emotion rushing through her was so overwhelming that she couldn't deny what she felt for him. Love. There, she thought as she allowed herself to relax into his embrace, she'd said it, if only in the silence of her own mind.

She wrapped her arms around him and held on tight, letting go for once, borrowing his strength as the storm raged through her. She could have stayed there like that forever, letting him take care of her. If only it had been an option.

Dex Keegan, with his mystery and his hot looks and irritating and unwelcome interest, wasn't her salvation. The way he'd moved on her when she didn't want him to, the way he'd kept poking at her until she couldn't ignore how much she wanted him. And now, when she was feeling raw he stood there like a rock, one she couldn't hold onto just because she was raw and lonely.

She'd thought flying was her talent, but apparently she was a genius at impossible relationships. Her father would never love her for who she was.

And Dex, she thought as she eased out of his arms, might never love her at all. But even if he did, his life wasn't on Windfall Island.

Thank God, Maggie thought after her father was gone, that she didn't have to fly. With her nerves stretched to the breaking point, she didn't belong in a cockpit, ten thousand feet in the air. She belonged alone.

Dex still wasn't getting the hint.

He followed her home, but when she went to the big table piled with papers, he took himself into the kitchen, muttering something about being hungry. Lunchtime had come and gone; she ought to be starving, too. Her stomach wasn't getting with the program. In fact, her stomach was as far from hungry as a stomach could possibly get.

In the world Dex came from, food would be one of the ways they dealt with sorrow, and besides, he was a fixer. If only what was wrong with her could be cured by opening a can of soup.

She sighed as she placed the papers back on top of the stack they'd come from, and laid her hand on top of it. "I'm sorry about before. My father."

"Nothing to apologize for," he said from where he stood beyond the wide arched doorway that led to the kitchen.

"It must be hard for you to understand, coming from a normal family."

"I don't think there's any such thing as normal when it comes to family."

"Very diplomatic. At least yours cared about each other."

He looked over at her for the first time, but only, she could see, because she'd surprised him. "How do you know?"

Because it all but shimmered around him. His confidence told her he'd never had to wonder if he was loved, if he belonged. "Tell me about them."

He shrugged. "Mom, Dad, me, a sister, like I said, and a brother." His mouth widened into the kind of smile, she imagined, that graced her face when she thought about her island family: fond, indulgent, a little long-suffering and a lot grateful. "Sometimes they're batshit crazy, but yeah, we care about each other. In spite of."

"You said your father was in the military?"

"Gulf War. When he got back he went into law enforcement, just like his father, and his father before. Boston Irish, three generations back it was either cops or mafia." He gave a soft snort. "Still is for a lot of the families in my neighborhood.

"When I mustered out, I went into the family business, but

I didn't have…I won't say the heart for it. Being a cop takes a lot more than heart. I guess I didn't have the patience."

"There are rules," she said with a smile to take the sting out of her observation.

"Maybe that's a part of it. More like I wanted to help, and I didn't feel like I was doing any good riding around in a squad car handling petty crime and domestic disputes." He laughed softly, derisively. "I wound up handling nothing but domestic disputes, as it turns out."

"But they were your cases," Maggie said, beginning to understand. "You don't arrest somebody and then turn it over to the courts, or discover a dead body and hand the case off to a detective. You get to fix something that's not right."

"Yeah, that's what I thought. What I got was wives who wanted to take their cheating husbands to the cleaners, one party trying to catch the other with their pants down, usually so they could beat a prenup."

"You said you did some insurance work."

"Yeah," he exhaled heavily. "People on disability trying to cheat the system."

"So, basically you dealt with liars."

He kept layering cheese between slices of buttered bread, then, after a minute, he said, "You're thinking I learned a thing or two about the truth from them."

"I'm thinking this case must be the answer to your prayers, and you did what you had to do in the interest of finding the truth."

He did a double take, held her gaze, and made her feel ashamed for making him think she didn't respect him. "That sounded suspiciously like approval."

"It's understanding," she said simply.

He walked over, set a bowl of chicken soup in a spot free of papers. She'd thought she wasn't hungry, but when she took a spoonful of soup for his sake, it hit her stomach so warmly. Food, she guessed, did fill an emotional void, as well as a physical one.

Dex came back with his own soup and a plate filled with enough grilled cheese sandwiches for half the town, which he proceeded to plow through as if the hollow leg were a real thing and he had two of them.

Maggie had to admit she felt better after a half bowl of soup and a half sandwich, enough that she was able to slog her way through a couple of the journals.

Dex worked across the table from her in companionable silence until, when her eyes were too bleary to focus anymore, she rose and walked around the table, holding out her hand to him.

"Are you sure?" he said quietly. "You've had a pretty emotional day."

"You could take my mind off it."

He reached out and curled his fingers around hers, kept their hands linked as they walked to the stairs, turning lights off as they went.

Maggie turned into Dex as soon as the bedroom door shut behind them. She wanted the dark, wanted the fire Dex brought her, needed both to sweep away the dregs of the day. It was oblivion she sought, a span of time, however long, when she might forget the pain of walking away from a father she loved, the heartache of babies lost to a disease that was all but wiped out now, the worry over what finding Eugenia might do to the place and people she loved.

She wanted heat, sensation; she wanted to be taken over so she couldn't think, only feel.

Dex, however, wasn't cooperating. Oh, he kissed her back, but while there was heat in the mating of his mouth with hers, there was also gentleness. He framed her face with his hands, and when she tried to push for more, his mouth left hers, nibbled its way down her throat. And stopped.

"If you're trying to drive me crazy—"

"Shhhh," he kissed her again, soft and chaste, but his hands slipped down, caught the hem of her sweater, and whisked it and the tank beneath over her head.

She reached for his jeans, and again he stopped her.

"I assume at some point you're going to let me participate," she said, the slight hitch in her breathing ruining her attempt at dry sarcasm.

"In good time," he said, and even in the dark she could tell he was smiling.

"Okay, you want to drive the train, strap on your engineer's hat and let's go."

Dex chuckled, a low sound that only notched up her frustration. She groaned, spun away, but he caught her up, bore her to the bed.

"Finally," she breathed, losing herself to his kiss, to the feel of his hands running over her.

He left her for a second or two, and she took the opportunity to shove her pants off, lose her bra and panties. When Dex came back she felt the warm slide of his skin against hers, but he didn't bring urgency with him.

His mouth took hers, shooting her into a whirlwind of heat and need. Reality fell away, replaced by the feel of his mouth trailing down her throat, his fingers feathering across her aching nipples, his body covering hers.

She ran her hands down his back to his butt, pressed him against her, moaning at the feel of him, hot and hard. "Now," she panted, "I need you now."

Dex caught her wrists, staking them to the pillow above her head. And set to work driving her mad. His free hand ran over her in long, soft strokes. He feasted on her, mouth nipping, tongue soothing after, leaving little shivery patches of cold against the fire building inside her.

She heard a voice begging, realized it was her own, but couldn't seem to stop herself as he took one rigid nipple into his mouth, as his hand dipped between their bodies and shot her to a climax that left her shattered, gasping for breath then moaning as he joined his body to hers in one long, lovely stroke that pushed her halfway up that mountain again. And held her there, balanced on the almost painful point between the glow of what was and the magic of what he brought her. What they brought one another.

"Look at me," he ground out.

And she was helpless to deny him. Her eyes opened, met his in the pale silver light from the crescent of moon outside her window. He began to move. She shifted a little, and he released her wrists, only to take her hands in his and lay them at either side of her head, his fingers twining with hers.

"Be with me, Maggie." He whispered it against her lips, kissed her once as he began to move. "Let go."

And without intending to, she opened herself to him, felt him tremble as she trembled, muscles that wanted to race held to a brutally slow pace. His hands clenched around hers, tighter and tighter as pleasure bloomed and lifted them. His gaze held hers until his eyes glazed over. And when he locked himself inside her she went blind and deaf, lost to everything but the ecstasy ripping through her, and the echo of it tearing him to pieces.

He slid down, shifted to one side. But his legs were still a welcome weight over hers, his breath was hot at her neck, and his hands left hers, slipping down to gather her close as he planted a soft kiss at her temple.

And her heart fell at his feet.

Chapter Twenty-One

Days passed—days of sleeping together, eating together, working together. Days of hands brushing absentmindedly, of meals shared, of conversation and laughter. And yet, Maggie thought, it wasn't all circling hearts and singing birds. There was a shadow looming, a...lack, she thought, a missing emotional component that she wanted badly to find.

And if it scared her to death? She'd learned a long time ago that fear was to be faced.

So she'd made comments about the inconvenience of going to the Horizon for clean clothes, observations about how Dex was spending most of his time at her house anyway, broad hints about saving the price of a hotel room. And okay, she hadn't come right out and asked him to stay with her, but she'd beaten around the bush so much there was nothing left of the damn bush except a pile of dead brown leaves and broken branches.

Dex was always ready with some excuse, most usually the lack of privacy with Hold in the house. The truth was, though, Dex was holding back. So was she, Maggie thought. That was another truth because, since the day of the Admiral's … invasion, she'd had a hard time looking Dex in the eye. Not because of her father; it was the moment after. That moment in Dex's arms, of comfort offered and comfort taken. That moment when, for the first time, she'd begun to realize just how deeply in over her head she'd gotten.

She'd turned a corner that night, shattered boundaries, stepped over a line into something she wanted to retreat from, and couldn't. It scared her to death.

"Where's Dex?"

Maggie looked up from the page she'd been pretending to read, and when she saw Jessi staring expectantly at her, she wanted to blurt out all the insecurity, all the fear and worry and sadness over what the future might bring. But she just wasn't ready yet. "Dex went into the village, Jess; said he wanted to put in a little face time, keep any lines of communication open."

Jessi's response was a long "Hmmmmmm" that Maggie refused to read into.

"Making any progress?"

"No." She put the page aside, picked up the next. "There's a reference here and there to running illegal liquor, a few passages about the epidemic, but nothing to do with Eugenia. At least not that I can decipher. What's up with you?"

"I just came over to tell you I booked a charter for Monday. It should dovetail nicely with the errands that have been piling up."

"Mmm-hmm." Maggie put another page aside, waiting for Jessi to get to the point.

"You haven't been to the office for two entire days, Maggie."

"I've been working my way through these damn journals."

Searching desperately for the information that would solve Dex's case so he'd leave. Or stay. Either way it would tip the scales, and she'd have an answer.

"You should come over and see how much we have done on the genealogy. It's really coming along."

"Yeah, I'll do that first chance."

"I think the thing you need to do first chance is admit you're falling in love with Dex Keegan."

Jesus, it showed? Maggie kept her eyes on the page in her hand, her trembling hand, managing to remind herself that Jessi knew her inside and out. Dex was pretty insightful, too, and that gave her another bad moment. But he hadn't been looking any closer at her than she had at him.

"It's only been a few weeks."

"Your life is here and his isn't." Jessi leaned a hip against the table. "You can't trust him because he lied to you. Any other excuses you can think of?"

"How about I don't have time for this." Maggie shoved her chair back, took to her feet to pace. "Talk me out of it."

Jessi crossed her arms, amused. "How?"

"I don't know. Tell me I'm crazy."

"Fine, you're crazy, but Maggie, love is crazy. If you do it right."

Maggie stopped, scrubbed both hands back through her hair. "I don't know how to do it right."

She wanted to, though. She could have hated Jessi for making her feel the way her stomach burned and her throat ached, the way her head took one long, confusing spin because she wanted so desperately to be loved it pared her down to a big ball of need.

She stared at her fisted hands as if they belonged to someone else. Someone weak and wounded. Someone helpless, empty.

Someone who'd look to the first man who really attracted her to fill that emptiness? "Maybe I only think I'm...I might be starting to feel that way because I've never done it right. Maybe I just want it so badly—"

"Stop it," Jessi snapped, harshly enough to slap Maggie out of her funk. "If you were that kind of person you'd have gone through men and marriages like the Atlantic chewed up ships two hundred years ago. You haven't dated in at least six months, and by dated, I don't mean scratched a mutual itch without getting emotionally involved."

"Well, that's flattering. I've gone from an emotionally-driven nutcase to an unfeeling slut."

"You know what I mean, Mags. You don't walk around looking for love with every man you cross paths with. The fact that you're in love—" she held up a hand when Maggie would have taken issue with that assessment, "it's not just about sex anymore, is it?"

Maggie chewed on that a minute, but when she tried to convince herself Jessi was wrong, she felt Dex's arms around her again, the peace and comfort even the sound of her father's departing Huey had been unable to shatter. And she accepted. "It doesn't mean I should make it worse by dragging Dex into the insanity."

"You have to at least give him the option, Maggie."

"He doesn't feel the same way—"

"Who doesn't?" Dex appeared in the doorway, Hold Abbot standing behind him like a big, handsome shadow. "What way?"

Maggie fielded Jessi's pointed look, ignored the slight, encouraging tip of her head in Dex's direction. "Time and place," she murmured to Jessi. *Not here, not now.*

Jessi nodded slightly, and it gave Maggie a different kind of comfort to know her best friend understood that she had to live with it a little while before she could take the next step. She looked over at Dex. The next, completely scary step.

"Are you two going to use actual words at some point?"

Hold just stood there, smiling archly and giving Maggie the sick feeling he knew exactly what was going on. But Hold wasn't her problem.

"Ummm," Jessi began, "I came over to tell Maggie she has a new charter. With Jim Oldham. Maggie had a crush on him in school. He, uh, moved to the mainland, so we haven't seen him for a while. We were just reminiscing," she broke off, giggled as she slanted her best friend a look. "He had this mole just here," she pointed to the small of her back. "You know how guys like to wear their pants at half mast. Remember, Mags?"

Maggie opened her mouth, shut it when Hold caught the scowl on Dex's face and grinned even wider. "How about we all get to work? I know Dex wants to solve this case as fast as humanly possible."

"Well, we all have lives outside of…" Jessi glanced at the table littered with papers, "this. But that doesn't mean we can't, well, bond over it. Right, Dex?"

"I wouldn't want to interfere with business."

"A girl's gotta make a buck," Maggie shot back, stung by his snotty tone.

"You're going to charge an old friend like Jim?"

"Sure. I don't let anything interfere with business."

Dex moved in on her, lowered his voice. "What crawled up your ass?"

"Nothing. What crawled up yours?"

"Maggie," Jessi interjected, giving Dex a meaningful look.

Maggie narrowed her eyes, and then it hit her. "Oh. *Oh*."

Jessi and Hold laughed.

"What the hell's so funny?"

"Well, son," Hold said to Dex, "I could explain it to you, but I'm thinking you won't see it as such a laughing matter."

"How about you let me be the judge of that?"

Hold opened his mouth, but Jessi took his arm and started to pull him out of the room.

"Now, if you want my company, Jessica," Hold said to her, "all you have to do is ask."

"Fine, Holden, would you come with me, please?" She shot Dex a look. "And keep your mouth shut while you're doing it."

"With pleasure. Ma'am," he said, tipping an imaginary hat to Maggie.

"Wait a minute," Dex yelled after them. "What the hell is going on here?"

"I'd like to help you, Dex, but I think my assistant is right. She's not the one who should do the explaining here."

"It took you long enough to figure that out," Jessi called from the entryway. "And I'm not your assistant."

Hold's response was nothing more than a murmur, cut off when the door shut behind him.

Maggie took her customary chair at the table, then got to her feet again when she couldn't settle. Not with Dex watching her so carefully.

"Maggie—"

"Jessi thinks I should admit I'm in love with you." She blurted it out fast, like ripping off a bandage.

He stared at her for a second, deer in the headlights.

He might as well have hit her. It wasn't just hard to breathe; the mere attempt to draw air into her lungs made her feel like she'd swallowed razor blades. She pressed the heel of her hand over her heart. The pressure helped a little. "I knew this was a bad idea."

Dex caught her arm when she turned to go. "Maggie, wait, you can't just say something like that and walk away. You have to give me a minute."

There were a dozen reactions he could have had. *I love you too* came to mind, or even *Thank you*, which would have been painful enough. But this? "You needing a minute pretty much says it all, Dex."

He shoved his hands back through his hair, fisting them for a minute. "Jesus, Maggie, let me think. I mean, your father was just here and you're still hurting . . ."

"So I'm looking for someone to lean on?"

"No. Hell, you don't lean on anyone. It's just . . . Do you get how big a step this is?"

"Yeah, I do. But you don't think so. I don't have the foundation, so I can't understand what real love is." Funny, she would have thought her background made her uniquely qualified to understand love—when it was real, and when it wasn't.

"Stop putting words into my mouth."

"Fine. You talk."

But he didn't, and she couldn't bear the silence.

"Let me toss out a subject or two," she said. "We've already established that I'm only reacting to my father being here, how never having his love makes me incapable—"

"Stop. Just stop."

She lifted her eyes to his, met his gaze, and made herself hold it even when she recognized the emotion she saw there as pity.

He reached for her, but she moved away.

"When I told you about my family, I never expected you to use it against me."

"I'm not using it against you, Maggie, it's just that I've seen what that kind of...environment does to people. To kids especially."

"So the real problem here is you." And recognizing that was so very little comfort. He'd grown up with love; it was a shame he'd forgotten that. "Despite your *environment*, you choose to believe that the few people who've used your services represent the vast majority of humanity."

"You're the one who told me not to fall in love with you."

"Well, this is a hell of a time to start taking my advice."

Dex shoved his hands in his pockets, looking trapped and confused and miserable. "I can't seem to say the right thing."

"You got your point across all the same," Maggie said, heading into the entryway.

She just couldn't stand there in the same room any longer, wanting him so desperately she ached with it, even after he'd broken her heart. Hell, she couldn't even blame Dex. He was right. She had warned him not to get emotionally involved with her. Worse, she'd known he wouldn't stay on Windfall Island. She was the one who'd tripped; whatever got broken in the fall was her own fault. "I think you should go."

He dropped his gaze from hers, turned away, turned back. Hope filled her, and everything inside her lifted, soared.

Then he spoke.

"Maybe you're right about me. Maybe my work has jaded me. God knows I've seen the damage people do to each other in the name of love."

"Is that supposed to—" She broke off, reminded herself it wasn't Dex's place to make her feel better. "If you lo...If you felt anything for me, you wouldn't be looking for ways to convince me I don't know what I feel." He wouldn't be turning her love back on her.

"I'm sorry for putting you in this position." She smiled slightly, sadly. "That's three times I've apologized to you. A hat trick. That ought to give you a foothold in the village. They'll tell you I don't apologize easily."

"Christ, Maggie, let's take a step back."

She did just that because he reached for her again, and if he touched her...If he touched her she'd shatter, into pieces so small she'd never put them all back together again. She'd given him her heart, he'd refused it. She wouldn't give him her tears, too.

"There's no stepping back, Dex," she said quietly. "There's only stepping away now."

"And that's what you're doing."

"Is it?"

He scrubbed his hands over his face. "I'm the one who stepped back, Maggie. I get that. But if you think—"

"I think you should keep going. The door is right behind you."

He met her gaze again, finally. "This isn't over."

She stared right back at him, knew he'd see the pain in her eyes, the sorrow. And the resolve. "I'll work with you, Dex. I made a commitment."

"But there won't be anything personal."

"I hope we can be friends." But not just now, she thought. Not until she'd had time to...What? She'd never loved any man before, she'd never loved anyone or anything, even flying, the way she loved Dex Keegan. She had no idea how it would hit her when he was gone. But she knew how to handle it now, with him watching her so carefully.

She pulled open the front door, and held it for him.

Even feeling like everything inside her was shredded and screaming with pain, she refused to let him see it.

"I'm sorry," Dex said as he went through it. He turned to face her. "I didn't mean to hurt you, Maggie. I didn't know I could."

She lost her breath at that, very nearly doubled over before pride put iron into her spine. Bad enough that he didn't love her back, but he didn't think her capable of love? "I'm responsible for my own feelings," she said as she closed the door on him.

And it was going to hit her now, she realized. It was going to hit her hard. She went into the living room she never used and sank into a big overstuffed easy chair, pulling her feet up and letting her head sink onto her knees. That chair had been in that room since the day she'd moved into the house, and she'd sat in it maybe twice before. Her house was as empty as her heart, she thought, so broken and cold and sad she couldn't even cry.

The sun started to set, the room grew dark and chilly, and still she sat, numb finally. When her cell chimed, she answered it out of habit, then wished she hadn't.

Still, she thought, as she got stiffly to her feet, she couldn't stop living because she'd fallen in love with Dex Keegan, and he didn't love her back.

Dex didn't remember making the walk from Maggie's house to the office, but somehow he found himself there, with Hold and Jessi both staring at him.

Jessi said something; her lips moved, but he didn't hear anything over the roar of his heart thudding in his ears. He felt a little shell-shocked, disoriented, not quite sure what had happened, let alone how he was supposed to feel about it. About Maggie.

Someone—Jessi—tugged at his arm, and the room snapped into painfully sharp focus. Sharp and loud.

"*Dex.*"

He brushed her off, sank into a chair.

"Dex." Jessi crouched down in front of him. "What happened?"

"I'm not sure." But he told Jessi. Maybe she could explain it to him, he thought, as he stumbled his way through the surreal conversation with Maggie—it couldn't be termed an argument, not when they'd both been so fucking polite.

As a cop and PI he'd trained himself to remember details when he wasn't in a position to write things down. He wanted badly to forget, but every word came back to him now, every emotion he'd seen in her brilliant blue eyes.

She'd looked so young, he thought, so impossibly young and fragile when he'd tossed her feelings back in her face, but she'd been implacable and clear-minded when she opened the door and invited him to walk out of her life.

And her poise. How much grace and sense of self, how much strength had it taken for her to say she hoped they could still be friends when he'd . . . God. He dropped his head into his hands.

If he'd been hoping for sympathy, he wasn't going to get it.

"You used her father against her," Jessi said through her teeth. "You told her she had no idea what it meant to love because of him."

"Jessi, I—"

She held up a hand. "Then you implied she wasn't capable of love."

"No, I . . ." He remembered telling her he didn't want to hurt her, didn't think he could—and it hit him. "Jesus, I meant I never thought she'd let me in enough to hurt her."

"Yeah, that would make her a cold, closed-off bitch instead of a damaged, unfeeling bitch. So much better."

Dex closed his eyes, but he couldn't shut out reality. No wonder Maggie had looked like he'd struck her. He had, with words, and words, he knew, could be the hardest blows of all. "I have to apologize."

"No you don't, not now."

"I can't leave it this way." He appealed to Hold, who spread his hands and gave him a *poor-bastard* look.

"I'd suggest you listen to Jessi," Hold said. "She knows Maggie better than anyone."

"But I have to take it back. I have to explain what I meant."

"Words," Jessi sneered. "Do you feel any differently?" She huffed out a breath when he only stared at her. "Do you love Maggie?"

"Give me a minute to think."

"Thinking? What is it with men?" She rounded on Hold, who had the good sense to keep his mouth shut. "What are you going to say to her that you didn't already say in your stupid male fashion?"

He could only stare at her, speechless.

"Exactly. All you'll do is cause her more pain. Stay the hell away from her." She turned her back and flounced back to her desk, plopping into her chair. "Honestly, men," she said with great disgust. "We don't need you anymore," she said, rounding on Hold. "You're the genealogist; you should know we can make babies without you."

"What did I do? Besides being born male."

"That's enough," she said darkly.

"And just so you know," Hold added, taking his life in his hands, in Dex's opinion, "You still need us to make babies. Humans haven't been cloned successfully."

"Yet. And they probably have cloned human beings, except it's being hidden from the public by some secret government agency. Run by men."

Hold opened his mouth, but Jessi said, "Oh, just go somewhere else. Somewhere Maggie isn't."

Wisely, Hold got to his feet.

"And take genius over there with you."

Chapter Twenty-Two

Dex followed Hold back to Maggie's tiny office, grateful there was little of her left there. Her desk had been cleared of her things to make room for the family Bibles and papers Jessi had been quietly collecting throughout the community, in some cases "borrowing" them without permission so the rest of the Windfallers wouldn't put two and two together and figure out why Dex had come to the island.

"You want to talk about it?" Hold asked him.

"No." He just wanted to put it out of his mind, forget how hollowed out and brittle he felt.

"Glad to hear it," Hold said. "That would make us girls, and despite Jessi's current disgust for the entire male gender, I'm not ready to switch sides."

"Work," Dex said shortly. Work would take his mind off the mess of things he'd made with Maggie. Work would set him to rights...or as close as he could get.

He turned to the chart that took up an entire wall of the small office. And gave up trying to forget about Maggie when her name jumped out at him. "*Jessi*."

She came to the doorway, looking like a pissed off pixie.

"I am not at your beck and call," she said. "Yell at me again and—"

"Shut up."

"Shut up?" she sputtered. "Shut up? Maybe you should take your own advice, Mr. Keegan. Maybe—"

"Why is Maggie's name on here?"

That stopped her, verbally and physically, as she halted in mid-stride, her gaze shifting to the chart. She crossed her arms, glared at him. "Why wouldn't it be?"

"Lose the snotty attitude and pay attention. She told me she wasn't from the island."

Jessi frowned. "I'm not letting you off the hook for the snotty attitude comment, but you must be wrong."

"She told me . . . Shit, she told me she moved here in high school."

"There, you see? She's absolutely right. But her mother was born and raised here. You just misunderstood her."

Misunderstood, hell. Dex ran a hand back through his hair, paced away, then back, which didn't take long as the room was barely eight by ten. It also didn't help him arrive at a plan of action.

Under normal circumstances, he'd have been at her house by now. He'd have tossed the lie in her face, and they'd have had a nice argument, some name calling, maybe a little yelling before she went sullen. Under normal circumstances.

He looked over at Hold.

"Jessi called over to the house. Maggie's on her way."

"Good," Dex said. "We can get to the bottom of this." And he could find out why this time she'd lied to him, and if she'd done it because she realized just what hiding her ancestry meant.

*   *   *

Maggie took her time walking over to the office. She'd splashed some water in her face, done what she could to get some color back into her pale skin. The bleakness in her eyes she could do nothing about, but she didn't want to appear any more pitiful than she had to. It was going to be difficult enough to see Dex again so soon.

Jessi met her in the lobby and folded her into her arms. The hard, long hug nearly ruined her efforts at putting on a brave front.

"What can I do to help?" Jessi wanted to know. "Booze, ice cream, male bashing? I could make a little wax figure of Dex and you can stick hat pins in sensitive areas."

"I'm fine," Maggie said, working up a slight smile to go along with the lip service. "I've had a lot of practice."

"There's no practice for this."

"Maybe not, but let me have my illusions for now. We can eat ice cream and bash men later."

"It's a date."

She looked toward the sound of subdued male voices coming from the open doorway. "What's so important?"

"The genealogy, Maggie. I'm sorry."

"Shit," she said, still too numb to feel much more than a little mild disgust over forgetting that sooner or later Dex would see her name on Hold's chart and realize she'd kept the truth from him. "He's probably not going to be at a loss for words this time."

"I'm sorry," Jessi said again, "If I'd known—"

"How could you when I didn't even know it mattered myself until just recently."

"And you've had other things on your mind."

"Yeah. He won't believe that."

"To hell with him."

Maggie would have agreed with that sentiment, except she was already in Hell, and she didn't want to run into Dex Keegan there, either.

"Let's just get this over with."

Maggie walked in, Jessi following close on her heels—hovering, Dex decided. But it was Maggie's face he couldn't take his eyes from. She was pale but dry-eyed. Absolutely dry-eyed. Her expression was so placid it baffled him, as much as the pain that had him rubbing at his breastbone—which he stopped when she glanced at his hand and her mouth twisted up in a faint smile.

"Not going to yell at me?" she asked him, lifting her eyes, her starkly cold blue eyes, to his.

"Yeah, I'm pissed that you lied to me," he said, his voice just as even as hers.

"I told you I didn't grow up here. That's not a lie."

"You left out the part about having relatives on the island. An omission is still a lie, Maggie."

"You mean like asking me to omit the truth to Jessi?"

"Damn straight," Jessi put in. As if Maggie needed any help.

"Why didn't you tell me?"

"It was none of your business at the time. It's none of your business now."

Dex swallowed that, and while it made him feel better that the whip in her voice proved she wasn't as calm as she looked, there was still that pain in his chest, still the knowledge that he'd hurt her, and that even though he hadn't done it on purpose it was still on him.

"Don't," she said, reminding him of something else about her; how well she'd learned to read him. "Don't make this your fault. It isn't about you."

"That's not what you said a little while ago."

"Well, you managed to convince me. Thank you for that."

"Pretty easy to change your opinion, Maggie."

That got her. She turned away, left him feeling like even more of a heel. Jessi shot him a look that promised retribution, slow and bloody retribution, before she went to Maggie.

Maggie shrugged her off, turned back, still pale, still in control. But she wasn't looking him in the eye anymore.

"So my name's on your chart. What's the big deal, Hold?" she said in a voice so steady Dex wanted to shake her until that control snapped and she cried or punched him, anything to make her stop being so damned cold, so damned different from the woman he'd come to...like and respect.

But if he put so much as a finger on her, he was afraid he'd be the one to shatter.

"We've traced a few of the families still on the list you and Dex gave us," Hold answered Maggie's question. "But before we had the list, Jessi started with the families she knew fairly well."

"Including mine."

"Yes. Your grandmother would have been a baby around the time Eugenia Stanhope went missing."

"Me and everyone else in my generation."

"Exactly. It didn't mean much to Jessi or me, but when Dex saw your name and who you connected back to—"

"The Finleys."

"Emmett Finley, to be exact," Dex put in.

Maggie shrugged. "Emmett is my great uncle. So what? His name wasn't on the list. Nobody in my family died in the measles epidemic of '31 and '32."

Dex studied her face. All he saw was puzzlement. "You said yourself it's likely the name isn't on the list we found,

Maggie. If Eugenia was substituted for a child around the same age who died, the family might have kept it a secret, even from the other Windfallers.

"Emmett recalls the night the *Perdition* blew up," he continued when she only stared at him. "He described it to us, remember? I think it's likely he saw it firsthand."

"Or he's embellishing on a story he heard a long time ago."

"I don't think so. He remembered how it smelled, even from twelve miles away, how the ground shook, the hiss of the burning timbers as they fell into the water."

"You're jumping to conclusions." But she cupped her elbows, and moved a little closer to Jessi.

"I'm sorry, Maggie," he said, "I can imagine how upsetting this is for you, but it's a possibility we can't afford to overlook."

"There's no concrete evidence," she insisted. "Nothing on this chart or in the journals points to my family. All you have are the ramblings of an old man whose mind is...blurry."

"Jesus," Dex bit off.

"Like I said," Hold jumped in, "it's not a conclusion, just a possibility."

"A strong possibility," Dex said, reigning in his temper. "If Emmett was helping the bootleggers the night the *Perdition* exploded, and if Eugenia survived and somehow got off the ship with them—"

"That's a lot of ifs."

"Not when you string them all together."

"There's one more thing," Hold put in. "Your eyes, Maggie."

"I blew off the resemblance because Maggie said she wasn't from the island," Dex said.

Maggie ignored him, talking to Hold. "What about my eyes?"

"If you've ever seen one of the Stanhopes in person, you never forget their eyes." His gaze shifted to Maggie. "Vivid, brilliant blue, like the sun on tropical waters."

Maggie folded her arms, but Dex could see the upset beneath her calm exterior, even if she did manage to keep her voice steady. "Why didn't you say something before this?"

"I had no idea this case was about the Stanhopes when I came. After Dex told me..." Hold spread his hands, "I wanted to be sure. Your eye color is rare, but it could have been a coincidence. I wasn't certain until Dex saw the chart and made the connection to the Finleys."

Maggie blew out a breath, squared her shoulders. And didn't look at Dex. "So test my DNA," she said to Hold. "Rule me out and that's that. The two of you can go on searching for the real descendant, if there is one, and I can get back to my life."

"Unfortunately, it's not going to be wrapped up as tidily as all that."

Maggie snorted softly. "Spit it out, Mr. Private Investigator."

Dex inhaled, exhaled, managed to find a small store of patience. Jessi was right; there was no talking to Maggie now. Whatever else she was feeling, she was on the way to working up a good head of anger, and it was focused on him. "My room was ransacked."

Jessi clapped her hand over her mouth, but Hold just shook his head and said, "You sure know how to bury the lead, son."

"He didn't just bury the lead," Maggie said, "he buried the whole thing."

"I told you about it at the Horizon, the night we had dinner."

"Because AJ let the cat out of the bag. And you said it was no big deal."

"I didn't have anything connecting me to the Stanhopes, and nothing was taken."

"And you think the rock slide is connected?" Hold said.

Dex rolled his shoulders. "Yeah. Whoever broke into my room was definitely looking for something, but chose a time when the room would be empty. The rocks were meant to cause harm."

Maggie, still holding herself a little ways apart, said, "When did we establish that the rock slide wasn't an accident?"

"Like I pointed out at the time, it's a little too coincidental," Dex said.

"Then who's the target?" she shot back, still angry but not so much she couldn't be logical.

"Me," he said bluntly.

"And who do you think pulled the trigger? Because it had to be one of us. A Windfaller. There aren't any outsiders on the island. Except you."

Jessi jumped into the tense silence. "Even if it was intentional, Dex, how could it be aimed at you? Any one of us could have come along that road."

Maggie shook her head. "Mort stays out here more often than not, and you always take the easier road in from the village, Jess. I take that way on occasion, but I was here the night before the rock slide. Dex is the only one who could have taken the road that morning," her gaze shifted to meet his, "driving too fast to stop in time."

Jessi blew out a breath. "Tell me it was just a warning."

"I'd like to," Dex said. "We can't be sure until we know who's behind it."

"How serious do you think this threat is?"

"As serious as the Stanhope fortune and that's hundreds of millions of dollars."

"The descendant could be in line to inherit a chunk of that," Maggie added. "If Dex is right, someone is willing to kill to prevent it from happening."

"I wouldn't say no to being a Stanhope, and sure, that's because of the money, but it would also mean..." Jessi broke off, terrified as understanding dawned. "I have to get Benji."

Hold stepped into the doorway. "First, he's in school, so he's safe. Second, you're not going anywhere by yourself."

"Because I need a big, strong man to protect me? Please."

Maggie smiled faintly. "Take him into the village, Jess. Let the women get a good look at him. You won't have to worry about him following you around. He'll be busy trying to keep his virtue intact."

"Who says I want my virtue intact?"

Jessi scowled. "Come with me, then, and get yourself... debauched."

"Try not to talk about why you're here," Dex put in.

"He is pretty free with information," Jessi said. "Pillow talk would be right up his alley."

Hold grinned. "Honey, when I'm in bed, ain't a whole lot of talking going on."

"Big words," Jessi said.

"Words ain't the only big—"

"No, there's your ego," Jessi said with a conspiratorial smile for Maggie—who wasn't in a conspiratorial mood.

"If you two are finished, we were agreeing to keep this from the rest of the island."

Dex shrugged when they all looked to him. "The Stanhope family has waited this long, a few more days or weeks won't mean anything."

"So what do we do now?" Hold wanted to know. "I'm new to all this life and death stuff."

"You should go pick up your son, Jessi, but only because I think it'll make you feel better. I doubt either one of you are in danger. The threat seems to be focused on me, and if it is an islander, that's just another layer of assurance you won't be a target. As for the rest, I don't know yet. Let me give it some thought and we'll meet back here tomorrow."

Maggie made her opinion of Dex's plan clear. She didn't use words, she used the door.

He followed her through it. "Why didn't you tell me your mother was born here?"

"Seriously, Counselor?"

"Fine. I get why you kept it to yourself in the beginning."

"We've been over this. My answers haven't changed." Maggie shoved through the lobby door, stepped out into a freshening wind. She closed her eyes for a second or two, let it wash over her and carry away some of the pain that seemed to swirl around her like a dense, heavy fog.

Knowing Dex was right behind her, she didn't give herself long, and when he fell into step with her she ignored him. Until he followed her up the steps and through the front door of her house.

"Get out."

"Not until you tell me what's going through that stubborn, contrary brain of yours."

"I'm thinking about getting my gun."

"Bullshit. You're thinking about taking matters into your own hands."

She froze with her foot on the first stair riser, looked at him.

"That's some imagination you have there, Mr. Keegan."

"Stay out of this, Maggie. Don't do anything rash."

She turned, looked him dead in the eye. "Because I'm a pathetic, self-destructive female scorned by the man she loves?"

"Because you want me gone."

"You're not wrong there."

"No, I'm the one who was wrong." His gaze lifted to hers, held. "What I said about you and your father."

"Your opinion changed so easily, Keegan?" she said, and oddly enough, with sarcasm she wasn't just playing at. It felt good to know she was already coming back, at least a little, to herself.

"I had a life before you showed up. I'll have a life after you're gone. A good one," she added, even if the way she looked at the world had changed—for the better, she decided. Dex had shown her that she had a capacity for love. He'd opened up the possibilities for her—even if she wasn't up to thanking him for it quite yet.

"You're right in the damn middle of this now, Maggie, no matter if either of us is happy about it."

"I gave you a solution. You refuse to take it."

"Jesus, are you pissed enough at me to put your life on the line over something you don't even want?"

"Who says I don't want it? Who wouldn't want big piles of money? Isn't that why you lied to everyone in the first place? We're all a bunch of greedy lowlifes who'd do anything to get their hands on part of the Stanhope fortune, right? Any mainlander could tell you that."

"They'd be wrong, at least where you're concerned. If you were willing to take a handout, you'd be toeing Daddy's line. You built this place with nothing but your own blood, sweat, and tears—if you'd ever give anyone the satisfaction of shedding one, that is."

He was wrong, Maggie thought, she was on the edge right now. Her only defense, her only weapon, was anger, and she was holding on tight to the ragged end of hers. "At the risk of being repetitive," she said mockingly, "I'll tell you again. Get out."

"This is my case."

"But it's my life."

"And I'm not allowed to be involved anymore."

"By your own choice."

"Jesus, Maggie, give me one damn minute to think here." Dex paced a little away, running a hand back through his hair like he did when he was working his way through some frustration.

Maggie could understand, but she wasn't inclined to sympathize. Thinking wasn't the problem. Feeling was, and if she'd allowed herself a little more time to let her brain talk her heart off the ledge, she might not be in this predicament.

And that, she thought with a slight smile, was bullshit. Telling Dex she loved him was non-negotiable. If not today, she'd have told him before he left Windfall. She'd always been a risk-taker because without risk there was no reward. And no loss. But better, she decided, to lose before she loved Dex Keegan any more than she already did.

"Don't trouble yourself, Dex. Everything's been said that requires saying."

"Not if you're going to do something stupid."

She laughed. It was easier than she'd thought it would be. But then, she was laughing at herself. "I try not to be stupid more than once every twenty-four hours or so. I think I've met my quota for today."

Chapter Twenty-Three

Emmett Finley picked up a package of Oreos, offered it to Maggie for the third time in the ten minutes since she'd arrived at his ramshackle old house on the edge of town.

Maggie dipped in, took one to placate him. She didn't eat it, didn't have the stomach for it. She hadn't had much of a stomach for anything the last couple of days. She wished she didn't have a heart anymore.

Having Dex throw her love back in her face, having him tell her she was damaged, incapable of understanding that emotion... She couldn't put the pain of it into words. She wished she could stop feeling it, but she knew it would take a lot of time to get over him. Distance would have helped, but distance was something she couldn't have on an island the size of a postage stamp. Unless Dex solved his case and got the hell gone.

Which was what had brought her to her uncle Emmett's house on a brisk fall morning, with the sky as dull and gray as her mood.

Hard on the heels of a broken heart, she'd been hit square in the face with the possibility she might be the long lost Stanhope descendant. It hadn't sunk in then, when she'd been numb and angry. She felt the weight of it now, a weight in her stomach and on her heart. Family connections had never played a positive role in her life. The Stanhopes, with their wealth, their history, their position, would almost certainly expect her to live up to their image. Maggie had no intention of living according to anyone's rules but her own.

Emmett Finley was her great uncle, and the only family she had who might be able to help her confirm her ancestry one way or the other. He'd have been no more than eight years old when Eugenia Stanhope went missing, but eight was old enough to understand what was going on around him. If he could remember it.

Thankfully, he was too deep into one of his stories to notice her nerves. As it was a story she'd heard countless times, she was free to search her mind for a way to ask him, to ask an uncle she loved, if he'd had a hand in concealing the kidnapping of a helpless baby.

She didn't want to distress Emmett, but she had to discover the truth. She would, Maggie decided, even as she heard a knock on Emmett's front door. Finding Dex Keegan on the other side of that door worked wonders for her emotional upheaval, paring the conflict raging inside her down to a fine point of white-hot anger.

She stepped back, met his eyes as he walked by her. She'd given Dex everything she had to give; he wasn't getting anything but her indifference from now on.

"Never thought I'd see the day you'd back away from a fight," he said.

She shrugged. "It's worth it as long as it gets me closer to the day you'll be gone." And because she'd forced herself to hold his dark, challenging gaze, she saw the flash of anger. So, she'd won a battle after all, she mused, allowing herself to feel the satisfaction of victory without acknowledging there'd been hurt in his eyes, as well.

"Two visitors in one day," Emmett said, oblivious to the tension. He offered Dex the Oreo bag.

Dex took one, held it much as Maggie had. But he wasn't having any problem getting to the point. He hunkered down by Emmett's chair, waited until he had the old man's attention. "What do you know about the kidnapping of Eugenia Stanhope?"

Emmett gasped, mild curiosity shifting to shock as his face drained white.

Maggie took the hand that groped for hers, sank down on the arm of his easy chair and wrapped an arm around his shoulders. She leaned close, murmuring reassurances until she felt the pulse under her fingers start to quiet.

Then she seared Dex with a look. "Jesus, Keegan, why don't you just punch him in the face?"

"You want me gone, there's a price."

"So you use an old man to make me pay it? Whatever's between us, I wouldn't have believed it of you."

Dex shot to his feet, every bit as furious. When he spoke, though, his voice was even, coldly even. And he didn't speak to her. "I'm sorry I upset you, Mr. Finley."

"Emmett," he corrected. "I like you, boy, but I don't know nothing about the Stanhope girl."

"Then I can't protect Maggie."

"Maggie?" Emmett's hand tightened on hers. "What's he on about? Somebody after you, child?"

"No—"

"Yes," Dex said over her. He hunkered down by Emmett's chair again, laid his hand on Emmett's other wrist. "I came here to find out what happened to Eugenia Stanhope. I think you may know."

"Don't," Emmett said stubbornly.

"Don't or won't?"

"Amounts to the same thing, boy."

"Even if your silence puts Maggie in danger?"

Emmett's face folded into belligerent lines. But he looked up, and Maggie saw the hint of doubt in his eyes, the shadow of an old, sad secret. And God help her, she used it.

"You know I can take care of myself, Uncle Emmett. Don't you think it's time to let Eugenia rest in peace?"

Dex started to speak. She cut him off with one warning glare.

"You and Aunt Jane were so good to me when I moved back here."

Emmett smiled fondly. "She used to show up at our place at all hours," he said to Dex. "Nancy was my niece, family, but she was a poor judge of character. Latched onto that Solomon character the minute he stepped foot on the island. She got what she wanted, but she should have spent less time blaming you for putting her back here, and more time being a real mother."

Maggie swallowed away the tightness in her throat. "She just wanted to be loved, Uncle Emmett. I don't think I ever really understood that before."

"You loved her. I loved her. It should have been enough."

"Yes," Maggie said. She had people who loved her, and it *would* be enough. But not today. As long as she had to be faced with Dex Keegan, she knew the ache in her chest, the tears that constantly threatened, would be with her as well. And she'd feel this huge, consuming yearning for something she knew she could never have.

Yes, she understood her mother, at long last. It did neither of them any good.

There was, however, one wrong she could right. "Tell me what happened on the night of October 16, 1931," she said to her great uncle, and when he remained silent, she prompted, "Your father was running illegal alcohol from the ships docked off shore, wasn't he?"

Emmett's jaw bunched.

"It's important, Uncle Emmett. You know I'd never upset you this way if it wasn't necessary."

Emmett shoved unsteadily to his feet, and for a second Maggie thought they'd be leaving none the wiser. Then he sank back into his chair and began to talk.

"Things were always tight when I was a kid, Maggie, before this got to be such a blessed tourist attraction." He said it with equal parts pride and disgust, and made Maggie smile. "Windfall Island has always been a place where necessity dictates. When Prohibition became law more than one Windfaller started running booze in from the big ships, always in crews, as it took more than one pair of hands to make quick work of the runs before the Coast Guard caught on. My da partnered most times with Norris, Meeker, and Gifford, but others floated in and out of the group."

"What about that night?" Dex prompted.

"Let him tell it his way," Maggie said, giving her uncle's hand an encouraging squeeze. If his mind went sideways, they'd just have to wait until the next time he was lucid to get the rest of the details. Pushing would only make him clam up. "Take your time, Uncle Emmett."

"We're out of time," Dex said, although he had the good sense to keep his tone calm and reasonable. "Forgive me, Mr. Finley—Emmett—but waiting could mean we never get the truth."

Emmett snorted. "Because my mind is blinking on and off like a faulty lightbulb?"

Maggie made a sound of denial, and he used his other hand to pat her wrist. "Don't think I don't know, child. Sometimes." Emmett smiled wryly. "The blessing of it is, a lot of the time I don't realize I'm a rambling old fool."

"You're not a fool, Uncle Emmett, just old. I'll take you to the mainland—"

"Been to the doctor, and I'm taking the pills he gave me."

Maggie gripped his hand, held on tight, her heart aching.

"I'm near ninety years old, Maggie. Body's about give out, no reason why my mind shouldn't be showing its age." He settled back into his chair, took a deep breath and let it out heavily.

"October 16, 1931," he began, smiling as he visited the past by choice instead of wandering there in confusion. "Like I said, my da used to work with a crew running booze in from the ships parked at what they called the Rum Line. Was three miles at the beginning of Prohibition, government moved it to twelve." He grinned, winked at Maggie. "They thought it would stop folks like us, but what's a little hardship to a Windfaller? Hell, we even had dealings with Bill McCoy—the real McCoy, he was called, and that's where the saying comes from, for not watering down his liquor like most of the others did to stretch supplies and pad profits.

"Norris and Gifford went out to the big ships that night. They were the usual pair. Hank Gifford—"

"Giff."

"That's right," Emmett said to Dex. "He used to like to chase the ladies, gold band on his finger notwithstanding."

"Another quality the current generation seems to have inherited," Maggie put in, pleased that it brought a smile to her uncle's face.

"Can't blame a man for chasing after you," he said fondly. "Just their bad luck you're so picky."

"I guess I'm comparing every man I meet to you. I thought I found one who measured up, but I rushed to judgment."

Emmett slid a look in Dex's direction. "Maybe you should take it a little slower next time, child."

"My thoughts exactly," Dex muttered.

"Next time?" Maggie shook her head. "Go on with your story, Uncle Emmett."

"It was a floating party, my da used to say. Music, gambling, booze flowing like water, women with their stockings rolled down. Floozies they were called back then. Always thought it was a shame my da wouldn't let me go out and see for myself, but I had to be satisfied with hearing the stories."

"Your mother probably would have skinned him alive, you being all of eight years old."

"Nearer to nine, and precocious to boot," he said with a grin. "Hank Gifford, now, he was the one telling the stories, more often than not. Ran into a girl that night—"

"Sonja Hanson," Dex murmured.

"Never did hear her name," Emmett said. "I'm not sure Gifford knew it, either, as Sam Norris—the elder Sam Norris—dragged him back to the boat once they'd made their deal. Weather was wicked that night. I remember that much, and crossing twelve miles of ocean when the Atlantic's in a bitch of a mood is risky, even without the Coast Guard breathing down your neck."

He rested his head against the chair back, and for a second, Maggie thought he'd had enough for one day. Though she wanted to push for the rest of the story, she started to get to her feet.

Emmett pulled her back down next to him. "My father

took me with him that night as much to get me out of the house as for the extra pair of hands. My baby sister, your grandmother, Maggie, was bad sick with the measles. My mam had her hands full, and Da thought to get me out from under her feet.

"We were unloading when we heard what sounded like a baby crying. The men, they all froze, kind of looking at one another, you know, like they didn't believe their ears. So I went over to the boat, and there she was."

"Eugenia," Dex said.

Emmett hesitated, then sighed. "In for a penny, in for a pound, my old Mam used to say. The babe was wrapped in a blanket, finer than anything I ever saw, before that day or since. Had a big, curlicued S stitched on the pink satin edging, with an E and an A on either side of it. And there was a necklace around her throat, rubies, diamonds, though I didn't know it then, and don't know to this day what became of it, let alone if it was real or paste."

"Real." Dex surged to his feet, pacing across the small room then back. "And an eight-month old baby wouldn't have been wearing jewelry like that. Sonja never mentioned it. Neither did the Stanhopes."

When he looked over at her, Maggie met his gaze. "They kept the necklace secret, and that makes it another way to track her."

He nodded, and she could feel the excitement pumping off him.

Maggie could understand, at least a little, how he must be feeling. She'd only been on the hunt for Eugenia Stanhope for a few days, but she felt hope rising up inside her, making it a little hard to breathe.

"Can you tell the rest of the story, Uncle Emmett, or are you too tired?"

Emmett rested his head again, but mixed with the weariness on his face was what she thought might be relief.

"You've been keeping this to yourself for a long time."

"I have," he said, sitting forward again. "You won't tell anyone, will you? Dex?"

"It'll have to come out, Mr. Finley." Dex came back, knelt down in front of Emmett. "Her family has a right to know, don't you think?"

"They've never stopped looking for her, have they?" Emmett scrubbed age-gnarled hands over his face. "I didn't think about that when I was a kid, and by the time I grew up, well, I guess I put it out of my mind, like I was told."

He looked at Maggie, said apologetically, "They were afraid, you see. Finding her in their boat while they were breaking the law, and then the *Perdition* blowing up that way. We'd've been blamed, Maggie. Bad enough these days, the way people look askance at us, but back then?" He shook his head. "Our men'd get hauled off to jail and nobody woulda give a rat's ass about evidence or guilt."

"Nobody's judging, Uncle Emmett."

"I understand the reasons it was kept quiet," Dex added, "But that time has passed. Can you tell me what happened to the baby? One of the island families took her in, right?"

"I'm sorry," Emmett said. "She came home with me and Da, but I don't know what happened after that."

Again Dex stood, paced.

"You have to understand," Emmett said, "The measles were running like a plague through the island. Every kid was either getting over the sickness or coming down with it. Half of them were hovering at death's door, most of them babies too young and weak to fight off the disease. Wasn't a day went by we didn't hear of a loss.

"That baby—Eugenia—wasn't in a good way, either, in

that boat God knows how long, then riding twelve miles in damp, frigid air with only a blanket to keep her warm. Da had me put her inside my coat while they finished unloading the crates, and I kept her warm as I could, but she was chilled to the bone, no doubt about it."

"What happened when you got home?" Dex pushed.

"He was just a kid," Maggie reminded him, keeping her voice even for her uncle's sake. "It's not like they would have consulted him, or told him what they planned to do."

"You have the right of it, Maggie. I...I don't know what happened to the child." He shook his head. "If she didn't die of exposure, she'd have been placed with one of the families who'd lost a child to the epidemic."

"Do you remember any of the families that would have fit the bill?" Dex asked him. "One with a baby girl about the same age?"

The way Emmett looked over at her had Maggie's blood running cold. He squeezed her hand, but it didn't lessen the blow she knew was coming.

"Your grandmother, Maggie, she'd have been about the same age as Eugenia Stanhope. Is she the only one?" Emmett, frowning a little, looked over at Dex. "Do you know?"

"There'd have been several other families with little girls around the same age," Maggie said soothingly. "Jessi's for one." The Walker family would be another, which put Paige squarely in the crosshairs as well. And they wouldn't be the only ones.

"It might be a moot point if Eugenia didn't survive that boat trip," Dex said. But his gaze strayed to hers, not just considering now, judging.

Maggie ignored him, trying to reconcile what she'd just learned. When Dex had told her the truth about why he'd come to Windfall, she'd known someone's life was going to be turned upside down. She'd never dreamed it might be hers.

"Can I trust you to keep this a secret a little while longer?"

Dex spoke to Emmett, but he was still studying her face. She didn't like the pity she saw in his eyes now.

"You'll keep it to yourself, won't you, Uncle Emmett."

"Secret?" Emmett sighed wearily. "Did you tell me a secret?"

Maggie managed a weak smile as she got to her feet. "I'll send Mort over tomorrow to look at your oil burner."

"I'd be grateful, child. These old bones don't hold the warmth like they used to."

She bent, kissed his wrinkled cheek then put her hands on his shoulders. "Thank you for the cookies."

"Don't be a stranger."

"Never. You and Han are the only family I have."

She hoped.

"Maggie," Dex called after her as she headed out the front door. If she heard him, she didn't show it.

He thanked Emmett and hurried out after her, catching her arm before she could slide into the driver's seat of her Mustang.

She looked down at his hand, her expression as coldly furious as her voice. "You'll want to move that."

"Not until you tell me what you're thinking."

"None of your damn business."

When she tried to brush him off, he yanked her out of the door opening, put her up against the car, and caged her in. "I started this mess. That makes it my business."

"Back off," she snarled, punctuating it with a two-handed

shove that wouldn't have budged him if he hadn't allowed it—which he did because he saw the pain in her eyes.

Pain he'd put there. He was just beginning to understand how deeply he'd hurt Maggie, just allowing himself to think about why he'd needed to believe she didn't know her own heart.

"What more proof do you need?" she said, her words, her demeanor so cold he wondered he didn't get frostbite. "The next step is to have my DNA tested."

"No." The word was out before he gave it conscious thought. And when he did, he decided it was the right response. Even if it sabotaged his case.

Maggie's chin came up, her tone remained even, reasonable. But the bleakness in her vivid blue eyes sliced at him. "Not getting squeamish on me, are you? Where's the guy who'd do anything to solve a career-making case like this one?"

"Damn it, Maggie."

She stepped away, and he let her. He needed the distance as much as she did. He couldn't be close to her and pretend he still didn't want her like he needed his next breath. And he couldn't pretend she wasn't more important to him than his case.

"My great grandfather brought Eugenia home that night, weak and sick from exposure. His daughter was deathly ill with the measles. One of them survived to become my grandmother."

"Or Eugenia could have been placed with another family that lost a daughter about the same age."

"Then the test will rule me out."

"Or put you in immediate danger. Somebody knows why I'm here, Maggie. Whoever broke into my room wanted to find out what kind of progress I'd made on finding an heir for Eugenia. There's no other explanation. And if they're watching me I have to assume they're watching the lab. The minute we send off your DNA, you'll be a target."

"And you think I'm going to stand around wringing my hands if he comes after me? I'm not the kind of defenseless little woman you must be used to dealing with."

"No." Dex rubbed at one of the shoulders still aching from the shot she'd given him. "I wouldn't call you defenseless, but he's not going to give you fair warning, Maggie."

"Then I'll have to be careful."

"And I'll have to be your shadow."

That stopped her. She turned, her gaze so caustic she all but stared holes through hm. "I don't think so."

"Try to stop me."

"I'm just supposed to sit around in limbo? For how long?" she demanded, though she knew as well as he did that he had no answers to give her. "Sooner or later, and my guess is sooner, your bad guy is going to start nosing around out here. My office locks, but it isn't exactly Fort Knox, and I won't be the only possible descendant on that chart your genealogist is putting together. How many lives are you going to risk while you're busy watching my back?"

"We'll get rid of the chart for now."

She stepped back, crossed her arms, and when he met her eyes he could see he needn't have worried about her drawing any conclusions about why the idea of her being in danger made him want to hurt someone.

"Putting off the DNA test won't accomplish anything."

"That's my call."

"Try to stop me."

"You're already stopped. You don't know where to send the sample, or who to test it against."

"I don't imagine the Stanhopes will be hard to find. And I have a plane."

"That would be stupid," he said bluntly. "Which one of them wants Eugenia's descendants to disappear?"

"I thought they were the ones who sent you."

"But why did they send me? If I find descendants, will they be welcomed into the family or eliminated?" Dex could see he'd gotten his point across, but he felt a need to drive it home. "Going to the Stanhopes is the fastest way to get yourself killed."

"I want this over with."

"So you can go back to your nice, comfortable, closed-off life?"

"I'm closed off?" She stepped up to him, toe to toe. "You're the one who comes from a tidy, safe little world. You're the one who's afraid to risk, but you can stand there and accuse me? All I've ever done is risk and work—" Her voice hitched and she turned her face from his.

Dex almost hated himself for breaking her even that much. He reached for her, but she slapped his hands aside and walked away. "Maggie."

She paused, one foot already in her Mustang, and looked at him with eyes not just bleak but drenched now, too. "Stay away from me, Keegan. Just stay the hell away from me."

He caught the door, stopped her from closing it. "Promise me—" He stopped, words jumbling in his mind, feelings clogging his throat at the idea she might be hurt. And it hit him, with all the speed and explosive impact of a freight train. "Jesus, Maggie, I think I'm in love with you."

She laughed. It was a truly heart-breaking sound. "Right, throw me a bone and expect me to fall in line like a lovesick fool. You should have thought of that a couple of days ago. I might have fallen for it then."

She dropped into the driver's seat, flooring the car as soon as it turned over. The door ripped out of his hand, and all Dex could do was stand there, staring after her.

Like a lovesick fool.

Chapter Twenty-Four

Dex made good on his promise. A fool he might be, and a lovesick one at that, but a little discomfort didn't absolve him of his responsibility for putting Maggie in harm's way. Whatever he was feeling now would be nothing to what he'd suffer if she was hurt—physically—because of him.

He'd have slept on her front porch if necessary, but thanks to Holden Abbot, Dex had moved his things from the Horizon to Maggie's house. Until they found out who wanted Eugenia's descendants to disappear, Maggie's shadow was what he'd be.

That was just how she treated him. When she did have the misfortune to notice him, he was completely ignored.

Not that he didn't deserve it. He'd fucked up in a variety of ways. The list was long, beginning with him throwing her love back in her face, and ending with her returning the favor.

Dex leaned against the pillar supporting the roof over the wraparound porch, stared past the side of Maggie's house and out over the silver-gray chop of the bay under equally leaden skies. The wind had real teeth today, biting through the jeans and hooded sweatshirt he wore. He barely felt it. The Atlantic in a wintry mood was no competition for Maggie's particular brand of cold shoulder.

He blew out a breath, stuffed his hands in his pockets. If she'd cry, he could comfort her. If she'd lash out, he could fight back until her anger turned to a different kind of heat. If she'd throw his insults back in his face, he could agree with her. If she'd only talk to him, he could...

What? he asked himself, as he'd done so many times he'd lost count. What words could possibly be said that would erase the damage he'd already done?

I love you?

He'd tried that. She'd laughed at him. She'd believed he was trying to play her. She'd been right on both counts.

Where the hell did he get off proclaiming his feelings, let alone expecting her to fall at his feet in gratitude? He'd done nothing but lie and use and manipulate her since the moment he'd walked into her life. He'd threatened everyone and everything she loved, pushed her into a corner, and forced her to lie to her best friend, not to mention everyone else on the island. He'd done nothing but hurt her.

None of that changed how he felt, but his heart wasn't the one that mattered. Hers was. He'd broken it; he'd find a way to fix it before he left her alone. There was no other option.

"I hope you're thinking about what a jackass you are."

Dex turned, saw Jessi standing just behind him.

"A spineless, miserable jerk of a jackass," she continued, taking one step on each syllable, punctuating the last one by drilling a finger into his chest.

"What is it with the women on this island and physical assault?"

"We have a lot of experience with jackasses. Cowardly,

slow-witted jackasses, who don't get a point unless it hits them over the head."

"That's the second time you've called me a coward."

"I'm not trying to be subtle." She held up a finger when he tried to talk. "I don't want to hear any whiny defense or simple-minded justifications."

"I don't whine."

That earned him a small smile, as he hadn't troubled to deny any of her other insults. Except, "Slow-witted? Simple-minded?"

"Maybe short-sighted would be better, and I forgot self-delusional, so you can add that to the list. Don't you think it's about time you faced up to the truth, Dex? You're terrified."

"And we're back to cowardly."

Jessi looked away, murmured, "It takes one to know one. And you have no idea what I'm talking about," she said loud enough for him to hear her. "Love, Dex. You love Maggie and it scares the pants off you, doesn't it?

"You know how I know? Because I feel the same way. All the time. Terrified I'll fall in love with some jerk who will break my heart." She rubbed a hand over her chest in a way that told Dex more about her luck in love than any words she could have used.

"Benji's father?"

"Yeah. The idea of trusting anyone like that again makes me want to kill everything with a Y chromosome on the face of the earth."

He smiled, just a crooked twist of his mouth. "There's that bloodthirsty streak again."

"I was being dramatic for effect. Maggie..." Jessi sighed. "Her heart has been broken all her life, but she still chooses to love. She's so brave, Dex, so fearless. She's known the worst kind of pain there is, but she still risks her heart." She shifted enough to lean against the railing. "I could hate her for it, but mostly I'm just in awe."

"So you're saying she won't pine over me forever?"

"Maggie, pine?" Jessi laughed.

Dex had to smile, too, a real smile. Maggie Solomon wasn't the kind of woman who would sit around moping and sighing. She'd go out and live her life—hell, live was too pale a word. Maggie didn't just live. Maggie *was* life, vital and breathtaking, filled with a spark that was impossible to resist. Some day she'd find a man, settle down as much as she was able to, and have a couple of kids.

Dex caught himself frowning over that notion. Or maybe it was the way green crowded around the edges of that happy domestic picture.

"Well, now, that's not terror I see on your face."

Dex snapped back, caught sight of Jessi's self-satisfied smirk, and popped up a brow.

"So," she said, making her expression suitably serious, "Still afraid?"

"Absolutely," Dex said, "But I'm no coward."

She rested her hand on his arm. It amazed Dex how comforting he found the simple touch. "I never really doubted you."

"She won't even talk to me, Jess."

Jessi gave his arm a bracing squeeze. "I know Maggie. There'll be a moment, Dex. When it comes, you'll know it."

Jessi's confidence in him was highly overrated, Dex thought. Or maybe it was her faith in Maggie.

He could see it wearing on her as much as it was wearing on him, this…impasse they were at. He could understand that she wasn't the kind of woman who waited patiently. He should take the DNA sample and put them both out of their misery.

He couldn't bring himself to do it, though, knowing it

would put her firmly in the cross-hairs of whatever weapon was trained on his investigation.

The front door swung open, and Hold and Maggie stepped through it.

"We're off to the village," Hold announced. "Maggie's promised to buy me supper."

"I've been feeding and housing you since you arrived," Maggie said to him in an easy, sarcastic tone. "I think it's about time you picked up a check."

"I'm only too happy to, darlin'." Hold slung an arm around her shoulders, and every muscle in Dex's body clenched, except the one bunching in his jaw.

As they went down the steps, Maggie looked over. Her gaze didn't make it as far as Dex, he noticed, but she caught Jessi's eye. A look passed between the two women, and Jessi nodded slightly.

"What was that about?" Dex asked Jessi.

"Nothing, Sweetie, just a little girl talk. How about you come home with me and have a hot meal? It's only leftover night, but it beats eating alone."

"I'm not fit company tonight," Dex said, his eyes following Maggie's taillights until they disappeared. "Tell Benji I said hi."

He didn't hear Jessi's response, had no idea she'd gone until he heard the rumble of her old Explorer putt-putting out of the parking lot. Darkness fell before he tried to move and found himself all but frozen where he stood.

He shook off the cold, squared his shoulders, and sloughed off the malaise that had settled over him for the last two days. He didn't know how or why, but he was going to deal with Maggie, get her to see reason, and figure out a way to deal with her possible connection to Eugenia without putting her in danger.

And while he was at it, he'd end world hunger, he thought with a grim smile—which would be easier than getting Maggie to talk to him.

Maggie led Hold through the Horizon's lobby door rather than the one that opened directly to the restaurant. It had occurred to her on the short drive into the village that no one knew about him. She should have known better.

Not five seconds after they stepped inside Helen Appelman poked her head around the doorway.

"What, do you have radar or something?"

"We have a doorbell," she said to Maggie. But her eyes were firmly on Hold, and they were giving him a very thorough and appreciative once over. "This must be Holden Abbot. Mort," she said to Maggie's frown. "He mentioned you had a new fellow staying out at the airport, and what with Dex moving out there..." Helen smiled. "It'll be interesting to see what happens when you walk in on this one's arm."

Hold cocked his elbow obligingly.

Maggie ignored him. "I'm not on his arm."

"Okay, but see you take your customary booth," Helen said. "And keep your back to the wall. I'll try to keep the lunatics away." She took another long visual tour of Hold's tall, lean body. "I'll expect a full explanation later."

Hold grinned. "Name the time and place, darlin', and I'm yours."

Helen's cheeks pinked.

"Don't let AJ hear you say that," Maggie warned.

Helen snorted. "Are you kidding? I'd pay you to say that in front of him. Not to mention the rest of the barracudas who are here tonight."

Hold laughed, long and loud and infectious, and as

Helen ushered them into the dining room, every eye in the place swiveled to him. Several of the women got to their feet in order to get a better look.

Maggie met their gazes, each and every one of them, satisfied when butts reconnected with chairs.

Helen brayed out a laugh. "I don't believe you'll need me to keep the peace. George and a cocked pistol couldn't keep folks at bay the way you can with a look."

"I'm in no mood for the normal craziness," Maggie said, cursing under her breath when Helen took a closer look at her.

"You sure you want to share a table with her, Mr. Abbot?"

"I'll risk it," Hold said, "and it's Hold."

"Now, is that a name or a suggestion?"

Again with the laughter, and the women, and the quelling looks, which Maggie had to turn up a notch this time. "What are you, the Pied Piper of horny women everywhere?"

"I like to think of myself as a magnet, a big, strong one, and women are just pretty bits of glitter."

"With real sharp edges, around here anyway. Any one of them could rip you to shreds in a matter of minutes."

"But I'd enjoy every second of it. And I have amazing recuperative powers."

"Great, they'll erect a statue to you." She held up a hand. "Don't comment on my choice of verbs."

"I'll just say it was an apt one."

Maggie rolled her eyes, took him by the arm, and dragged him to the corner booth she favored. "Come on, I need to get my back to the wall before one of your glittery little admirers shanks me to clear the field."

"You and me're just friends, more's the pity."

"They don't know that."

Maggie slid into her customary seat. Hold took the one opposite her and picked up the menu.

"Don't bother," Maggie said. "You'll be getting the daily special, and you'll love it."

"Anything would be good about now. But we're not here for the food, are we?"

Maggie only half heard him, her gaze winging to the door, stalling there.

Hold touched her hand, brought her attention back to him. "You wanted me away from Dex for a reason, Maggie."

"It didn't exactly work," she said, tipping her head to where Dex stood by the entrance, staring at them.

Hold looked over the back of his seat, started to raise a hand in greeting. Dex ignored him, heading across the room. It took him a while, seeing as he stopped at nearly every table on the way.

"I thought he might want to join us," Hold said.

"He'll have no trouble finding a partner for dinner." But Maggie watched him refuse every offer, then take a seat at the bar.

He turned sideways on his stool, leaned one elbow on the bar, and stared in their direction.

"He doesn't appear to like being the consolation prize."

Hold looked over his shoulder, and when he turned back he was grinning. "Is that what you think he's mad about?"

Maggie shrugged.

"I'd say there's a green tinge to that glare he's aiming my way."

"Yeah, right, I shouldn't go by what he says, I should read into his expressions."

"You strike me as a sterling judge of character, Maggie."

"And?" she said cautiously.

"When have you ever met a man who knows what's in his own heart?"

Being that she'd grown up with a man who didn't know he even had a heart, she had to give Hold that one. She glanced at Dex, felt the beginnings of what she thought might be hope, and squashed it. She knew what hope could do to a person—had done to her. She wasn't going there again.

AJ provided just the distraction she needed to keep her from sliding back into the dark mood she'd finally begun to shed. He slid a plate in front of her, and one in front of Hold, before hurrying away at the call of his name.

"Good, old-fashioned Yankee pot roast," Maggie said. It smelled like heaven, but tasted like dust in her mouth.

Hold was clearly enjoying it, though. "It's not fried chicken and grits, but it does kind of hit the spot. Now if I could get you to tell me why I'm here, eating this truly amazing meal with a beautiful woman, my evening will be complete."

"Do you always take three times as long to say everything as the next person?"

"I come from a place where language, like everything else in life, is something to be savored at leisure. And you're evading."

"Fine, here it is. I want to submit my DNA for testing. I could go about it myself, but Dex won't tell me where to send the sample."

"And you want me to help you."

"I'm hoping you will, but if you're going to do the male solidarity thing, I'll find another way."

"By letting it be known you sent the test, even if you didn't."

She bumped up a shoulder. "It's going to come out anyway, but I'd rather do it the right way, Hold."

"And if I don't help you, you'll stick your neck out and

see who shows up to chop your head off. I get it, and you can keep your pretty little head on your shoulders. I'm all for the male solidarity thing, but in this case I happen to disagree with Dex."

Maggie opened her mouth, then shut it. "You'll help me get the sample in for testing?"

Mouth full, Hold nodded.

"Why?"

"For all the reasons I imagine you gave Dex when the two of you argued about it. I don't like using you as bait any more than he does, but it's the only option we have at the moment."

She stabbed a finger at him, vindication zipping through her like an electric charge. "Exactly. Dex is the damn professional; you'd think he could see that."

"Maggie. You really don't understand why he can't put you in danger?"

Her eyes wandered toward the bar.

"You don't want to see. He hurt you, and you won't be hurt again," Hold said as if he'd read her mind. "No one can guarantee that, Maggie, not even Dex. But are you really better off this way?"

"I'll be better off when this business is finished and my life gets back to normal."

"You don't believe that. Neither does he. You both just have to face up to it." He held up a hand. "Before you get all het up, I'll see to the DNA test because I agree with you. But I won't run interference between you and Dex."

"I'm not—" She blew out a breath. "Yeah, I guess I am. But—"

"He's sticking close because he's worried about you, Maggie. Maybe you should ask yourself why that is."

She settled back into her seat, knowing she was sulking

and not caring. "Maybe he should work up the nerve and tell me."

"You've never been a man, have you."

She snorted softly. "I've never been crazy, either, but it sounds about the same to me."

Dex watched Maggie make her way to the door, stopping to greet people much as he had when he walked in. Although it was tempting to confront her, he knew she wouldn't talk to him. So when Hold held up two fingers then gestured him over, he ordered a couple of beers and made his way to the booth.

"You could've brought the beers," Hold said when Dex slid in across from him.

"Now that you're alone you're free game."

Hold looked around the room, shrugged. "I don't see that as a problem."

"You will when you've had a little more experience on Windfall."

"I don't need more experience, son," Hold said with the kind of wicked smile that made Dex glad the man had his back to the room. If the women in the room saw that smile there'd be another riot.

"You invited me over, remember?"

"Sure, and I'll get right to the point. I'm going to send Maggie's DNA to the lab. Save your objections." Hold snagged one of the beers Helen dropped off on her mad race around the room, took a long pull. "We both know why you're holding off, and we both know you can't protect Maggie from a bullet if you don't know who's firing the gun."

The word *bullet* made Dex's blood run cold; he'd been on the receiving end of a sniper's rifle, and there was nothing quite as terrifying as taking fire when you didn't know where it was coming from. Unless the target was someone you loved. He took a swig to cool his suddenly burning throat, but he couldn't quite manage to banish that picture from his mind. "I've been trying to come up with a way around it. Can't find one."

"There is no way around it, Dex. She deserves to know the truth. She'll either match or she won't. Question is, which outcome are you afraid of?"

Either, Dex thought. *Both*.

If she was related to the Stanhopes, she'd become a member of one of the richest families in the country. It would change her, no matter how strong she was. When the truth came out, and the media descended on her, she'd have no choice but to run, either to the Stanhope family or to someplace she could find obscurity. Both destinations would take her from Windfall Island, and either way she'd hate him for ruining everything she'd built.

If she wasn't a Stanhope, she'd hunker into her life and shut him out. Hell, she'd already shut him out. And either way, there was someone out there trying to ensure that Eugenia's descendants never came to light. Someone who wouldn't wait for the outcome of a DNA test to see that Maggie didn't survive for her ancestry to be an issue.

"Let's put the lady out of her misery, and drag the black-hearted S.O.B. who's causing trouble out into the open before somebody gets hurt." Hold took Dex's silence as agreement. "'Course, that's not Maggie's only misery."

Dex got to his feet. "Stick with science, Abbot."

Hold looked over his shoulder, saw several pairs of female eyes glued to him, and said, "Biology always was one of my stronger subjects."

Chapter Twenty-Five

Maggie heard the distinctive throaty rumble of the Roadster as it pulled up in front of her house. *Never should have repaired the thing after the rock slide*, she thought bitterly. Then it wouldn't grate so much that he continued to drive her car, now that they were...apart. But she'd be damned if she gave him the satisfaction of knowing it bothered her by asking for the keys back. She could have locked her front door, but that would have been cowardly. She wasn't a coward. Stupid, yes, misguided, certainly. Foolish enough to fall in love with a man she'd known would never love her back? Definitely. And it would be a whole hell of a lot easier to deal with her own folly once Dex Keegan was gone.

Until then, she'd handle it, and him, face to face.

"Are you ever going to talk to me again?"

His voice, so close behind her, was bad enough. He touched her, and it was worse. Just a fingertip feathering over her shoulder, and she began to tremble. She sidled away from him, then turned when she had enough distance.

Face to face didn't have to mean toe to toe. She could still see Dex, still hear him, but he couldn't touch her.

"I love you, Maggie."

Okay, he couldn't touch her physically.

"This is where you tell me you love me, too."

"What would that accomplish?"

He shrugged slightly. "We could kiss and make up."

"And sleep together?"

His lips tipped up, just at the corners. "I could convince myself."

"I wouldn't object to the sex, but I think we need to get a few things straight first."

"That's what I've been trying to say, Maggie. We need to talk."

"No, you just have to listen." Without thinking, she took a step forward, wanting desperately for Dex to hear her this time, hear and understand why she couldn't let him in again. "You were right about me. I learned about love from a man who doesn't have the first clue what it is. You were there the other day. You heard him use love as a bargaining chip. If I were a good, dutiful daughter, if I loved him, I'd be willing to do what he wanted when he wanted it and be ignored the rest of the time."

"Maggie—"

"There's no use tilting at windmills, Dex," she said over him. "People are who they are, and they don't change."

"They can fall in love."

"Maybe that's true, but I won't leave here, and you won't stay."

"Shouldn't that be my decision?"

"You made it before you ever set foot on this island, and you made it clear to me before I fell in love with you."

"So it's your fault I hurt you?"

Her eyes lifted to his, and in them she saw a world of regret. "Yes."

"Bullshit."

"You may be close to solving a case that will make your career. Are you telling me you would turn your back on that now?"

"I'm telling you I can make my life anywhere." When she opened her mouth, he said, "No, my turn to talk."

She snapped her jaws closed, bit back on the argument she'd been about to make. The sooner Dex had his say, the sooner he'd leave her alone.

"People go missing all over the world, Maggie," he began, dark eyes imploring hers, deep voice washing over her like a warm, soothing blanket she hated to shrug off.

"No matter where I live I'll have to do some travelling. Or hell, I can take on cold cases like the Stanhope kidnapping. There's something about closing the books on a case no one else has been able to solve, bringing peace to a family that has been searching for a lifetime."

"There's probably not a lot of money in that," Maggie pointed out coolly.

"So I'd be thankful to have a wife who's bringing home the bacon."

Her ears began to buzz, her heart to pound. She swayed as her mind took a long, dizzy whirl. None of it convinced her she hadn't heard what Dex said. Or understood his meaning.

And when it finally sunk in, she backed off a step, then a couple more for good measure. "Jesus, now who's jumping the gun?"

He gave her that one-shoulder bump she used all the time. It only pissed her off coming from him.

"I love you," he said. "You love me. What else matters?"

She threw hands up in the air, started to pace. "How about the fact that you don't want to live on a tiny little speck of real estate, populated by people who think the world isn't right without a little crazy in it? How about there's someone out there watching and waiting to see if a Stanhope heir is found, and it's probably one of those crazies? One of my friends," she amended, "who may be ready to kill." The thought of it, along with all the other emotional upheaval, was almost enough to break her.

Instead she fought back the tears, ruthlessly steadied her voice. "How about I'm not the easiest person to live with? I'm a pain in the ass at the best of times, contrary, sarcastic, hardheaded, and I'm focused on building something here. I don't have time for a husband, let alone kids."

"How about this?" He crossed the room in a flash of movement she failed to anticipate before he caught her around the waist, pushed her back against the wall, and kissed her.

She tried to fight him off. But her heart wasn't in it.

Dex swung her up into his arms, headed for the stairs.

"No," she said simply. She could withstand his words, she could even make love with him and stick to her guns, as long as it was fast and hard and physical. If he was gentle with her, she'd be lost. "Put me down, Dex."

He dropped her feet to the floor. He didn't let her go. "We love each other, Maggie. We'll figure the rest out as we go along."

His fingers rubbed a circle, warm and soothing, on the side of her waist, his eyes met hers, and she wanted to believe him. "I don't know…"

"Then I'll convince you."

He held out his hand.

Maggie froze; even her heart stopped beating. But as Dex's fingers started to curl over his palm, she couldn't stop herself. Maybe it was understanding the pain she was causing him, maybe it was impossible for her not to hope one more time. Either way, she moved into his arms, felt them tighten around her, and with a small sigh, she surrendered.

And still he waited.

She eased back, looked into his eyes, and saw everything in the midnight depths. Need tempered by control, patience warring with hunger, vulnerability bolstered by the strength to let her set the pace.

She held out her hand this time, and when he took it, led him up the stairs. When they got to the top she turned into his arms, just held him and let him hold her while the sorrow and heartache of the last few days slipped away.

"Dex," she began, but he took her mouth, pulled her into a kiss of such sweet tenderness everything in her seemed to bloom.

She wasn't a woman who'd ever dreamt at all, let alone in terms of flowers and bluebirds and little circling hearts, but she could see it all now, and her heart simply sang.

"Let me," he said, brushing her hands aside to remove her flannel shirt, feathering his fingers along her shoulder and making her tremble. Then her tank was gone, her bra, too, and he was touching her everywhere with hot hands and hotter lips. He bent and took one aching breast into his mouth, running his tongue across her nipple as he drew her deeper into the heat, and she felt the tug of his mouth everywhere.

Need gathered, filled her, building into an ache that only grew as he slipped a hand into her jeans, beneath her panties, inside her. And shot her to peak where she stood.

And when her knees gave out, Dex swept her up again, and it felt like she was floating, even after he laid her down on the bed. He touched her again, everywhere this time, and the need rose in her, impossibly higher until she twisted her body against his just to feel his strength.

She slid her hands over him, smooth skin and hard muscle, drifting down to wrap her hand around him. Dex groaned, head thrown back, the muscles in his neck corded. He caught her wrist, and she said, "I want you inside me," and then he was, surging into her, deep and hard. And not moving.

"Dex," she gasped, shoving at his shoulders, right on the edge again and desperate.

"Shhh," he said, gathering her close, holding her tight. "What's the hurry?"

The hurry? The hurry was everything, Maggie thought. It was the slide of her skin against his, the way their bodies fit and moved together, the race of her heart, the burn in her blood. The haze over her mind. It was letting go of the pain and being with the man she loved.

She kissed him, poured herself into it as she eased Dex onto his back and rose over him, filled with so much love she wanted only to share it. She let Dex fill her body as he'd filled her heart, moved with him in a dance as old as time and as new as the morning to come.

She told Dex how she felt, not with words, but with her body, the same way he told her, giving and taking until they rose and crested together, then drifted back to reality in each other's arms.

Chapter Twenty-Six

Dex woke up, blinking and stretching in the bright morning sunshine streaming in Maggie's bedroom windows. He rolled toward her. And shot out of bed when he realized she was gone. He dragged on some clothes and went racing out onto the tarmac, pants unbuttoned, juggling his shirt, jacket and shoes. And there was Maggie, clipboard in hand, brilliant blue eyes focused like lasers into the engine compartment of her Piper.

She pulled back, made a check mark on her checklist, and glanced his way. "What's with the stupid grin?" she asked, closing the compartment and stepping down from the ladder.

"You. Us."

"I haven't agreed to be an *us* yet."

Dex just kept grinning. Maggie was clear-eyed and annoyed—and blushing, just a little but enough to tell him he'd wormed his way through her defenses. He sidled up to her, whispered in her ear.

She pushed him away. But she was grinning now, too.

"So what's on the agenda?"

"I have souvenirs to drop off and mail to pick up in

Portland, along with a charter down to New York. Plus a quick stop in Boston; a courier is meeting me at the airport there."

To pick up her DNA test, Dex knew, squashing the urge to ask her not to go. "Can I brush my teeth before we take off?"

"You're not going with me."

"Yeah, I am."

She stopped what she was doing, set her clipboard on the top step of the ladder, and came over to stand beside him. "It's too soon for anyone to take a shot at me," she said, keeping her voice low though there was no one but the two of them around. "Once my DNA hits the lab, then you can worry."

"Somebody has already taken a shot at you. Those rocks."

"Were more likely aimed at you."

"We can't be sure of that, Maggie. Somebody is paying attention, somebody with bad intentions."

"I don't disagree," Maggie said, retrieving her clipboard and going back to work. "But the quickest way to tip your hand is to stick to me like glue, Dex. Protecting me puts a pretty big target on my back. Besides, I haven't loaded enough fuel to compensate for your body weight."

"So load more fuel."

She gave him a look, part exasperation and all stubbornness.

He could be just as stubborn. "Your only other option is to stay grounded."

And now he saw anger storm across her face. "You don't get to dictate what I do or when I do it."

"If I had my way you'd be in a locked room, wrapped in cotton wool," he shot back. He took her by the shoulders, shook her enough to get his point across. "I'll do whatever it takes to see that you're safe. You're going to have to deal with that, and me, from now on. You fly, I fly."

She turned back to the plane, gave herself a minute to fight off tears. Dex had all but crushed her heart and she hadn't cried, but the man showed her a little concern and she was mush. Which didn't change reality. "I don't take chances with my equipment, Dex. My plane is air-worthy or it doesn't go up." She held up her clipboard. "That's what this checklist is about. That's why Mort slept on a cot in the hangar last night—the locked hangar. I'll be damned if I let the coward threatening us ground me. I do that and I've given up more than my life."

"Then you'd better load more fuel, Maggie."

She shrugged. "Fine. I'm leaving in ten minutes."

He took her clipboard, saw she was only halfway down the list. "We both know you won't be taking off until you've finished this, and we both know I can be ready in less time."

She snatched the clipboard back from him, ripped the half-completed sheet off and let it go. "Watch me."

Dex caught the page before it could flutter away, held it out to her.

She looked at it, at him, and crossed her arms.

He held her eyes for a moment, let his lips curve. "You love me that much?"

She tore the page out of his hand, slapped it back on her clipboard. "Who said anything about love?"

"You did. You just didn't use words." And at her disgruntled glare, he grinned. "It's just a matter of time before I convince you to marry me. Until then, I'll settle for the pleasure of your company."

Maggie watched Dex walk off. After last night, the way she'd, well, blossomed in his arms, she'd needed some time to herself. She wasn't going to get it, but she didn't stew over it for long. Sure, Dex had boxed her into a corner, but you just had to admire a man who could be as hard-headed, as focused, as much a pain in the ass as you were, she decided.

That didn't mean it was a good idea for them to shackle themselves to one another permanently.

Still, spotting Dex striding across the tarmac, dark hair wet and sleeked back from what must have been a very quick shower, sent her heart on a long, slow roll in her chest.

As he neared he said, "For a second there I thought you were happy to see me."

"That's quite a fantasy world you're living in," she replied. The sarcasm felt good, normal—to Dex, too, judging by his grin.

"I'm under no delusions where you're concerned."

"Good thing, because I'm not the pipe and slippers-fetching type."

"I don't smoke, I prefer my feet bare, and I can fetch for myself." He stepped up, brushed a hand over her hair. "But if that's a yes—"

She snorted softly. "You're lucky I didn't leave without you."

He cupped her cheek, ran his thumb over her skin. "Then I guess I'd have had to grow wings." He grinned. "Can't have my woman going off without me."

She looked into his laughing eyes, wanting so desperately to believe what she saw there. "Dex—"

"Maggie—" Mort came around the back of the plane, stopping short when he saw Dex.

Maggie swung around, thought she caught the heat of a glare in the look Mort directed at Dex before his gaze dropped to his feet, the toe of one boot digging into a crack in the pavement. "What's up?" she asked him.

When he lifted his eyes again, they latched onto Dex. And they were definitely filled with anger.

"Mort," she began without any idea what she could say to ease whatever hurt she'd caused him.

"Weather's kicking up down the coast," he said on a rush.

"I checked the forecast, Mort. It's just a little squall, nothing I can't go around."

"And I'm going with her," Dex put in.

"Can you control the weather?" Mort sneered.

"Down, Fido."

Mort snapped his mouth shut, his gaze shifting from Dex's face to Maggie's. "You'll be fine. You've got Superman with you." He turned on his heel and shuffled off.

"Mort," Maggie called after him.

He never looked back, but she watched him until he disappeared into his little tool shed.

"He has a crush on you," Dex said.

"No, but I'm about the only friend he has." Maggie sighed a little, rubbed a hand over the back of her neck. "His mother isn't doing well; he's fixating. He'll get over it."

"Sure, right after he rips out my heart and feeds it to me."

She rolled her eyes. "You're a bit of a drama queen, Keegan."

"I object to the word 'queen.' "

"Sure, that's the part you should object to. Get in the plane, Elizabeth."

They popped down to Boston and dropped off the DNA test to a courier Hold had waiting at the airport. After that they picked up the mail and delivered the souvenirs in Portland. They were back in the air in under an hour, Maggie breathing a sigh of relief as she turned the Piper for home.

"What happened to the charter?" Dex said once they'd taken off from Portland, hit altitude and leveled off.

"I called a friend while you were making yourself pretty. He'll get the executive to his meeting in New York, and he'll think Solomon Charters took him there."

Dex skimmed right over the dig. "He? How good a friend?"

She slanted him a look. "Are you going to give me a personal history?"

He smiled, settled back into his seat.

"I'll take that as a no."

"It's history, Maggie. For both of us."

"You're taking a lot for granted."

He met her gaze. "I'm trusting you to forgive me."

She looked away.

"I'm not expecting it to happen overnight."

She smiled slightly. "We're almost ho—, uh, back to Windfall."

She'd almost said "home," but Dex only grinned over it. He'd pushed her enough for the time being. He looked down, saw the familiar mosaic of islands separated by narrow channels of water. And home was what he felt.

"Was that a sigh I just heard?"

"More like fatalism," he said.

"Windfall has that effect on people," she said. "You're happy to see the place, but you kind of wonder why."

"I know why," Dex said. "You're there."

She let that sink in as silence fell, or as much silence as possible in a small plane with a turbo-prop. "We're a couple of idiots. Most people who fall in love are."

"Put this thing on autopilot."

"What?"

"Never mind." He wrapped a hand around the back of

her neck, met her halfway between the two seats for a kiss that went hot and deep, sizzling in her bloodstream and shorting out brain cells so that the world lurched, and then everything went silent and soft and hazy, and it felt like they were falling...

"*Shit!*" She jerked away from Dex, pulling back on the wheel as the engine sputtered and the Piper lurched again, fighting gravity. Maggie consulted the instrument panel, her breath hitching as she watched the needle on the fuel gauge sweep down to empty.

The propeller gave a couple of weak chugs then stopped turning, and quiet descended. "I think we blew a fuel line."

Dex just sat there in his seat, looking relaxed, all except his eyes, which were glued to her.

"Jesus, Dex, did you hear me? I checked every connection, every wire, every inch of that engine—" Her breath sobbed out, muscles screaming as she fought to pull the Piper's nose up. Fought and lost. The plane dropped closer and closer to the surface of the Atlantic, nothing she could do. "Parachutes?" Dex said.

"No time." She unhooked the radio speaker, oddly calm in the face of the inevitable. "Mayday, mayday," she said into it, giving their coordinates while Dex unhooked his belt and disappeared into the back of the plane.

"There's this," he said from behind her.

She looked over her shoulder and had to smile. "You aren't Indiana Jones."

"It was worth a shot."

"You just hang onto that raft," Maggie said, "And get back in your seat. I'm going to try a belly landing on the water, and we'll need to be strapped in for the impact. If I pull it off, we won't have much time to get out of the plane before it sinks."

"And if you don't pull it off?"

"I'll be damned if I let some backstabbing son of a bitch—" But she had to break off, focus all her strength to keep the nose up, keep the Piper in a glide as gravity dragged them toward the unforgiving surface of the Atlantic—deceptively smooth, but like concrete, Maggie knew, if you slammed into it.

Skimming it now, that was the ticket, and skim it she did, the plane bouncing back up with a screech of metal that told her something had torn. Something on the belly, she hoped, fighting to keep them level because if one of the wings caught the surface they'd be pulled into a cartwheeling spin. Belts or no belts, she and Dex would bounce around the inside of the plane like pinballs. They'd be dead before the Piper came to a stop and there was even a ghost of a chance of getting out and into that raft.

Dex was yelling, feet braced on the dashboard and reaching for her. She shoved him off, pissed that she had to take a hand off the wheel for even a second.

"Touch me again, and we're both going to die," she shouted, knowing he couldn't hear her any more than she could hear him.

The belly of the Piper hit for the second time, jerked her against the harness and she felt something tear again, in her this time. She felt a screaming pain along her left side, hoped it was just a cracked rib. As they hit again she bore down on the wheel, ignored the pain and the possibility the strain would turn a cracked rib into a broken one, maybe puncture her lung. The plane skipped off the surface of the ocean, bounced up, then dropped down again, softer this time, followed by a series of increasingly smaller bounces, like a stone skipping over water as the plane lost momentum.

Fire shot along her ribs with each jolt, and then they were down, the Piper nosing in as it finally came to a halt. And began to sink.

"Crack that door," Maggie ordered Dex, barely waiting for him to climb out of the passenger seat before she was up and making her way into the belly of the plane.

Water began to pour in around her boots, quickly climbing up her calves to her knees.

"Hurry, Maggie, Jesus," Dex shouted, pulling at her arm.

The Piper was already listing badly, pain and frigid water were stealing her strength, but she hauled the canvas bag up to the cockpit and shoved it at him. "Take this."

"What the hell?" But he shoved her in front of him and out of the plane, dragging the sack as he followed her.

She had to duck under the surface of the water to get out, then fight the suction of the plane as the water dragged it down. And she was losing. She fought with her one good arm, kicked frantically with her feet, but the freezing blue-green water closed over her head, stung her eyes and nose, pressed on her lungs as she was pulled down in the wake of the Piper.

She looked up, spotted the life raft on the surface, Dex's feet disappearing into it, and thanked God he was safe. And then he was swimming down to her, his expression murderous. She reached for him with her good arm, his hand closed around her wrist, and she swore, though his mouth never moved, she could hear him yelling at her to fight.

Fight she did, drawing on reserves she never knew she possessed to force her frozen muscles to kick and struggle, her lungs to hold out just a few more seconds. Her head broke the surface just as she surrendered to the need to draw something, anything, into her lungs. What she got was a combination of air and water as Dex dragged her into the life raft, cussing her out the entire time.

She ignored him, draping herself over the side of the raft, coughing and retching the water out of her lungs as huge air bubbles boiled to the surface, gradually tapering off until there was nothing to show what she'd lost.

"That was my first plane," she murmured, not the least ashamed of the tears burning her eyes.

"You're my first wife," Dex said. "I almost lost you, too."

"First?" She rolled over, closed her eyes, remembered to count her blessings. "Cheesy, Keegan. And that better be *only* wife."

Dex dragged her over and into his lap. She wrapped her good arm around him, burrowed in for a minute. Now that she wasn't fighting to keep them alive, the fear tried to creep in, and it felt so good to be held, even bobbing around in the middle of nowhere, freezing to death and with her life in shambles.

"You can let go now," she said when she tried to pull back and he wouldn't let her.

"Just another minute," he said, but he eased back, kissed her, long and deep, then rested his forehead on hers. "You nearly died, Maggie. The plane was sucking you down."

"No, Dex—" She hissed in a breath when he only tightened his grip.

He eased her back, searched her face.

"I think I cracked a rib or two," she explained, earning herself a few more choice curses, not to mention an insult or two.

"Swear at me all you like," she said, mostly amused, "But I have to object to being called stupid."

"Yeah?" He kicked the canvas bag at the other side of the small raft. "What's with the luggage that you'd risk your life for it?"

"Nobody messes with the U.S. Mail. I got paid to pick

that up. I'll be damned if it's going to the bottom of the Atlantic, just because somebody tried to kill me."

"Idiot." And although she knew he was teasing, he held her tight enough to make her ribs complain again.

She bore the ache, even managed a slight laugh as she turned her face into his neck and said, "Maybe there's something to this marriage thing after all."

That made him let go, but only enough so he could see her face. "Is that a yes?"

"Well, you did save my life."

He took his jacket off and wrapped it around her. "You saved us both, Maggie. If we'd been on our way to New York, we'd have been over land when we ran out of fuel."

She closed her eyes, ignored the pain when she clung to him a little tighter. "That would have made the landing a little more difficult."

Chapter Twenty-Seven

Maggie picked up the single stingy oar included in the life raft kit.

Dex took it out of her hands.

"So, are you going to marry me?"

She settled gingerly back against the side of the raft, both arms wrapped around her middle. "Tell me you have a phone, and I'm yours."

"Not only do I have a phone, it's waterproof."

"I knew it," she shouted, but had to settle for only imagining pumping her fist into the air. "You're such a boy scout."

Dex left the phone in his wet back pocket. "We can't call anyone to come get us."

"What? We're at least ten miles from shore," Maggie said. "And I'm not going to be much help rowing."

"Then I'll row."

"We could call Hold and Jessi."

His eyes cut to hers. "If you call and tell them we're alive, he'll bolt."

"Who'll bolt?"

"Mort."

Maggie lowered her eyes, not ready to see the truth in Dex's. *Not Mort*, she told herself and her breaking heart. How could a kid she loved like a brother try to murder her? "Even if we assume the Piper was sabotaged—"

"Maggie. You checked that engine from one end to the other, you said so yourself."

"Even if we assume," she repeated, "Mort isn't the only person on the island who could have done it."

"He's the only person who would know how to get it past you. Do you want to risk it?" he added when she remained silent.

"You know Jessi has to be going crazy right now."

"And you know she's not a good enough actor to hide her relief from Mort."

"Yeah." If Mort was the one behind the malfunction of her Piper—and who was she kidding, Maggie thought as her eyes filled? Mort was the only one with both the knowledge and the opportunity to sabotage the plane. "For what it's worth, he tried to stop me."

"He didn't try very hard." Dex dipped the oar in the water. His muscles, cold from the water and freezing wind, protested immediately. "Next time, bring along a raft with a motor."

"Next time?"

Dex blew out a breath. "Just tell me which way."

"West," she said, swallowing back her tears so she could read the compass from the raft's survival pack. "Into the sunset."

The sunset was just a fond memory, and Dex's arms were like rubber by the time they made it to the small sandy shingle of shore behind Maggie's house—which had cost him an additional mile.

Windfall Airport was lit up like Christmas, the landing lights on and every window in the office blazing.

"You ought to work on that upper body strength a little more," Maggie teased.

"Just in case I have to row ten miles again?" Dex said, not buying her light tone for a second. Not with her teeth chattering.

She was freezing, they both were, but Dex hoped the fact that she was still lucid meant she wasn't heading into shock.

"The runners used to do it several times a week, Dex. Twelve miles out, twelve miles back, without motors when the night was still and the Coast Guard was out."

"Been doing your research?"

She jerked up a shoulder, hissed a little at the pain.

Dex pulled her close, rubbed at her arms, her back. "Let's go in the house and get you into some dry clothes."

"I'd rather just get it over with. Before anyone realizes we survived."

Since Dex agreed, they made their way across Maggie's lawn, rimed with frost. It was deathly quiet inside the lobby of the Windfall Island Airport. For a minute Dex didn't think anyone was there. Then Jessi appeared in the doorway, eyes swollen and red from crying. She sobbed once, and launched herself at Maggie, shoving her back against Dex.

"You're alive," Jessi whispered, stepping back at Maggie's pained gasp.

"What happened?" Hold demanded.

"She's hurt, give her a minute."

"It's okay, Jess," Maggie said, then answered Hold's question. "Busted fuel line, I think."

"Busted?"

"With a little help, in my opinion," Dex put in. "Maggie managed to ditch the plane in the water, prettiest bit of flying I'll ever see, and I'm not just saying that because she saved both our asses."

"You kept me from drowning."

Jessi held up both hands. "Wait, you almost drowned?"

Neither Dex nor Maggie were paying attention to her anymore.

"Not happy to see me, Mort?" Maggie said, hurt clear in her eyes.

Mort's gaze, completely unapologetic, lifted and slid to the door.

Dex shifted over to block him just as he saw George Boatwright appear out of the shadows at the far side of the office.

George's eyes, dark and shadowed in his pale face, went to Maggie. "Jessi called me when she thought you were..." He crossed the room in three strides, caught Maggie up into a hard hug that lifted her off her feet, and made her gasp in pain.

George put her down, but kept his hands on her arms. "What the hell is going on, Maggie? Start with why you think Mort sabotaged your plane."

Dex came over, wrapped his arm around Maggie's waist, and drew her over to sit. "Why don't we let Mort explain that?"

"Got nothing to say," Mort muttered.

Dex turned and punched him in the face.

Mort staggered back, fell on his ass.

"That's for trying to kill Maggie. And me, even if you didn't plan it that way."

Mort picked himself up off the floor, pulled his sleeve over his hand to dab at his bleeding lip. "Maggie was a paycheck. Killing you would have been a pleasure."

"Who hired you?" Dex said flatly.

"Hold on a minute." George stepped between them, his hands curling into fists. "You just admitted you tried to kill Maggie."

Mort cringed back, but George had more self-control than Dex. Only a little more. He caught Mort by the shirt-front, lifted him off the floor and launched him into a chair.

"Not that I'm unimpressed with all this macho behavior," Maggie said, "but can you leave him in one piece long enough to explain why he damaged my plane?"

Mort's gaze shot to her, but he only went sullen and silent.

Maggie shot to her feet, shoving George and Dex aside to get right in Mort's face. "You tried to kill me, after... Jesus, you're like my brother."

"Brother." He shoved to his feet, knocking Maggie back a step. "The only family I have is dying. Like you give a damn."

Maggie closed her eyes for a moment, her face a study in misery. "And this is how you show your mother you care?"

"I can save her if I have enough money."

"So you traded her life for mine."

Mort sat, put his head in his hands.

Dex almost felt sorry for him. Almost. "What I want to know is how you found out Maggie was the focus of my investigation."

"All I did was pay attention. Nobody ever notices me unless they need me." He shot Dex a hate-filled glare. "When you moved out here, I got a phone call."

"From?"

Mort leaned back, crossed his arms. "Not answering questions 'til I talk to a lawyer."

Dex scrubbed a hand back through his hair, pissed at

himself for being so obvious, for being so lost in Maggie that he hadn't stopped to think about what it might say to someone on the outside looking in.

"Whatever you're thinking," Maggie said tightly, "stop it."

"I should have known after the rock slide." His eyes cut to Mort. "That was you, too. And you went through my room before you were told to take Maggie out. Who gave the order?"

Mort ignored Dex, and although Mort kept his eyes downcast, Dex could see that the kid seriously hated him.

"I should have figured it," he said again. Even though his interest in Maggie had been personal rather than investigatory, whoever was behind the murder attempts wouldn't know that. When there was so much money involved, even the rich went a little crazy. "Who paid you?"

Mort looked up at George. "You can take me to jail now."

Dex stepped toward him, only to see Maggie's eyes roll back, and when she fainted, he managed to scoop her up before she crumpled to the floor.

Jessi rushed over, hands fluttering, but Dex was already heading for the door.

George got there first, held it open. "I'll deal with Mort, you take care of Maggie," he said, though Dex could see he wished it were otherwise.

At the moment Dex could have cared less about Mort, or George, or the Stanhope case. Especially the Stanhope case. He carried Maggie to her house, and into her bedroom, thankful his watery muscles didn't give out halfway up the stairs.

"You have a doctor on the island?" he asked Jessi, who was already pulling off Maggie's boots.

"No."

"What the hell do you do when somebody is sick?"

"Maggie flies them to the mainland."

Dex huffed out a breath, set to helping her undress Maggie so they could get her warm.

"We could go by boat," Jessi offered.

"The trip would do her more harm than good."

"But—"

"I know enough first aid to tell she only fainted. Her breathing is good, her heart rate is steady." He set a hand on her forehead. "She's not feverish, just exhausted and in pain."

"Mother Appelman has a way with healing. But we'd have to take Maggie to her."

Dex shook his head. "Sleep's the best thing for her. We'll have to wrap her ribs, though."

He sent Jessi looking for a sheet that he cut into wide strips. Jessi helped him wind them around Maggie's ribs, not easy now that he'd seen the livid bruises along her left side. For a minute all he could think of was getting his hands around Mort's throat and squeezing until the image of those dark purple smudges on Maggie's pale, perfect skin faded.

"I'd like to kill him myself," Jessi said, patting the hands Dex had fisted so tightly they ached. "Let's take care of Maggie for now. Mort will still be there in the morning."

Maggie stood under the hot water, let it beat over her head for a couple of minutes before easing back to put her mid-section directly under the spray. She stayed that way until her skin started to prune and the water began to cool.

Twenty minutes later she was dried, dressed and trying to figure out a way to re-wrap her ribs when Dex staggered to the bathroom door and leaned against the jamb, blinking in the light.

"Why didn't you wake me?"

"Same reason you let me sleep last night."

He yawned, rasped his fingers through the growth over his jaw. "I could use a shower and some coffee."

Maggie held out the strips of sheet. "Help me with this, and you can have the first while I see to the second."

He took the cloth from her, but when she lifted her arms, he simply slipped under them and pulled her close, carefully.

Surprised, touched, Maggie turned her face into his neck and held on for a minute. Just a minute. There were still loose ends to tie up. "Let's finish this," she said, giving herself a moment to let him pull her into a kiss that rejuvenated her more than anything else could have.

Less than an hour later, Dex guided her Mustang into the village. Neither of them had had much of a stomach for food, but Dex had forced Maggie to choke down a piece of toast, and she was grateful for it now, when nerves had her stomach pitching.

No matter how somber their purpose, though, neither of them had been prepared for what they found inside George's little station house.

"Mort hanged himself in his cell last night," George said as soon as they walked in, even before they saw the blanket-draped form in the tiny cell.

Maggie sank into the single chair, let her head drop into her hands as sorrow weighed heavy on the load of worry and regret she was already carrying.

Dex rounded on George. "What the hell happened?"

"Guilt, regret—my guess is he couldn't face what he'd done, couldn't stand the thought of everyone finding out he tried to harm Maggie."

"That didn't occur to you last night?"

"I took his belt and his shoelaces," George rasped out, his jaw so tight it was a wonder he could talk at all. "He used the sheet from the cot, wrapped it around the bars and his neck and—"

"Mort is dead," Maggie cut in, too exhausted and sad to even raise her voice. But it got through. "Someone has to tell his mother."

Dex and George backed off from each other, and fists were relaxed.

"I'll handle it," George said, "right after you tell me what's going on."

Dex would have refused, but Maggie met his eyes, shook her head, and he relented. The story took an amazingly short time, considering how much her life had changed in the few short weeks since Dex had walked into it.

"I always knew Alec sent me here on behalf of the family," Dex finished, "but it looks like one of the Stanhopes doesn't want a descendant found. They must have hired Mort to see to it. Now Mort is dead, and he took the name of the master-mind with him. Unless you got it out of him last night."

George sighed heavily. "He asked for a lawyer. Can't question him after that. Which, being a former cop, you know."

"Yeah." Still it took Dex a minute to swallow his disappointment before he said, "It could be any one of the Stanhopes. Even the one who hired me."

"They'll all need to be investigated," Maggie said wearily.

"Digging into the family history?" George asked her with a little edge to his voice.

Dex pulled out his cell. "Suppose we find out?" He kept his eyes on Maggie as he punched in the number, as it rang, as he told the voice on the other end why he'd called.

Maggie saw the answer on his face and closed her eyes, relief blowing through her like a fresh breeze.

"Not my family history," she said, and sank down on the edge of George's desk, taking Dex's hand as he came over to stand in front of her. "I'm not a match. I'm sorry, Dex."

Dex swiped away the single tear that was tracking down her cheek. "I'm not."

"But your case—"

"Isn't solved. Yet."

"So you'll be sticking around," George observed coolly.

"I was sticking around anyway," Dex said, still holding Maggie's eyes, "Case or no case."

"Well, at least your romance will keep people from wondering why you're staying on Windfall." George sat back, then forward again, his gaze going from Maggie to Dex. "I'm not happy you didn't bring me in from the beginning, but you were right to keep this quiet. I'll do the same," he continued. "I don't want to cause a frenzy. But I'll be keeping my eye on both of you from now on."

Chapter Twenty-Eight

It took George even less time to relate what had taken place since Dex's arrival on Windfall Island than it had taken Dex to tell him. But then, George's audience was infinitely more knowledgeable about the case—and able to show it as he hadn't been.

"How are you going to handle the mother?"

George shifted in his chair, the quiet voice bringing him back to the conversation at hand. "She's under hospice care on the mainland, not expected to last the week. It's a blessing she doesn't know."

"It may be a blessing for her, but it was cruel to use Mort, to play on his hopes."

George let silence provide his agreement. "I'm sure I can convince Maggie to keep Mort's part in all this quiet. She won't want his memory tarnished."

"Not going soft on me, are you?"

"There's already been one death here."

"There might be more. Can you handle it?"

"I know what I signed up for, what it might mean to the community here." He wouldn't mourn Mort, not as long as he recalled that the kid had nearly killed Maggie.

George didn't delude himself that it might not be so black and white if there was a next time. "Doesn't mean I have to like it."

"But you're still in."

"Yeah, I'm in." George scrubbed a hand over his face, but it did little to ease his conscience. "As far as Keegan knows, I'm keeping his business here a secret. What about your family?" he countered. "Keegan knows it has to be one of the Stanhopes. He'll be trying to find out which one of you wants Eugenia to stay dead."

That was met with silence, the considering kind, and George knew the person on the other end of the line was not prone to rash and thoughtless actions. "Your Maggie is safe, in any case."

"She's not my Maggie, not anymore."

"She's a friend."

"A friend who's no longer in danger." But when he thought about what had nearly happened—

"George?"

He sighed. "Yeah."

"It was a risk to try to take her out before the results were in. A very large and ill-considered risk."

"Desperation," George said, "is a hard taskmaster."

Maggie sat on the back porch, swaying gently on her creaky old porch swing, staring out at the Atlantic. It had nearly taken her life, and now the restless waves seemed to remind her to live every day to the fullest. She'd be hard pressed to do it with Dex around. When she'd wanted the fresh air, even though it came with thin sunlight and cold wind, he'd insisted on wrapping her in every blanket in the house. But she was happy where she was—unspeakably sad over the loss of her first plane, but already thinking of ways to move forward, already excited over what her future might bring.

And trying really hard not to wonder if Dex would be a part of it.

He'd been gone all day—where, she didn't know—and she'd refused to ask him. It was a matter of pride. She wouldn't be the type of woman who had to know her man's every thought, every move. If he still wanted to be her man...

She shook that off. Just because he hadn't brought up the idea of marriage again didn't mean anything. Besides, it wasn't like he was leaving permanently any time soon. Not until he solved his case.

None of them seemed to have much heart for it at the moment, not after Mort. She sighed heavily. There was a cloud without a silver lining. She should have felt angry, betrayed, but she was simply hurting, for his mother, for herself. Most of all for Mort, for a friend who'd only been looking for a way to save a mother who was his entire world.

"It's been a hell of a day," Dex said.

She kept her face turned toward the ocean, but closed her eyes, just a moment while she absorbed the relief and the joy that swirled through her as he settled at her side on the swing. "It's been a hell of a week."

"Think you can stand a little more drama?"

"I think I've had enough drama to last me the rest of my life. Or I will have had by the time you close your case."

"And after I close my case, what then?"

Maggie rested her head back, looked up at the slice of sky she could see between the porch roof and railing. "It will be a while before I can replace the Piper, even with the insurance. I don't think I should be making any big decisions until—"

His hand appeared under her nose. Something sparkled in the palm of it.

"Dex." She eased back against the side of the swing, wrapped her arms around herself to keep from shivering. Not all the tremors were due to the cold. Who the hell knew a round of white gold circled with channel set diamonds could be so frightening?

And although her heart leapt, she had to be certain before she let herself grab the ring, and him, and hold on forever. "Are you sure, Dex? I meant it when I said I won't be easy to live with, or easy to love. Sometimes," she qualified when he started to object. "It's not false modesty, and I'm not fishing for compliments."

Dex picked up her left hand and slipped the ring on her finger. "Yeah, you're moody and irritable and stubborn and you always want to do things your own way."

She curled her fingers over the proposal she still hadn't formally accepted. "I can compromise."

Dex snorted.

"You're no prize, either, you know." But she didn't take the ring off. Instead, in a rare girly moment, she held her hand up and watched the diamonds sparkle in the meager sunlight filtering through the cloud cover. It was exactly what she'd have wanted if she'd chosen for herself, something simple, understated, that wouldn't catch on things while she was working, because God knew she'd forget to take it off. Or refuse to.

"That's it? I'm no prize?"

"Give me a minute. I'm sure I can come up with an insult or two." But she glanced at her left hand again and thought, what else could she do with a man who understood her so well, except marry him?

Dex slipped an arm around her and pulled her close.

She rested her head on his shoulder. "There are a lot of small airports in the Boston area. I can find one, rent some hangar space. It'll even be cheaper as long as I'm down a plane."

"We've been over this, Maggie. My job is portable. And your family is here. You're just as important to the people of this island as they are to you."

"Well." She swallowed against the tears clogging her throat, but not out of pride. This was too important a moment to waste on a useless activity like crying. "What about your family?"

"You're necessary to me. My family will understand."

She smiled. If they were anything like him, she'd have her hands full. "I'd like to meet them sometime."

"You will, over Christmas."

As the blood drained from her face she shot upright and twisted around to gape at him. "This Christmas? In like two months?"

"Yeah, Christmas is non-negotiable in my family."

Maggie slapped a hand over her stomach. "That means I'll have to shop. What the heck am I supposed to get people I've never met?" She flounced back against the seat. "If things had turned out differently I could have bought a mall or something, then they could make their own choices."

Dex laughed, pulled her close again. "You're not sorry about the money."

"At the moment? Yeah, I am." She sighed, leaned into him. "Seriously Dex, am I what they want for you?"

"They want me to be happy, Maggie. You make me happy."

"I won't, not all the time."

"And I'll drive you crazy once in a while."

She grinned. "Don't give me reasons to change my mind. I haven't said yes yet."

He grinned back at her. "You said yes in the life raft."

"I didn't think you remembered that."

"Near death experiences always stick in my mind."

They both fell silent, thinking about how close they'd come to a very different reality.

"Are you?" Maggie said at length. "Sorry about the money, I mean." She'd never wanted it, and all the complications it would bring along with it. But Dex might feel differently.

"No," he said, and sent relief breezing through her. Not that she'd needed confirmation, but still, it felt good to hear him say he didn't care.

"We're alike there, Maggie. Half the fun of having anything is the satisfaction of looking at it and knowing what I put into getting it."

"We." Maggie looked at up at him. "What we put into building it, Dex."

"We," he agreed. "It's going to take us a while to build what we want, Maggie. I was thinking a lifetime. Want to sign up?"

She lifted her hand, let the ring catch the light for a second or two before she laid her hand on his cheek. "I already did."

Genealogist Holden Abbot arrives
on Windfall Island to uncover the
identity of the mysterious Stanhope heir.
But when he meets the stunning
Jessi Randal, his investigation takes
the most personal turn . . .

Please turn this page for a preview of

Hideaway Cove.

Chapter One

Jessica Randal, Jessi to her friends and family, had been born and raised on Windfall Island, Maine. At the tender age of seventeen, her high school diploma so fresh in her hand the ink was still wet, she'd found herself pregnant and engaged. Nine short months later, the boy she'd thought her soul mate had left her high and dry, and she'd given birth to the real love of her life.

Benjamin David Randal arrived with little fuss or fanfare, a contented, happy baby who'd refused to cry even when the doctor slapped him sharply on the bottom. Seeing as he possessed the dreaded Y chromosome, Jessi knew for certain he'd give her trouble. She vowed he'd be the only man who would—as he'd be the only man in her life.

Almost eight years had passed since that life-altering day, and she'd made a good life for herself and her son. She didn't have a college degree, but she took enough online courses so that when her best friend, Maggie Solomon, started her charter business with nothing more than a used airplane and a drive to succeed, Jessi had climbed on board and never looked back.

Maggie owned two planes and a helicopter now, along

with a pair of ferry boats. She spent as much time as she could in the air. Jessi made that possible.

As ten percent owner and one hundred percent business manager of Solomon Charters, Jessi handled the scheduling, drummed up business, kept the place stocked in everything from toilet paper to aircraft fuel, and juggled the bills to keep the wolves from the door—for the business, and for herself and her son.

All in all, she was pretty proud of herself, satisfied in her work, and fairly content with her personal life.

"Mom?"

She turned toward the sound of that voice and thought, make that deliriously happy. Looking into the face of her son, how could she not be?

"What's up, Benj?"

He paused in the act of loading his backpack. "Where are we going on vacation next summer?"

"I'm not sure." She gestured to his pack. "Work while you talk or we'll be late. How about Boston, or maybe Gettysburg?" she tossed out, because summer was a long way off and she hadn't given vacationing even a passing thought. "What do you think, Freedom Road or battlefield ghosts?"

Benji stuffed some papers in his backpack, flopped in a book, and heaved a sigh. "History stuff again?"

"I thought you liked history stuff."

"It's okay." He sent her a sidelong glance. "They have history in other places."

"Oh? What other places?"

He shrugged. "Everywhere, even Disney World."

Jessi bit back a smile. "I don't know, Benj. Disney World?"

"It's not just rides and cartoon stuff, Mom. I looked it up in school." His little voice rose with excitement as he made his pitch. "They have animals, like in a zoo but they get to wander all over and you have to look at them from a train kind of thing. And there's stuff about countries and presidents and science."

"And this idea just came to you out of the blue?"

He hunched his shoulders. "Danny Mason is going with his family."

And Danny was bragging on it to all the other kids in school. Not that Jessi could blame him; Disney World was the Paris of the pre-teen set.

"Auntie Maggie could fly us there," Benji said, "And some of the hotels are pretty cheap—I mean," he screwed up his face, "affordable. Some of the places are affordable, Mom, like for families, you know? So we could still stay in the park."

But there was airline fuel, airport fees, a rental car, admission tickets and meals for a kid who ate like he had two hollow legs—and souvenirs, because why go all that way and bring back only memories? And she kept those details to herself. Bad enough that Benji had gone to the trouble of researching hotel prices; she wouldn't have him worrying about money, not at his age.

"You've never said anything about Disney World before. Do you want to go just because the Masons are going?"

He thought about it for a second, which made her smile—and tear up just a little. How many seven-year-olds took the time to think through an answer—an answer about a proposal he'd clearly already put considerable thought and study into?

"I don't know. I want to be a pilot, like Auntie Maggie. I guess that means I kinda want to go everywhere."

"London? Moscow? Budapest?"

"I'm just a kid," he said, and though his back was turned

she could tell an eye roll went along with the comment. Then he zipped his backpack and turned, giving her a sunny smile. "I'll hit those other places when I grow up. *We'll* hit them, Mom."

And the tears filled Jessi's throat so she could only smile and ruffle his hair as she nudged him toward the door. The way he assumed they'd always be a unit warmed her heart, and broke it a little, because she knew he'd leave her one day. She intended to do everything in her power to make sure he could and would. Children were meant to grow up and lead their own lives, and it was the task—and burden—of their parents to make sure they were prepared. When the time came, she'd swallow back tears again as she saw him off.

But that day was a long time coming, she reminded herself. For now, for all the days until then, he still belonged to her. Only her. "I've always wanted to go to Budapest."

"Really?" He looked up at her, brown eyes alight with curiosity. "Where is that, 'xactly?"

Jessi sighed loudly and for effect. "It's a good thing you're going to school for a few more years if you don't even know where Budapest is."

"I can look it up only . . . how do you spell it?"

Laughing, Jessi gave him the letters after they'd climbed into the car. Benji copied them down on a scrap of paper, barely finishing before they pulled up in front of Windfall Island's little school.

He stuffed the paper in his pocket and opened the car door, but instead of getting out, he turned to her. "We could get a dog," he said. "Instead of going to Disney World, I mean."

Jessi shook her head, amused. "Consolation prize?" He'd asked her for a dog at least a thousand times, but somehow he always managed to find a new angle. "Only you, Benj."

He gave her a bright, mischievous smile. "I'll talk you into it," he said, tossed in a "Bye, Mom," and jumped out of the car, too old to kiss her in front of his friends anymore.

She'd gotten used to that, even if she waited until he'd gone inside before she turned the car—and her thoughts—toward work. Best to concentrate on what she could have, what she could do. To remember that while it would be amazing to give her son a once-in-a-lifetime dream, by getting through every day, every week, every year, by sending him to college, she'd be giving him the tools to realize all his dreams.

Windfall Island perched just off the coast of Maine, a long, narrow, unforgiving spit of land edged with rocks too damn hard for even the relentlessly pounding surf of the Atlantic Ocean to wear down. Her people were just as hard and just as unforgiving, not to mention they ran the gamut from mildly eccentric to downright off-kilter.

Holden Abbot had come to Windfall Island to do a genealogy of the residents. All the residents. According to his research, the island had been settled by those on the fringes of society, sailors who'd jumped ship, men who'd broken laws, runaway slaves and fugitives from justice. They'd left a legacy of insularity, paranoia, and a severe dislike for any form of law enforcement—maybe because, over the centuries, breaking the law had often meant the difference between survival and starvation for the people of Windfall.

Laws weren't broken on a regular basis anymore, at least not the big ones. Nowadays tourism provided. The season, however, had ended with the falling leaves and dropping temperature. The last tourist had vacated the island long before the wind became cutting and the surf turned deadly.

Hold wasn't a tourist, but he was an outsider—which

had proved even less tolerable to the citizens of the island. At least the male citizens. The women tended to be a lot more welcoming. Rabidly so.

Except the one he wanted to get to know.

Jessi Randal seemed mostly oblivious to him, friendly, helpful, and sort of vaguely flirtatious without putting any real intent behind it. Without ever saying no, she kept him at arm's length. Then again, he'd never outright asked her for a date because hearing her say no, well now, that would be a true rejection.

She walked in, petite, pretty, and looking so fresh and so sunny it seemed she brought spring in with her. And there, Hold thought, his blood sizzled, his nerve endings tingled, and there seemed to be a weight on his chest that made it just a little hard to breathe.

"What's new, Mississippi?" She peeled a puffy coat the color of fresh lemons off her curvy little body, and when she turned and leveled her bright smile and dancing green eyes at him, he couldn't have kept a thought in his head with duct tape and wire mesh.

"I know you Southern boys like to go slow, but it can't possibly take this long for you to come up with an answer. You only need one word, like *fine* or *good*."

Being from the South, Hold generally took his time over, well, everything. Jessi made him feel a powerful impatience; he just didn't want her to see it. So he sat back, folded his arms and played it cool.

"Unless you're up to something nefarious and you don't want to tell me about it."

"Not me." Unless, Hold thought, she considered it nefarious to picture her naked. Which she probably did.

"Okaaay, so let me try this again. What's new?"

"Not a blessed thing, darlin'."

"Well, then." She sat at her desk, and although the phone began to ring, she only looked over at the old-fashioned wall clock, which stood at one minute to eight.

She waited, watched the second hand sweep its measured way around the dial to dead on the hour, then plucked the receiver off the ancient black desk phone and said brightly, "Good Morning, Solomon Charters. Hold Abbot?" She looked over at him, grinning hugely. "Let me see if he's around."

Hold slashed a hand across his throat, shook his head, even got to his feet, prepared to beat a hasty retreat before he had to talk to the Windfaller on the other end of that call, probably female and ready with a proposition he'd have to find a non-insulting way to fend off. He'd just about run out of charm, and for a man who hailed from a part of the county where charm was as much a part of the culture as pralines, that was saying something.

Jessi rolled her eyes, but said into the phone, "He's not here, Mrs. Hadley." After a "Yes," a couple of "Mm-hmmms," and some scribbling, she said, "Good-bye," and hung up the phone, holding out a pink message slip. "How about dinner?"

Hold crossed the room to brace his backside against her desk, just near her right elbow. "Sign me up, sugar."

"Boy, you're good at that," Jessi said. "The little lean, the eye contact, and the way you call me sugar in that slow, easy Southern drawl. Smooth as Bourbon. Laureen Hadley is a goner."

"Who? What?"

"Laureen Hadley. You're having dinner with her tonight." Jessi handed him the pink message slip. "Eight sharp, which is quite the sacrifice for Mr. Hadley since, according to Mrs. Hadley, eating that late will wreak havoc on his digestion.

Mr. Hadley is always one taco away from complete intestinal meltdown, so that's really no big surprise."

Hold stared at the slip a minute, then wadded it up and tossed it in the trash. "I'm not having dinner with the Hadleys. I'm busy tonight."

"Of course you are," Jessi said in a way that told him she thought she knew exactly what he'd be busy doing. Or rather whom.

She reached into the top drawer of her desk and pulled out a stack of pink message notes and handed them over. "Take your pick."

Hold dropped them in the trash. "I'm busy then, too."

"Why do you encourage them if you're not interested?"

"I don't encourage them."

She twisted around in her chair, rolling it back a couple feet so she could stare at him, brows arched. "What do you call flirting?"

"Harmless fun. A way to pass the time, make a woman feel good about herself."

"Harmless for you, maybe. Around here it's like making yourself the only bone in a roomful of starving dogs. Once they get done swiping at one another, the last one standing is only going to feel good once she ..."

"Gnaws on me a little while?"

She gave him a slight smile. "For starters."

"You made your point, Jessica. From now on I'll only flirt with you."

"At least I know you don't mean it." She rolled back to her desk, pulled a stack of paperwork over in front of her.

"What makes you think I don't mean it?"

"I don't know; maybe the fact that you flirt with, oh, every woman between legal and dead? What would make me any different?"

"I don't know," he parroted, "maybe the fact that I'm attracted to you?"

She rolled her eyes.

"It's true, Jessica, I'm saving myself for you. Ask any woman between legal and the grave. They'll tell you I'm all talk and no action."

"I have no interest in your love life."

Not for long, Hold thought as he pushed off her desk. And he was running out of patience. Sure, he'd only been there a couple of weeks, and while he'd wanted Jessi from the moment he saw her, he'd decided to give her time to get used to the idea. She was, however, being purposely, *stubbornly*, obtuse.

Or maybe there was something more at work this morning.

Hold slid the stack of papers out from under her unseeing eyes. "Want to share your problem with Uncle Hold?"

"You're not my uncle."

He grinned, settled beside her again. "Glad you noticed."

She shot him a look. "It's not that big a deal, just something Benji sprang on me this morning that I'd like to make happen."

"Maybe I can help."

"It's something I have to do myself."

"Why?"

"Because Benji is my responsibility."

"I get that, but why do you have to do it alone? Maggie would do anything for you, no questions asked—Maggie and Dex," he said, referring to her best friend and majority owner of Solomon airlines, and her fiancé. "So would I."

"Then it would be Maggie and Dex doing it. And there's no way I'm asking you for help."

"Why?"

"Because I hardly know you."

"And you don't want to admit you're attracted to me?"

"Back off, Abbot." She shot to her feet, did the backing off herself. "Benji is my son, and if he wants to go—whatever he wants, I'll damn well make it happen without going begging to my friends. Or complete strangers with egos the size of..." she tossed her hands in the air, "something really big," she finished, clearly at a loss, but so damn gorgeous he wanted to scoop her up and kiss her until all that glorious temper turned to a different kind of heat.

"What are you grinning at?"

"You," he said, holding himself back with what could only be called a Herculean effort. "You're beautiful when you're mad."

Her mouth dropped open. "You...I...Stop saying things like that."

"I'd rather show you anyway, sugar."

She lifted her hands to her cheeks, not just pink now but hot red. "Hold—"

"Why don't you tell me what Benji wants?" he said because he'd pushed her too far, and he didn't want to hear her give him a single reason why they couldn't be together.

"It's just so..." She dropped her hands, laughing a little, "ridiculous."

But it had upset her, and it didn't take much for him to reason out why. "It can't be easy to raise a kid by yourself, no child support."

Jessi sat back, crossed her arms. "Really? Do tell."

Hold smiled indulgently. "I know you own ten percent of Solomon Charters, but you're plowing most of the profits back into the business if you want to grow it at all, and especially right now, when you've just lost the Piper..." He trailed off at the look on her face—a look that had nothing to do with being reminded of Maggie's near-death just a few days before, resulting in the loss of her first airplane. And when the tone of her voice matched the look, he knew. He'd just made an ass of himself, a supercilious, condescending ass.

"Oh, don't stop now," Jessi said. "I find it just fascinating how you can tell me all about my life without ever asking a single question."

"Uh…"

"Let me guess. You've been asking questions, just not to me."

"How do I respond to that observation without putting your back up any more than I've already done?"

"Apologizing would be a good start," she said with a perfect mix of disappointment and reproach.

Hold suppressed the urge to hang his head, dig his toe into the carpet, stuff his hands in his pockets, or otherwise give physical presence to the guilt he felt. "I wouldn't have to apologize if you'd talk to me once in a while."

"I talk to you all the time."

"Not about anything personal."

"That's because my personal life is none of your business. Which I keep telling you, and you keep ignoring."

"Doesn't that tell you how serious I am about getting to know you?"

Jessi just shook her head, turned back to her desk. "You want to get to know me? Start with my genealogy, Hold. Maybe I'll turn out to be the long lost Stanhope heir, and all my troubles will be over."

Money, Hold thought sourly.

He could have told her it didn't solve every problem, but that would raise questions he wasn't ready to answer. Jessi believed him to be a simple researcher; he hadn't told her, or anyone, that he came from one of the wealthiest families in the country.

Because he'd yet to meet anyone it didn't matter to on some level.

He could honestly say the women he dated didn't always go into the relationship because of his money, but once they found out, they changed. Every last one of them.

What he felt for Jessi...He didn't know what he felt for Jessi, or what she felt for him. But he wanted a chance to find out before his money complicated everything.

Jessi sighed. "It's a nice dream, inheriting a fortune. Not having to live from paycheck to paycheck would certainly make life easier."

"Money isn't everything," Hold murmured, although he couldn't brush off the ease it put into his life—the freedom, for instance, to be here on Windfall Island for who knew how long, working a job that didn't even net him a paycheck.

But he understood there were people who would do anything, say anything, be anything, to get it. He had firsthand proof.

THE DISH

Where Authors Give You the Inside Scoop

From the desk of Jaime Rush

Dear Reader,

DRAGON AWAKENED and the world of the Hidden
started very simply, as most story ideas do. I saw this sexy
guy with an elaborate dragon tattoo down his back. But
much to my surprise, the "tattoo" changed his very cel-
lular structure, turning him into a full-fledged Dragon.
I usually get a character in some situation that begs
me to open the writer's "What if?" box. And this man/
Dragon was the most intriguing character yet. I had a
lot of questions, as you can imagine. *Who are you? Why
are you? And will you play with me?* This is the really fun
part of writing for me: exploring all the possibilities. I got
tantalizing bits and pieces. I knew he was commanding,
controlling, and a warrior. And his name was Cyntag,
Cyn for short.

Then the heroine made an appearance, and she in no
way seemed to fit with him. She was, in the early version,
a suffer-no-fools server in a rough bar. And very human. I
knew her name was Ruby. (I love when their names come
easily like that. Normally I have to troll through lists and
phone books to find just the right one.) The television
show *American Restoration* inspired a new profession for
Ruby, who was desperately holding on to the resto yard

she inherited from her mother. I knew Ruby was raised by her uncle after being orphaned, and he'd created a book about a fairy-tale world just for her.

But I was still stumped by how these completely different people fit together. Until I got the scene where Ruby finds her uncle pinned to the wall by a supernatural weapon, and the name he utters on his dying breath: Cyntag.

Ah, that's how they're connected. [Hands rubbing together in anticipation.] Then the scene where she confronts him rolled through my mind like a movie. Hot-headed, passionate Ruby and the cool, mysterious Cyn, who reveals that he is part of a Hidden world of Dragons, magick, Elementals, and danger. And so is she. Suddenly, her uncle's bedtime stories, filled with Dragon princes and evil sorcerers, become very dangerously real. As does the chemistry that sparks between Ruby and Cyn.

I loved creating the Hidden, which exists alongside modern-day Miami. Talk about opening the "What if?" box! I found lots of goodies inside: descendants of gods and fallen angels, demons, politics, dissension, and all the delicious complications that come from having magical humans and other beings trapped within one geographical area. And a ton of questions that needed to be answered. It was quite the undertaking, but all of it a fun challenge.

We all have an imagination. Mine has always contained murder, mayhem, romance, and magic. Feel free to wander through the madness of my mind any time. A good start begins at my website, www.jaimerush.com, or that of my romantic suspense alter-ego, www.tinawainscott.com.

Jaime Rush

♥ ♥ ♥ ♥ ♥ ♥ ♥ ♥ ♥ ♥ ♥ ♥ ♥ ♥ ♥ ♥

From the desk of Kristen Ashley

Dear Reader,

I often get asked which of my books or characters are my favorites. This is an impossible question to answer and I usually answer with something like, "The ones I'm with."

See, every time I write a book, I lose myself in the world I'm creating so completely, I usually do nothing but sit at my computer—from morning until night—immersed in the characters and stories. I so love being with them and want to see what happens next, I can't tear myself away. In fact, I now have to plan my life and make sure everything that needs to get done, gets done; everyone whom I need to connect with, I connect with; because for the coming weeks, I'll check out and struggle to get the laundry done!

Back in the day, regularly, I often didn't finish books, mostly because I didn't want to say good-bye. And this is one reason why my characters cross over in different series, just so I can spend time with them.

Although I absolutely "love the ones I'm with," I will say that only twice did I end a book and feel such longing and loss that I found it difficult to get over. This happened with *At Peace* and also, and maybe especially, with LAW MAN.

I have contemplated why my emotion after completing these books ran so deep. And the answer I've come up with is that I so thoroughly enjoyed spending time with heroes who didn't simply fall in love with their heroines. They fell in love with and built families with their heroines.

In the case of LAW MAN, Mara's young cousins, Bud and Billie, badly needed a family. They needed to be protected and loved. They needed to feel safe. They needed role models and an education. As any child does. And further, they deserved it. Loyal and loving, I felt those two kids in my soul.

So when Mitch Lawson entered their lives through Mara, and he led Mara to realizations about herself, at the same time providing all these things to Bud and Billie and building a family, I was so deep in that, stuck in the honey of creating a home and a cocoon of love for two really good (albeit fictional) kids, I didn't want to surface.

I remember standing at the sink doing dishes after putting the finishing touches on that book and being near tears, because I so desperately wanted to spend the next weeks (months, years?) writing every detail in the lives of Mitch, Mara, Bud, and Billie. Bud making the baseball team. Billie going to prom. Mitch giving Bud "the talk" and giving Billie's friends the stink-eye. Scraped knees. Broken hearts. Homework. Christmases. Thanksgivings. I wanted to be a fly on the wall for it all, seeing how Mitch and Mara took Bud's and Billie's precarious beginnings on this Earth and gave them stability and affection, taught them trust, and showed them what love means.

Even now, when I reread LAW MAN, the beginning of the epilogue makes my heart start to get heavy. Because I know it's almost done.

And I don't want it to be.

Kristen Ashley

♥ ♥ ♥ ♥ ♥ ♥ ♥ ♥ ♥ ♥ ♥ ♥ ♥ ♥ ♥ ♥

From the desk of Kristen Callihan

Dear Reader,

In SHADOWDANCE, heroine Mary Chase asks hero Jack Talent what it's like to fly. After all, Jack, who has the ability to shift into any creature, including a raven in *Moonglow*, has cause to know. He tells her that it is lovely.

I have to agree. When I was fifteen, I read Judith Krantz's *Till We Meet Again*. The story features a heroine named Frederique who loves to fly more than anything on Earth. Set in the 1940s, Freddy eventually gets to fly for the Women's Auxiliary Ferrying Squadron in Britain. I cannot tell you how cool I found this. The idea of women not only risking their lives for their country but being able to do so in a job usually reserved for men was inspiring.

So, of course, I had to learn how to fly. Luckily, my dad had been a navigator in the Air Force, which made him much more sympathetic to my cause. He gave me flying lessons as a sixteenth birthday present.

I still remember the first day I walked out onto that small airfield in rural Maryland. It was a few miles from Andrews Air Force Base, where massive cargo planes rode heavy in the sky while fighter jets zipped past. But my little plane was a Cessna 152, a tiny thing with an overhead wing, two seats, and one propeller to keep us aloft.

The sun was shining, the sky cornflower blue, and the air redolent with the sharp smell of aviation gas and motor oil. I was in heaven. Here I was, sixteen, barely legal to drive a car, and I was going to take a plane up in the sky.

Sitting in the close, warm cockpit with my instructor,

I went through my checklist with single-minded determination and then powered my little plane up. I wasn't nervous; I was humming with anticipation.

Being in a single-engine prop is a sensory experience. The engine buzzes so loud that you need headphones to hear your instructor. The cockpit vibrates, and you feel each and every bump through the seat of your pants as you taxi right to the runway.

It only takes about sixty miles per hour to achieve liftoff, but the sensation of suddenly going weightless put my heart in my throat. I let out a giddy laugh as the ground dropped away and the sky rushed to meet me. It was one of the best experiences of my life.

And all because I read a book.

Now that I am an author, I think of the power in my hands, to transport readers to another life and perhaps inspire someone to try something new. And while Mary and Jack do not take off in a plane—they live in 1885, after all—there might be a dirigible in their future.

♥ ♥ ♥ ♥ ♥ ♥ ♥ ♥ ♥ ♥ ♥ ♥ ♥ ♥ ♥

From the desk of Anna Sullivan

Dear Reader,

I grew up in a big family—eight brothers and sisters—so you can imagine how crowded and noisy, quarrelsome and fun it was. We all have different distinct personalities, of course, and it made for some interesting moments. Add in a couple of dogs, friends in and out, and, well, you get the picture.

I was the shy kid taking it all in, not watching from the sidelines, but often content to sit on them with a good book in my hands. Sometimes I'd climb a big old elm tree behind our house, cradle safely in the branches, and lose myself in another world while the wind rustled in the leaves and the tree creaked and swayed.

Looking back, it's no wonder how I ended up a writer, and it's not hard to understand why my stories seem to need a village to come to life. For me, the journey always starts with the voices of the hero and heroine talking incessantly in my head, but what fun would they have without a whole cast of characters to light up their world?

The people of Windfall Island are a big, extended family, one where all the relatives are eccentric and none of them are kept out of sight. No, they bring the crazy right out and put it on display. They're gossip-obsessed, contentious, and just as apt to pick your pocket as save your life—always with a wink and a smile.

Maggie Solomon didn't grow up there, but the Windfallers took her in, gave her a home, made her part of their large, boisterous family when her own parents turned their backs on her. So when Dex Keegan shows up, trying to enlist her help without revealing his secrets, she's not about to pitch in just because she finds him…tempting. Being as suspicious and standoffish as the rest of the Windfallers, Maggie won't cooperate until she knows why Dex is there, and what he wants.

What he wants, Dex realizes almost immediately, is Maggie Solomon. Sure, she's hard-headed, sharp-tongued, and infuriatingly resistant to his charms, but she appeals to him on every level. There must be something perverse, he decides, about a man who keeps coming back for more when a woman rejects him. He enjoys their verbal sparring, though, and one kiss is all it takes for him to know he won't stop until she surrenders.

But Maggie can't give in until he tells her the truth, and it's even more incredible—and potentially explosive to the Windfall community—than she ever could have imagined.

There's an eighty-year-old mystery to solve, a huge inheritance at stake, and a villain who's willing to kill to keep the secret, and the money, from ever seeing the light of day.

The Windfallers would love for you to join them as they watch Dex and Maggie fall in love—despite themselves—and begin the journey to find a truth that's been waiting decades for those with enough heart and courage to reveal.

I really had a great time telling Dex and Maggie's story, and I hope you enjoy reading about them, and all the characters of my first Windfall Island novel.

Happy reading,

Anna Sullivan

www.AnnaSulivanBooks.com
Twitter @ASullivanBooks
Facebook.com/AnnaSullivanBooks

VISIT US ONLINE AT

WWW.HACHETTEBOOKGROUP.COM

FEATURES:

OPENBOOK BROWSE AND
SEARCH EXCERPTS
•
AUDIOBOOK EXCERPTS AND PODCASTS
•
AUTHOR ARTICLES AND INTERVIEWS
•
BESTSELLER AND PUBLISHING
GROUP NEWS
•
SIGN UP FOR E-NEWSLETTERS
•
AUTHOR APPEARANCES AND TOUR
INFORMATION
•
SOCIAL MEDIA FEEDS AND WIDGETS
•
DOWNLOAD FREE APPS

BOOKMARK HACHETTE BOOK GROUP
@ WWW.HACHETTEBOOKGROUP.COM